THE REDEMPTION MAN

THE FIRST DEVLIN THRILLER

JAMES CARVER

PROLOGUE

He sprinted through the rain, weaving in and out of the mesh of branches nearly invisible now in the darkness. He had long ago lost any sense of how much ground he had covered or how long he'd been running for. It had been dusk when he'd entered the forest. Now a moonless night had fallen and closed in around him like a tomb. Must have been a couple of hours at least, he guessed. But it felt like an eternity. His body and his nerves were beginning to give. And yet it wasn't completely hopeless. Not completely. After all, he had speed, agility, and youth on his side. If anyone could do it, he could. He had to. He just couldn't keep running forever.

The rain that had started out as a fine drizzle was hammering down. The waterlogged forest floor felt like it was moving under his feet. Just in the nick of time, he skid-braked into a hard stop and stood panting on the brink of a bank. Below him was a steep slope. He looked back over his shoulder. In the far distance, he could see tiny pins of light bobbing and winking at him through the trees and slicing rain. His heart burned with fear. There was no way back. He slid his foot down the side of the bank, trying to get a firm hold. With a hand placed on the top of the ridge, he crouched and cautiously placed his other foot on the wet incline and began to sidle down. Very quickly he found himself accelerating, gravity and frictionless, wet mud taking over. He slipped onto his backside and began surfing the sodden earth. Faster than he could register and faster than his hands could react, his foot caught on a root, and the weight of the top half of his body pulled him over into an uncontrollable spin. He started to tumble at speed, speed that kept increasing until eventually the slanting bank evened out into flat ground and he rolled to a stop in the middle of a clearing.

Soaked to the skin and covered in dirt and blood, he scrambled to his feet and scurried back into the cover of the forest. Moving quickly in these circumstances needed constant concentration and fast reactions. But he was hitting exhaustion, and his reflexes were deteriorating. Suddenly, out of nowhere, his brow collided against a bough, and in a white flash he found himself spread-eagled on the forest floor. He sat up cradling his head and began to panic.

Jesus. How long had he been out for? Seconds? Minutes?

He struggled to his feet, but his head ached and his balance was off. He looked back in the direction he'd come from and saw the lights again. But now he could hear voices too—men calling to each other. He turned and flew off again, choking on the rain. The voices and lights were not so far behind him now, closing in. Not for the first time, he considered surrender. Throwing himself on their mercy. But he knew there would be no reprieve. These people didn't even think of him as human.

Another low branch struck his body, slamming him onto his back and embedding him in mud. By the time he had gotten to his feet, the pack of men was so close he could see cones of light sweeping the trees and hear branches being broken as they forged their way toward him. Desperation began to overwhelm him. This was their land, their forest. He was lost.

He managed to stand and swayed, breathing unevenly. Then, at the edge of his vision, something twinkled and caught his attention up ahead. Something at last that wasn't darkness or more forest. Through a small gap in the dense woodland, a white light flashed. Not the swing of a flashlight though... There it was again. A white light that zipped by. And another. Not flashlights... No...headlights. Cars. On a highway. And then he heard it, above the sound of the rainfall, as if plugs had been removed from his ears: the thrum and buzz of traffic. He made one last lurch into a walk, not running but using the trees as crutches, throwing himself forward from one trunk to another until he stumbled onto open ground, drenched grass underfoot that rolled down toward a busy highway. He blinked away the tears, blood, and rain, and his blurred vision made out a police cruiser pulling over, then coming to a stop. A door opened and a uniformed figure stepped out.

He fell to his knees. He had made it. He would live after all. The police officer walked up the bank of grass toward him. Through a sheet of tears and warm blood, he made out an outstretched arm. Was he being beckoned? Yes. An arm was reaching out to beckon him forward. Protection. His nightmare was over. He wrenched himself to his feet and began to walk toward the police officer.

Now, as his terror receded, his mind slowly began to take control of his raging emotions and to piece together what the officer was doing. Something wasn't right.

The officer's outstretched arm was holding a gun. Why was a gun being pointed at him? He wasn't any kind of threat. Then the officer spoke, with a soft voice just audible over the falling rain.

"Turn around."

He looked at the cop and then at the gun in the cop's hand that shook a little from being gripped too hard. It wasn't within his power anymore to live, but he sure as hell would decide how he died. With one last breath he summoned all the courage and strength he had left and ran at full tilt, screaming at the top of his voice, a ragged, lunatic death rattle.

Three shots did it. Two to stop him in his tracks and one last one to the head as he lay twitching in the wet mud. And he was grateful for each one of them.

1

The figure in black leaned against the hood of his beat-up Ford Explorer, tilted his head up toward the blue sky, and let the midday sun warm his face. He was standing in front of St Patrick's Church on G Street in Washington, DC. One hand held a lit Cohiba Corona, and the other was buried into his jacket pocket, gently rolling a rosary bead between his thumb and forefinger. Silently he mouthed the Fatima Prayer to himself: "O my Jesus, forgive us our sins. Save us from the fires of hell. Lead all souls to Heaven, especially those most in need of thy mercy." He pulled on the cigar, sucking in a thin ribbon of heat and smoke that seethed between his teeth and curled down the back of his throat, baking his lungs.

The silver Chevy Impala was a 2004 3.8-liter model. It was the LS with rear spoilers and leather bucket seats. This particular Impala had red and white Ohio plates. The man in black knew all this because it was the same Chevy that had followed him from Baltimore down to DC. It was the same Chevy that had followed him all the way down New York Avenue, and it was the same Chevy now parked up half a block away along G

Street, sitting outside some gaudy, billion-dollar-making clothing store for people so young it made the man in black tired just thinking about it all. It was possible of course that they weren't following him. It was possible it was just a coincidence. When you have something to hide, everything looks different.

He stamped out the cigar, grinding it with his heel into the sidewalk. He was dressed entirely in black save for the square of white at his throat, which he fingered with hands that trembled. He waited for the shakes to ease off, then headed up the church steps, entering through the ornate limestone arch.

Father Hector Hermes had finished his last confession of the day. He was reflecting on the sins he had heard when the booth door opened and the darkly lit frame of a large man slid onto the seat behind the screen.

"I'm afraid I've finished taking confession for the day. The red light was..."

"Hello, Hector." Father Hermes instantly recognized the voice, a deep, distinctive rumble, and looked up in surprise.

"Gabe? Gabe Devlin? Where have you been? I called you a dozen times. Why haven't you answered?"

"I've had some thinking to do."

"They told me you quit your church? Is that true?"

"Yes. Yes, it's true."

"Why?"

"Because I was no longer fit to minister."

"No longer fit? Since when?"

"Since I made a decision that I could not honestly perform the duties of a priest. It was a kind of sudden decision..."

"No kidding. Gabe, you can't just quit. Are you doubting your faith? Every priest I know, every cardinal I know has doubts. Quitting isn't the answer."

"I'm not quitting the priesthood, Hector. Not yet anyhow. I'm taking some time off. I just wasn't fit to lead my congregation.

Any congregation. Not right now. And I have a short-term plan. Of sorts. I'm heading to Georgia. An old Air Force friend said there might be an opening, training paratroopers at Jump School. Just for a few months. Some space is all it is. Beyond that, I can't say."

There was a silence. Hector's eyes narrowed. "Have you been drinking?"

Devlin clasped his hands, not in prayer but only to keep them still. "Yes."

"Gabe, it's been seven years since you touched a drop."

"Have been drinking, Hector. Have been. I stopped three days ago, but I still have these damn tremors. I'm off it now. That's an end to it. But it had nothing to do with quitting St. Jude's."

"So what happened, then, Gabe?"

"I fell."

"You fell? What does that mean?"

"What it means is, I'd like you to hear my confession, Hector."

Hector didn't respond for a moment. His dark, lined eyes, overhung with the odd stray hair from his thick brows, locked onto Devlin, making him out in the shadows of the confessional for the first time. Devlin, Hector observed, was a big, impressive man not easy to place in years with a thick shock of black hair swept back from the temples. His large frame and strong features gave him presence and authority, but there was still a suggestion of a youth not so long gone around his blue eyes. Middle age had not quite arrived yet. When he spoke, if you listened very, very carefully, you could hear the thin seam of an old, soft Belfast accent that had refused to be entirely forgotten. The sharp downward light, what little there was of it, gave his deep-set eyes a haunted, almost tormented appearance. And there was something else too, something slightly extraordinary about Devlin. His presence was charged with an energy. It had a crackle about it. Hector thought of it as a troubled divinity. And it troubled Hector as much as it seemed to trouble Devlin. Hector worried at the unknown consequences of this overflow of spirit.

"Are you in trouble, Gabe?"

"Yes. But it's my responsibility to live with what has happened and mine alone. Something's happening to me, Hector. I can feel it. I'm not who I was. I can't explain it any other way... Hector, you picked up the pieces when Jane died. You mentored me through seminary. You are the only person in the world I wholly trust. Will you take my confession?"

"Of course, my son." Hector dropped his head and made the sign of the cross.

The light outside on the confessional booth went red.

An hour later Devlin reemerged into daylight. It was now just after two, and the lunch rush was dying. The sun beat down, so Devlin shaded his eyes making a quick scan up and down Tenth Street and up over to G Street. The Chevy was still in the same place. He could just about make out two figures sitting in the car, both wearing sunglasses.

Okay, thought Devlin, let's see what the deal is here.

Devlin got into his car and set off down Tenth Street, eventually turning onto Pennsylvania Avenue heading southeast out of DC. He kept checking his mirror for the Chevy nosing about in the run of traffic behind, but there was no sign of it. Maybe he'd lost them. Maybe it was his paranoid imagination at work. Or maybe they'd held back and, for the first time since he'd seen them, done a decent job of tailing him.

He drove on for a couple of miles toward the Beltway and turned right down Southern Avenue. He kept driving until the neighborhood took a steep dive, and he found himself cruising past empty row houses that stood in weed-lined streets with liquor stores on the corners. And then, finally, he hit on exactly what he was looking for—a bank. It was a Sun Trust bank, and it sat in a run-down stretch of retail and industrial estates. Devlin pulled up in the parking lot and waited. After a couple of minutes, the Chevy appeared and stopped over on the other side of the highway, opposite the parking lot. Devlin got out of the car and strode toward the bank, a modest, slim brick building with two white faux-classical pillars either side of the door topped with a pediment. As he approached the entrance, he straightened his collar, buttoned his suit jacket, and once inside made for the counter.

"Hello, can I help you, Father?" The teller gave him her warmest smile.

"You surely can. I would very much like to open an account if that's possible."

"Oh, we can absolutely help you with that. I'll call an account manager for you. Would you like to take a seat?"

"Of course. Thank you." Devlin sat waiting for a minute or two until an impeccably dressed young man with gold wire glasses and thin brown hair parted to the side approached him, extending a pale hand.

"Father, my name's Martin. I'm the assistant branch manager. I understand you wish to open an account?"

"Yes, that's right."

"Come with me."

They sat down at a desk by a front window, and Martin logged in to his desktop. "Now, I'll need to see some ID of course."

"ID?"

"Yes, driver's license or passport will do."

"Oh, I don't have one of those with me."

"Right. We can't open an account without identification, Father. You understand that would be impossible?"

Devlin clasped his forehead in horror. "Of course you can't. You must think me a complete fool."

"No, no. You wouldn't be the first. People just don't think of these things," Martin lied.

"It's been so long since I've opened an account. Well, a priest only needs the basics, financially speaking. I'll have to go back home and pick up my driver's license."

"And social security number, please. That's another one folks forget."

"Yes, of course. You know, I only intended to come out here for the bank, but I got caught in that wretched dollar store and spent about seventeen dollars on absolute trash. I tell you, they're an addiction with me."

"Really, Father, forgive me but..."

"I shouldn't be allowed near them. My congregants joke that I'll make myself bankrupt—but I shouldn't be telling you that, should I?"

"It's fine, really, Father." Martin stood. "I'm sorry, do you mind? It's just I have another customer waiting."

"Of course." Devlin stood, hesitated for a moment, then sat down and said, "There was another thing I thought I should mention."

Martin sighed and sat down. "Yes, Father?"

"I've been walking up and down, doing a bit of window-shopping."

"Is this really important? Because Saturday is very busy for—"

"And there's this car over on the other side of the highway. It's been parked outside the bank with two men in it for at least as long as I've been parked here. That's got to be an hour and a half, more even." Martin was suddenly on his feet and peering anxiously out of the window.

"Can you see it? Two men with sunglasses sitting outside a

bank for nearly two hours. Now, I'm no Columbo but..." Devlin didn't have time to finish. Martin had already gone. He was behind the counter on his cell talking hurriedly, the blood drained from his face. On the other end of the line, the District Heights Police radio dispatcher recognized the address and the caller's name and sighed. Martin had raised the alarm at least half a dozen times since the last armed robbery.

Devlin returned to his car. He tilted his rearview mirror to get a ringside view of the Chevy and made like he was talking on his cell. This would shake things up. If they were undercover police, there would be a quiet conversation, nods of heads, and the cop car would be back on its way. If they weren't, well, then the gloves were off.

It took a little under eight minutes for the police to respond. Two black-and-white Ford Police Interceptors arrived in quick succession and pulled up in front of the Chevy. Four officers got out, and one of them, tall and overweight, approached the car while the others stood back, watching for how things would play out. Devlin didn't miss his cue and wheeled out back onto the highway.

Inside the Chevy, the driver, a weaselly-looking guy with a thin oily face, watched Devlin disappear down the highway and out of view. He threw up his hands and cried, "What the hell? I don't believe it. Do you think he saw us and called the cops?"

"Maybe he did," hissed his partner in the passenger seat, who was a good deal heavier and bald with a carelessly shaved goatee. "I told you we shoulda hung further back. We got no choice now. We have to let him go. Just sit tight, Bradley, and don't say anything. It might be a nosy cop just fishing."

The cop signaled for the skinny guy to wind down his window. He complied.

"May I ask what your business is here, sir?" asked the cop.

"Uh, we were just parking up to pick up a coffee and a bite to eat, Officer."

The officer looked unimpressed with the answer and asked for IDs, which were duly handed over. "So, Mr. Bradley, Mr. Otterman, you boys came all the way from Ohio for a bite to eat?"

"You don't know how hungry I get," said Otterman.

The cop took a look at Otterman. "I could take a good guess. Please step out of the vehicle so I can search it."

"Uh...well, is there a reason why you need to search my car, Officer?" said Bradley.

"Please just step out of the car, sir. Or we can talk this out back at the station if you'd prefer. It's really up to you."

DEVLIN HAD SETTLED a few blocks back up along the highway, out of sight on the grass bank of a slip road. He watched the two guys standing by looking agitated while the cop searched their car. It was pretty clear by now that they weren't undercover, and he was able to check them out properly as they stood on the roadside. Sunglasses and badly fitting suits. Difficult to say for sure, but from the look of them and the Chevy, Devlin's money was on private detectives. If they were PIs, they weren't high-end; they looked more like they made the bulk of their living from the spousal surveillance racket. Bottom-feeders.

Devlin could see the cop hadn't found anything and was giving them some sort of talk. The two PIs got back into their car, waited for the cop to go, and took off. Devlin waited too and then followed some way behind.

"DAMN," rasped Otterman. "We got no idea where he could be. What a mess. Who's going to tell Stein?"

"We need to pull over for some gas first. Then we'll flip for it," Bradley replied. He rode on for a couple of miles until he spotted a Red Top and pulled off the highway and stopped by a pump.

"Get a receipt this time, Bradley," said Otterman.

"You think we're gonna get expenses on this? For the day's work we've done?"

"We caught some bad luck is all. That's what we tell Trayder. Get me a Pop-Tart, will ya?"

"Since when do gas stations sell frickin' Pop-Tarts?"

"If they do, then get me Wildlicious Cherry...no, wait, Brown Sugar Cinnamon."

"Who eats Pop-Tarts anyway? They're goddamn terrible for you. Just scalding slices of sugared cancer."

"Well, it ain't you who's..." Otterman broke off midsentence and craned across Bradley to peer through the driver's window. "Would you look at that. Some dumbass is paying at our pump."

"What the hell is he—?" But Bradley was cut short as the driver's door was whipped open. The dumbass in question was Devlin.

Bradley reached for the ignition, but before he could get to the key, Devlin cupped his hand around the top of Bradley's head and bounced it off the wheel. Bradley shrieked in pain and bent double into his own lap. In the confusion, a panicked Otterman froze, staring in disbelief at his partner, who was rocking back and forth clasping his forehead. Suddenly the stench of gasoline filled the car. Thick, heavy liquid was splashing onto the back of Bradley as he groaned, spilling into Otterman's lap, covering the dash and dripping down in the footwells. Devlin was holding the pump nozzle and flicking liters of gas over the occupants of the car.

"What the hell are you doing, you maniac?" shouted Otterman. "You're crazy!" Bradley was gagging on the liquid as it ran over his head and into his mouth and nose. Devlin dropped the nozzle and pulled out a plastic lighter from his jacket pocket.

"I have to confess, I've taken a guess at the octane rating. Tell me why you're tailing me, or I light you both up and you burn like it's a hot day in hell."

"What kind of priest are you?" Otterman squealed.

"The kind of priest that was in Air Force Special Investigations for ten years. You guys really should have done your homework."

"Please! Oh God, please! Don't...don't do it!!" begged Bradley, still choking and spitting out fuel and saliva. "We were tailing you for a client, some guy out of Ohio. I swear, that's all we knew. Please!" Devlin could see the cashier behind the till looking out of the glass front onto the forecourt, trying to work out what was the commotion was about.

"Run," said Devlin, standing back from the door.

"What?"

"You wanna live? Get out of the car and run. Go. Now!" Devlin held the lighter high in the air.

"You'll blow us all up! There are vapors everywhere!" screamed Bradley, wheezing and retching.

"I'm ready to meet my maker." Devlin flicked his thumb and a small flame glowed in his large hands. "Run."

Bradley slid out from his seat, snaking through the narrow space between priest and the car, and backed away. Otterman fumbled at the door handle, finally pulling it open and clambering out of the door. In his desperation to get out, he skidded on the sill and fell out of the car onto the concrete forecourt, then scrambled to his feet and sprinted after his partner.

"*Run,*" bellowed Devlin.

The two men scampered off down the highway in their dripping suits, looking back from time to time until they disappeared out of view.

Devlin pocketed the lighter and took his card out of the chip card reader. It was a risk using his card for the gas, but instinct told Devlin that these guys were unlikely to go to the cops for the same reasons they'd been attempting to covertly tail him and not give themselves away. And the risk had bought him the chance of a snoop in their car.

Other customers at the pumps were looking over. They hadn't got to their cells yet. They were mostly terrified for their own safety, standing still, hoping to God they weren't going to be involved. The fact that Devlin had his clerical collar on created more confusion and bought a fraction more time. But all the same, he figured he had seconds, a minute at most. He leaned into the stinking car, pulled down the driver's sun visor, and found an Ohio Class A private detective's license registered to a Rick Bradley. What was a PI from Ohio doing tailing him in DC? He pulled open the glove compartment and scrabbled around the contents, cursing his shaking hands. In amongst phone chargers, pens, and receipts he found an envelope. It was addressed to Mr. Ed James. This discovery stopped Devlin in his tracks and immediately set alarm bells going. He punched the dash.

"For the love of God! Ed? You moron! This is about you?

Devlin had known Ed when they served on Osan Air Base in South Korea. They had gotten to be close as brothers, but he hadn't seen him in nearly five years. Inside the envelope was a Greyhound bus ticket from Springfield Ohio to Massachusetts. On the back of the ticket, Ed had scribbled the words "St. Jude's," Devlin's church. Ed must have been planning to come see him.

Devlin took the ticket and slipped it in his jacket pocket. The cashier had come out through the sliding door to take a closer look. People were staring while they filled up, looking over, trying to work out what was going on. Devlin replaced the nozzle, walked out of the forecourt, and wove his way across the four lanes of traffic back to the safety of his car.

As he drove off back toward DC, he took out his cell and scrolled through his contacts until he found Ed James's number. It was a number he had from a while back. When he called, it rang and someone picked up but didn't speak.

"Ed? That you?"

There was a pause. Devlin could hear deep breaths, then a reply, strained and whispered. "Who's that?"

"It's Gabe."

"Gabe? Gabe Devlin?"

"Yeah. What the hell's going on, Ed? I just had two guys tailing me all the way from Baltimore to DC. PIs. They had a Greyhound ticket you bought to come see me."

"Two PIs were down in DC ...? Listen, Gabe, I know it looks bad, but it's nothing to concern you, I swear."

"Nothing to concern me? Two private detectives follow me for forty miles and I shouldn't be concerned?" There was a pause. More deep, rasping breaths. "Ed?"

"I don't know why they're following you, Gabe. I don't know who they are, but you gotta believe me that it's okay, Gabe. It's... it's a gambling thing. That's all. I got into debt...I thought I might need to borrow some cash, so I was going to go see you, ask you for some dough. But it's fine...I got it covered now..."

"Where are you, Ed?"

"I gotta go, Gabe."

"Who do you owe money to?"

"I don't...anymore... Like I say, I was in a bit of trouble...but... but it's in order now."

"Oh yeah? You want to tell that to the two guys who hauled their asses all the way over from Ohio to find me?"

"C'mon, Gabe, what do I have to say? It's okay..."

"It's not okay, Ed. I can tell it's not okay." Devlin couldn't be sure, but it sounded a lot like Ed was holding back from sobbing.

"Tell me where you are. I'll come and help you."

"Gabe, I got it worked out..." Now Ed's voice was beginning to break up, cracking with emotion, maybe fear.

"Let me come see you, Ed. Whatever it is I can help fix it—"

"You're not listening to me. It's okay. It's all okay! So leave me the hell alone."

"Ed?"

There was a silence, and then the cell went dead. Devlin redialed, but it went straight to voice message. He looked at Ed's address on the envelope. It was a place called Halton Springs, north of Dayton, Ohio. He knew Dayton; he'd been stationed there at Wright Patterson Airbase for a while in 2005, and Ed's last posting had been there too. Devlin pulled over to the side sharply, causing the car behind to sound its horn.

He turned the engine off and studied his hands. They were still, at last. He angled the rearview mirror to look at himself. His eyes looked tired and worn, seeking desperately for meaning, for an answer, for a purpose. For absolution. He had to pull himself together. The two men tailing him was just a crazy coincidence. It had nothing to do with Devlin. Nobody knew what Devlin had done, and nobody was coming after him. His actions were just a matter for his conscience and his conscience alone.

Devlin knew from Ed's voice and from all the things Ed hadn't told him that something was deeply and badly wrong. He would go help his old friend no matter how bad things were. Even if it ended in pain. Maybe because it ended in pain.

Devlin put the Halton Springs' zip code into Google Maps on his cell phone. Jump School could wait. He was going to Ohio.

2

Congressman Clay Logan was tall, lean, and toothy. Blessed with a generous helping of breezy Midwestern charm, he was movie-star good-looking with a face that was tanned and sculpted. A successful businessman and rising-star Republican, Logan possessed an enviable mix of talents that inspired unusual resentment amongst his peers, even by Capitol Hill standards. He stood with effortless poise wearing one of his many elegantly tailored suits in front of the assembled guests at the Logan Ranch, beaming that toothy grin, emanating assurance and charisma.

"I wanna give a heartfelt thank-you to everyone here for accepting my invitation to come up to the family ranch in Halton Springs. You do us a great honor. For some of us just venturing outside Washington may be a cold bath in itself." A hum of laughter traveled the room. "Tonight is all about how good business can support, lift, and energize a community. Freedom Medical Care currently runs seven hospitals in the state of Ohio and has an economic impact that runs into the billions of dollars." Logan turned to his left, acknowledging the lady sitting beside him. She was trim, poised, and the right side of glamorous for a serious businesswoman and gave the firm impression of being as smart as whip and twice as quick. "Under the enlightened leadership of their CEO, Marie Vallory, they have reached out and given their assistance to drug rehabilitation and funded research into childhood cancers. And tonight we are celebrating another landmark for Halton and for Freedom Medical, the opening of Freedom's eighth hospital in Dayton." There was a burst of applause. Logan paused to let it die and raised a glass. "So I'd like to propose a toast. To Halton Springs and to Freedom Medical—a progressive partnership making each other stronger. Here's to good business." The audience took to their feet, glasses in hand, and Logan basked in the adulation.

After the speeches and toasts at the Logan Ranch, people began to network. They pressed the flesh and moved amongst each other, seeking out anyone who might be of any use at all in the continuing push to advance their careers even an inch forward. Marie and Clay, however, had retired upstairs to Clay's office to carry on cementing their partnership. Marie was backed against Clay's oak desk with Clay pressed up against her, nibbling at her neck. Marie moaned. Then Clay stopped. Stopped still..

"What's wrong?" asked Marie.

"I think someone's coming."

"Damn." Marie quickly smoothed down her dress and checked herself against the large window that framed the oak desk. She sat in one of the two chesterfield armchairs that faced the desk, entwining her lower legs. Clay likewise straightened himself up and relaxed into the chair behind his desk just as there was an impatient rat-a-tat-tat at the door.

"Come in," answered Clay. The door swung open and Earl, Clay's younger brother, entered. He was beanpole tall with a head that hung to one side, like he was expecting incoming fire at any moment. His dark brown eyes were mean and narrow and sat under a thick lick of yellow hair that crested over his long forehead.

Earl registered Marie sitting by the desk but, apart from a flicker of disgust, didn't give her even the tiniest acknowledgment. His presence instantly made Marie tense, and she did her best to disguise it. She could feel the boiling, swirling rage that seemed to be the one force keeping him alive, but she noticed too that Clay seemed oblivious to it. Maybe because he'd known Earl all his life, he'd gotten so used to his brother he didn't see it like everybody else did. Or maybe it was because that was how Clay was, so assured in himself, so self-possessed that Earl's anger didn't reach him.

"Everything okay, Earl?" asked Clay.

"No. No, it's not goddamned okay. You roped Packer into the fertilization lab. He's my foreman—get someone else."

"Sorry, Earl, but I need Packer. He knows the business, and I can rely on him. I gotta have him, Earl. I need his experience."

"Get your own foreman; he was mine first."

"Earl, the only person who knows our stock better than Packer is you. And you made it quite clear you wanted nothing to do with the lab. So if you won't help me, then I think it's unfair that you won't let me use Packer. Unless you've changed your mind?"

Earl's knuckles whitened as he curled his fists tight. "No. I haven't changed my damned mind."

"Well, what am I supposed to do here?"

"Get your own foreman, and stop sucking off of me like a parasite."

"We both know that's not true. The side of the business that's keeping our raggedy asses in profit is the lab, Earl."

Earl's expression didn't change, and he spat back, "Packer's mine. End of." And then he left, slamming the big oak panel door so hard that the framed photos along the wall jumped on their hooks.

"It's hard to believe he's your brother," Marie said stonily, her former ardor now vanished completely.

"Yeah, he's a tricky son of a bitch, that's for sure."

"Tricky? Are you crazy? He's an animal, Clay. He's dangerous."

"What can I do? He's my brother. He's okay; his bark's worse than his bite."

"When somebody has a bark that bad, that really isn't any reassurance. No. You gotta do something about him."

"What can I do? I can't throw him out of the business."

"Why not?"

"Because he's family."

"Oh, please."

"And because he's a part owner. The business was split between both of us when dad died."

"There wouldn't be a business without you, Clay. How many times have you cleared up the mess he's left behind? How many beatings has he given out? If you weren't his brother and your dad wasn't who he was, he'd be at the state penitentiary, in solitary. Or death row. I mean it, Clay—he's a psycho." Marie stood. "His behavior is a risk to your career, and therefore it's a risk to mine." She walked to the door and turned to give her parting shot.

"Do something about him."

Marie left but her words hung in the air, and Clay swung his chair round to look out the window, taking in the clear night sky, the wealth of visible stars, and the spread of the ranch below. His gaze drifted over the dark outlines of the trailers and barns and up to the highway. As he weighed up Marie's ultimatum and the intractable difficulty that Earl's personality presented, his eyes idly tracked a pair of headlights in the distance that approached and passed the main ranch entrance at high speed, spearing along the dark landscape like a shooting star. *Kids*, he thought, *damn kids, high on something or other and tooling around like maniacs. They'll get someone killed.* Then he swung back to his desk and resumed picking over his private troubles.

The car out on the highway all by itself was an old Ford Explorer, and the occupant wasn't some stoned kid. He was a weary priest, gripping and leaning into the steering wheel. Devlin looked up at the lights on in the ranch house, a grand building that sat some way back from the highway.

A feeling was growing in Devlin, a sense of purpose, maybe even destiny, that he had been searching for a long time. For the past few weeks, he had been possessed by a strange feeling. Maybe it was guilt, maybe it was the dawning realization of what he had done, maybe he was straight out losing his mind—whatever it was, it coursed through his body. And then there was the dream. The same dream night after night. He closed his eyes momentarily to try and forget and then forged ahead. Halton Springs was surely where he was meant to be.

3

Devlin drove by the ranch that stretched out along the highway for about five or six miles. After that he passed a group of trailers that looked like a small encampment of travelers. And all the while he drove, in the background, sitting on the skyline, was the forest. It had become a constant companion on Devlin's journey toward Halton. All the way from the ranch to Ed's house and beyond, never out of sight from the highway, a dark edge of dense woodland that climbed up and away into the far night sky.

Devlin could see on his cell's Google map he was coming up on Ed's address, so he slowed to a crawl by a row of trees that screened Ed's house from the highway. Where the line of trees ended, he found a turnoff that led up a gravel path. He stopped short of the house, cut the engine, and took a good look at it.

Cloaked from the road by ash trees and lit only by moonlight was a shabby one-story house. It had a modern white-wood exterior with a sloping, ribbed metal roof. The windows were old and dirty with faded, peeling, dull green shutters, some of which had come off their hinges. The garage was up at the north side of the house, the side farthest from Devlin, and was open.

From where Devlin stood, he could just see the back of a cargo van parked inside.

The house was dead quiet. And dark. Not a single light was on. Devlin walked across the path up to the porch, rang the bell, and waited. No answer. He looked in through the living room window. It was hard to make anything out, so he pressed his face up against the cold glass. There were the shapes of a couple of armchairs and beyond them a rectangle of countertops marking out the kitchen diner. He scouted around back, looking in through the other windows, but at night, without any light inside the house, he couldn't make out much else. He circled back around and stopped in front of the open garage door and the cargo van.

Inside the garage, Devlin tried the handle on the van's door. It clicked and released. He pulled it open, slid in, and turned on the cab light so he could take a look around. The van stank of tobacco. The seats were battered and marked from heavy use, the dash was scuffed, and there were Styrofoam cups and junk food packaging lying around in the footwells.

Devlin scanned the dash. It was fairly basic: AC controls, CD player and radio, and three cup holders in a row. The clock showed just under a hundred thousand miles. He sat facing the steering wheel and reached across to the glove compartment and pulled it open. Inside the compartment were a bunch of receipts for gas, a couple of pouches of tobacco, and a slim GPS unit. He took the GPS and looked it over. To Devlin it seemed kind of old-fashioned to have a separate GPS unit; they'd been mostly superseded by smartphones. He turned it on and it flashed up a logo and then a home screen appeared, but there was no list of recent journeys. Devlin turned it off and slipped it into his pocket, then twisted round to look into the cargo part of the van. There was an empty liquor bottle lying on its side, discarded cable ties, a coil of yellow tow rope, and nothing else. Devlin swung back around and got out of the cab.

At the back of the garage was a service door to the main house. Perfect for a way in. Then he noticed that someone else must have had the same idea: the frame by the lock had been busted and splintered. The house might not be as empty as it appeared, thought Devlin. He pushed the door and it creaked open a few inches. He paused for a moment; if he was going in, he was going in prepared. He stepped back and took a look around the garage. Below the fuse box and propped up against the back wall was a two-by-four. He picked it up to feel the weight in his hand. It was good enough. Solid. He turned the flashlight on his cell phone on and slid through the service door into the main house.

The service door opened onto the living room with the breakfast bar and the kitchen diner to the right. There was a heavy, unpleasant odor in the house, a rank mix of cigarettes and stale food and sweat. He shined the light around. To his left, in front of the living room window and front door, was a sofa, a couple of armchairs, a coffee table, and a TV housed in a tall cabinet. Straight ahead, in the older part of the house, he could see a hallway that had to lead to the bedrooms and bathroom. The only sounds were the tick of a clock and the hum of the refrigerator. He found a light switch on the wall and flicked it on. The shadeless low-watt living room bulb hummed and flickered into life, its flat yellow light revealing a room covered in dirty plates, greasy discarded pizza boxes, half-empty cups, and open beer cans. There were overflowing ashtrays, piles of old car magazines, and a couple of stray socks left by the armchair that hadn't made it to the laundry basket. The place looked and smelled like it belonged to a lonely middle-aged man.

Devlin walked through the living room, his feet moving between the islands of mess on the carpet, and stood at the top of the hallway. He put his right shoulder against the wall and slid along till he came to the first door. He pushed it wide open and stepped in, his weapon ready at shoulder height, flashlight in his other hand. He flicked the light switch on. It was the bathroom, and it was empty. He then moved along the wall to the second door and pushed it open with a foot, stepped across to the other side of the doorway, and craned in. It was a small, simply furnished bedroom. He entered, turned the light on, and checked the closet and under the bed. Nothing. The last door was on the other side at the end of the hall. Devlin figured it was the master bedroom that ran the length of the hallway. Again, he gently kicked it open with a foot. No movement. Nothing. He eased inside, flicked the switch on, and moved over to the closet, swinging open the doors and rifling through the rack of clothes with the length of wood. Empty. He checked under the bed. Clear. All clear.

It began to look to Devlin like the person who had broken in had long gone. Or maybe he had just jumped to the wrong conclusion. It was as likely, knowing Ed, that he had lost his keys at some point and had had to break in himself.

Devlin allowed himself to relax, pocketed his cell, and walked back out into the hall. As he stood pondering his friend's deserted home, he heard a long, deep creak of old wood, like the first note of a sad song, coming from the ceiling. He looked up and had a split second to register two legs dangling from an attic hatch before he was flattened under the massive bulk of a falling body. Someone north of two hundred and fifty pounds had dropped onto Devlin, ambushing him from above and knocking him to the ground.

Devlin found himself struggling for breath and trapped on the floor. The guy holding him down was huge. He wore a black leather jacket, black pants, and a black balaclava, and he stank of rum, like that Bay Rum lotion old men use. He had to be nearly three hundred pounds. The two-by-four had gone flying out of Devlin's grip, and his arms were pinned down by two enormous legs, doubled up and kneeling on his biceps. Instinctively Devlin opened his jaws wide and sank his teeth into his attacker's inner thigh. Fabric tore and flesh filled the small space between Devlin's front teeth. His attacker gave out an animal-like roar of pain. He sat up and fell forward, frantically trying to pull his leg away, allowing Devlin to slide out from under him and grab the two-by-four. Devlin turned, ready to bury the piece of wood into the other guy's head, but he'd already hobbled up to the other end of the hallway. He was big, but he wasn't so fast right now with Devlin's teeth marks still burning in his thigh.

Devlin got up after him like a sprinter out of the blocks and rushed him, shouldering him in the back. The intruder rocked forward, stumbling over cups and cans, overturning the coffee table, and staggered back toward the living room window. He came to a stop and drew out a hunting knife from a leather sheath hanging off his belt. Devlin dropped the two-by-four and grabbed the two uppermost legs of the overturned table, lunging forward with every ounce of force, speed, and strength he could muster, holding the table rigidly out in front of him like a battering ram. Devlin and the table went crashing into the assailant and on through the windowpane. The knife was forced out of the assailant's hands as he went backward through the shattering glass and rotting wood. The two of them plunged into the sudden chill of the night air, shards of glass raining everywhere.

Devlin rolled to a halt in the midst of chunks of wood and a carpet of sharp, broken glass. The intruder had rolled on a little farther. Devlin tried to pick himself up, but the layer of glass around him slowed him down. He was too late getting up on his haunches, and the other guy was already taking a run-up. There was no time to form any kind of protection from the low kick to his guts that lifted Devlin's body off the ground and back down onto the glass. Devlin squirmed on the ground, gulping at the air like a fish out of water, knowing that once he was down, he stood next to no chance of being let up. Then Devlin felt his hair being grasped and pulled, his face yanked up toward the stars, and glimpsed the shadow of a huge fist somewhere in his peripheral vision before his head was hit by a freight train that arrived out of nowhere. A fist like a side of beef, cold, raw, and solid, slamming into his cheekbone and jaw. Then he was lying on the broken glass and damp earth again, spitting blood onto his chin. He felt his hair being yanked up once more. He waited dangling in midair for the knockout blow, but instead of oblivion, he was thrown back down on the ground. He heard heavy feet scramble and hit the ground running, off into the distance.

A moment passed. Could have been an hour, could have been a minute. Devlin reflected that he had been in many, many fights but that he'd clearly gotten a little rusty. What mattered was he was still alive and hopefully in working order. The next time he went up against that gorilla, so help him God, he'd rip his head off. Whoever he was.

One thing was for sure though: Ed definitely wasn't home.

And then the ground lit up blue like an underwater grotto.

4

The three of them sat around a square, gray table in a charcoal carpeted interview room with washed-out yellow walls. Devlin initialed each of the Miranda rights on a piece of card and pushed it back across to the lead cop, a young guy, probably not even thirty.

The door to the interview room had been left ajar, and as the lead cop was scanning the arrest report, Devlin noticed a small group of uniformed officers heading out of the lineup room on the opposite side of the hallway. A moment passed and two other more senior officers came out of the lineup room and followed. From their rank insignia, Devlin had them down as the sergeant and the deputy.

The arresting cop broke off from his papers and asked, "You sure you don't want to get proper medical attention?"

"No, thank you," said Devlin.

The lead cop's name was Miller. Officer Gray, his partner, was a young black cop, probably in her early twenties and serious. She had cleaned Devlin's cuts, administered a few Band-Aids, and given him painkillers at Ed's place.

"You're lucky—all our patrol cars got individual first aid kits and we got training," said Gray.

"I feel real lucky right now. Looks like I couldn't have chosen a better place to have the hell beaten out of me."

"That's right, Mr. Gabriel Devlin..." Miller glanced down at the arrest report. "Or would you prefer Father? But I'd say you're a long way from church right now." Devlin had taken his collar off when Gray had dressed his cuts, so right at that moment, Devlin didn't much look like a priest—more like a guy with a liking for black.

"Are you a Catholic, son ?" Devlin asked.

"No," replied Miller.

"Do you believe in God?"

"Nope."

"Then I don't think it matters either way to you, does it?"

Miller bristled a little but shook it off and continued. "Mr. Devlin, let's get down to brass tacks...your account of this evening's events. So, you came to Halton Springs looking for Ed James, who you knew from the Air Force where you worked in...?"

"Office of Special Investigations."

"On discovering he wasn't at home, you noticed that there were signs of forced entry at his residence?"

"Correct."

"On examining further, you encountered a male of approximately six foot eight and three hundred pounds dressed in black. You both fought, resulting in damage to the window and furniture and injuries to yourself, which we treated at the scene, injuries which you refused any further treatment for and for which we have completed a medical refusal report. Your assailant escaped on foot before our arrival."

"Yep."

"I know this is a long shot, but...do you think...could it have been a Bigfoot, Mr. Devlin?" Devlin didn't laugh and Officer Gray never laughed at anything, so an awkward silence followed until Miller followed up with a question that he also intended to be a warning.

"You sure you don't want that lawyer?"

"Positive."

"If I were in your position, Mr. Devlin, I'd definitely want the services of a lawyer."

"I don't need 'em."

"Perhaps you'd care to explain why? After all, some of us aren't big shots who worked at OSI."

Devlin shrugged. "If you really need me to tell you, well then, I guess I better tell you."

"Oh yeah, I really need you to tell me."

"Okay." Devlin leaned forward, eye to eye with Miller, and clasped his hands together on the desk. "I'm just gonna ride this thing till the charges die, son. I haven't got anywhere I need to be. No deadlines. No budget to meet, no figures to explain. As you pointed out, I used to work, albeit a way back, in Air Force Special Investigations, so I can see where this pans out to. My relationship with Ed will check out. My injuries and the damage to the property are consistent with my account of events. Now, admittedly, I don't know the specifics of Ohio law, but B and E is likely to be a relatively low-level felony and, without any evidence of intent, very hard to make stick in a court of law. Equally, I don't know the specifics of this station, but I've rarely seen one this size this busy. With this many cops on shift, someone's on overtime, so something has just gone down, and even on a slow night my case would be a bad bet. Tonight? The odds are astronomical. So my educated guess is that you're going to consult with your superior officer, and he's gonna tell you exactly what I just told you. Son."

Miller gave Devlin a long bitter look and just about swallowed down his bile. He looked at one of the papers in front of him and back up at Devlin.

"You were taken into protective custody last week in Boston for..." Miller looked down at his sheet. "Public intoxication."

"Is that a question or a statement of fact?"

"Doesn't paint a picture of a law-abiding citizen or a good priest."

"No law was broken. That's the only picture you can look at, Officer."

Miller glowered at Devlin. Devlin's cool pale blue eyes stared back with the simple confidence that Miller did not have it in his powers to touch or affect Devlin in any way. Eventually, Miller became self-conscious and turned red, then abruptly gathered up the arrest report and walked out of the interview room down the hall to the deputy's office.

Miller intercepted the deputy as he came out of his office pulling his coat on. He looked like he had the troubles of the world on his shoulders.

"Everything okay, Greg?" asked Miller. "Looks like you got your hands full."

The deputy didn't answer immediately. Instead he beckoned Miller back into his office.

"You might as well know, Todd, we've just had a homicide called in, couple of miles out east, over by Long Pine National Park. About one hundred and fifty meters from the highway."

The priest was right, thought Miller, *Smart-ass.* "Wait, up where the Gypsy camp was?"

"Around there, yes."

"I bet those sons of bitches did it."

"Well, let's not jump to conclusions, Todd. The crime technician's on her way over. I've called in the rest of the patrol and Sergeant Taylor, and they're heading over to the crime scene. What did you want?"

"Uh...well, we have this guy booked in, name's Devlin. We were called out to the corner of Thirty-Sixth and Franklin due to a neighbor's report of a disturbance and found him all beaten up, and damage to a Mr. Edward James's property. There was a smashed window, signs of forced entry. This guy says James is a friend of his and he discovered an intruder inside the property who attacked him and ran off..."

"Right..."

"I made an arrest 'cause I think he's playing us and spinning a story. I think there's more to this..."

"Thing is, Todd, we're stretched like a rubber band here."

"Yeah, but I really think—" Deputy Stevens's cell phone started buzzing, causing him to almost jump out of his uniform.

"Hold on, Todd, it's the chief." Stevens answered his cell. "Chief...yes, that's right...I've got them going out there to meet with the crime technician...That's right...I'm about to head up there myself to get a handover...Okay, I'll meet you there. Oh, also, we've had an incident at a property up on Franklin. At an Edward James's property. Someone claiming to be the occupier's friend was found at the scene of a break-in...Right." Stevens broke off and addressed Miller. "Any evidence of intent?"

"Uh...well...not really."

"No, Chief," said Stevens back on the cell. Miller watched his boss nodding to a string of instructions coming down the other end of the line. "Okay...Sure...Okay...Will do..." Stevens got off the phone. "Chief Walker says we're unlikely to be able to make the charges stick, and we've got a suspected homicide to deal with. He knows Ed James and is of the opinion that he's a drunk with nothing to steal. Maybe hold him over till the morning in case Ed James turns up. But otherwise, let's not resource it any further. Okay, Todd? Sorry."

Todd was unable to hide what he thought of the deputy's decision. He shook his head then headed back to Gray and

Devlin muttering to himself, "'Let's not resource it.' Spineless moron."

Miller stood over Devlin and said flatly, "We're keeping you overnight to check out your story. I tell you, if I were running this place I'd make sure we got you to court and made you explain yourself to a judge."

Devlin got out of the chair, stood to full height, and peered down at Miller. "And that's why you'll never run this place."

Gray was finally jolted out of her silence. "Wow. It's no wonder you had the hell kicked out of you."

"Yeah. For someone so smart, you didn't see that coming." Miller snorted. "Take him to holding cell four. The one by the broken heater."

"First I want to fill in a missing person's report for Ed," demanded Devlin.

"Who the hell says he's missing?" exclaimed Gray.

"He ain't missing! The chief says he's a drunk—more than likely he's sitting in a bar or sleeping it off in a ditch somewhere," added Miller.

"I want to file a report," insisted Devlin. "At least then I know he'll be on the NCIC database, even if you do nothing about it." Miller and Gray looked at each other and rolled their eyes.

"You take the details, Gray. I gotta file his arrest report," said Miller.

"Crap! C'mon, Miller," Gray protested. "I got to go home, get a couple of hours' sleep, and then drive up to Mount Carmel Hospital to pick up my mother."

"Look around you," said Miller. "It's just us two here, so if we split the work it gets done quicker."

Gray gave a sigh and said to Devlin, "Come with me, will you?"

Devlin followed Gray out of the interview room to her desk

where she logged into her PC, all the while sighing and huffing about it.

Devlin had already been booked in and searched, so after Gray had filed the missing person's report, she took him straight to the holding cells.

Devlin walked into the narrow concrete twelve-by-six cell, and Gray threw him a blanket.

"I'm sorry I've kept you from getting away to see your mother," he said.

Gray looked at Devlin wearily. "Breakfast's at seven. Right now it's lockup time, Father." And she closed the cell door and turned the key.

Although it was the early hours of the morning, there was still a low-level light on. The painkillers were wearing off, and Devlin's face and the right side of his body were pulsing with pain. He was damn hungry too as he hadn't eaten since nine o'clock when he'd made a halfway stop just south of Pittsburgh. The mattress was a thin blue plastic affair covered in a rough single sheet which sat on a concrete ledge. He said a night prayer from the Liturgy of the Hours followed by a prayer for Ed and lay down as carefully as he could, covering himself in the blanket that Gray had tossed him. Then, despite the pain and the stabs of hunger, sleep descended like a heavy cloak, a powerful drug overwhelming his weakened body.

It took minutes for Devlin to drop to the lowest level of consciousness, to begin dreaming. He was walking along a crowded street, a street he knew in downtown Baltimore. Limping toward him came a pathetic figure holding a dirty rucksack that no longer had any working straps. He wore a wool hat and an army surplus jacket. His jeans were dark with filth, and his sneakers just battered bits of canvas without laces. And, as he approached, just like every other night, he asked Devlin the one question that Devlin feared the most:

"Father Devlin, are you ready to repent?"

5

The rain had begun to fall at around one o'clock in the morning, a sudden solid downpour making work slow, difficult, and not particularly rewarding. The team of Halton officers along with a crime scene technician called in from Miami Valley crime lab had managed to secure the area. Although hidden within a copse, there had been enough of a clearing around the body to erect a white forensic tent. In spite of the rain and the waterlogged earth, the crime scene technician had evaluated the physical evidence, established a basic narrative of the scene, and walked it through with Deputy Stevens. Then she started taking photographs. Her camera flashes lit up the hillside along with the white bars of the flashlights held by the police officers brought on-site to comb through the wider crime scene.

Stevens stepped out into the open to get a moment away from the body and heard a voice barking at him from a little way off.

"Greg!" It was Chief Walker staggering up the grassy incline. In his haste to get out of bed and over to the site of the homicide, he had thrown on jeans, a shirt, boots, and an old high-vis jacket. Stevens could see Walker's Lexus parked up on the highway below, tucked in behind the police cruisers.

"Greg! What's the situation?" Walker shouted up to his deputy. "I want a full update, everything we know."

"Evening, Chief—or morning I guess. We got the body of a male, late teens or early twenties probably."

"Ethnicity?"

"From what we have left of the vic, Caucasian. But I don't think we could be specific."

"I know what I'd bet on," said Walker as he stopped to get his breath back. His small eyes drifted across to the piles of garbage and debris left by the recent camp which dotted the open ground only a hundred meters away.

"This happened right under the nose of those damn Gypsies. Coincidence? Highly unlikely I'd say."

"Chief, it's impossible to say for sure what happened. Thing is, it's nasty, Chief. Real nasty. The body has been decapitated and hands and feet also severed off and taken from the crime scene."

"Good God."

"It looks like there's been a concerted effort to prevent any identification of the victim."

Walker had now climbed the grassy bank and was standing beside Stevens, breathless and rasping. Stevens caught a faint whiff of liquor and gathered Walker must have had a tolerably good time at Congressman Logan's dinner up at the ranch.

"Do we know the time and cause of death, Greg?"

"There are two bullet wound entry points, one to the stomach and one to the chest. No exit wounds. CSI seems to think the time of death was about twenty-four hours ago from the body temperature and taking into account it's been outside. Dismemberment occurred after death. Apparently, there'd be a lot more blood if it took place antemortem, even accounting for the rain. So he was probably dead before they started cutting him up."

"That must be the definition of small mercies."

"We got a bad break with the weather last night and tonight. The forest floor has been swept clean by the downpour."

Walker sniffed and wiped raindrops away from his eyes. "And no witnesses either."

"No. No witnesses. Body was found by a trucker who stopped for a comfort break."

"A comfort break? He came all the way up here in the rain for a leak?"

"It wasn't a leak he needed, Chief."

"Oh, right...I see...well, when you gotta go, you gotta go."

"Looking for a tree to crouch under. Got more than he expected."

"I'll say."

"He's being questioned down at the station, but his truck's clean, his log sheet checks out, and his employer says he only left Cincinnati an hour and a half before he called 911. He found the body in the crop of trees." Both men glanced over to the dark tangle of trees and the forensic tent nestled within it. "Looks like the head was sawn off, and the hands and feet."

"Sawn?"

"It's a very clean cut. To be frank, Chief, the crime scene isn't telling us a hell of a lot at the moment. We don't know for definite if the homicide took place here. We don't even know if the dismemberment happened here. We can just hope the coroner gives us something to go on."

"Pah! They won't. They never do. They never stick their necks out on anything up at Miami Valley. They'll produce the safest, most open, and unhelpful conclusions they can."

Chief Walker thought for a moment, and his eyes darted over to Stevens and away to the forensic tent and back again. He rested a hand on his hip and brushed down his drenched mustache with his thumb and forefinger a couple of times.

"Greg, I think it's clear we're dealing with Gypsy business here."

"Are we really sure...? Because there could be other explanations we need to rule out."

"Greg, the camp uprooted today, the last of them left only hours ago. We had trouble with them fighting down in the town only last week for God's sake, had to pull a bunch of 'em in and dry 'em out. They were out of control. This is a Gypsy feud gone bad. I'd bet my badge on it. You know the score—someone's brother slept with someone's sister, or something like. I don't want anyone getting all Sherlock Holmes over this. Greg? Do you hear me? I'm not gonna get the Bureau of Criminal Investigation pulled in to go over this when it's plain who's responsible."

"But is it plain, Chief? I mean, it's tidy—"

"Greg, there hasn't been a homicide in Halton in over five years. Hell, the last one wasn't even a proper homicide; it was a firearms accident up on Kip McGrath's farm. A community of Gypsies turn up, to use the politically correct parlance we all have tug our forelocks to these days, and bang! What do you know? We've got a decapitated body on our hands. When you do the crime scene debrief, let's make it clear that this is our main and only lead and we do not expect there to be others. With a bit of luck and a following wind, we can turn this over to whatever police department has the dubious pleasure of seeing this motley crew roll up into their municipality."

"But the homicide is in our jurisdiction. Nothing can change that, Chief."

"Sure, sure. We'll have to process the forensics. But the manhunt and investigation will be wherever the Gypsy camp ends up next. That's where the resources will go. Halton PD's a small operation, and we cannot lend any help on that account. I see this one slipping very easily into some other PD's in-tray." Walker gave Stevens a challenging glare. "Do you understand me, Greg?"

"Fully, Chief. Do truckers crap in woods?"

"Ha! Very funny! Good man. Greg, I've got a meeting with the mayor first thing in the morning to brief him, so if you're okay to carry on here...?"

"Absolutely."

"I know I can depend on you."

Walker gave Stevens a solid pat on the shoulder. As he slipped and sidled off back down to his Lexus, he muttered, "Do truckers crap in woods?" to himself a couple of times and chuckled. But Stevens cursed his good nature and his geniality. He felt a twinge of shame that yet again he hadn't found the resolve to challenge his chief.

6

Devlin was woken by the scrape of iron on concrete. He peeled the side of his face off the mattress and saw the holding clerk standing in the doorway of the cell swinging a bunch of keys.

"Get up, you can go. They're not going to press charges."

Devlin ran his hands through his black hair, sweeping stray curls back from his forehead. He swung his legs onto the floor, gripped his knees, and exhaled slowly and evenly in a bid to cope with his tiredness and body aches.

"Let's go. We haven't got all day," said the clerk.

"I see you treat innocent people here the same way as suspects. I don't even get breakfast?"

"I wouldn't complain. The honey bun and juice aren't that memorable."

The clerk took him to the booking room, signed Devlin off on the system, and handed back his belongings in a plastic bag: wallet, watch, car keys, cell phone, cigars, cigar cutter, lighter, rosary, the cross he wore around his neck, and Ed's GPS.

Devlin made his way out of the station and crossed the tree-lined parking lot. The next thing would be to get a cab out to Ed's and retrieve his car. He'd already lost a night, and now it would be midday before he could resume any meaningful search. As he emerged onto the street, he almost ran flat into a bleary-eyed Greg Stevens. Devlin immediately recognized him as the deputy he'd seen the night before. In daylight and up close, he also noticed he'd lost some weight compared to the department photo hung up on the wall in the lobby. Stevens apologized and was about to move on when it clicked with him who Devlin was.

"Hey, you're the guy we booked last night," said Stevens.

"That's right," replied Devlin.

"They let you go?"

"They never should have kept me. I was just up visiting a friend when some goon jumped me."

"What's the name of your friend?" asked Stevens, trying to recall the conversation he'd had with Miller in the early hours of the morning.

"Ed James." Devlin could see Stevens was curious about this stranger that had just rolled into town and was looking to make his mind up about him.

"How do you know him?" asked Stevens.

"I was in the Air Force with him. Investigations."

"You still in investigations?"

"No. I'm a priest now."

"No kidding?"

"No kidding."

Stevens titled his head to the side, looked Devlin up and down, frowned, and asked, "Where's your collar?"

"In my pocket."

Beaten up and after a couple of hours' sleep in a cell, Devlin didn't exactly look like priest material. He pulled out his celebret card, his clerical ID, from his wallet and handed it to Stevens, who studied it, nodded approvingly a couple of times, and said, "You're Roman Catholic?"

"Yep."

"I'm Catholic too, Father...?"

"Devlin. Gabe Devlin."

"Good to meet you, Father Devlin. Deputy Stevens." He extended a hand and they shook.

"Good to meet you too, Deputy."

"Where's your parish?"

"Dover, Massachusetts. St. Jude's Church." Devlin left out the part about him having just quit. Best keep things simple.

"We go to Sacred Heart in Springfield, me and the family."

"I'm very glad to hear it. Going today?"

"Well, actually... No, not today. See, I got to be back here later...for something quite serious. I know, you're thinking it's a mortal sin to skip mass."

"From all the activity at the station last night, I trust you have a serious enough reason. Probably not even a venial sin I'd say."

"Thanks, Father. I'll take that as my official pardon."

Stevens rubbed his chin and considered Devlin for a moment "Say, you're beat up pretty bad... Listen, you want to come back to my house? You could use my bathroom to clean up."

"Oh, I don't know," Devlin replied, unsure whether he wanted to be hanging out with a cop right now.

"And I could fix you some breakfast."

"It's an imposition."

"Not at all. Look at it as my way of making amends for skipping mass. And I hate to see a man of God going around looking like you do right now."

After another moment of uncertainty, Devlin decided to

accept. He couldn't spend his life avoiding the law. And if he was going to find Ed, he needed a way into this strange new town, and the deputy was a good start. And, equally importantly, Devlin was nearly faint with hunger. So he accepted graciously.

"Sounds like the best invitation I've had since I got to Halton."

"It's the only invitation you've had since you got to Halton, isn't it?"

"Yep."

"My car's just over there." Stevens pointed back to the police parking lot. "Follow me."

DEVLIN COLD SHOWERED, a habit he'd gotten into in the Air Force. It was a discipline and a kind of shock therapy to jump-start his body and mind. It was especially needed after the small amount of sleep he'd managed to get in the cell the night before. While Stevens cooked up breakfast, Devlin changed into clothes Stevens had lent him: a T-shirt and jogging pants along with socks and old sneakers that were just wide enough to fit his feet without laces. He sat at the kitchen table in the borrowed clothes, which were almost comically tight, his hair wet and combed back and his face freshly shaved, the cuts and bruises from last night dressed anew from a first aid box that Stevens had dug out.

Stevens served up a tower of pancakes and bacon, which Devlin demolished and washed down with nearly a pot of coffee.

The deputy watched this broad, imposing figure hunched at the table eating. His raw, square-set features, the coal-black hair, and searching blue eyes. There was a physicality about him a little at odds with people's regular idea of a priest. Devlin looked more like your old-time preacher, carrying the word of God out to a frontier town. As handy with a Smith and Wesson Schofield as he was with a sermon. And he definitely looked like he'd lived some.

Stevens's wife had taken the kids to a playdate, so they had the place to themselves. Stevens had changed out of his uniform into shorts and a T-shirt and looked even more exhausted than Devlin. He ate only a couple of pieces of toast and mainly played with the salt shaker. For a long while Stevens didn't say much. He seemed caught up in himself. Distracted.

Eventually, he asked, "So, who do you think the guy was you ran into at Ed James's place?"

"No idea, but he was one tough son of a gun. It's been a long while since I was in a fight, but I can handle myself. This guy was a powerhouse. And I'm not just saying that because I got whipped."

"Kind of odd though. Burglars don't usually stand and fight if they have an opportunity to get out. And he could have just slipped out through a window in the dark. It's like he was trying to scare you. Or worse."

Devlin wasn't anxious to blow this thing up or get into a detailed conversation about it, so he shrugged and said, "Maybe. Or maybe he felt cornered."

"Mmmm...maybe." Stevens toyed with the salt shaker some more and then asked, "Why did you become a priest? If you don't mind my asking?"

"I don't. My wife was a worrier, so I quit special investigations to settle down so she would quit worrying...and then she died. It was sudden; we didn't see it coming."

Stevens stopped playing with the shaker and looked up at Devlin. "I'm sorry."

"So I rethought everything," Devlin continued. "I'd been

brought up a strict Catholic, so I returned to my faith because nothing else came even remotely close to making sense."

There was silence. Stevens looked like he was absorbing what Devlin had said. Some salt had scattered onto the tabletop, so Devlin deftly took a pinch, threw it over his left shoulder, and muttered, "Blind the devil."

"Do you believe in hell, Father?"

"I don't want to."

"But?"

"But I believe we are held accountable for our actions. Somehow. If that's hell or not, I don't know."

Stevens refilled both their cups. Devlin sloshed a mouthful down and asked, "What was all the fuss at the station about last night? It was full of cops when I was there."

"Oh." Stevens hesitated for a second and then shrugged and spoke. "Well, I guess I can tell you now it's being reported. There was a body found up in Long Pine."

"Long Pine?" said Devlin, suddenly alarmed and thinking of Ed.

"Yeah, the woods north of Halton. Kinda gruesome. The victim had been dismembered."

"Dismembered? Have you ID'd the body?"

"No. All we know is he was a kid. In his late teens, early twenties. Not much more to go on than that."

"A kid? Damn." Devlin masked his relief and shook his head. "Any clue who did it?"

"Well, there was a Gypsy camp by the spot the body was found. They only just moved on last night, so that's the way the investigation's headed."

"Are they Roma Gypsies?"

"Yeah, they are. Why?"

"Just curious. The word 'gypsy' gets used for lots of different people. Any reason why it happened?"

"We don't know for sure. Chief thinks it's a feud. Family dispute gone bad. I'm not so sure, but it's the only line we're pursuing at the moment." Devlin nodded. "You want some more pancakes?" asked Stevens. "There's some left over."

"You not eating?"

"Nah. I don't eat much after pulling an overnight."

"Listen, don't let me stop you if you want to get some sleep."

"No. Stay, please. It's good to have company, not to have the house so quiet. You want those pancakes?"

"Actually I will, thanks."

Devlin ate some more and then between mouthfuls said, "They don't kill for revenge or for wrongdoing."

"Who don't?"

"Roma Gypsies."

"How do you know?"

Devlin swallowed down the last scrap of pancake and took a sip of coffee before replying. "Because I've spent time with them. With Roma Gypsies. I went to Lourdes after my wife died. It was a pilgrimage to test my faith before I decided to train to be a priest. When I went happened to be the same time as the yearly pilgrimage made by Romanies. They go in honor of a Gypsy saint, Sara la Kali. Thousands of them turn up, year in, year out. I got friendly with a group of Kalderash from Romania and traveled back to Paris with them. I was their guest. I ate with them, drank with them, slept in their bed. It was...illuminating. They know about our laws, but we know nothing about theirs."

"So what do they do if there's a dispute? A serious dispute? What's their law?"

"They have a pretty developed form of internal justice. Death is not a recognized sanction. It wouldn't even compare to the seriousness of their strongest punishment."

"Which is what?"

"'Marime.' Banishment. Social death. The loss of their honor, their identity, is far worse than capital punishment. They become impure or defiled. No longer clean. That's what happens in the most serious disputes."

"When you were in investigations, did you work homicides?" asked Stevens.

"Many. You?"

Stevens shook his head. "This is my first one."

"I have a feeling, Deputy, that you'll do better on your first than some do on their hundredth."

"Why do you say that?"

"I think you have integrity, and I think your instincts are right. This isn't a Gypsy-related homicide. But you didn't invite me back here to discuss a police case, did you?"

"No...no. I didn't."

"Why did you invite me back, Deputy?"

"So you could get cleaned up and have something to eat. What other reason would there be?"

"I don't know. But in my experience priests are usually houseguests for a more personal or spiritual reason."

Stevens's eyes darted back and forth, like he was making up his mind whether to say something or not to say it. He looked down into his lap for a second. Then he looked up, his tired, red eyes reddening some more. He clenched his teeth and braced himself. "Okay. Yes. You're right. There is another reason..."

"What is it? What's troubling you?"

"I'm...I'm dying, Father."

Devlin leaned forward. "Do you know how long you have?"

"It's months."

"Are you getting any treatment?"

"No...it's metastatic pancreatic cancer. Too late for intervention. All that's left is palliative care. When I get to that point. I got another scan booked in today, but it's already so far gone that it's really just a formality. The scan is just so's we have an idea of how quickly the end might be coming."

"Are you talking to your priest about this?"

"Yeah, but Father Francis is...well...a bit stiff. Not the most comforting of men."

"Do the other cops know?"

"Not yet. But I was working up to it." Stevens stopped and took a moment to consider Devlin. "You don't seem surprised?"

"I guessed it must be serious, whatever it was," said Devlin.

"How?"

"Inviting a priest you hardly know round for breakfast, the interest in hell, the fact you were obviously preoccupied with something of significance...and the weight you've lost."

Stevens nodded. "And I thought I was being discreet... Thing is, Father, most of the time I try to act like it's all okay, for my wife and kids, but...I'm afraid. I'm really, really afraid."

Devlin laid a hand on Stevens's hand and said gently, "Of course you are, but you have faith, and so the Lord will be holding your hand just as I am now when your time arrives." A single tear trickled from the side of Stevens's eye. "Would you like me to pray for you, Deputy?"

"It's Greg. And yes, Father, I would. Very much."

Devlin brought out his rosary. Both men clasped their hands in prayer, and Devlin recited the Chaplet of the Divine Mercy for Stevens. As they sat and Devlin prayed, again the priest laid a hand on Stevens's hand, and he felt a gentle, warm flow of force, a rising energy in his chest that radiated out into his limbs. It was so subtle and natural, he wasn't sure whether it was real or imagined.

After the Chaplet, they sat in reflective silence for a while, a dying man and a priest who was sure he was going to hell.

Slowly Stevens's thoughts returned to the life he had left to live. He thought about the man who'd been murdered up in the woods. He thought about what the chief had said. About the likelihood of anybody in the station actually working the homicide properly. He knew that likelihood was zero. Definitely. Chief Walker ran the department like a fiefdom. Stevens looked over at Devlin and saw a potential ally. And he did something he'd done too rarely in his life up until now. He took a gamble.

With a resolve that was new to him, he asked, "Would you do me a favor?"

"Depends. But I am a priest. Favors are more my line than most."

"Would you take a look at the photos from the crime scene with me? You may have a more seasoned eye than I do."

Devlin wasn't expecting the invitation, but he saw an opportunity immediately and replied. "Sure. Of course I would...if you could help me out finding Ed?"

"You think Ed's missing?"

"Yeah. I do. I think he's upped and left because he was... unhappy," said Devlin, deciding to be thrifty with the facts. "He'd had his ups and downs...problems. It's not uncommon with ex-service personnel. His marriage had broken down, he was estranged from his wife and daughter. I need to find him and make sure he's okay...because nobody else sure as hell will."

"You think you can find him?"

"I do. Detective work is what I used to do for a living. So I'll do it again."

"Okay. It's a deal," said Stevens. "I'll help you with Ed, if I can." Stevens went to fetch his laptop, and when he returned, he set it down on the table.

"Have you said to your chief you disagree with his line?" asked Devlin.

"No. No, I haven't. Not yet. I will if I need to. Right now all I want is an opportunity to follow the evidence. Saying a Gypsy feud is our only lead means we keep it in Halton PD and close the case before it's opened."

"You gone against the chief before?"

"No. Never."

7

Stevens opened up his laptop and clicked on the attachments he'd got from the crime technician.

"Before we start, I should warn you, it's not pretty. The victim has been decapitated and hands and legs likewise removed."

"You really don't have to worry on my account," replied Devlin. "I think I've seen most everything there is to see."

Stevens opened the first photo. It was of a naked male torso with arms and legs but no head, hands, or feet. It was partially embedded in the surrounding mud, and there was no significant decomposition. The flash of the camera gave the skin tone an unnatural paleness that exaggerated the exsanguination caused by the dismemberment. There were two neat, black round holes, one in the gut and one to the right side of the chest. Nicks and scratches covered the torso. Although, considering the extent of the butchery, there was a lot less blood on the surrounding soil than Devlin would expect. The last few nights' rains must have washed most of it away. Devlin clicked through more photos that had been taken of the body from every conceivable angle and close-up and medium shots of the wounds. But the crime scene was really only the body. There were no other objects in the vicinity. The only other set of significant photos were close-ups of fly larvae on the genitals and wounds.

Stevens gave Devlin the information that had been gathered so far. "So it's a young male, looking like late teens or early twenties. In all probability Caucasoid. But skin tone may possibly suggest Hispanic or other ethnicity, though the skin discoloration prevents us being anywhere near certain. But that could prop up the Gypsy theory. From the bullet wounds it looks like they used a small round, maybe even a .22. It's by no means certain either of the shots were lethal. So, maybe there was another shot to the head or another cause of death entirely. There are no exit wounds, so the bullets that caused the two wounds to the trunk are almost certainly lodged in the body. We haven't found any other bullets or casing at the crime scene. The guess is they've amputated the body parts to prevent identification."

"Where exactly was the body found?" asked Devlin.

"Here." Stevens opened an aerial satellite map with a pin marking out the clump of trees near the highway where the body was discovered.

"Right on the edge of the forest?"

"Yeah."

"Had the body been moved?"

"CSI says it's unlikely from the pattern of lividity."

Devlin thought for a minute. Then a minute turned into two and he began to sink into a state of deep concentration. He sat with his head lowered and his fists in his lap. Moments ticked by, but Devlin was not now conscious of duration, only the images and connections firing and flashing through his mind. More time passed in silence until Devlin exhaled heavily and returned to the present and to Stevens.

"Can I smoke?" he asked. "Outside?"

"Yeah. Sure."

They both headed out through the porch into the hot sun bearing down on the backyard. They sat around a wrought iron table in matching chairs under the shade of a sycamore tree. Devlin bit the end off a cigar, lit it, and breathed in the burning ropes of delicious smoke.

"So?" asked Stevens eagerly.

"I saw a young man running hell for leather in blind panic through a forest."

"What, like a vision?"

"No. No vision. I saw it because the body has cuts and tears all over it. Cuts and tears from running through the dense forest in the dark. Running without care for their own safety. Running from somebody, or something."

"But he was caught."

"Yeah. He was caught all right. He ran straight into his killer." Devlin raised his hand that held his cigar and shaped his thumb and fingers like a gun. "Boom, boom, straight into his front. He was corralled into the path of the person who shot him. And whoever caught him was in a hurry."

"How do you figure that?"

"If you were going to dump a body in a forest, where would you dump it? Would you dump it on the outskirts? Next to a highway and a Gypsy camp?"

"No. I guess I wouldn't. But why kill him there? Why cut his body up there? That's a lot of work to do when you got cars and people not so far away."

"I don't think they chose for it to happen there. For some reason, it had to happen there. Maybe that's where they finally caught up with the victim. And in the weather conditions they would have had two nights ago, it would have narrowed down their options. It's raining, it's dark, traffic flying by in one direction, people milling around in the other. They didn't have the time to dig a deep enough grave to be confident that the body wouldn't be dug up by animals. They were in heavy rain on a sloping forest floor; it had to be muddy and waterlogged as hell. No good for digging. So they hacked off the limbs. They knew it was a matter of time before the body was found. They made it so it didn't matter that it was found. They took what they needed, the face, the prints, and the dental evidence, left what they didn't...but they didn't take the DNA."

"No. So the coroner should give us something on that."

"Yeah...or maybe they weren't worried about the DNA."

"Why would that be?"

Devlin paused for thought, and then he said, "I'm not sure."

Stevens hesitated for a moment. He knew he shouldn't involve Devlin any further, that professionally he'd said more than enough and it should remain solely a police matter, but already he'd given Stevens more to go on than any of his own team.

"Would you come with me to the coroner's office when the autopsy report is in?"

"Are you sure that'd be okay? With your superiors?"

Stevens shrugged. "Maybe not. But I want to do the right thing here, not the correct thing. I'm the only one keeping an open mind on this case, and I could do with some help. So you let me worry about that. Okay?"

"Okay. Sure. In that case, yeah. I'd be happy to help. Now it's my turn. Ed... Think I might need a bit of local information." Devlin pulled out the GPS unit he'd taken from Ed's cab and turned it on. "It's Ed's," said Devlin.

"Where d'you find it?"

"His truck." Devlin flicked through the home page to the list of favorite destinations. There were just two. Apart from Ed's own address, nearly all his journeys began and ended in two places: a zip code on Route 36 and a full address in Columbus.

Devlin handed the unit to Stevens. "You know either of these two places?"

"That's the Logan Ranch," said Stevens, pointing at the spot along Route 36. "Clay and Earl's ranch out east from Halton."

"I saw the ranch coming into town last night," said Devlin. "Looked like there was something going on there. Some kind of party. Place was lit up."

"Yeah. That's Clay. He's congressman for the 10th District—a star on the rise, and he throws high-powered get-togethers. He's like Halton's own movie star. His brother, Earl, is the one to watch. He's a mean son of a bitch. Tall and skinny with a nasty sneer plastered across this face. We had to pull him off more guys in more brawls than I can count. It's a miracle he hasn't killed anyone. He hasn't just got a temper; he's borderline psychotic."

Stevens handed the device back to Devlin. Devlin tapped on the Navigation button on the screen and then on Recent Destinations. A list of stored journeys came up, and nearly every one started at the Logan Ranch. Devlin passed it to Stevens to see. "Have a look at that. He's spending a lot of time driving out from the ranch. Maybe Ed was doing some kind of deliveries for the Logans," said Devlin.

"Could be."

Devlin considered Stevens for a moment, how much he felt he could trust him. "You've been straight with me, Greg, so I'm gonna be straight with you."

"Okay."

"Truth is, I think Ed's in danger. I was tailed down to DC yesterday by two guys. I noticed them in Baltimore, but I think they could easily have followed me all the way from my church in Dover. They were after Ed. I called Ed to check in with him, and he was a very frightened man. I haven't been able to contact him since. I think he's on the run from people."

"Why?"

"Maybe he owes them. Gambling debts. At least that's how Ed told it. Whoever I ran into last night at Ed's is one of those people. I guess what I'm saying is, if you pick up anything that might help me, can you let me know?"

"Okay. No problem. You got it."

A text alert sounded from Stevens's cell phone, and he swiped it to see who it was from.

"What now?" said an exasperated Stevens.

"What's up?"

"You'll have to excuse me. It's Brendan. He's been at the front door ringing the bell. He's a kid, lives in Halton. In and out of trouble, drugs mainly."

"I should go anyway. I need to pick up my car, get a hotel room somewhere."

"You can stay here. Not a problem."

"That's very kind, but you don't need any extra impositions right now. And I'm here in town anytime you need me. For anything. I mean that. I'll text you my number."

"Thank you, Father."

Devlin made to rise and then had second thoughts. "Greg, could I use your laptop? Just for research."

"Sure, no problem."

"Thanks. Oh, and you don't have a notebook and pen to hand, do you?"

"Yeah. I'll get them from the office."

Stevens fetched Devlin the pen and paper and then went to the front door. Devlin sat at the table, googled Clay Logan, and got his congressional website up. He read through the press releases that had been uploaded and which went back ten years. They outlined the local issues he was most involved with. Then Devlin clicked through to the list of Clay's Caucus memberships, making notes of any he found most useful. Devlin noticed that Clay had been heavily involved in projects at the Wright Patterson Air Force Base, where Devlin was briefly stationed and Ed was posted. If he rolled up to the Logan Ranch uninvited, he would need to have something to reach for, depending on his reception, a backstory. He shut the laptop and slipped the GPS into his pocket. About half an hour had passed, and Stevens hadn't returned. He picked up his dirty clothes that Stevens had packed into a grocery bag and made his way to the front door.

Outside he ran into Brendan and Stevens, who were sitting on the porch. Brendan was a pale, thin, and delicate-looking teenager, maybe seventeen or eighteen at most. He wore skinny jeans, a sleeveless top, and sneakers with no socks. His hair was crew-cut at the sides with a thick quiff combed up and back at the top. Around the top of his left arm was an elaborate Celtic cross tattoo. There was a cherubic look about him mixed with a premature world-weariness, and his eyes were red, like he'd been crying.

"Thanks, Greg," said Devlin. "I'll be on my way. And just let me know when you need me to help out with that thing we were discussing."

"Will do. By the way, Father Devlin, this is Brendan. Brendan, this is Father Devlin."

"Hello," said Brendan warily.

"Hello."

"You going running, Father? " Brendan asked, and Devlin realized he was talking about his clothes.

"Maybe."

"You been in a fight?"

"I fell."

"Oh. I see. Onto someone's fist?"

"Yeah. Onto someone's fist."

"While you were running?"

"Stop it, Brendan," said Stevens, half smiling and half admonishing.

"It's fine, Greg…see you." Devlin walked to the front gate.

"Oh, listen, do you want a ride anywhere?" asked Stevens. "It's a way back into town."

"You've been up all night. I'm happy to walk," said Devlin.

"I can give you a ride back," said the kid. "I gotta head to work at the coffee shop."

"You drive?" asked Devlin.

"Sure, I'm seventeen; I got a probationary license."

"His license is clean if that's any reassurance," said Stevens.

Devlin shrugged and said, "Okay. In that case, show me to your chariot."

"No need to be a wiseass; it's me doing you the favor," Brendan said as he stood and took out his car keys.

Brendan's car was a twenty-year-old Honda Civic. Devlin managed to squeeze into the passenger seat, but his knees were practically up around his chest. Brendan started the engine while pulling a carton of Marlboro out from his pocket, and with one hand on the wheel, he pecked a cigarette out with his mouth.

He looked at Devlin. "You object?"

"On the contrary," said Devlin, pulling out a Corona.

"Damn, look at the size of that thing. Don't only the mafia smoke those?"

"Less talk, more smoke. Light me up, already." Devlin bit off the cigar end, rolled down the window, and spat it out. Brendan passed Devlin the car lighter, then lit up his own cigarette and planted it back in the dash.

"Jesus!" Brendan said as Devlin let out a thick, pungent cloud of smoke. "Now I know how nonsmokers feel."

"Can I ask you not to take our Savior's name in vain?"

"Yeah, you can ask." Brendan pulled out into the road with a jolt, heading north, up toward West Main. "Where you want me to drop you off?"

"I need to pick up my car. It's parked up on the other side of town, just off the 36."

"Why'd you leave it out there?"

Devlin kept the explanation evasive and short. "I was at a friend's house. Had a couple of beers. Better safe than sorry."

As they drove back into the main drag, Brendan put on a CD and cranked up the volume. A short percussive rhythm started up followed by a loud twisting and straining chorus of electric guitars. Brendan glanced sideways to check if the priest sat next to him was reacting with predictable distaste. But Devlin was grinning back at Brendan, his arm resting on the rolled-down window and his relaxed hand tapping the rhythm out on his cigar.

"*Loveless*. Great album," said Devlin.

"What? You know this? You know My Bloody Valentine?" Brendan said with astonishment.

"Yeah. I saw them in North Carolina in 1992."

Brendan stared back at Devlin and said in frustration, "What kind of priest are you? I don't know whether to like you more or My Bloody Valentine less."

They turned onto the main strip, passed by the police station, and continued back out east. Brendan lit up another cigarette. Devlin had let his cigar go out and looked out the window, studying each store and building as they flashed by. From time to time, Brendan sniffled and wiped his eyes and nose on his sleeve. He was clearly still upset about something.

Eventually, Devlin asked, "You okay?"

"I've been better. I just broke up with someone."

"Did they do the breaking up?"

"No. I did."

Devlin considered this and blew a trail of smoke out of the window. "I know it's an obvious thing to say, but it gets better."

"You're right, it is an obvious thing to say..." Brendan sniffed again and said, "I'm sorry, I don't mean to be snappy, but everything just looks like crap to me at the moment."

"I know. That's the way it is when you're at the end of something."

Brendan sucked hard on his cigarette and blasted out a thin spurt of smoke through pursed lips. Then he asked, "You ever been...at the end of something?"

"Yeah. Yeah, I have," replied Devlin.

"You had your heart broken?"

"Yeah."

"Who was it?"

"My wife."

"She left you?"

"She died...so, yes, she left me."

"Oh, God, I'm...I'm sorry."

"It's a long time ago, and I'm better now. So all I'm saying to you is, anyone who hasn't been in pain because of love doesn't have a certificate for being a fully paid-up human being."

"I'm in pain all right... But it had to end...it wasn't right. In fact, it was about as wrong as it could be."

"Sounds like you did the very best thing. And the pain goes. I promise."

"Does it?"

"Yeah. Like you wouldn't believe."

"You're not in pain about your wife?"

"Nope. Time. It's all about time, Brendan."

But of course, Devlin was lying.

8

The silver Chevy's engine died, and Bradley put his head back against the headrest. "Pretty."

"Picture-postcard pretty," replied Otterman. "Seems like only yesterday we were here."

"That's 'cause it *was* yesterday, dumbass," said Bradley.

They were sitting in front of a pristine whitewood church. A tall bell tower protruded from the middle of the building and divided it into two halves. On the left side of the tower was the church hall which was end on. On the right was a single-story house with two windows either side of a double door made out of light cypress wood and shaded by a pillared portico. Laid out in front was a glimmering green lawn, tidy and striped from recent mowing. Around the house was a low natural-stone wall. Behind the wall was a neat garden hedge that an elderly man in slacks, a short-sleeved shirt, and sandals was pruning back with great care.

"He looks about a hundred years old," murmured Otterman.

"Yeah. Happy though." Bradley sniffed the air. Then he sniffed again, and his expression soured. "Damn! It still stinks of gas in here. I hope to God we get our deposit back on this thing."

But Bradley's concern about their car rental was cut short by the chorus of "La Bamba" suddenly blaring out.

"Change your ringtone for crying out loud," barked Otterman. Bradley noted the number coming up on the screen and straightened up in his seat, clamping the cell phone to his ear.

"Mr. Stein, hi..."

Eight hundred miles away, Trayder Stein sat in his cream leather, high-backed, executive swivel chair. He was looking out through his tinted office windows over the busy six lanes of East Broad Street in downtown Columbus.

"Morning. Where the hell are you?"

"We're in Dover, Massachusetts, like you said, Mr. Stein. Outside Devlin's old church."

"Okay. Well, he ain't there."

"What?"

"My client got a helpful call from their inside guy at Halton Springs PD. Apparently, he turned up there last night looking for Ed James. The cops picked him up at Ed James's place. Say, you guys didn't give anything away to Devlin yesterday?" Bradley's stomach turned a somersault. He was pretty sure Devlin turning up in Halton was down to him having taken Ed James's Greyhound ticket, but he instantly went into full denial.

"No way. Absolutely not, Mr. Stein. James must have got in contact with him somehow."

"Yeah. Maybe so. Fortunately, though, Devlin doesn't seem to be any wiser about his whereabouts than we are."

"So, I guess that's it. There's nothing more for us to do." There was a silence at the other end of the line. "Mr. Stein?"

"Mmmm, I'm thinking. If Devlin's looking for Ed, then he's a live threat. Maybe it'd be useful to do a little digging. I've been looking into this guy Devlin's history. It's quite a formidable track record. Before he got the God bug, he started out as pararescue, a medically trained paratrooper, like a male nurse with wings. He got bored with that and then trained as a special agent with Air Force Special Investigations, joining Region Seven—counterintelligence and special access programs, high-up stuff. If he's in Halton sniffing around Ed, then it might be a good thing to find out a bit more about who he is. Above and beyond the public military record—more...personal information."

"How do we do that?"

"You're the PI, Bradley. You work it out. And you have the best day, y'hear?"

"Wait—Mr. Stein?" But Stein had hung up.

"Anything I need to know?" asked Otterman.

"Devlin isn't here," Bradley replied.

"What?"

"Apparently he's back in Ohio looking for Ed."

"Oh, man. The ticket."

"It's okay. Stein doesn't seem suspicious. Looks like we're in the clear on that. But he wants us to do some digging on Devlin. Get some dirt. Christ knows how though."

Otterman scratched his ragged goatee thoughtfully and said, "I reckon we go with the 'kind visitors' schtick."

"You think?"

"Yeah, I think."

"It's a bit of a reach, isn't it?"

"Nah! Come on! What happened to Narcotics Detective Second Grade, Bradley? Huh? The guy who worked a case until it squeaked? It's one of your favorite plays." Bradley looked over at the old man gardening and then back at Otterman. It was true; Bradley was better than this. Better than just some guy sitting in a car with a fat moron like Otterman for twelve hours at a time, listening to him break wind and whine nonstop about 9/11 conspiracies. Just one stupid procedural error in a drugs case laid bare in court had got him ejected prematurely and unfairly from the work he loved: the work of police law enforcement. He was better than this, and he was certainly better than Otterman.

"Okay. Let's do it. But I do the talking," said Bradley.

"That's my boy!"

They got out of the car, and Bradley opened the trunk. Under their carryalls, cases, coats, and gasoline-riddled suits he found what he was looking for, a square box wrapped untidily in gaudy gold and purple paper. He blew the dust off it and did his best to wipe it clean with his jacket sleeve. Then they walked toward the church with Bradley carrying the box. The old man who had been hunched over and moving at the speed of tai chi suddenly leaped into life when he saw the two men approaching and scuttled toward them waving his hands and shouting, "Off! Off!"

"What the hell's he—?" Bradley began before realizing what the fuss was about. "Oh nuts, we're on the lawn!"

Bradley and Otterman shouted sorry a couple of times and tiptoed apologetically off onto the asphalt that ran up to and around the church.

"I just did the lawn this morning!" whined the old man.

"We're really sorry," said Bradley.

"So sorry," said Otterman.

"Can I help you?" asked the old man.

"Well, Father, perhaps you..."

"Oh no. I'm not a priest. I'm the sacristan. Name's James Barroso."

"Oh, okay," said Bradley. "Well, Mr. Barroso, we were just looking for a very old friend of ours. Father Gabriel Devlin."

"Father Devlin?"

"Yes," said Bradley, turning on all the warmth he possessed. "We knew Gabriel...I mean Father Devlin...back in the Air Force, and we had a get-together with some of the other guys recently but couldn't get hold of him. So we were traveling down through Massachusetts and decided to come look him up."

"Oh. Well you won't find him here I'm afraid," said Barroso.

Bradley feigned disappointment. "You're kidding... Why not?"

"Well, he's...well, the truth is he decided he wanted a break from his duties here at St. Jude's. He's left." Both Bradley and Otterman's eyes lit up at this new piece of intelligence.

"Oh no!" Otterman said with all the feeling he could muster. "When did he leave?"

"He resigned from the post formally a few weeks ago. But he didn't really leave properly until yesterday in fact."

"So sudden," said Bradley sympathetically.

"Yeah, it's a real shame. He was a great priest. A great man. We're all broke up about it," said Barroso.

"Yeah, he must have been an amazing priest," agreed Bradley.

Barroso chuckled and replied, "He was. Although a little eccentric. But that's Gabe."

"Oh, yeah," chimed in Otterman. "They broke the mold..."

"Yeah," agreed Barroso as he took a step forward conspiratorially. "He went off the rails a little with the drink too...just the once, you understand."

"Hey, who hasn't been there?" guffawed Otterman.

Bradley stiffened at his partner's casual response and tried to maintain the concerned and understanding tone. "He's a man of...complexity...is how I'd put it, Mr. Barroso."

"That's right. You're right. That's a good way of putting it. Though when he told us he didn't necessarily believe in God, that riled some people up. Ha!"

"He said he didn't believe in God?" Otterman said incredulously.

"Well, not in the way most people did. He believed God was

a symbol for the unknown. He was always a bit of a radical. Thing is, people took it; mostly they went with it. Mostly. He had a sort of power, Father Devlin. He had a gift for truth, that's how I'd put it."

"Yeah, a gift for the truth," said Bradley. "I couldn't have put it better myself. He is a fine man. We all think the world of him —all the guys too. Well, actually, that's why we're here, to give him a present from the guys...in Region Seven."

"I see. Well, I don't know what to say," said Barroso. "As you can see, you can't give him the present. He's not here."

"Do you have any forwarding address we can send this on to?"

"No. He said he'd be back at some point to tie any loose ends up though. Pick up the rest of his stuff from the office in the rectory. But I don't know when that would be."

Bradley's eyes widened. "He has an office?"

Barroso led them through to the priest's study at the back of the rectory. It was a modest room with a desk facing the window and walls lined with books nearly up to the ceiling. There was no sign of a laptop or PC, but there was a small iron lock key safe tucked in the corner. Bradley and Otterman shot each other a look.

"Would it be okay, Mr. Barroso, if we wrote a little note to leave with our gift, for when Father Gabriel gets back?" asked Bradley.

"Sure. But look, I need to finish the hedge and then attend to the sacristy before mass. Do you mind if you write your note and let me know when you're done?"

"Not at all, Mr. Barroso. Not at all. We don't want to impose any more than we have already. Just give us five minutes and we'll be done."

Barroso shuffled out and Bradley and Otterman listened for the click of the front door like it was a starter pistol. As soon as the doors shut, Otterman was down on one knee by the iron safe with his pick set in his hand while Bradley stood guard.

"A double bit key. No problem." It took less than a minute to open the safe door. "Jackpot," croaked Otterman, trying to keep his voice down.

"What's in there?" whispered Bradley urgently.

"Hold on a second, I'm looking... Jeez, he keeps a gun. Obviously, he doesn't place all of his trust in the good Lord. And half a bottle of whiskey. A twenty-one-year-old single malt."

"Leave it where it is, Otterman."

"Sheesh! All right already, Elliot Ness."

Otterman took the bottle and the gun out, which had both been resting on a row of bound books filed side by side, and placed them on the stripped wooden floor. He pulled out the book on the end of the row to his left and opened it. It was a photo album. The first page was filled with a photo of a young, very beautiful woman, tall and lean-limbed with long brunette hair. She was ice-skating and performing a comic arabesque. He flicked through the rest of the pages; many of them contained photos of the girl with Devlin, who looked much younger, photos of the two of them together as young lovers. Lovers on holidays, at home, in restaurants, with friends and family. Otterman picked out the next one along.

"Well? What have you got?" asked Bradley impatiently.

"I think they're all just photo albums."

"Photo albums?"

"Yeah, I think they're mostly of Devlin with the same woman. A girlfriend."

"Okay. That's a bit odd for a priest. Maybe there's something in it? Like he was having an affair?"

"Looks like old stuff. A few years back. Like before he became a priest. Why doesn't he keep this stuff on a PC like everybody else?" Otterman was now frantically searching through each album and stacking them on the floor, but every album and every page was of the same woman.

"Wait. I Got something..." Otterman had found a thick folder wedged between two of the albums.

"What is it?" asked Bradley.

Otterman opened it and flicked through. "It's personal stuff —receipts, credit card statements, personal documents."

"Take it!"

OUTSIDE BARROSO HAD STOPPED PRUNING. Something about the two men was starting to make him uneasy. They hadn't offered their names. And they had called Father Devlin "Gabriel." Nobody called Father Devlin "Gabriel." He was always Gabe. He always introduced himself as Gabe. Always and without exception. He realized he might be being paranoid, but maybe it wasn't wise to have left two strangers alone in the rectory. He reprimanded himself for being so loose with his tongue and gossiping about Father Devlin.

"Barroso, you old fool..." he muttered to himself. "Always too willing to trust."

Inside the rectory, Bradley stood in the office doorway looking down the hallway and out through the front door windows so he could keep an eye on Barroso. He started getting itchy.

"He's stopped pruning the hedge."

"What?"

"The old man's stopped pruning the hedge... Hurry up and put it all back... Oh, Jeez. He's looking back at the house. I think he might come back in... Put the albums back... Oh no, he's walking back to the house."

"Damn." Otterman started cramming the albums back into the safe. Bradley jumped down beside him and helped. They had just about stuffed the last one in when they caught the sound of the front doors clicking open. Bradley rushed out of the study, checked his pace, and sauntered down the hall to intercept the old man.

"Mr. Barroso." Bradley shook Barroso's hand warmly. "We're done now. Thanks so much. I was just wondering how you kept your lawn in such good…?"

"Where is your friend?" Barroso interrupted.

At that moment Otterman glided out of the study and into the hallway, greeting Barroso enthusiastically. "Thank you, Mr. Barroso." He too clasped Barroso's hand. "Thank you so much. Well, we'd best get going. We have to be on the road; we got a ways to drive."

"Yes, that's right," said Bradley. "Thank you, Mr. Barroso. I hope Father Devlin enjoys our gift. If you see him before we do, please say hello."

Bradley sped up once they were out of sight of St. Jude's. Otterman used one hand to lever himself up off his seat and the other to reach down the back of his pants and pull out the folder they'd found in the safe.

"It's heavy." Otterman felt around inside the folder and pulled out a gold medal on a red, white, and blue ribbon.

"What's that?" asked Bradley.

Otterman held up the medal and read the inscription. "It's a medal for boxing. Says the National Collegiate Boxing Association 1996. Devlin's name's on it. Damn. This guy really isn't any regular kind of priest."

"What else is there?"

Otterman put the medal back in the folder and carried on looking. "Well…there's receipts, a car insurance document… Hey, there's some kind of court record here… Whoa! It's a petition for expungement in Georgia. It's for assault…committed March 1995."

"Assault? You think he had to get the expungement so he could become a priest?"

"Maybe. What do we do with this?"

"We tell Trayder. This is good stuff, Otterman." While he drove, Bradley began counting off on his fingers what they'd discovered. "He's had trouble with drink, he doesn't believe in God, he was convicted of assault. That ain't the usual stuff if you're supposed to be a man of the cloth. That, my friend, is a good day's work. We really turned up the goods on this one, Bradley."

"We certainly did," Otterman agreed. "And you know what? Something tells me this is just the beginning. Something tells me Father Devlin isn't the paid-up saint he pretends to be. Revenge will be sweet...so damn sweet."

9

After Brendan had dropped him off, Devlin dumped his dirty clothes in his Ford and got his case out of the trunk to unpack a change of clothing. Then he walked back up to Ed's house.

The damage he had caused in the fight had been cleaned up. Somebody had boarded up the broken window and swept away the glass on the driveway. If Ed hadn't returned, then likely it was the police or maybe Ed's landlord. Devlin tried the bell, but there was no reply. He went round to the garage. The van was still there, and the service door was still open. Devlin went in through the door and took another look around the house. Everything had been left like Ed had just disappeared from the face of the earth. No preparations, no sign of a man about to leave whatsoever. His coat was hung up by the door. Devlin checked the pockets and found Ed's house keys. Dirty laundry had been left in the washer, and cups and plates that had made it to the sink sat unwashed in an inch of brown water.

From the moment Devlin had spoken to Ed over the phone, he hadn't quite bought the gambling line he'd been fed. Now Devlin started putting into words why that was. If Ed did have gambling debts, then why would he leave his belongings behind? His TV, his truck, all the things he might be able to sell to raise some cash? When you were in debt to people, however bad those people were, all they were interested in was getting their money back, however long that took and however much interest there was on top. Just like everybody else, bad people took a pragmatic view when it came to dollars. Gambling and debt didn't explain Ed's behavior.

Devlin changed into the clean clerical shirt, collar, fresh suit, and spare shoes he'd unpacked and was walking back out through the garage when he heard the engine of a car slow as it passed the house. He ran out of the garage and glimpsed a black sedan idling at the end of the drive. On seeing Devlin emerge, the sedan suddenly picked up speed and squealed off. He sprinted after the car, but by the time he'd swung out onto the sidewalk, it was already far too far away to make out a license plate. It looked like someone was keeping a close eye on the place.

Devlin walked back to his car and drove a few miles farther out east to his next stop, the place where nearly all Ed's GPS routes had started from. It was time to visit the Logan Ranch.

10

In daylight, the ranch looked more utilitarian than it had lit up at night. From the highway, Devlin followed a dirt track up through a stone arch and stopped in a dusty clearing that was used to park ranch trucks and all-terrain vehicles. There were a collection of buildings dotted around one side of the clearing: barns, the shop where the pickups and ranch machinery were maintained, and a row of trailers painted different colors but which had faded and peeled badly out in the elements. There was also a long wooden bunkhouse with stovepipe chimneys and a tar paper roof, and farther up, looking down on the working part, the ranch house. "House" was an understatement; mansion was nearer the mark. It was an old nineteenth-century ranch house idealized by a well-paid twenty-first-century architect. Judging by the mint condition it was in, it couldn't have been all that old. It was three stories of pale brown brick topped off with elegantly curved limestone gables. It was handsome with tasteful flourishes done in the Dutch colonial style. But it stuck out a mile, like it didn't belong. In Devlin's eyes, it had an excess that was alien to its own surroundings.

Five ranch hands were clearing out the jugs in the calving

barn and dumping the used hay into the bed of a pickup. Three of them looked Hispanic, maybe brought up from ranches in Mexico. They didn't pay much attention to Devlin and kept on with the job at hand until the rhythm of the work was broken by an all-terrain vehicle that came tearing around into the clearing. The rider stopped to yell instructions at the ranch hand operating the pickup and caught sight of Devlin standing by his Explorer. He motored over, drawing up a few meters short of Devlin and dismounted. He was tall, slim with blond hair and a look of permanent disgust. Like he'd just got the bad news he'd been expecting all his life. Devlin guessed from Stevens's description that this was Earl Logan.

"This isn't a guest ranch if that's why you're here, Father," Earl said in a businesslike tone devoid of any courtesy but full of the sneer Stevens had spoken of.

"No. That's not the reason. Name's Devlin. I've come over from Boston way, on a mission of sorts."

"If you've come to save us, you're way too late. Been a long time since God came up here. I don't think he's interested in us. Not if last winter was anything to go by."

"No. I'm not here to save souls. At least not those that don't want saving." As Devlin spoke a Range Rover with darkened windows appeared, winding up the dirt track into the clearing. As it rolled by the two men, Devlin saw Earl glance up at the car and quickly affect indifference to the occupants.

The Range Rover drove on, and Earl snorted and spat a wet missile into the ground a few inches from Devlin's right foot.

"What are you here for, then? I told you, this isn't a dude ranch—we got work to do."

"An old Air Force colleague of mine lives in Halton. I'm trying to track him down, and I believe he worked doing deliveries for a farm or ranch. So I figured it might be this one."

"You been to his house?"

"Yep. But he hasn't been in."

"You tried his phone?"

"He isn't answering."

"Maybe he's avoiding you."

"It's possible. His name is..."

"I can't tell you. I can't give details of any staff here to strangers who roll up out of the blue whether they're priests or Supreme Court judges. That sort of information is confidential. Now you just turn around and walk back to your car and go on back to Boston or wherever the hell you're from. We're busy." Devlin could see in the distance that the Range Rover had pulled up in front of the ranch house, and a suited figure and a smartly dressed lady were getting out.

"Okay, well, you've made yourself clear. Say, is that gentleman over there Congressman Logan? I would like very much to talk to him..."

"Did you hear me? Get the hell off my ranch, priest."

Devlin considered Earl's response and then silently turned and walked back to his truck with Earl's eyes boring into his back.

Devlin got behind the wheel and started up the Ford. But he wasn't going anywhere. He muttered through gritted teeth, "Manners maketh man," and, instead of turning back down to the highway, drove straight on past Earl who was mounting his Honda and accelerated up to the ranch house.

As Devlin sped by, Earl was filled with a volcanic rage. He could see that Devlin was heading toward Clay, and he swept his Honda around, taking off after him. Devlin, however, had already covered the short distance, come to a halt, and got out to intercept Clay, who was walking from his Rover.

Earl was going to kill the priest. He was going to rip his face off and snap his neck. He could see Clay now talking to him, in an animated conversation of some kind. A red mist had descended; he skidded to a stop and got off his bike, heading straight for the priest.

"Earl!" exclaimed Clay. "You're not going to believe this. This is Father Devlin—he headed up the Air Force detail that got the real-time counterintelligence team up and running at Wright Patterson."

Earl came to a sudden halt. "What?" he spluttered.

"I got the funds for it in an Appropriation Bill. When was that, Father?"

"2005. That's the main reason I dropped by, while I was in Halton, to say thank you. As a special agent in the field, it was a big thing for us, Mr. Logan. I guess I never got a chance at the time. Well, we were all so damn busy." Devlin flashed Earl a smile. Earl's heart burned with hate.

"Clay. Please, call me Clay. You did a great job. It got some big wins which proved to be a real turning point for me on the Air Force Congressional Caucus. I'm grateful to you. In fact, I owe you. Pleasure to meet you, Father. Bit of a career change you had."

"I like to think I serve in other ways now."

"Of course, of course. Very admirable. You been in a fight, Father?" Clay said jokingly.

"This?" Devlin said, pointing to his face. "I got this walking into a door. A choirboy slammed the chapel door in my face rushing to confession."

"Wow..."

"Don't worry. I forgave him." Clay laughed loudly, and Earl seethed. The initiative had been taken from him. Every nerve in his body was shrieking at him to do real damage to this priest that had waltzed past him onto his land. But even Earl knew there would be another time, a better time to settle this than in front of the ranch hands.

"In fact, I think a friend of mine worked for your ranch," said Devlin. "And I was hoping to catch up with him too."

"Oh, really? Well, why don't you come in for some tea or coffee?" said Clay. "Y'know, I'd love to talk to someone who was on the ground at Wright Patterson. I'm a big supporter. I'm co-chairman on the Caucus, partly due to you and your team's efforts. Besides, I've always got time for an Air Force veteran."

"I'd be honored."

"Great, come on in." Clay was about to turn to enter the ranch house when he paused and looked back at his brother. "Are you okay, Earl?"

"Oh, I'm fine. Just fine. And I'll be seeing you, Father." Earl's face was neutral, giving away not a flicker of the white-hot hatred roiling inside. "I'll definitely be seeing you."

Inside the ranch house, Clay introduced Devlin to the lady he'd rode in with, Marie Vallory. She was a slim, handsome-looking woman, cool and self-possessed. Clay explained that Vallory was CEO of a company called Freedom Medical, an organization that ran six hospitals in Ohio and was a big contributor to the town's social projects. He then asked Vallory if she wouldn't mind going up to his office while he talked with Devlin, promising that he'd join her shortly. He called for the maid and asked for tea and coffee to be sent to the library. Then Clay guided Devlin into a spacious book-lined room that had been fitted and furnished with mahogany. In the middle of the library was a large glass case about five foot by three foot and set on steel legs. It contained a scale model of the ranch house and grounds.

The two men sat opposite each other by tall windows that looked onto the ranch and which threw large, bright rectangles of gold onto the Persian carpet that squared the room. Clay, a long-limbed, charismatic man with a toothy grin and quick bright blue eyes, was in a genial mood and keen to continue the conversation.

"So, Father Devlin, although it was quite a while ago, it's still useful to have your view on how Wright Patterson was run. How did you find it? Were there any concerns you had about the staff or operationally?"

"At Wright Patterson? No. I can say honestly I had no involvement with or knowledge of any criminal investigations while I was stationed on the base. My work was solely about the CI program we were setting up. As far as I was aware, that base was in good order. I'm in touch with officers who still work on Wright Patterson, and they have had no cause to air any concerns you would want to know about."

"Glad to hear it. As someone who puts an awful lot of time into representing the Air Force's needs at a federal level, I take any intel where I can get it. Homeland was very happy with the results of the work your team did and its in-field applications."

"Glad to hear it. "

"Those were the days, hey, Father? Exciting times in a new world. Real-time hacking and trailing of online security threats. When we traveled far and wide by our own lights. We thought it was the answer to 9/11. Turned out life is never that easy."

"We were operating in a technological Wild West. It was all new. There were no rules. No accountability. No oversight. The west doesn't stay wild for long."

"Too true. Anyway, Snowden happened and that put a stop to that. That's the trouble with people—they want it all, but they don't want to know about the consequences."

The maid arrived and poured coffee for Devlin and tea for Clay.

"I was actually here on other business when it occurred to me to look you up," said Devlin. "The idea was put in my head because an old Air Force friend of mine was working up this way, I think on your ranch. And I was hoping to hook up with him."

"Oh, what's his name?"

"Ed James. He was running deliveries I believe." Clay thought for a moment, dipped his gaze, and searched his memory. Eventually, he said, "Short salt-and-pepper hair, maybe five ten and skinny. That him?"

"Yeah, that sounds like him. He work for you?"

"Yeah...well, for my brother Earl. You're right, he drove supplies. I think he was casual labor though. Not on our books as a ranch hand. You don't have an address for him?"

"Well, funny thing is I do, but he isn't there. And I can't get him on his phone. To be honest with you, ex-service personnel can have difficulties settling back into a role in civilian society, and Ed had his troubles. Drink, gambling. I'm just a little anxious to check in with him and make sure everything's okay."

"Does he have any relatives? Friends who might be in touch with him?"

"He wasn't a great one for keeping in touch with friends. As for his family, he has a wife and daughter, both estranged. As I say, he's had his troubles. In fact, I have to be honest with you, I'm afraid the story about how I got these injuries was a little invention. I was up at Ed's place, and someone had broken in. I discovered them there, and they jumped me."

"Dear God. Did you report it to the police, Father?"

"I did."

"That's terrible."

"So you can see why I'm interested to make sure he's okay."

"Yes, I can." Clay pressed his fingertips together and thought for a moment "But the truth is, Father, we have a lot of casual labor passing through the ranch. I'm afraid to say we don't keep records, and they come and go without leaving any kind of footprint. My suggestion is that you take this back to the police."

"I have done. I've filed a missing person's report. But with the homicide here, I just feel it'll be way down the bottom of any police priorities."

"That's true I'm afraid. They are up to their necks right now." Clay drummed the arm of his chair for a moment. "I'll tell you what, I'll have a word with Earl and the guys and see if I can't turn something up. Maybe another ranch or place he works at, an address...hell, even if it's a bar he goes to...who knows? Could be useful."

"That's kind of you. I know you're a busy man."

"Not a problem. I owe you anyway, Father. Now, I'm afraid I've got to take a meeting upstairs in my office."

"Of course. This is some place you have by the way," Devlin said as they rose.

"Thank you."

"Ranching is tough. But you seem to have made it into a successful business."

"Oh, it is now. Believe me, about ten years ago this place was about to go to the wall."

"What happened?"

Clay paused for a moment and said with a twinkle in his eye, as if he couldn't resist the chance to show off, "What happened? I'll show you what happened. Have a look at this."

They walked over to the scale model in the glass case.

"This is the Logan Ranch," said Clay. "When my father first brought business up to Ohio, it was a smart move. There was all this reclaimed mine land that was cheaper than dirt. But then margins got very tight on our produce. Low-price imported meat flooded the market, and things were looking very bad for a time. So I just had this instinct, we had to gamble big or die slow. I looked into other methods of selling stock, and we took a deep breath and got into preparing and trading frozen embryos. We set up a lab—here." Clay pointed to a modern aluminum structure behind the ranch house. "We developed our own system whereby frozen embryos are thawed and implanted into host cows. Well, I don't have to tell you, the economies of shipping frozen embryos as opposed to live cattle—it's a real win."

"Do other ranches use this system?"

"Oh, yeah. But there's been little movement in terms of yield for decades. The industry standard is fifty to seventy-five percent. We have got to a point where we're getting ninety percent. Part of that is down to managing the recipient herd, but a big part is our own very secret process for inducing superovulation and freezing embryos. I took the decision to push a wall of money at R & D, and it's saved our asses and then some. This here," said Clay, pointing to the model lab, "this is our Area 51. A lot of people would pay a stack of money, or hell, even do something illegal to see how we operate. It's state-of-the-art and completely green. Lighting and heating run off solar panels during the day and are powered at night by a hundred-and-fifty-kilowatt generator that runs off animal waste. It's the future, and we guard this baby with our lives." Clay was beaming with pride, his charming, white-toothed grin. "Now, I really do have to take this meeting."

"Of course." Devlin walked to the door with Clay following behind. Devlin was about to let himself out of the library when he turned to Clay and said, "You know, there's one thing that's bugging me. It's bugged me ever since I got here."

"What's that, Father?"

"Where are the springs?"

"Excuse me?"

"This town. It's called Halton Springs. Where are the springs?"

"Oh..." Clay let out a long, deep laugh. "The answer to that is simple. There aren't any!"

"Then why the name?"

"It was a lie, Father. A big fat lie. The town was founded by a guy called Joseph Halton. He purchased the land the town sits on. Before they knew there was coal and iron here, this guy Halton wanted to attract people to stop over and spend their money. Make it a tourist place. So he built a lake, right where the fire station is now, and said it was a spring. He put a hotel right by the fake spring too. He tried to peddle a story that the Native Indians believed the spring held magical qualities, that it granted long life. But once they found there was actually coal here worth extracting, the idea of the spring wasn't important anymore. It fell into neglect and was eventually filled in. So, that's how the town got its name—after a spring that never was."

"Funny story," replied Devlin.

"Isn't it though?' And with that Clay was gone, ascending up the staircase into the higher reaches of his mansion.

11

Devlin parted company with Clay and walked to the entrance. He was about to get into his car when he saw a piece of paper fluttering in one of his windshield wipers. He pulled back the wiper, picked out the paper, and read it. Scrawled on the page were the words "You won't have to wait for the next life. I'll make sure you pay in this one, Father Devlin." Devlin looked around, but there was no sign of Earl, just a couple of guys fixing up a pickup in the shop.

A voice calling out from the bunkhouse broke the calm of the afternoon. Devlin looked over and saw one of the Hispanic workers set his wrench down on the hood of the truck he'd been working on and shout back, "It's not my turn, Campbell!"

The voice coming from the bunkhouse belonged to a hand in his forties who had now appeared on the porch. He was gnarled and sun-beaten with short gray hair that was dry as hay. His wiry body was hard, compact, and knotted from a life of ranch work.

The wiry guy shouted back, "Yes it is! Reeves is out checking the drop. Come on, Alvarez! You need to clean up the kitchen! Now, Alvarez!"

Alvarez walked truculently over to Campbell, who had now caught sight of Devlin watching, and suddenly got all shy and snuck back inside. Devlin followed after Alvarez and called over to him.

"Can I speak to you?" asked Devlin.

Alvarez tried to up his pace and get away from Devlin, but he didn't want to look like he was breaking into a run. Devlin caught him up, and Alvarez wheeled around and put his hand up. "Get away from me," he hissed, almost in desperation, and turned back toward the bunkhouse. Devlin called out again and caught up walking side by side with him.

"Hey," said Devlin. "I just wanted to talk to you about a guy who worked here."

Alvarez was only a kid, seventeen or eighteen, and was shaking like he was really scared. "I can't talk to you. Please. I'll get into real trouble if I do. Please, Father."

"Are you Catholic? I'm a Catholic priest. Father Devlin."

"Sí, padre. I know."

"What's your name?"

Alvarez looked up at Devlin. He had stopped walking, and his gaze fell and lingered on Devlin's white collar, before he replied, "Miguel. Miguel Alvarez." Alvarez had calmed down briefly, but now a new wave of fear overtook him. "But I've been told not to talk to you. That you pretend to be a priest, but really you're a detective."

Devlin was taken aback for a moment. How did anybody here know he used to be a detective? Maybe the men who worked here had friends down at the police station, thought Devlin. Word was likely to spread pretty fast in a place the size of Halton.

"I'm not a detective," he replied. "I'm just looking for a friend, Ed James. That's not anything that'll get you into trouble. Did Ed James work here?"

The Mexican looked around and said quickly, "He used to, up until about a few days ago."

"You know where he went?"

"All I know is he left quickly, like it was a surprise to everyone. He was a nervous guy. Didn't speak to any of the hands here. Only spoke to Packer."

"Who's Packer?"

"The ranch foreman. That's it. That's all I know. I gotta go, padre. If you keep talking to me, you will be putting me in danger. Please, padre."

"Okay. Okay, Miguel. I get it." Devlin backed off, and Alvarez walked quickly into the bunkhouse. The kid was terrified.

12

Stevens had slept for six hours straight when he was woken by the buzz of his cell phone. He checked it and saw he'd missed three calls from Walker. He must have been out cold. He sat up in bed and didn't feel too bad. Then he swung his legs out onto the soft carpet and attempted to stand but fell straight back on his ass. He felt awful—dizzy, nauseous, and faint—so he lay back down. Fifteen minutes passed and he felt a little better. His wife and kids would be back soon, and he wanted to get himself presentable so he wasn't a cause for concern, so Rachel would feel she didn't need to ask him if he was okay. He showered, had a strong cup of coffee, and checked his messages. Four missed calls from Walker and a message asking him to meet at eight o'clock at the station to brief the mayor. He knew immediately that Walker was going to want him to keep selling the Gypsy story. He got into uniform, left a note for Rachel, and grabbed his car keys.

A light rain had returned, and he could hear the tiny cracks of hundreds of wet drops landing on his windshield. As he drove, he kept recalling his conversation with Devlin. He recalled what he had said, that he was sick of who he was, sick of being scared of doing the wrong thing. He wanted most of all to be a good father and a good husband. If he couldn't be those things, then how could he expect his two sons to have any chance? It was not good enough to do just enough. It was not right. He would steer the truest course he could. That would mean, for the first time in his life, riding through the storm, instead of around it. It would take all the energy he had, but he knew too that it would not be for long. After Brendan and Devlin had left, he'd driven to Miami Valley for his scan. The full results would take a few days, but the face of the technologist told him all he needed to know. He had only met Devlin this morning, but he badly wished Devlin was here right now. He needed to draw upon his certainty for what was to come.

WALKER AND THE MAYOR, Jim Cutter, were sitting at one end of the long table in the meeting room next to Walker's office. They were both relaxed and talking amiably when Stevens entered. When they saw Stevens, they broke off and gave him a restrained but friendly enough greeting. He gave out hard copies to the two men of the Dayton crime scene report that had been emailed over. They read in silence, skimming through for the most part, occasionally stopping on a page to examine it more carefully. Cutter was slouched, in contrast to Walker's more erect bearing. He was bald with light brown hair at the sides that was swept back untidily over his ears and down to his collar. Cutter was a politician. Not of the movie star stature that Clay Logan had. He was a town politician who had a knack for saying what needed to be said in order to stay in the office to which he had been elected.

Cutter threw his copy of the report onto the table and asked, "So, what's the department's take on this?"

Walker leaped in, seeking to make sure this was put to bed

right away. "Well, Jim, there is only one line on this. The evidence strongly indicates a homicide amongst the traveling community that was camped here until a day ago. The body was found right by their camp on the night they moved out. The victim is from an ethnic group that points to him being from that community. We have had a number of incidents in recent weeks where our officers have had to deal with drunken and antisocial behavior from this group. I'd say in fact that there was a pattern of escalation. An escalation that matches a brewing internal feud. The crime scene has thrown up no other lines of inquiry. According to the *Dayton Sun*, the travelers have moved on to Cleveland and set up camp—on a football field for crying out loud." Cutter shook his head and raised an eyebrow at Stevens as Walker carried on. "I suggest we turn our evidence over to Cleveland PD and let them investigate. We carry on with our investigations and it'll just mean stepping on another, bigger department's toes."

"Good stuff, Caleb. Great. I'll tell the press office to prepare a line and I'll run it by you. Something to fend off any wild speculation. Okay?'"

"Just what I was going to suggest, Jim."

Cutter turned to Greg. "When are we expecting the autopsy results, Greg?"

"We're expecting it to be emailed over midafternoon tomorrow. But I've booked in to head down there myself tomorrow lunchtime so I can talk it through with the coroner and follow up any other lines of inquiry the report throws up."

"What the hell do you mean, Greg?" snapped Walker. "What do think the report is going to 'throw up'?"

Greg gritted his teeth. Beneath the table his hands were balled up into fists.

"Well, Chief," started Stevens, "I want to see if the coroner's report gives us anything else to go on, any other lines of inquiry that we might not have covered."

"You don't think the homicide is related to the travelers?" asked Cutter very slowly and clearly as if he thought Stevens was intellectually deficient.

"I'm not sure...well, actually, I think the evidence we have is circumstantial only. That's not enough to hand the case over to Cleveland. In fact, I think it may turn out to be a very tough sell."

"An easier sell than we don't damn well know, Greg."

"That's why I'm holding out for something from the autopsy. Something better than circumstantial or 'we don't know.'" Walker was now openly looking at Stevens like he was a dead man walking. Which he was but not the way Walker had it down.

"I thought you had this under control, Caleb?" said Cutter. "That we had a definite position that I could give to the press this evening?"

"We do. This is a Gypsy killing, and all other talk is fanciful and careless speculation."

"With all due respect, Caleb, that's not the message your own goddamn deputy is giving out. I expected to come in here and be told this was settled." Cutter turned his focus onto Stevens. "Greg, I could just overrule you and issue that press line anyway."

"You could, but it's a big gamble. Issuing a press line you may have to go back on. That might turn out to be...embarrassing."

"Only if you're looking to find empty leads and create a motherload of pointless police work," yelled Walker.

Stevens held firm. "I strongly suggest we hold back until the coroner's report is in and we've exhausted other leads."

Cutter looked at Stevens, unable to hide his displeasure. He leaned forward and jabbed a finger at him. "Listen to me very carefully, Deputy, so you understand exactly what's going on here. This is the highest-profile case we've had in all three of our careers, and it's now about public confidence in this department and this mayor. The town's already talking of nothing else, from the young moms in the fair-trade coffee shops to the pensioners watching the local news bulletins from dawn to dusk. This is as serious as it gets, so don't even think about starting to suddenly play hotshot detective with a conscience at the expense of a homicide investigation and my goddamn career. Do you understand me?"

"Yes. But we can't close this case before the autopsy..."

"Yes, yes, Greg, the autopsy...change the record for crying out loud." Cutter rubbed at his forehead and sat back in his chair. "Fine. We will wait for the autopsy, and I expect to be told tomorrow afternoon that, on the basis of the coroner's report, we have a line of inquiry and it is the only line of inquiry and it is a line of inquiry that all of us—" Cutter eyed Stevens. "—all of us can live with. Caleb, have another meeting arranged with my assistant for tomorrow afternoon. In the meantime, I'll have to tell the press office to put that response on ice."

Cutter left and there was a terrible silence. Walker and Stevens stood. Walker approached Stevens purposefully and squared off with him. His face was red, and a vein running up under the sun-damaged skin on his forehead was raised and angry.

"Well, you blew that you idiot."

"I'm not convinced it's the—"

"I don't give a damn what you're convinced of. I'm the chief, and I don't expect to be undermined by my own deputy in front of the goddamned mayor. Do you understand?"

"I was asked my opinion—"

"I don't care about your precious opinion." Walker moved

forward and up into Stevens's face, his hot, stale breath spreading into Stevens's mouth and nose. "You picked a hell of a time to be a maverick, Greg." Then Walker marched out the door, slamming it shut behind him.

Well, thought Stevens, *that could have gone worse.*

13

Night had fallen on Halton Springs, and the highways, rooftops, cars, forests, and fields were covered by a thin residue of rainfall. Soft, gentle, but persistent rainfall. Out on the Logan Ranch, Miguel Alvarez was finishing off a draining thirteen-hour shift: mopping the bunkhouse floor, changing oil and busted tires in the shop, hosing down the pulling room floor, cleaning the mud out of the drain. It was endless. A calf wasn't able to suck on its mother, so his last job was to put the cow in the head catch to be milked so the calf could be fed. That last task done, he was hauling his tired ass to the end of the barn when he spotted a tall thin figure with a slight stoop at the entrance. The harsh barn lighting painted him yellow, making his features appear pale and washed-out and his eyes look like sharp, dark angular slits. He had his hands dropped by his denimed snake hips and stood with his feet a little apart.

"Hello, Mr. Logan," said Alvarez.

"Alvarez. You done with that heifer?"

"Yes, Mr. Logan."

"You changed the hay?"

"Yes, Mr. Logan."

"The bunkhouse clean?"

"Yes, Mr. Logan."

"Anything else you need to tell me?"

"I don't think so, Mr. Logan."

"Anything happen today you want to tell me about?"

"Nothing specific..." Alvarez walked up past Earl. "Good night, Mr. Logan." Earl stopped him with a thin, long-fingered hand spread out on his chest.

"What did you say to the priest, Alvarez?"

"Nothing. I told him nothing."

"You're lying to me."

"No. I'm not. I swear." Alvarez had heard many stories about Earl Logan's brutality. He was breathing fast and shallow, and he felt terrified and trapped. Earl's big, alien-like hand pressed into his chest and his small, dark eyes bore down on him.

"I know you're lying," said Earl. "One of the guys was in the kitchen and overheard you talking to the priest, telling him about Ed."

"I just said he worked here. That's all. Nothing more."

"Where are you from, Alvarez?"

"Morelia. West..."

"Yeah...a wetback. Packer and my brother brought you in; I didn't. Seems I can't help that, but I can teach you how things work on this ranch. Okay? I said, okay?"

"Okay," whispered Alvarez.

"Okay," said Earl and slowly took his hand away from Alvarez's chest. Alvarez breathed out, and his body deflated. Suddenly there was an explosion in his stomach and he collapsed, first onto his knees on the barn floor, and then he sunk over, sprawling onto his side. Earl had planted a fist right in his guts.

"We do not tell anyone about what goes on in this ranch. Okay?" Earl snarled.

"Okay," whimpered Alvarez as a sharp boot drove into his lower back, sending screaming pain shooting up the side of his body. He heard the heels of Earl's boots clicking into the night. Then Alvarez curled into a ball and began to spasm and vomit onto the cold concrete floor.

14

Devlin had woken, as he usually did, at five hundred hours. He said his morning prayer from the Divine Office and prayed the Rosary, dwelling on the sorrowful mysteries. Then he cold showered, shaved, and dressed in his clerical collar and shirt.

After he'd visited the Logan Ranch, Devlin had driven around until he found a suitably cheap place to stay called the Country Inn Motel that proclaimed "Hospitality Halton Springs Style." The decor had been unrefreshed for some time. The cheap wooden furniture was chipped, the carpet looked dull with wear, and the flowery pattern on the bedspread was not Devlin's style. But it was reasonably priced and clean. Then he had set off to the Sacred Heart in Springfield for Sunday-evening mass. Father Francis, an earnest and good man, had given the mass and read from the Book of Acts. The message of the homily was that God gives endlessly. That God showed no partiality. Where to begin with his personal struggle with that message, thought Devlin. Then he returned to the hotel and passed out on the bed.

By the time he'd gotten into the Explorer in the motel

parking lot, it was six thirty. The light rain that had fallen in the night had passed, but the town was still damp. Morning sun had just broken through, but it was still fresh rather than warm. Devlin pulled a piece of paper out of his pocket with an address taken from Ed's GPS. The address was in downtown Columbus, an office on East Broad Street. Devlin left the hotel parking lot and headed east out of Halton, then south before turning onto a near gridlocked I-70 where he hit heavy morning traffic. After a grueling drive on the interstate, he came off on Cleveland Avenue and arrived in East Broad Street by nine o'clock.

The offices at this address were definitely on the grand side. Four stories of clean granite with wreaths and other decorations reminiscent of Imperial Rome were sculpted into the stone facade. The plate by the large steel and glass entrance announced that these were the offices of "Trayder Stein and Associates. Financial and Legal Consultants."

Devlin walked into the lobby which was as pristine and as well-appointed as the exterior. The high walls were covered with gold and brown white-veined marble. There were low, round, dark wood tables placed here and there surrounded by white, low leather chairs with dark wood frames that matched the tables. Opposite the entrance, past the tables and chairs and next to the elevator, was a high reception desk. The desk was a curved white block that looked like a modern sculpture. Behind the desk stood a young man and woman who were immaculately turned out.

Devlin's cell buzzed. It was Stevens texting him to tell him to meet at Montgomery County Coroners for half past three. Devlin checked his watch, still only a little after nine—plenty of time. Then he heard the receptionists call out almost in unison, "Morning, Mr. Stein."

A man not far off Devlin's height, just a little under, with a ponytail and wearing a double-breasted suit, a cowboy string tie, and carrying a leather briefcase, walked in. He reminded Devlin of Penn out of Penn and Teller, but less classy. Devlin saw an opening, and before Stein had reached the elevator, he had caught up and was walking side by side with him.

"Mr. Stein?" Stein wheeled around and caught sight of Devlin alongside him. Before Stein could react, Devlin said, "I'm so sorry to bother you, Mr. Stein. I'm Father Devlin." And in that moment, as cool and as self-possessed as Stein was, he gave away something to Devlin—a glimmer of recognition and surprise at the mention of Devlin's name. But Devlin was so intent on making the contact with Stein that he didn't quite catch it.

"Hello, Father," said Stein, quickly assuming an innocent and slightly confused expression.

"Hi," replied Devlin. "This is going to sound very strange, I know, but I'm looking for a friend of mine. Someone I'm having trouble locating, and I think his work might have taken him to your offices."

"Okay...well, I'm not going to be able to help you. A lot of people come here, and most of them I don't even get to see."

"His name's Ed James."

"No. Never heard that name," Stein replied without hesitation. "You're probably better off asking the receptionists. They're the ones that see everyone come and go. Now, you'll really have to excuse me, I have a meeting for nine which I'm already late for..."

Stein was about to go when it caught up with Devlin—Stein's first flicker of a reaction, a reaction so easy to dismiss as a product of one's own imagination, but Devlin saw a flash of something important there.

"Have we met before?" asked Devlin.

"I'm sorry?" said Stein, his manner stiffening.

"Something in your look...when I said my name... Sounds

crazy, I know, but it was as if you knew me...or knew of me."

"No. I tell you what it is..." Stein blustered. "You look very much like a business associate of mine out of Michigan. Very handsome-looking guy too—you should be flattered."

"Well, I believed you right up until handsome," said Devlin. Stein laughed a little unsurely. "Is he a priest too?" asked Devlin.

"No, it's more an aspect of your face than your"—Stein made a flourishing gesture with his hand—"garb. Anyhow, I do hope you find your friend."

"Oh, I will Mr. Stein. I will." Devlin grabbed Stein's free hand, placing it between his own, pressing firmly and looking directly at him. It made Stein deeply uncomfortable. "Thing about me," continued Devlin, "is I don't let go of things. Ever. It's a flaw really. Always been the way, a motor that keeps on whirring inside me pushing me on, forcing me to ask questions, interrupt busy men in their own lobby. Anyway, you'll definitely recognize me if we meet again." He let Stein's hand drop. "Tell your friend out of Minnesota he's got a doppelganger."

"I will." Stein turned to the elevator in haste; then he paused and turned back, calling after Devlin. "Except it's Michigan, Father."

"Of course it is, Mr. Stein. Of course it is."

STEIN EXITED THE ELEVATOR, stormed down the corridor, and burst past his secretary, ignoring her greeting, and went straight into his office. He flung his leather case against the wood-paneled walls.

"Son of a bitch. Oh? He thinks he's gonna spook me out? 'If we meet again'?"

Trayder fell into his cream swing chair and chewed at his manicured nails. The whole search for Ed James had stalled. He hadn't managed to turn up a thing. And now this man Devlin that he'd paid good money to track had turned up on his doorstep unannounced. He took out his cell and ran through his contacts.

FIVE HUNDRED MILES away in a Boston motel, Rick Bradley sat at a desk hunched over a pile of credit card statements and letters. They were a wad of Devlin's personal paperwork that the two PIs had removed from the key safe at St. Jude's. Bradley had been obsessively sifting through the documents since they'd checked into their rooms, looking for anything, any chink of light that might give a view of Devlin's real self. His private self. At first, Bradley had been filled with the thrill of a voyeur. But now, after many hours of solitary, painstaking work, his resolve was beginning to wane.

Otterman was laid out on the bed behind him playing Call of Duty on an iPad.

"You know they serve the breakfast here on paper plates, Bradley?"

"Yeah, I know," said Bradley, barely paying attention.

"Paper plates. Like being at a children's birthday party. I half expected a clown to turn up and start handing out candy."

Bradley was spooling through papers about to reply with another "Yeah, I know" when a chorus of "La Bamba" blared out and Bradley's cell shook from side to side on the hotel comforter. Otterman cursed. Bradley reached over and picked the cell up, looked at the number, took a deep breath, and answered.

"Hello, Mr. Stein?"

"Okay. So here's the latest," said Stein. "I just got the priest ringing on my doorbell playing the concerned holy man, and I didn't like it, not one bit."

"What?"

"Yeah, spinning me a number about how he's looking for Ed

James. I have no idea how he got hold of my address, but I never, ever put myself in a position where someone else knows more about me than I do about them. Listen, I liked what you two dug up on Devlin yesterday. It intrigued my client, and my client likes to be intrigued..."

"That's good news, Mr. Stein."

"So get me some more."

"Er...okay. Like what?"

"I don't know 'like what'—like something we can use on him. Comprendes?" But Bradley wasn't so sure he did "comprendes."

"Mr. Stein. It is just possible that there is nothing we can dig up on him."

"You and I both know there is nobody—*nobody*—in our long association that we haven't been able to get the goods on. Everybody has something they don't want entering the public arena. Maybe it's a busty widow he got friendly with, maybe it's a particularly alluring choirboy, or maybe there's a hard drive somewhere with images on that would entail a lengthy prison sentence and great shame. He is a Catholic priest for crying out loud. You did good. Now I want you to do better. Come up with something that will wipe this guy out of our lives. For results on this, I'll pay double."

"Right. Okay, Mr.—" Bradley began, but Stein had rung off, and Bradley put down the cell.

"How'd it go?" asked Otterman.

"You know, it wasn't too bad. He almost sounded subdued. For Stein."

"What's subdued mean?"

"Never mind. He said we get double if we get something he can use on the priest."

"Double? Holy cow. He was impressed with what we did at the church, see? I told you it was the right thing to do. Course, if he had a computer... I know a guy who works in a computer repair shop in Columbus who make things appear on a person's cell phone that would make your heart stop."

"No, Otterman. We need to turn up something more...robust."

"Well, short of bugging the guy's confession, I don't know how we'd do that."

Bradley's eyes suddenly widened, and he swiveled around in his chair so quickly that Otterman actually looked up from playing Call of Duty.

"What?" said Otterman. "Why are you looking so weird?"

"Confession..." Bradley was looking intently at Otterman with a wild gleam in his eyes. "Of course. Confession."

"I was only joking about bugging his confession."

"No, no. Listen, Otterman. Why did Devlin go all the way down to the church in DC? When we tailed him down from Dover?"

Otterman looked deeply confused. "I don't know...to talk about God I guess."

"No, Otterman. What did he do when you followed him into the church?"

"'Oh, he went into the confession box thing."

"That's right. He must have confessed." Bradley sat back in his seat and grinned. "And it had to have been something pretty major. I mean, priest or no priest, you don't travel over four hundred miles to confess just for cussing. Oh boy." Bradley stood, walked to the bed, grabbed Otterman's round shiny face, and planted a kiss on his lips.

"Hey, get the hell off me!" Otterman protested.

"Otterman, we're taking a trip back to DC."

Bradley was ecstatic. It felt like he'd never left the force. Like the procedural error had never happened. If you could call excessive force and alleged torture a procedural error.

15

After the meeting with Stein, Devlin had returned to his car and waited. He waited through the rest of the morning, and at about ten past twelve he saw Stein exit his building and head west down East Broad Street. Devlin got out of the car and followed half a block behind. Stein took a right up North Fourth Street and entered the Renaissance Hotel. Devlin followed in behind and watched him walk over to the hotel restaurant. Inside the restaurant, Stein joined a man already sitting by at a window table, a man with pale skin tinged with a yellow hue and thin, pitch-black hair oiled back across his head.

Devlin walked straight on through and out of the exit onto North Third Street. Across the road was a steakhouse with window blinds. Devlin walked in and asked for a table by the window which gave him a direct line of sight onto the two men. He ordered a steak sandwich and coffee, and through a narrow slit in the blinds, he watched their food arrive in the restaurant opposite. They ate and then talked for about twenty minutes longer. Finally, they shook hands and the man with the greased black hair left while Stein stayed to order another drink. Devlin decided to hang on for Stein. As he watched Stein drink and talk on his cell, he noticed a sparkling new silver Jaguar XFR come up from the underground parking lot exit by the restaurant. In the driver's seat was the man that had been eating with Stein. Devlin watched the Jaguar drive north and memorized the license plate. Then he texted it to Stevens and asked him if he could run a check on it. Devlin was finishing his sandwich when his cell buzzed. It was Stevens.

"You ran the license plate already?" asked Devlin.

"Yeah, I figured it's to do with Ed, so I gave you the premium service."

"It is."

"Well, the car comes up as registered to a Dr. Claude Lazard. Home address is Beverly Park, LA."

"Fancy."

"Isn't it? But I also got something else. Something interesting. There was a traffic violation recorded against the license plate a few weeks back. But it wasn't issued to Lazard. It was issued to a Mr. Ed James."

"That is interesting. Why would Ed take a ticket for him?"

"Must've been driving Lazard's car."

"It's an expensive car. I wouldn't lend it out if I were him."

"You think you got something?"

"Not really. Just painting a picture, that's all. Brushstroke by brushstroke. Thanks for checking it out so fast. I know you gotta be busy."

"No problem. Speaking of which, where are you?"

"I'm in Columbus."

"Columbus? You better get a move on. We got that meeting at three thirty."

"Relax. I'll make it."

After Stein had finished at the restaurant, Devlin followed him back to his office. Then Devlin walked back across to the lot, got into his car, and headed west to Dayton to meet Stevens at the coroner's office. While he drove he thought about Ed, about how he came to be mixed up with Stein and Lazard. And his gut told him that they weren't the kind of company a man would wisely or freely choose.

16

The Montgomery County Coroner's Offices were situated in a big, plain-looking concrete building with narrow and dark glass windows. Devlin pulled up around the side in the parking lot. When he got inside, he found Stevens already sitting in the reception area waiting. Devlin sat down beside him.

They both waited a few more minutes until the receptionist called them and led them through to the coroner's office. After another short wait, a disheveled-looking guy in his fifties with no shoes on shuffled in holding a mug of coffee and muttered a couple of hellos. Bald with a half-hearted attempt at a comb-over, he wore a colorful and thickly striped shirt with a wide knotted wool tie. He sat in his chair and swung to face the two men.

"Jack Carr, chief coroner, how do you do?"

"Hi, I'm Greg Stevens, deputy up at Halton Springs. I hope you don't mind, I brought along Father Devlin. He was an investigator with the Air Force and has some knowledge of Romani Gypsies, which is a lead at the moment. I've been consulting with him on this investigation."

"Father Devlin," said Carr, leaning forward to shake Devlin's hand. "Well, gentlemen, safe to say this isn't one that comes across yours or my desk every day. Decapitation is...well, let's just say this is my second in a long and not particularly illustrious career. I'll email the full report over after lunch. Shall I take you through the headlines, Deputy?"

"Please."

"Okay. The victim's age and gender as the CSI at the scene reported. Male, well nourished, late teens. No evidence of recent sexual activity. The head had been severed from the trunk between the first and second cervical vertebrae. Both hands had been separated from the forearms at the wrists, both feet at the ankle joints. We retrieved two 9 mm bullets in the thorax. But neither would have caused death. Possibly there was another shot to the victim's head, but we don't know the cause of death. Looking at the description of blood loss at the scene, it would appear the dismemberment occurred postmortem. There is a distinguishing mark, a red elongated birthmark on the collarbone. But not a huge help in identifying the victim given the absence of prints and teeth."

"What about a DNA match?" asked Stevens.

"I'm afraid not, Deputy. Whoever this guy was, he doesn't show up on our database."

"What about other countries' databases?"

"You'd have to push a request like that up through your chief and the Bureau of Criminal Investigations I'm afraid." Stevens' heart sunk. He knew that would only happen if Walker and Cutter allowed other lines of inquiry to be opened.

"Any clue to the victim's ethnicity?" asked Stevens.

"It's not really possible to say anything definitive with what we have of the body. The most we could get to saying is that the victim is likely non-white Caucasian. As unhelpful as that might be, it's as much as could be stated without being willfully misleading."

"Do we know if the body was moved?"

"I don't think so. There was pronounced lividity along the back and buttocks consistent with the victim having lain since time of death in the position he was found. We found the presence of Cochliomyia larvae that had hatched. It's not likely that blowfly eggs would hatch in the host body so quickly if it had been disturbed and moved from another place. The only material found on the body was soil and insects native to Long Pine. No matter was found that would indicate another site."

"Is there anything to tell us what was used to dismember the body?"

"Well, yes, I think so. There are persistence marks on the bones."

"Persistence marks?"

"Marks on the bones either side of the actual cuts. Where someone has made cuts to the left or right, false starts, or where they have missed the main cut. So that would point to a saw or large knife. However, I don't think it was a saw. You see, it's all about the kerf."

"Kerf? Doesn't that have to do with wood?"

"Usually yes; it's the pattern of a slit made by a cutting tool, and it holds for bone as well as wood. You see, saws leave a squared cross-section kerf floor at the bottom of the slit. The marks here are V-shaped and consistent with the V-shaped kerf floor that bevel-edged knife blades create. So in my view, it was done with an extremely sharp knife."

Devlin, who had been silent during Carr's briefing, spoke up. "Isn't the orthodoxy that decapitation is very rare in homicide? That homicides ending in corpse dismemberment are most commonly committed by a person close to or acquainted with the victim?"

"Yes. And I'd agree, except here the trauma is consistent, measured. It's a very clean cut."

"So not likely to be done in the heat of rage or passion?" asked Devlin.

Carr folded his arms and crossed his socked feet. "No. I wouldn't say so. The cuts aren't ragged at all. They're quite precise. I would also say from the direction of the marks that the person making them was right-handed."

"Okay. That's helpful," said Stevens. "Don't suppose you want to come to the briefing with the mayor at Halton PD this afternoon?"

Carr smiled and took a sip from his steaming mug. "I don't think so. I got two more autopsies booked in today, my friend."

"Worth a try. Anything more to report?"

"There is something…something else…"

"What?" asked Stevens.

"The first round of toxicology results showed up a trace amount of ketamine."

"Ketamine? Was he high?"

"Possibly. It's conceivable it was taken for recreational use shortly before the estimated time of death. It'll take another few weeks to establish precise levels, and we don't know the exact time of death or the initial dose, so we have to treat these first results with great care. But that's what it looks like to me."

STEVENS AND DEVLIN stepped out into daylight. Stevens sighed. "Well, it ain't much, but it's something. Something we can take back."

"We?" said Devlin in surprise.

"Yeah, to Walker and Cutter."

"Listen, Greg, I don't know that I should be getting involved…"

"I think I can ask for a bit of professional and moral support. I'm a dying man, after all."

"You do know, Greg—the Lord's infinite compassion notwithstanding—that there are only so many times you can play that card?"

"Come with me. Please. I'll do the talking, but it would sure as hell give me the moral support I need if you were there. Do this and I swear, I won't lay any more dying wishes on you. I promise, Father."

Devlin wasn't keen to walk into the middle of a homicide. Right at the moment, he wasn't keen to be walking into police stations period. But Stevens was a good man trying to do the best thing. If he was pleading with him for his help, then he didn't see he could turn him down.

"Okay. But you do all the talking. And you can drop the 'Father' thing too. Call me Gabe. My friends call me Gabe."

"Thanks, Gabe."

17

"I see you've brought your spiritual counselor with you, Greg," quipped Walker. The chief was sitting back in his chair alongside the mayor around the meeting table in his office, looking smug and comfortable.

"I brought Father Devlin along as he has valuable experience of Romani Gypsy culture and a background in investigations with the Air Force. I'd very much like him to sit in on this meeting." Walker and Cutter exchanged glances, but the mention of Devlin's knowledge of Gypsies seemed to placate them.

"I'm Jim Cutter, mayor of Halton, Father Devlin. This is Chief of Police Caleb Walker."

Devlin nodded acknowledgments, and he and Stevens took their seats before Cutter kicked things off.

"Well, where does the coroner's report on this put us?"

"I've read it," said Walker quickly. "And it pretty much reinforces our position yesterday. It opens no other lines of inquiry. Wouldn't you say, Greg?" Walker stared directly at Stevens. His dull, bloodshot eyes narrowed in anticipation of Stevens's reply.

"I wouldn't, Chief. I think it poses serious questions for our investigation."

Walker snapped forward in his chair and slammed the table. "God's sake. Jim, this is a load of crap. The victim was decapitated and dismembered. It points to a murder by someone who knew the victim well. These kind of mutilations are almost always the act of someone known to the victim."

"I don't think so," interrupted Devlin.

"Oh? And what light could you possibly have to shine on this, Father?"

"Romani Gypsies do not kill their own. Their strongest punishment is banishment. And the method of dismemberment here points to a methodical act, not one of passion or revenge."

"None of that is in the damn report," countered Walker.

"It's implicit in the coroner's analysis of the striation marks on the bone," said Devlin. "The cuts were not rushed. It was done competently and with a sharp beveled knife. Whoever did this cut up the body to prevent identification, not out of rage. It is not compatible with a feud, revenge, or crime of passion theory."

Stevens leaped in. "And that's why we need to check other countries' databases for DNA as we didn't get a match on our own..."

"An international DNA check?" Walker exploded. "Go through the BCI? Without any evidence or reason? Jim, this is insane. And why the hell are we listening to a priest tell us how to investigate. What's next, we get Oprah in?"

"Because he's right," said Stevens.

There was a heavy silence. Cutter looked angry and spoke slowly in near to a whisper. "This is the biggest investigation this department has ever handled," said the mayor. "And it's also turning out to be the biggest mess I've ever witnessed." His voice was beginning to rise as he got into speech mode, but he was cut short by his cell buzzing on the table. He leaned forward to see what it was.

"Jim, you have my word that this is the same case it was yesterday," said Walker. "And today's report changes absolutely nothing. I have informed deputy Stevens that he is to be—" There was another buzz. This time it was Walker's cell that vibrated, and he paused to take a look too. Cutter already had his reading glasses on; he had clicked on a link and was watching a video. Stevens and Devlin looked at each other.

"You got it too, Caleb?" asked Cutter

"Yeah...I got it," replied Walker. Cutter looked up at Walker, who was evidently watching the same video that Cutter had just seen. There was a knock at the door, and Miller appeared.

"You got my link I sent you, Chief?"

"Yeah. Thanks, Todd."

"It looks like it was taken outside Charley's last week," said Miller. "It's a great shot of the guy with the knife. Just what we need." Miller turned to Stevens, and Devlin unable to hide the smirk breaking out across his face. "You two gentlemen will want to take look too, I'm sure. We've been able to spec the knife, Chief. With any luck, the weapon will match the injuries to the vic."

"Great police work, Todd," added Walker. He had watched through to the end and put his cell down. He looked triumphantly across the table at Stevens and Devlin and with evident pleasure said, "Someone's just posted a video on YouTube taken a few weeks back of a Gypsy brawl outside Charley's, and one of them is holding a large knife about to attack one of his...what's the term?" Walker looked at Devlin. "Brethren. Looks like he's about to rip the other guy apart until he's held back. I think this is becoming a slam dunk. I told you, Jim, this has always been going one way."

Cutter took off his reading glasses and slid his cell to Stevens. "There's the link; have a look yourselves."

Stevens and Devlin watched it through. Right enough, there was a brawl between about four or five young men. One of them had been filmed brandishing a knife before being restrained and pulled back by friends.

"This proves nothing about the case," said Devlin. "All it proves is someone desperately wants it to be a Romani killing."

"It's more circumstantial evidence," added Stevens.

"Yeah, but Greg, it's evidence. And yet again, I don't see any coming from your end, of any kind. Jim, the momentum of this case is clear. I propose my officers put together a summary of all the evidence we have, including any information we can find identifying the guy with the knife, and our recommendations. We will then send that to your office and to Cleveland PD where the Gypsies have moved on to. We'll promise to send an officer to Cleveland as a gesture. To commit resources. Hell, we're a small department; one officer is a hell of a gesture. Send Gray out there. With that sour face of hers, it won't be long before they'll be begging us to take her back. And that will be the end of the road for us as lead in this investigation. It will be effectively off our books."

Cutter leaned back in his chair with the air of a condemned man who'd just got a reprieve. "Yep. I agree." He looked at Stevens and Devlin, his mind running through the next steps he needed to take. "I think the three of us need to discuss how this case has been handled. Father Devlin, this is now an internal personnel discussion, and due to confidentiality, we'll need to keep this meeting just between the public officials in this room."

Devlin nodded and stood to leave. In a manner that was plainly meant as a goodbye rather than a show of gratitude, Cutter said without looking at Devlin, "Thank you, Father."

"The best thing you can do for us, Father Devlin, is pray," added Walker drily.

"I'm afraid I don't have a prayer for the blind," said Devlin. Walker's eyes flashed with anger, and Cutter looked up to watch the priest leave the room.

Cutter breathed more freely once Devlin had gone. "Greg, I think you have come perilously close to wasting police resources and public money on investigations which are frankly ill judged and which unnecessarily undermined the Office of the Chief of Police."

"Thanks. I agree, Jim. I'll suggest Officer Miller put together the evidence summary."

"Wait a second," interrupted Stevens. "Okay, so you're sidelining me—that I understand. But Miller? Sergeant Taylor is the obvious choice."

"Time I think to jump a generation," said Walker. "We need a level head on a high-profile public case like this. He's a capable officer who has sensible judgment, and who turned up the video we just saw."

"He's ambitious and he won't question your command," replied Stevens.

"That's right, Greg—both qualifications you don't happen to have. I also want to say for the record that I'm unhappy with the way in which my deputy conducted this case. It has given me cause to doubt his investigative ability."

"No, Caleb," Stevens shot back. "That's not true. I happened, for the first time in my career, to voice an opinion that differed from yours. And that's something you can't abide. If there's a reason for my abilities not being suited to the role of deputy, it's that the main requirement is that he or she kiss your ass."

"That's enough, Greg! You're out of order," barked Cutter. "And, if I may say so, you're missing Caleb's point. The problem is you've chosen to go against your superior officer on the biggest case we've ever faced. And after an established track record of toeing the line, that shows a concerning lack of judgment."

"Maybe it's because it's the biggest case we've ever faced," said Stevens. And with that, he grabbed his report and left.

With Stevens gone, Cutter and Walker exchanged unguarded looks.

"I'm really sorry, Jim. This was a departmental matter that should have been handled and contained by me. I'm sorry it affected the case."

"It's not your fault, Caleb. Don't blame yourself. Let's just move on as fast as we can. I'll have the information officer issue that press line."

DEVLIN WAS SITTING on a bench outside Halton PD smoking a cigar when Stevens finally joined him. It was early evening, and the two sat side by side looking philosophical about the whole thing.

"What happened?" asked Devlin.

"I'm not lead on the case, and Miller's effectively taking over. I'll be sidelined and pretty much a busted flush in this department. That smug son of a bitch Miller will be like the cat that ate the canary."

"You did what was right. So Walker and Cutter don't like it, but you might be surprised how it changes the way the officers working for you see you."

Stevens didn't answer and didn't look wholly convinced. Then he reached into his jacket pocket and said. "Oh, hey, I almost forgot, Sergeant Taylor gave this to me." Stevens gave Devlin a leaflet.

"What is it?"

"A leaflet for the Halton Medical Center."

"What's that?"

"It's a free clinic out on South Oakland Drive, just off West Main. I asked Taylor to see if he could turn anything up on that Lazard guy you asked me to run a license plate on. Turns out he didn't need to look far; he saw leaflets being put out in the reception and picked one up out of curiosity. Lazard holds a surgery there a few days a week."

"He's got an expensive car for a guy who works in a free clinic." Devlin read through the leaflet and glanced at his watch. "Damn."

"What?"

"It shuts at six. I would have swung down there otherwise."

"You can try first thing in the morning. Did you turn up anything with Ed this morning?"

"I'm not sure. Nothing and something."

"You still don't know where he is?"

Devlin turned to Stevens and blew a line of smoke over his head. "No. I don't. Ed's tracks have been covered so well that nobody, not me or I think anybody else, can find him."

"What's your next move?"

"My next move? My next move is to hit a bar. You game?"

"Oh yeah. I got a thirst like a camel."

"So show me where people go to get relaxed in a place like this."

18

Clay had his hands pressed down on the leather top of his oak desk. He was breathing slowly and evenly, and his eyes were unblinking, unwavering. Not out of anger or fear, but out of the need for survival. This matter was nothing personal to him, even though it had every right to be personal. Marie Vallory watched with her arms folded from the side of the room. A spectator with a big stake. She had to admire Clay. It was never, ever personal. Feelings never came into it. It was all about how the outcome could be shaped in his favor. Experienced political opponents often didn't even know they were being played by Clay. He was that good.

"You attacked and nearly killed a ranch hand, Earl."

Earl sat opposite Clay looking surly and resentful. "I didn't mean to nearly kill him. I just roughed him up a little."

"He's lying in an intensive care bed in Dayton. He has grade one trauma to his right kidney. If he had been found any later, he would have died of internal bleeding."

"So why do you care all of a sudden? He's a beaner; no one knows he's here, and he wants it to stay that way. We had beaners injure themselves before, and we didn't take any responsibility. This is a load of crap, Clay. You're just showing off in front of your new girlfriend."

"Dear God, how old are you?" said Marie. She was exasperated. Emotionally, Earl was a like a child. He had never progressed beyond his teens in his view of the world—a view that began and ended with a twenty-thousand-acre ranch. She couldn't have despised him more.

"No. Not injured," continued Clay. "No one was injured here. He was hours away from death. You would have killed him."

Earl looked indifferent; whether the indifference was affected or not wasn't easy to tell. He looked blankly at Clay and Marie. "So what anyway? He's okay. He'll live."

"So what? I'll tell you so what—Packer doesn't want to work alongside you anymore. He's had enough. The men are terrified of you, and he won't manage that any longer. He can't pick up the pieces. He says either you go or he goes, and I can't afford for him to go."

Earl's indifference vanished, and his features twitched uneasily. "You can't get rid of me. Half the business is in my name."

"No, Earl." Marie stepped in. "Not half of the whole business."

"Shut up and be quiet—this has nothing to do with you."

"It's everything to do with me. I am a partner with Logan Enterprises. I have millions of dollars wrapped up in your business. I am CEO of a company with a multibillion-dollar turnover, so when you do something like this, something criminal, I damn well won't shut up. I'll make sure we do the right thing."

Earl's eyes flickered at the hint of a threat. "What 'right thing'?"

This time it was Clay's turn to step into the ring. They were tag teaming, and Earl was only just beginning to see it. "Marie's right about you not owning half of the business," Clay said.

"No she isn't. Dad left half of it to me. No question."

"Yeah, half of the business then. Not the business now."

"What does that mean?"

"It means you own half of the traditional ranching business. The loss-making ranching business. I own half of that and all of the fertility plant, with of course investment from Freedom Medical. I own the profit-making part of the business, Logan Enterprises. And me and Marie are going to float that business. To raise more money. The ranch is just a withering stump on much bigger and far more powerful business."

"Look around you, Earl," Marie continued. "The old ranch hasn't changed in thirty years. But some things have changed. The building we're standing in, built by profits from the new business, the fertility lab. They're like space rockets ready to launch into the stratosphere, leaving all the broken-down barns and trailers behind."

There was a silence. Earl glanced from side to side. "I ain't going nowhere. I don't care what Packer or you say. This is where I was born—it's my home. And you're my brother, Clay."

"I know, and that's why I think we can come to a compromise. Packer will help me out with the lab. We'll get a new foreman in for you to train up. But you have to promise me, leave the hands alone. No more violence. This is a final warning. It isn't just down to me anymore. We're in a bigger world now."

Marie fired the final shot. "You stayed still, Earl. While everyone else was changing, adapting, doing what needed to be done, you stayed still."

19

Devlin had ditched his collar and was sitting up at the counter with Stevens in Charley's, a sports bar and grill on Main Street. Stevens had likewise ditched his uniform for a plaid shirt, jeans, and boots. Bob Marley was playing, and Devlin had ordered an orange juice while Greg supped on a beer.

"It's shit is what it is—pardon my French, Father," said Stevens.

"It's okay. You're right. Same everywhere you go. Gets to a point you're butting your head against a consensus."

"That why you left the Air Force?"

"No, that was down to Jane. She was happier with me not doing stuff that was dangerous or meant I had to travel."

"She sounds like a real worrier."

"She had plenty to worry about. Anyway..." Devlin raised a glass of orange juice. "Cheers. Here's to saying the right thing." They clinked classes and drank.

"You don't drink?" said Stevens.

"Not now. But boy I used to. I used to drink like I was afraid it would run out. I haven't had a drop though in seven years, apart from one slip." Devlin finished his juice and Stevens took big swigs of beer nearly draining the bottle. "You want another?" asked Devlin.

"Sure. I'm going for a leak. Keep my place free."

Stevens slid off his stool, and Devlin ordered another beer. He looked up at the long mirror behind the bar and scanned the room. The bar was loud and packed. It was a busy weeknight, and the place had pulled in a fair crowd. He caught sight of a lean, pretty, blonde woman, midthirties maybe, who was looking back at him. She was with some other guys about her age, office colleagues at a guess. He'd first noticed the group when he and Stevens had entered the bar. They were out partying and taking turns to do shots, and she seemed to be more than holding her own. The blonde smiled, and he smiled back. That was what being a priest got you sometimes, thought Devlin. Spontaneous, unforced friendliness. Except then Devlin remembered he wasn't wearing his collar.

Greg came back, and Devlin excused himself to go out for a smoke.

Devlin stood on the sidewalk outside the bar under an awning. He drew out a cigar from inside his jacket pocket and lit up. As he took a lung-busting pull, the blonde in the bar walked up and stood beside him, cigarette in hand. Even though she'd just thrown back a load of tequilas, she looked about as sober as a judge.

"Got a light?" she asked.

"Sure." He handed her his lighter. She lit up, took a drag, and handed it back.

"S'okay, it's only a cheap disposable. Keep it. I got another," Devlin said.

"Thanks."

"You can take your liquor."

"Uh-huh. I've learned to keep up. I'm competitive like that."

She put the lighter in her back pocket, took a lug on her cigarette, and glanced over at Devlin. "Closest a normal person gets to feeling like a criminal these days, what with all the public disapproval you get."

"Sure. Probably more acceptable to take up leprosy," said Devlin. "And cheaper."

"Yeah, especially with what you're smoking. That's a big cigar. You making a statement?"

"Freud would have a field day."

"Freud smoked twenty cigars a day. You're in esteemed company. Say, you been in a fight?"

"Nope. I took a fall."

"Hell of a fall."

There was a silence, and they both smoked as car headlights occasionally lit up the sidewalk.

"Where's the accent from?" the blonde asked.

"You have a keen ear. I was born in Belfast, but I left there a long time ago. When I was a kid."

"You live in Halton?"

"No. I'm from Boston way. I'm looking up an old friend who's proving resistant to the idea of being looked up."

"Oh. Who's that?"

"Guy called Ed James. Lived out east of Halton, on the corner of the highway going up to Fort Wayne."

"Don't know the name I'm afraid. Halton's small, but it's not that small. What'd he do here, for work?"

"He worked out of the Logan Ranch. Making deliveries."

"You been up to the ranch?"

"Yeah. But no one's talking much up there."

"It's a pretty closed shop. I never get anywhere with them."

"You have dealings with them?"

"From time to time. I'm a reporter on the *Dayton Sun*, and

they're the first family of the town. So they turn up somewhere in a lot of the news that comes out of Halton."

"What do you report on?"

"I'm public affairs."

"Right...so that's what? Everything?"

"Pretty much. Crime, health, public transport, high school football teams, arts, public finance. I'm Katy. Katy Fox." Katy extended a hand, and Devlin took it.

"Devlin. Father Gabe Devlin."

"Father? You're a priest?"

"Yes."

"What denomination?"

"Catholic."

"I see. You flash smiles at all the girls you see in bars?"

"Only the ones that smile at me first. And, flattered as I'd like to be, I think it hadn't escaped your notice that I'm with the deputy chief. So I'd say your interest is more professional than personal."

"Damn. Busted." She flicked her cigarette to the ground, exhaled, and looked up at Devlin. "So straight out, what's the deal on the murder up on Long Pine? Who uploaded that YouTube video?"

"You're talking to the wrong guy. I've got no idea." But something made Devlin stop in his tracks. A thought. A thought about this tough blonde who could take her drink and had her eye on the main chance. A thought about how she could be of help.

FOX HAD GRABBED a stool and pulled it up to the bar next to Stevens. Devlin sat down on the other side. Devlin did the introductions, but Stevens looked wary.

"Greg Stevens, Katy Fox. I met Katy outside," said Devlin.

"We know each other, Gabe. You're a journalist on the local paper, right?" said Stevens.

"That's right, Deputy Stevens. We've crossed paths a few times. You don't usually handle the press calls though?"

"No, that's Chief Walker's beat, thank God."

"Greg, I got talking with Katy," said Devlin, "and I think we could get to an agreement between the three of us that will be to all our advantage."

"What agreement?" asked Stevens.

"Okay. So, Katy, you know the department's view on the homicide?"

Fox had ordered herself a bourbon and Coke. She took a sip and shot back her answer. "Yeah, it was 'traveler related.' We got some weak-ass press line from the mayor's office this afternoon."

"But what if you could get behind the press line? Get to know what really happened in the police department?" said Devlin.

"And who would help me do that? You guys?"

"Maybe."

"Hey, hey, Gabe!" Stevens interrupted. "I'm not sure we should be leaking anything critical to the case. It's not professional."

"Greg, it's the only shot we got at the moment. We've lost our voice on this investigation; here's a way to get it back. If we don't do anything, Walker and Cutter are going to have it all their own way."

Stevens chewed it over and then said, "Okay." He took a slug of beer. "In for a penny, in for a pound I guess."

Devlin turned to Fox, "Greg could fill you in on what's really been happening. The divisions on the Long Pine case."

"What divisions?"

"If you agree to run the story, I'll tell you."

Devlin expected Fox to bite his hand off to get an exclusive like this, but Fox played it cool. "I'm interested..."

"Damn right you're interested," said Stevens. "On a case like the Long Pine murder that'll go down in the local history books an inside story could make a reporter's name."

"Yep. Your name," added Devlin.

"So what do you get, Father?" asked Fox.

"Greg gets a chance to air his case to the public," replied Devlin. "And maybe gets a shot at influencing the direction of the case. And, most importantly, a shot at justice."

"Yeah, I get that bit. Your sainthood's in the post, Father," said Fox, zeroing in on Devlin. "But what about you? What do you get? You said an agreement 'that will be to all our advantage.'"

Devlin smiled. He'd only met Fox ten minutes ago, but already he knew she was sharp as a razor. And that was why he knew she was a good bet right now.

"Okay," Devlin conceded. "There is something you might be able to help me with."

"I knew it! Come on, Father, spill the beans already."

"I told you about the guy I was trying to find. I think he was involved with a man called Trayder Stein. A businessman in Columbus."

"I know him. Big in finance, eccentric guy, does all sorts of good works, throws big charity galas that we cover."

"That's him. I think my friend has got himself in some sort of trouble, and it may be something to do with Stein. I haven't got a hell of a lot to go on at the moment, and I need all the help I can get figuring out what that trouble might be."

"What kind of help do you need exactly?" asked Fox.

"All it would be is seeing if there's anything your paper has on Stein. Anything...irregular. Doesn't matter how big or small it seems."

"You could just google that stuff."

"Sure, the stuff that's printed. But if you could have a nose around, talk to colleagues, see if there are any rumors about who this guy is, anything that hasn't made it to print. Anything the lawyers had struck down."

"Okay. I can do that. See what the buzz on him is, if anyone's running a piece on him, or had a piece dropped. I can't make any promises though."

"I understand," said Devlin.

"What time is it?" asked Fox impatiently.

Stevens glanced down at his watch. "Eight thirty."

Fox put out her hand. "Okay. It's a deal. I'll run the story."

The three shook hands. Fox fetched her rucksack from the table she'd been sitting at and pulled out a notebook and pen. Then Stevens ran through the events of the last few days in Halton Springs PD. While Fox wrote, he described the disagreements with Walker and Cutter and their desperation to pass the case off as a traveler homicide despite the lack of concrete evidence. Fox took every detail down, and when she finished, she drained her drink and hopped off her barstool like she was ready to sprint.

"I better go if I'm gonna get this in some kind of shape, past editorial, and get it in before the ten-o'clock print run of the morning edition. And it'll be online too and on our news apps for breakfast. See you, fellas. Pleasure doing business. And, Father, I'll look into that other thing for you."

Then she threw her rucksack over her shoulder, and in a flash, Katy Fox was gone.

20

Earl Logan didn't drink. Never had, never would. A teetotaler. Except for one time when he was fourteen. He'd drunk nearly a fifth of rum that he'd found in the bunkhouse, then puked his guts up and got one hell of a whipping from his dad. It was a bad experience, but that wasn't why he abstained. He didn't drink because it stopped him having the one thing he enjoyed more than anything else: control. Right now he didn't have control. He'd been humiliated by his brother and by that woman Vallory. After being rounded on by Clay and Marie, he had driven into town and sat in his pickup in the parking lot of a Best Buy. If he were asked how long he'd been sitting there, gripping the wheel and consumed by visions of violence, he would not have been able to say. Eventually he got out of his car and staggered into the night, panting like a wild animal. Earl was a storm looking for a ship to wreck.

He passed groups of people walking through Main Street from their nights out. Saw them coming back from restaurants, recently gentrified bars, and even some new place called the Little Arts Theater for Christ's sake. It had some foreign film on, probably French. What the hell did these people know about making things? thought Earl. Producing things? The world of real work?

If only Earl did drink, he could waste himself in liquor, dissipate all his rage in alcohol, and come around the next day, reborn. The trouble with Earl Logan was he had nowhere to put all the rage that the Lord had given him. Clay had got none of it, and Earl had been saddled with it all. But that rage had to go somewhere. It would not be quenched until it had done some terrible and incalculable damage.

And then he saw Devlin.

Earl watched Devlin walking along the sidewalk with his stupid cigar in his mouth. He knew all about Devlin, about his interfering at the police department. Earl had his sources. This was the guy who defied his orders. The guy who drove past him onto his own ranch. A trespasser. A trespasser that had made him look like a pussy. He was going to pay for that.

"Devlin!"

Devlin heard his name roared and stopped still. Up ahead he could see Earl standing with his feet apart and his fists gripped, staring him down.

Devlin took a split second to assess and plan. Earl looked like he wasn't carrying any weapons, but Devlin couldn't be sure. He glanced around. There was a group of five people behind him and cars passing by. He saw an alley that gave rear access between two stores, about six foot wide. He'd take the fight there, away from bystanders.

Earl saw Devlin throw his cigar down and duck into the alley.

"Chicken priest," he muttered. "I'll mow you down." He turned into the alley after Devlin and saw him standing halfway down, dimly lit with only a halo of light behind him. So much the better, he'd follow Devlin down to hell if it meant extinguishing him.

The scene was set and the moment of conflict decided. Earl felt a piercing thrill of adrenaline fork though his veins like lightning. He approached Devlin as if gravity as well as fate were pulling him toward the priest.

Devlin took a breath, slow and even, and exhaled. No panic. No fear. His heartbeat had slowed, and his thoughts were crystal clear. He had known this was coming, so let it come.

What followed next lasted at most twenty seconds, yet to both men it seemed to unfurl like a ballet.

Earl had approached to an arm's distance, and he suddenly pushed out at Devlin's chest. Devlin let the force take him back a few steps so he didn't overbalance. Earl took this as an opportunity to follow in on him, jabbing at Devlin's face with a sharp right fist and looking to follow with his left. Devlin lowered his face and held his arm up so that the punch dissipated against his forehead and fist. Earl came swinging in again with a looping blow aimed at Devlin's kidney, one of Earl's favorite targets. Devlin twisted his left hip back and let the blow catch him across the stomach. Not a direct hit, but it still took the wind out of him and gave Earl the chance to swing from the other side, up into Devlin's ribs. It was the first direct blow Devlin had taken, and Earl was following in with a stomach punch. Devlin saw his opponent's fists down and smartly popped Earl in the nose with a giant knuckled fist. Earl was flung back, his eyes smarting, and bright blood flowed over his mouth, chin, and neck.

"You son of a bitch!" Earl howled, his teeth bared and dripping with blood. "You've done it now!"

Earl came barreling at Devlin, his fists flashing.

Even though Devlin kept his arms up, he caught at least four or five blows to the head. Bright flashes sent his vision one way, then the other. *Don't close your eyes*, he thought, *don't close your eyes*. Devlin scooted back, retreating, and Earl took a split second to pause, draw a breath up through his nostrils, and pile back in.

Blood trickled into Devlin's eyes, some of it from the wounds from his fight up at Ed's place. He wiped it hurriedly away so he could see and held his position right up until the first blows of Earl's new assault were about to land. He put all his weight back on his left foot and snapped out his right leg, driving it into Earl's midriff, between the groin and the stomach. Earl groaned and collapsed. The downward trajectory of his head was stopped by Devlin's great hand grabbing a fistful of Earl's hair. Earl was yanked back up to feel the force of Devlin's forehead jackhammering into his nose and eye socket. Blood and snot exploded everywhere.

Devlin was wild now; he had a bloodlust. He grabbed Earl's shirt and held his useless lanky frame a foot from the ground, craning over him and screaming into his face.

"Where's Ed?" Devlin yelled. "Tell me where Ed is, or I'll break your head open!" But it was no use. Earl was nearly out cold, senseless to the world. Devlin loomed over him, his fist raised, ready to pummel his head into mush.

And then an image broke its way into Devlin's head—an image of a little man with a wool hat and an army surplus jacket, his jeans dark with filth and his sneakers just battered bits of canvas without laces.

Devlin dropped Earl on the ground and gasped, his heart frozen with guilt. His eyes closed shut, and his guts rolled with self-hate. "Father, forgive me."

He looked down at Earl, who had been stunned by the blow to his head and was prostrate on the ground. His shining eyes were just visible through his half-shut eyelids. Blood had run from his nose across his cheek and was dripping off his ear and neck onto the ground. Devlin suddenly felt an overpowering love and pity for this man, as painful and biting as if he were Devlin's own child, the child he had lost nine years ago.

Cold hatred had transformed into burning compassion. The priest placed his right hand on Earl's head very gently and began to recite the prayer for liberation from diabolical influences. As he uttered each line, the priest could feel a great heat building in his palms and fingers that then poured into Earl's body, making it arch and twist, not violently, but as if he were slowly being released of a great burden.

"Lord Almighty, merciful and omnipotent God,

Father, Son, and Holy Spirit,

Drive out from him all influence of evil spirits.

Father, in the name of Christ, I plead you to break any chain that the devil has on him.

Pour upon him the most precious blood of your Son.

May His immaculate and redeeming blood break all bonds of this man's body or mind.

I ask you this through the intercession of the Most Holy Virgin Mary.

Archangel St. Michael, intercede and come to my help.

In the name of Jesus, I command all devils that could have any influence over him,

To leave this man forever.

By His scourging, His crown of thorns, His cross,

By His blood and Resurrection, I command all evil spirits to leave this man.

By the True God

By the Holy God

By God who can do all,

I command you, filthy demon, to leave this man in the name of Jesus, my Savior and Lord."

The moment Devlin had finished, Earl let out a sigh as if he were greatly and finally eased and then descended into a profound sleep. Devlin sat back on his heels, shaking and spent. For a long time he gazed at Earl, and then he studied his trembling hands, searching for a remnant of the force that they had produced.

When Earl came around and got himself up off the floor, there was no sign of Devlin. He felt numb with defeat, sick with violence, and empty—empty like he had never felt before, like a blistering fire inside him had been snuffed out. He staggered from streetlight to streetlight and made his way through residential streets out to the northeast of the town, where the houses became grander and taller.

He was blinded, not just by injury but by a fatal sense of being utterly lost in this world. Utterly abandoned.

"Where am I?" he kept calling out again and again. "Where am I?"

He stood and roared it at full voice in the middle of the street. "*Where am I*?"

A couple walking by crossed quickly to the other side of the road. Lights went on in some of the houses, and drapes and blinds twitched.

But nothing changed. Whatever Earl did, nothing changed. And yet something had. Something within. Something fundamental to his sense of his own existence had shifted.

He shuffled on for few more yards until he saw a familiar house. The only place left for him. He rang the bell and a figure appeared in the hallway, visible through the frosted glass. Earl's heart leaped. The door opened. It was Brendan. Brendan's eyes opened wide, and he gasped in horror at Earl's appearance. Earl looked up helplessly, as if all his life had been poured into Brendan's power. Then he kissed Brendan full on his lips, tenderly and gratefully, like he was drinking up the cure to all his sadness. And he said, "Take me back...please."

"Earl? What happened to you?"

"I don't...know... I...please, you're all I have. I don't have anybody...anything." Earl put his bloodied head on Brendan's shoulder and began to sob and wail like a child. Brendan placed his arms around Earl's spent, shaking body.

"Come inside," he said.

Then the door closed, and the street was quiet.

21

It was a very fine May morning in Halton Springs. The sky was a flawless blue, and the town was energized by talk. Lots of talk. Talk of Earl Logan rampaging through the streets the night before. Talk of him being beaten up. Everyone was fascinated to know what was behind the downfall of the troubled younger son of Halton's first family.

And most of all there was talk of the article by Katy Fox in the *Dayton Sun* that had gotten picked up on local television news: The criticism of the police handling of the Long Pine homicide. Criticism too of the mayor's direction of the police department. Talk of stale, narrow-minded public officials at odds with the new, prosperous, outward-looking, and metropolitan town of Halton Springs, a town with cafes springing up selling chai tea lattes and playing world music, with an arts scene, with young moms pushing the most expensive strollers. A town on the up.

Cutter was sitting up in bed, his cell jammed against his ear, reading glasses on and the *Dayton Sun* spread across his lap. "Crap," he hissed. "Crap." His wife turned over sleepily and moaned, "Jim, don't shout..."

Cutter held the cell against his chest and snapped at his wife. "Shut up. This is serious."

His wife tutted and slurred, "Don't talk to me like that."

Cutter put his phone back to his ear. "When was the body found, Caleb?"

Walker was sitting at his kitchen table with a mug of coffee and the *Dayton Sun* flat out in front of him. "The cleaner found it this morning around eight o'clock. Time of death somewhere around three in the morning."

"This is the worst news we could have had," Cutter rasped. "On top of this damn article. That moron Stevens blabbed to the journalist I bet. Or that Rasputin guy he's started hanging out with, God's own detective, Devlin. This homicide has shot our only line of investigation dead in the water. It potentially makes us look like fools and gives credence to this wretched news story."

"We have to have grounds now to suspend Stevens, only he knew this sort of information," said Walker.

"No. No. We can't do that, Caleb. This woman, Fox, she'll have every right to keep her source confidential. Maybe we should consider another route. Damage limitation."

"Like what?"

"We need to distance ourselves from this investigation. It's a poisoned chalice. Whatever we do it's not good publicity. I say we make Stevens the lead on this investigation."

Walker nearly had a coronary. "Stevens? Are you out of your mind?"

"Wait. Calm down, Caleb. Think about it. Whoever has this investigation on their plate, if they don't solve it we can offer their head. And, let's face it, Stevens isn't up to solving this. We both know that. Even if he does get somewhere on this case, there are ways of...muddying the water. But my guess is he won't.

What I am saying is, it always makes sense to have a fall guy ready."

"I don't know..."

"Trust me, Caleb, it's better to run these things from the wings. Oh, and Caleb?"

"Yeah?"

"Who the hell is this Devlin guy? Run some background checks. It's in our interests to know that he's clean...or not."

STEVENS HAD SLEPT IN LATE. It was a school waiver day, and Rachel had the day off work, so she had slept in with him a while. Then the kids had come in and jumped up and down on the bed, and Rachel had gone downstairs to make breakfast. Greg knew he was very lucky, very lucky indeed. But he also knew that his luck would soon be running out.

He read Fox's article on his laptop and, on the whole, didn't regret leaking the information. He also read through the hundred-odd comments posted below it, and it seemed, when you stripped out the trolls, that they were broadly supportive. He didn't bother checking work emails. It was his day off. They could go to hell.

Rachel came up with breakfast, scrambled eggs and bacon with toast and coffee. Then she had watched him silently while he ate, and they both felt a pain in their hearts. After, while Rachel was clearing up downstairs and the kids were watching the TV, Stevens's cell rang. It was Todd Miller's number. Talk about a morning ruined, thought Stevens sourly. What pile of crap was he about to land on him? More fallout from yesterday? Maybe a summons to talk about the news article. Then what? Suspension? He took a breath.

"Morning, Todd."

"Morning, Deputy." Strange, thought Stevens, Todd usually

addressed him on first-name terms. "I know it's your day off," continued Miller, "but we got a situation."

"Todd, you better run this past Chief Walker. I think he's keeping me off any active investigations for the time being."

"Yeah, ah, actually he's the one who wants you out here."

Greg sat up on the side of the bed. "Why? What's happened?"

"There's been another homicide, sir. Another decapitation."

"What?! Have we ID'd the vic?"

"Yeah, we think so. It's not good, sir. The victim lived at 28 Fairfield Drive."

The address flashed up an image of a house in Stevens's mind. He knew that address. "But...but isn't that Brendan's address?"

"That's right, sir. We figure that's who the body is. It's Brendan McKenzie."

"I'll be right out there."

Stevens was winded by deep shock at the news of Brendan's murder, but even in the midst of this dreadful news, he had also grasped the game-changing nature of the event. It kicked the Gypsy theory into touch and made Cutter and Walker look like incompetents. For the first time in Stevens's life, he had stood up against the two men. And it had turned out to be manifestly the right thing to do.

Stevens called Devlin to tell him what had happened and to tell him to get over to the crime scene. Devlin didn't say much on the phone, but then Devlin wasn't always exactly Jay Leno when it came to conversation.

DEVLIN HAD WOKEN AT FIVE. He said prayers, showered, shaved, and dressed the wounds from the fight with Earl. Then he drove to the Sacred Heart in Springfield for morning Mass. After Mass,

Devlin left Springfield and was about to swing by Halton Medical Center and see if Dr. Lazard, the man he had seen meeting with Stein, was working there when he got the call from Stevens. In the grave circumstances, he dropped everything and drove to the address Stevens had given him. The new homicide confirmed everything they had been saying, everything that had fallen on deaf ears. Devlin couldn't help but feel that Walker and Cutter were partly responsible for Brendan's death. If they had looked for real leads instead of wishing the first murder away, then maybe, just maybe, Brendan might still be alive.

He drove back from Springfield as fast as he could taking the highway north. The address was in the northeast of Halton, and Devlin used the map on his cell to get there. As he got closer to Brendan's house, he found himself cruising along very pleasant, very quiet roads lined and bursting neatly with greenery. Clearly, he was in the better end of town. Houses in many different styles built before and between the two world wars were set back at a distance from the grass-covered sidewalk and covered from view by an assortment of hackberry, maple, and ash trees. They were houses that spoke of a particular kind of refined middle-class comfort. Toward the end of the road, Devlin could see police cruisers and several police officers posted outside one of the residences, a large, whitewashed foursquare with tall sash windows. It was an affluent neighborhood. Lots of space, lots of privacy, lots of opportunity for getting in and getting out without being seen.

He drew to a stop opposite and could see Stevens already in a white crime scene coverall talking to another officer. As soon as Stevens saw Devlin getting out of his car, he broke off his conversation and walked over. As he went to greet Devlin, he was taken aback by the new cuts and bruises Devlin had acquired overnight.

"Gabe, what the hell happened to you?"

"I ran into Earl Logan last night on the way back to the motel. Don't worry, I imagine this morning he looks worse than me."

"I thought you were meant to turn the other cheek?"

"I got some work to do on that front. It's definitely Brendan?" asked Devlin, keen to get off the topic of Earl. Stevens took the hint.

"Yeah, I mean, there ain't exactly a lot to go on, but he had a Celtic cross at the top of his left arm, which checks out with the victim. So, it looks certain to me."

"You okay, Greg?"

Stevens folded his arms and looked stubbornly into the distance. He was the commanding officer on site; he would not succumb to emotion.

"It's just the damnedest thing," he said after a moment. "I was supposed to go soon, and before him. That's how I had it down, and that was bad enough. He was seventeen; he hadn't even found out who he was going to be... There's just nothing anyone can say to make this better."

Devlin turned and took another look at the house. "He lives with his parents?"

"Yeah, they were on vacation in Florida. They're on a flight back. We got a road check on the main highways out of Halton, canvassing for information, trying to catch anything of use. You want to suit up?"

"I'm okay to go into the crime scene?"

"I'm the supervising officer here now. Brendan's murder has changed everything. Fox's article didn't hurt any either. You were right about that."

"They made you lead?"

"Yeah, don't worry. I know it's Walker and Cutter's way of offloading a headache. Any other officer would see it as potentially damaging to their career. But I don't have that worry, right?"

"I guess."

"You remember how to be a detective? Suit up, sign in, and let's get on with it."

Devlin zipped up into white coveralls and goggles, and his name was jotted down in the crime scene entry log. They walked passed Brendan's Honda Civic parked on the driveway and up to the front door. Stevens pushed the door fully open so Devlin got a view down the long, dark hardwood floored hallway. There was a thick stripe of dry blood starting from about halfway down the hallway floor and leading into the kitchen where he could see the same crime technician that had attended up at Long Pine busy going over the countertops inch by inch.

Stevens walked ahead and stood by where the red trail began. As he spoke, although his words were dry, clipped, and factual, they sat on a perpetually moving sea of grief.

"Here's where he fell initially. There were two shots to the back, possibly as he ran from the intruder down the hall toward the kitchen. One of those bullets would likely have been the cause of death."

"Did you find either of them?"

"That's the good part, yeah. We've found one lodged into the nick between the floor and wall. It's a .22."

"A subsonic round. Quiet. Did the neighbors see or hear anything?"

"No. It's a comfortable neighborhood, the properties are spread out and away from each other. If they used a .22, then they could be pretty confident the sound wouldn't have traveled."

They walked toward the kitchen, and Devlin caught sight of

one corner of a gourmet island, an object sitting on top of it. At first, he thought he was looking at a joint of pink, uncooked meat. He quickly recognized that he was actually looking at a raw and bloody stump. He also realized he was looking at the body from the neck end. The glossy granite countertop of the kitchen island had been used as a dissecting table.

They entered a large well-lit room with tall white cabinets and a wide arched window throwing light directly onto where the body lay. The skin was pale and static; suppleness and elasticity had departed. Dense red mass extruded from the neck and limbs. In truth, the corpse resembled nothing so much as an incomplete mannequin. Brendan had long departed; he was not here anymore. The white-tiled kitchen floor was a grotesque pattern of whirls. The blood that had drained and gushed off the table had been moved around into great concentric wheels like a work of abstract expressionism and had hardened in the daylight warmth. In the opposite corner of the kitchen below the window were a pile of sheets. What color they once were, it was not possible to tell for now they were a heavy, dark pile, crusted and soaked in blood with a broom standing on top and balanced against the wall.

"The dismemberment occurred postmortem, like Long Pine," said Stevens. "But there was still plenty of blood. Bed linen was taken from the washer and used to wipe away any trace of footprints. The murderer exited out the back door onto a gravel path, leaving some trace of blood but no prints. Then they must have fled by car. We're checking for tire marks to compare with the family's cars. It's all almost exactly the same as Long Pine. But there is one big difference: the murder weapon. It looks like they used a cleaver from the kitchen." He pointed to a bloody item that had been tagged and was lying where it had been discarded on the floor.

"What's the estimated time of death?" asked Devlin.

"Based on body temperature, about 3:00 a.m."

A voice hollered from upstairs.

"Hey, Greg!"

"That's Sergeant Taylor." Stevens and Devlin followed the voice upstairs into what looked like Brendan's room. The bed was unmade, curtains closed, and sneakers, pants, and socks lay strewn around the floor. On the walls were posters: Sonic Youth, Nirvana, Radiohead. Taylor's broad and stout figure covered in a white CSI suit was standing over Brendan's desk on which sat a MacBook and a collection of chargers and cell phones. He had an iPhone in his latex-gloved hand and was scrolling down the screen looking concerned.

"What you got, Keith?" Stevens asked.

"I think I found something. Kid had Grindr on his phone, the gay dating app. He's got eight favorites but only one he was chatting to last night, someone called 'Browneyes.' Here, that's the profile." Taylor handed over the cell, and Stevens and Devlin studied it. The profile had a background photo that was a pair of cowboy boots standing in grass. The text in the foreground said, "6 foot two inches, 30 yrs, 2.5 miles away."

"Brendan had broken up with some guy just recently," said Stevens. "This could be him. In which case we got a suspect and a motive."

"I think you're gonna want to take a look at the last messages he got," said Taylor ominously.

Stevens scrolled through Brendan's short chat history. It looked like he'd wiped everything up until last night, and he probably would have wiped his last conversation if he'd lived to make the choice. There were two messages. The first was sent at just after midnight by Browneyes: "I'm in a terrible way, I'm lost without you..." Brendan had replied two minutes later: "Hey Earl. OK. Mom and Dad away. Come over."

Stevens handed the cell to Devlin to read.

'What do you think, Greg?" asked Taylor. "It can only be one Earl. The ranch has got to be exactly two and a half miles from here."

"I think I better call Walker," replied Stevens. "Looks like we're going to pay the Logans a visit."

22

"Where the hell is he?" Clay glanced at his watch. "I said two o'clock on the dot."

"Not like Earl to be late," said Packer, his low voice rumbling through his huge barrel chest.

Packer was sitting in front of Clay's desk, making a spacious leather armchair look like it was constructed for a child. His giant frame obscured the back of the chair, his huge thighs were pinned between the sides, and his ham hands flapped over the armrests. Packer was a disconcerting presence and not only due to his size. His left eye was bright blue, but his right eye was cloudy and much paler with no discernible iris or pupil. It was the product of a fall from a bucking horse when he was a young ranch hand. The horse was one of a dude string that hadn't been ridden all winter. Packer had been called in to calm the horse down but ended up having his head stood on instead. But the fall was nothing compared to the intense pain he'd felt from a kicked-up stone that wedged between his eyelid and his cornea, causing blood and tears to weep from his eyes, leaving deep and lasting scarring. It had little effect on his vision except for a hypersensitivity to very bright lights. The effect on his appearance, however, was startling. When he looked down on someone, as he invariably did, his left eye was outward-looking, but his right eye seemed to be looking inward or, even more arrestingly, had the effect of possessing a spiritual, otherworldly quality. Generally speaking, nobody messed with Packer.

"I haven't got all day to sort this out. Listen, Packer, maybe we can do this another time—"

"I'd rather it got done now." It was said in a matter-of-fact way, but even so, everything Packer said sounded like an ultimatum. Clay paused. He wasn't particularly looking forward to this conversation with Earl, but Packer was right; the sooner it was done the better.

There was a knock at the door. Clay walked over to the door and swung it open. "Earl, where the hell have you—" He stopped midsentence when he saw Earl's busted face. One of his eyes was bruised and grotesquely swollen, his nose broken and his lip split. Even Packer raised an eyebrow.

"What happened to you?" asked Clay. Earl said nothing. He sat, crossed his legs, and said without emotion, "Let's get this done."

Clay sat behind his desk eyeing Earl anxiously. "You okay?"

"I'm fine," said Earl.

"The other guy?" Clay asked.

"He's not dead or maimed or anything else you have to worry about."

"Right. Right. Well, if you're okay to go on...?"

"I told you, I'm fine. Let's get this done."

"If you're absolutely sure?"

"Get on with it, Clay."

"Okay. So, as we discussed, Packer is to come work for the lab full-time helping to manage the recipient herds. We're going to bring in another foreman—"

"Fine."

"Good for me," growled Packer.

"—who I want to eventually take over your position, Earl."

"What the hell?" Earl exclaimed, his gaze flicking between the two men.

Clay was expecting a full-pitched outburst, and even Packer was uncertain about where Earl's reaction might go.

"I'm sorry, Earl, but I've had a rethink since yesterday. After the incident with Alvarez, I've had to promise the other guys that we'd get someone else in. I've given this a hell of a lot of thought, and I know it's hard, and as your brother I will make damn sure that you're looked after. I want you to know I would never, never abandon you." Clay hadn't expected to get this far without being shouted down, so it was already going far better than he'd expected. But Packer had noticed that Earl wasn't actually listening to Clay any longer. Clay, who was by now completely absorbed in his speech, his set piece to his younger brother, kept plowing on. "I mean that. But you have to understand, I cannot keep you working here managing the men. It is not an... Earl? Earl? Are you listening to me?" Clay had now also noticed Earl's complete lack of attention to what he was saying. He noticed too that not only was Earl not listening to him but instead was looking directly at the TV on the wall which had CNN on with the volume turned down.

Clay had never seen Earl like this before. His face had transformed. Clay had spent most of his life looking away from Earl, trying to ignore him. But for the first time in his life, he couldn't help staring at Earl. He was transfixed by Earl's face. Earl's bruised eyes were full of pain and vulnerability. The scowl that had almost scarred his brow had vanished, and his small brown coffee-bean eyes were wide and brimming with feeling. He almost looked angelic. A single tear had formed and was rolling over his fractured, bruised cheekbone. Clay finally tore himself away and looked around to see what had grabbed Earl's attention. A news headline about a murder in Halton was up on the screen. A photo of a teenager flashed up, and a chyron along the bottom read, “Young man decapitated in Halton Springs, Ohio.”

There was a sudden loud slam. Clay and Packer turned their attention back from the TV to find that Earl had gone.

23

Stevens's cruiser pulled up in front of the ranch house, and the three men got out. Taylor made a beeline for the calving barn where some of the men were doing a cleanup. He shook hands and high-fived with a few of them and powwowed for a while. Stevens had deliberately taken Taylor along for the common touch, to ease their way onto the ranch. He'd been in Halton all his life and knew everyone there was to know. He had an everyman quality about him that put people at ease, and for a cop, he was fairly popular.

Devlin was stood apart and had a good look up and down the barns and trailers, but there was no sign of Earl. Not particularly surprising—twenty thousand acres was a lot of places to hide.

Stevens and Devlin approached the ranch house as Clay Logan came out to greet them flashing a smile.

"Gentlemen. I saw your car coming up the track and was awful curious to know what brings a priest and a deputy up to this far, far end of town."

"Nice to see you, Clay," said Stevens, and they shook hands

warmly, despite the circumstances of Stevens's visit. Devlin could see there was a fair bit of familiarity between them.

"And I believe you've met Father Devlin."

"Hi, Father. Nice to see you again. I really should have called you up. I meant to, I'm sorry. I checked with the men here, and unfortunately I couldn't turn anything up on Ed."

"Thanks, and don't worry. I got another iron in the fire on that one."

"Glad to hear it. Any help you need, you just let me know."

"I will."

"Clay, we're actually here to see you about a very serious matter. Can we go somewhere private?"

"Sure, sure. Come on up to my office."

Clay perched on his desk with his arms folded, and Devlin and Stevens sat in two leather chesterfield armchairs facing him.

The flat-screen television on the wall flashed up Brendan McKenzie's face from time to time as they rolled out pretty much the same bulletin with the same information that they'd had this morning when the story broke.

"Terrible. Just terrible," said Clay solemnly. "This town is going mad. It's like a Greek tragedy. You got anywhere with this, Greg?"

"Actually, I think so. I've brought Father Devlin with me because he's been invaluable in helping me with this investigation."

"Well, of course—OSI, it's an elite body. I know that. And hey, he must be doing good; it turned out you were right about the traveler folk. Does a lot of good for your reputation, Greg. Especially with Walker heading for retirement in a few years." Nobody else would have noticed, but Devlin registered Stevens flinch at the mention of "in a few years."

Clay studied Devlin's new cuts and bruises. "You got another door slammed in your face, Father?"

"No. Not this time. I ran into your brother, Earl, last night, and he was out looking to give me a hiding."

A light went on in Clay's eyes. "Right. Oh boy. I'm so sorry, Father. Greg will tell you that I've pulled Earl out of more scrapes than we've all had hot dinners. Is this what this is about?"

"No," said Devlin firmly. "What happened between me and Earl was private, not a police matter, and I'm not looking to make it one."

"Clay, this is much more serious. But it is about Earl. We have information that puts Earl at the scene of last night's homicide at around one in the morning. Brendan died at three."

"What?... No... That can't be... That just can't be..." Clay stuttered and then fell silent. For once the congressman was speechless.

"Yeah. I'm afraid so. We really need to know where Earl is. We need to question him urgently."

"He's...he's out at a cattle auction in Hillsboro. I can call him?"

"No. Don't call him, Clay. We'll send a unit out there to pick him up right away," said Stevens. "If by any chance he comes back in the meantime, call me immediately."

"Of course...absolutely." Clay's reply was faltering. He was stunned, like all that wind and charm had been taken out of him.

"Clay, did you know Earl was in a relationship with the boy who was killed last night?" asked Stevens.

"No...I had no idea..."

"But you knew he was gay?"

"I...yeah. I knew. Sort of..."

"Sort of?"

"I knew. I knew. We just never, ever acknowledged it. Ever."

"I don't need to tell you how bad this looks, Clay. Earl has a relationship to the victim, and there's strong evidence he was at the scene of the crime shortly before the murder. That's before we take his track record into account. There are also strong parallels with the Long Pine murder. So we need as a matter of urgency to question Earl about that too."

"My God. Yeah, of course. I can't believe it's Earl. I know all about his temper and...but two murders? Like those two people were murdered?" Clay suddenly looked at Stevens, with a directness Devlin hadn't seen before. "But I'll do everything in my power to do what's right. If Earl did do these terrible things, then I'll do what needs to be done to make him face the consequences."

"We'll need to conduct a search of Earl's quarters."

"Whatever you need. Absolutely, Greg. Anything. Anything."

24

Katy Fox had been traveling along a lonely stretch of Route 40 for a while before she spotted what looked like her destination. Just south of the two-lane was an old building twinkling in the hard early sun. It looked deserted and in need of a fresh paint of coat, like an old gas station without any pumps. The only sign of life was a pink neon Open sign hung in the window. Fox took the exit and rolled up in front of the entrance, a small faded gray door.

When she got inside, she was relieved to see the interior was in much better condition than the exterior. It was sort of homely with wood-paneled walls and checked tablecloths. Apart from an elderly couple eating in the corner, it was empty. The only staff were one kitchen cook and the waitress who brought over menus. Fox ordered black coffee and apple pie and waited.

Ten minutes later, a thin gray-haired man in green-tinted aviators entered. He looked in need of a haircut and a shave, and his tweed jacket and trousers were worn and rumpled. He immediately recognized Fox and joined her, ordering a coffee for himself. As he sat down, Fox caught a whiff of liquor and cheap aftershave.

"Fox." The man nodded. He kept his aviators on.

"Well, well. Roger Webb, long time no see. Nice place. Your regular haunt?"

"It's cozy and not many people know it's here."

"I'm not surprised. It's like it doesn't want anyone to know it's here."

"I hear you've been busy since we last met. Divorced, aren't you?"

"Jeez. Does everybody know my business?"

"Best thing for people like us. Marriage is an unnatural state." Roger adjusted his aviators and chuckled. "I saw the Long Pine story by the way. Well, who didn't? Great stuff. About time someone double screwed Walker and Cutter. Couple of prize morons. Well done, Fox."

"Thanks, Roger." The waitress brought over coffee and filled both their cups up.

"So," said Fox, "how you keeping?"

"Unemployed is how I'm keeping. Man of my age getting a job is very unlikely."

"Sorry. If I hear anything..."

"You won't. Nobody does." Roger took a sip of coffee and sighed. "Sorry, Fox. I get bitter, can't help it."

"That's okay. I understand."

"You were always one of the good ones though. Not a brown nose like the rest of them. Speaking of which, how's Linda Chambers, the ice queen of the *Dayton Sun*?"

"She's the same.

You want some pie, Roger? My treat." Fox glanced down at her plate strewn with crumbs. "Gotta say, the apple pie here's pretty good."

Roger smacked his lips. "Yeah, that would be nice."

Fox ordered over another plate of pie, and Roger shoveled it down.

"So, Fox, I'm intrigued. I get a call from you, and of all things, it's about Trayder Stein."

"Yeah. I'm just dipping my toe really. Feeling my way around the subject."

"What's the interest?"

"Nothing very firm. Someone I ran into gave me a very loose lead, nothing more than vague rumor actually, that Stein might be into...something. That's all. That's all I got. And I don't think the guy who told me this has any idea what it might be. So I looked into any past stuff on Stein, and I saw you had something going on him just before you left. Must have been something pretty juicy 'cause it had been put on the legal risk list. But I couldn't find any evidence of an actual article by you."

Roger looked over the top of his aviators, his default pose as he sat stooped over his coffee. Always furtive, like someone might come looking for him at any time.

"Yeah. I had something. But someone on the editorial board got a call from Stein's lawyers telling us to back off."

"Really?"

"Really. And the paper and Linda Chambers were only too happy to let it drop. Everyone knew I was headed out of the building anyways. Didn't know they'd junked all the copies of the piece though. That's news to me."

"What was the story?"

Roger looked thoughtful and traced the rim of his cup with a finger. "It was about money. Money going from Freedom Medical to Logan Enterprises. Stein is the financial advisor who oversaw it. There were really huge sums transferring out into an offshore fund and then back across to Logan Enterprises."

"How did you find this out?"

"I got a lead from a friend in the Secret Service. It stunk of tax evasion or maybe outright corporate theft. They were looking into it but got shut down by the Secretary of State's

Office. So he let me feed from the trough for a while. But I couldn't make anything out of it either. Whatever Stein has got going on, it's like a fortress."

"So, you let the story go?"

Roger clenched his jaw and glanced sideways over his frames out of the window. "I had to."

"That's not like you, Roger."

"You don't understand, Fox, I had to let it all go. The story, the job. I'm hangin' on, baby." He looked back at Fox and pointed a finger at his temple. "I got mental issues. I'm on medication. Heaps of medication. I got paranoid. Kept having all sorts of crazy fears. Thought people were following me and, well... Turns out I'm too fragile for the job, Fox."

"I'm sorry, Roger."

"S'okay. All helped with my payoff. Anyway, I couldn't find anything, and I doubt you could either. It looked to me like one big dead end. So my advice would be to let it drop too. I wasted too much of my time on Stein; you shouldn't waste any of yours. Tell your friend the same. Besides, you've already started hunting bigger game: Halton PD and the mayor."

"Okay. If that's your advice, Roger..."

"It is."

The two talked for a while more and reminisced over the good times at the *Dayton Sun*. Then Roger said goodbye, leaving a disappointed Fox stirring her black coffee. She was sad to see a once talented and determined investigative journalist now a shadow of his former self and wondered why she was wasting time chasing down shapeless rumors. She heard Roger's car exit the lot and paid the bill.

As she made for the door, the waitress called after her.

"Excuse me, miss. You've left something." Fox looked back and saw she was holding an envelope.

"Oh, no...that's not mine..."

"Then it must have been the gentleman you were with. It was on the seat where he was sitting."

"Oh, okay. I guess he must have left it. Thank you." The waitress handed it to Fox. To her surprise the envelope had her name written on it. She opened it and pulled out the contents. There was a note inside that said, "I never did give you a wedding present. Love, Roger." And wrapped in the note was a USB stick.

25

Stevens had slept on the floor in his office in a sleeping bag he'd pulled from the equipment room. He was woken by Officer Miller knocking on his door to tell him a mixed bag of news. Earl had not been found at Hillsboro despite an extensive search, nor had he returned to the bunkhouse or the ranch house that evening. He had failed to respond to Halton PD's attempts to contact him, and no one on the ranch had reported seeing him. However, a search of Earl's living quarters had turned up a .22 revolver with his prints on. And, most importantly, Miami Valley Crime Lab had come back with a positive ID on Earl's DNA found in the blood at the crime scene.

As Stevens, aching just about everywhere from a night on a hard floor, pulled on the uniform he'd worn the day before, his cell went off.

"Hi, Greg, it's Clay."

"Hi, Clay. This is an early morning call."

"Yeah. Well, it's important. We think we know where Earl is. Come down to the ranch. Oh, and bring a big search team."

Clay finished on the phone with Stevens and turned to

Packer. They were standing in a pasture in the soft haze of the early-morning sun. Drizzle and mist hung in the air around them.

"This is turning out to be one unholy mess," said Clay as both men looked on at an abandoned all-terrain vehicle sitting by a stretch of broken fence. On the other side of the fence, a narrow dusty track led off into Long Pine.

"Crazy bastard's gone off into the forest. What the hell is he playing at?"

"Maybe he's planning to do himself some harm," said Packer in his matter-of-fact manner.

"Y'know, he used to head off into Long Pine when he was a boy and Dad was out to give him a beating. Did him no good then, won't do him any good now. Poor son of a bitch."

26

As soon as Devlin had got Fox's text, he raced out of Halton and east toward Columbus. The text she had sent just said, "Have got something. Unexpected" with the address of a diner in West Jefferson. Devlin found the turnoff from Route 40 and, like Fox before him, thought he'd come to the wrong place when he saw what looked to be a condemned building. He parked by the pink neon Open sign and walked in. It was early afternoon, and the place had got a little busier since Fox had first arrived that morning.

"Hello." The deep, rumbling voice shook Fox out of her trancelike state, and she peered up from her laptop to find Devlin standing over her.

"Hello, Devlin."

"Well, this is off the beaten path."

"Yeah, not my usual choice." Devlin sat, and Fox took off her reading glasses.

"You got here fast," she said.

"Your text got me here fast. What have you found?"

"I found something. I definitely found something. I did what I promised and went back over any stories we'd got on Stein."

Fox stopped dead when she saw the waitress come over. Devlin ordered coffee, and Fox had a refill. Then, when the waitress was out of earshot, she continued in a kind of urgent whisper, like she was afraid they were being bugged or in danger of being overheard. Like Roger Webb's paranoia had rubbed off on her.

"I found this one story we'd dropped about six months ago. It was looking into a financial link between Freedom Medical and Logan Enterprises. Stein is the financial advisor for both companies, so that's how he came into it. I spoke to the reporter who was investigating it; apparently massive and irregular funds were crossing from Freedom into an offshore account. He'd got Stein's copy of the Logan Enterprise accounts from a contact in the Secret Service who'd investigated but couldn't nail anything down. My friend was looking into it too, but the *Dayton Sun* board came under pressure from Stein's lawyers and dropped it. But he slipped me Stein's copy of the Logan accounts. And the accounts show the funds turning up on their books."

"What's bad about that?"

"There are only two reasons companies go through an offshore: taxes and transparency. And then there's the amount of money. Fifty million."

"Fifty million?"

"Yeah. From Freedom through a shady offshore and ending up in Logan Enterprises."

"Why couldn't the Secret Service nail this?"

"Because the Secretary of State's Office intervened and shut the investigation down."

As interesting as that all sounded, Devlin was more focused on one question. "What about Ed?"

"He's mentioned here." Fox clicked up a spreadsheet and scanned down it. "I've got a payroll with your friend Ed James down as employed by Freedom, not Logan Enterprises, as a chauffeur and delivery driver."

"A chauffeur? Of course. That's why he took the ticket for Dr. Lazard."

"Dr. Lazard? I know that name." Fox put her reading glasses back on, stared at her laptop, and scrolled through the file. "He's down as a consultant for Freedom Medical and works at the Halton Medical Center."

"Yeah, I knew about that."

"Well, the financial arrangement of the medical center is a bit unusual. It was set up the end of last tax year, a gift to the town from Freedom and Logan Enterprises. But it's just sitting there on the books, a joint liability with Freedom."

"What's unusual about that?"

"It could be tax exempt; it should be tax exempt. Given its purpose, it would be a shoo-in for status as a nonprofit organization. There's no earthly reason why it couldn't be set up that way. Any accountant worth their salt would advise it should be."

"So why isn't it?"

"There's only one reason I can think of: because then they'd be obliged to open their accounts for public inspection. They'd have to be completely transparent. Dr. Lazard is on the board of the medical center. In fact, I looked him up and he runs practices in LA, London, and Mumbai. Yet he's providing his services pro bono a couple of days a week seeing patients at the center."

"What's a rich, comfortable doctor with a lucrative international private practice doing bumming it in a free clinic in Ohio?"

"He's got form too. He's been up in front of the Medical Council of India three times on suspicion of taking money from pharmaceutical companies. Got off the hook each time."

"And Ed chauffeured for this guy? It's like Ed found himself in the middle of something that he didn't understand."

"Devlin, there's all this smoke here. There has gotta be some fire. I don't know why the secretary of state halted an investigation. And without Freedom and that fifty million, I doubt there'd be a Logan Ranch. In 2010 the Logan Ranch was close to bankrupt. The margins were really tight, and they couldn't have gone on like they were for long. It would have been curtains. Then Freedom starts pumping all this money into the ranch via the offshore company, expanding Logan Enterprises and the cattle fertilization part of the business. But what's in it for Freedom is anybody's guess."

Devlin sat back and sighed. He didn't look overjoyed.

"What's wrong? You said get something on Stein, I got something on Stein," Fox protested.

"You did a good job, Fox. Outstanding. But where's Ed? Everywhere I look for him, I see hints of him and people acting strangely, behaving in ways that tell me they're hiding something. Now I even see evidence of financial fraud on a huge scale. But I don't see Ed."

"You know what I think? I think you're looking for someone who wants to stay missing. Finding someone like that is nearly impossible. Trust me, I'm a journalist—this I know."

"It's more than that. All the people who knew Ed, that he worked with, they're all lying to me. Conspiring. I know it. I came here to catch a fish, and all I find are sharks." Devlin was now deep in concentration, hunched over the table and propped up by his elbows. He'd taken out a cigar and held both ends rolling it over.

"So? What you gonna do, Devlin?"

Devlin looked up, bit the end of his cigar off, picked it out of his teeth, and said, "I tell you what I'm gonna do. I'm gonna go see Lazard. Time me and the good doctor had a talk."

27

The only sound in the room was the tick of the second hand on the wall clock and every few minutes the slow and careful turn of a page. In his surgery office at Halton Medical Center, Dr. Lazard sat perfectly still at his desk reading through documents. Extraordinarily still. Stick insect still. In a trance like state that was shattered by his next patient knocking on the door.

Lazard tutted in frustration, shuffled his documents away into a plastic folder, and called out, "Come in!"

The door opened and a tall, broad gentleman dressed in black entered. A priest.

"Hello, Dr. Lazard. My name's Devlin. Father Devlin."

Lazard took a beat to respond, and when he did it was without courtesy or warmth. "Good afternoon, Father. I will of course honor this appointment, but doesn't your church provide medical cover? This is a free clinic, you know."

Devlin sat and stretched out his legs, making himself very comfortable, which irritated Lazard profoundly, having this big man taking up his space and time.

"As a matter of fact, it's not my health I'm here about."

Lazard stiffened. "If you are not here as a patient, then I don't have time to talk I'm afraid. As you will have seen in the waiting room, I am very busy."

"Yeah, I booked this slot with the receptionist. And I absolutely promise you I'll be two minutes. You're such a busy man it was the only way I could get a moment to speak to you."

Lazard glanced at his watch. "Well, please be quick. You are taking a genuine patient's time."

"I will be." Devlin's attention was caught by the orange plastic folder sitting on the desk by Lazard's elbow. From what Devlin could see, it looked like it contained patient notes. Lazard noticed where Devlin's gaze had fallen, and for a split second his usually expressionless face assumed a kind of panic. It was minute and fleeting, and Lazard immediately returned to his controlled, robotic self, but not before Devlin had registered it. Lazard hastily lifted the folder off the table, opened the top drawer of his desk, and dropped the folder in. The drawer was then firmly shut, making sure the documents were out of Devlin's sight.

"Now, please, what can I help you with?" asked Lazard impatiently.

"I'm looking for a friend of mine. We served in the Air Force together. He's gone missing. His name's Ed James."

Devlin let the name drop to see Lazard's reaction. But Lazard's face was blank. This time it didn't register a single thought or feeling. Like a reptile on a rock.

"Ed James..." Lazard replied after a moment. "Yes. He was my driver. Part-time. He drove me around when I came into Halton a couple of days a week."

"When was the last time you saw him?"

"Not since my last visit to Halton a few weeks ago. He was meant to pick me up from the airport on Saturday but didn't show."

"Why not?"

"I don't know."

"Did you try to contact him?"

"Of course. I phoned, but he didn't pick up."

"And you didn't think that was odd?"

"Odd? Of course I thought it was odd. I was very upset with him. But what could I do? He'd only worked for me for a month or so anyhow. I just have to find another driver."

"In the time before he disappeared, did you notice any change in his behavior? Anything he said? Anything odd? A name that he might have mentioned?"

Lazard's cold eyes gave no suggestion of his thoughts as he considered his answer. Then he casually replied, "No. Nothing like that. I just thought he'd had a better offer somewhere and taken a different job."

"Did he seem scared at all? Upset?"

"No."

"How did he come to work for you, Doctor?"

"I think he was recommended to me by someone."

"Who?"

Lazard crossed his arms and shook his head. "You know, I can't honestly remember... Someone at Freedom Medical perhaps. They booked my flights and hotel, so it would probably have been someone there. A secretary or what have you."

It was plain Lazard had decided to stonewall Devlin. The man barely bothered hiding his dislike of Devlin. So Devlin decided to take another tack.

"You're a heart and lung specialist, aren't you, Dr. Lazard?"

"Yes."

"You must be a very rich man."

"It's really none of your business."

"Why are you coming here a few days a week to work for no pay?"

Lazard had had enough. His delivery became even more clipped and staccato. "Father Devlin, I was born a long time ago in Sarajevo. Before I was rich, I was very, very poor. I was once an illegal immigrant, stateless and powerless. But my story has a happy ending. Many do not. You of all people, Father, should know about wanting to give something back to the community."

"So why Halton Springs? There are plenty of poor people in LA."

"Because Marie Vallory and Congressman Clay Logan wanted me. And I accepted. Now, I thought we were talking about Mr. James?"

"Your own fault, Dr. Lazard. You're just a very interesting man."

"I think our time has ended, Father," said Lazard, standing. "My many patients today aren't interested in my life story; they simply want a good doctor."

DEVLIN LEFT Lazard's office and walked out of the center. He got into his car and lit up a cigar. He took a deep chest full of smoke and blasted it up against the roof. He was so damn tired of rich men giving him short, unhelpful answers. He'd tailed around Halton, Dayton, and Columbus. He'd asked people very nicely, and it had got him nowhere. So now he was going to stop asking.

He switched the radio on and caught a news bulletin. A manhunt for Earl was in full swing. According to the bulletin, two teams of Halton PD police were heading into the forest, one from the southwest and another from the southeast, just by the Logan Ranch. Cops from Shelby County had begun to comb down from the north with more cops stationed along the east and west perimeter. Wright Patterson had supplied two Chinooks for air surveillance. And Stevens was leading it all. They were throwing everything at this, thought Devlin. It was a full-on assault on Long Pine. The irony wasn't lost on Devlin that the deputy was close to getting his man yet Devlin couldn't be farther away.

It was time to change strategy.

He rubbed out his half-smoked cigar in the ashtray and got out of the car. He headed back into the medical center and approached the receptionist.

"Hello, Father."

"Hi...again. I meant to use the restroom before, but I forgot. Could I...?"

"Of course. Just back down the left-hand corridor and last door on your right."

"Thanks."

Devlin entered the restroom, had a quick look round, and checked the stalls. Then he washed his hands and left. On the way back, instead of turning right and heading directly back to the reception, he walked along the back hallway, which connected up the two main hallways that ran the length of the building. Devlin passed an emergency exit door with a push-down bar that released the lock and gave access to the rear. He made a mental note of it and carried on around into the length-ways hallway on the other side of the building. Then he exited the medical center, walked back to his car, and called Fox.

Fox was watching WDTN in her office when Devlin called.

"Holy cow," exclaimed Fox. "Have you seen what's going down in Long Pine?

What's going on with Earl? They found his DNA at the McKenzie kid's place."

"Yeah, I've been listening to the news bulletins."

"It's like a war zone up there. Earl Logan, a killer...well, it ain't exactly a surprise."

"No. I guess not."

"How did it go with Lazard?"

"Not so great. I'm outside the center now. I just saw him. He's telling me nothing, but I know he knows something about Ed. I know he's lying to me. Both he and Stein are lying about Ed. And I hate being lied to."

"So, what you gonna do?"

"I got an idea. It's pretty radical though. You may not have the chops for it..."

"Give me a break. What is it?"

"We break in. Tonight."

"To the center?"

"Yep." There was a pause, and the line went silent.

Then Fox replied, "Why can't you do it yourself?"

"Because there's only one good way in, and I don't fit."

"But we'd be caught! We'll go to jail!"

"You'd be in and out in a minute. You just have to open another way in for me; then you can scoot." Fox didn't answer. "And I promise you, you won't get caught."

"You can't make that kind of promise, Devlin."

"Yes I can."

"How?"

"Because right now nearly every damn cop in Ohio is up at Long Pine looking for Earl. Tonight is the perfect night, Fox. There's never been one like it. All I need is two minutes in there to get a look at Lazard's office."

More silence.

"I got you a big story, Fox," Devlin added. "Career changing possibly."

"I got you the Logan accounts. We're even," replied Fox.

"When I find Ed, and I will, it'll be one hell of a story. It has to be. Like you said, there's so much smoke here, there's got to be one hell of a fire. Come on, Fox, don't make me beg..."

Fox hesitated, unsure of what her answer should be. Ever since she first encountered Devlin, the walls of Fox's small world had begun to crumble away. Each time they met took her a step further into some kind of adventure, away from small-town career paralysis. For the first time in years, life felt like a place of possibilities, a place where Fox could actually live. Against every sensible thought in her head, she heard herself replying, "Okay, Devlin. But you had better not mess this up."

28

The trees got so thick at times the officers on either side couldn't be seen, even though they were only twenty yards away. About fifty cops, most of whom were out-of-towners from Clark County Sheriff's Office, Xenia PD, Greene County Sheriff's Office, and Jamestown PD to name but a few, had now been brought in to form part of a chain. They began sweeping up through Long Pine toward another line of officers descending from the north. Every department that had a K9 unit had assigned a dog and a handler to the hunt and been provided with an item of Earl's clothing. But no scent had been picked up. Up above, the sound of helicopters flying over every half an hour brought a kind of comfort with them. It didn't take long to feel alone out here.

Evening had crept in and, at twenty-one hundred hours, nightfall was imminent. Visibility was down to flashlights with the aid of helicopter searchlights and the crews' night vision devices.

Although Caleb Walker was a self-contained man with a hard exterior, a formidable man who suspected any outward show of emotion to be a sign of weakness, he was having his own private struggle up there in the woods. The last time he'd been in dense forest at night carrying a rifle with air cover was over forty years ago in Cambodia, and it hadn't ended well. His mustache was wet with perspiration, and his damp uniform clung to his body. Increasingly he'd anxiously look down, sweeping his flashlight along the ground for timber rattlers. He made the routine call in on his radio with Miller, who was at the other end of their section of the chain, about twenty officers away.

"Miller, anything to report on your end?"

"Nope. No sign of Logan here."

Then the radio crackled out. Pity. Walker was uncharacteristically in need of conversation. He tramped on over the wet forest floor with a ball of hot fear sitting deep in his guts.

Miller, on the other hand, was in his element. Hunting was his great love, and he'd come up to Long Pine many times. On the years when the acorn crop wasn't so great, all he needed to do was find a tree that was producing, stay by it, and he stood a hell of a good chance of bagging a deer. Imagine if he could bag himself a Logan. Surely he'd get some sort of decoration for that. He quietly murmured to himself as he often did when out hunting, "Move quietly and into the wind, and keep your senses sharp. You might get lucky and have one wander into you."

The sound of whooping blades moved toward him. Miller looked up to get sight of the searchlights. He hadn't heard anyone except for Walker on his channel for about an hour. He guessed that Stevens must have moved out of range of the Motorola handhelds they'd been issued.

Out of curiosity, from time to time when a helicopter flew over, he tried the frequency the helicopters were making air-to-ground contact on. Communications between the aerial team and the ground tactical net were restricted to Stevens as the incident commander, but the channel was open for everyone to listen in on. This time when he tuned in, his radio crackled and a faint voice could be heard. Miller pressed the radio to his ear and heard the helicopter pilot calling for a response. There was no answer, and the pilot called in again. No response. Miller stopped still and his heart quickened. If the pilot tried a third time and Stevens didn't respond, then Miller would reply. After all, this was way too critical to stick to a protocol that obviously wasn't operating as it should. The third call came in, and nothing came back from Stevens. Miller clicked his button and spoke.

"This is Officer Miller, Halton Springs PD, on the ground." The radio hissed, and Miller squeezed his ear flat against it to hear the reply.

"Officer Miller, been trying to contact your incident commander, but our comms are all over the place. We got a heat signature showing on our thermal equipment up on the north ridge. Looks like someone hiding in a wooden shack of some kind. I don't know who it is if it isn't Logan."

Miller thought for a moment. Could it be this easy? He clicked the button and asked, "You sure it isn't a black bear or something?"

Again, a hiss, a buzz, and the voice responding. "Nope. Not the way the image is moving. I'm certain this isn't a wild animal. Can you let Deputy Stevens know? We're low on fuel, and we have to get back to Wright Patterson. There'll be a new shift flying out and making contact soon as. Hopefully, they'll be able to sort radio contact out."

"Leave it with me."

"Thanks. Head northeast toward Tar Ridge. We'll send another crew ASAP for you to follow to the exact location."

Miller left his position and ran up the chain of cops to

Walker. If they could get to Logan before that weak streak of piss Stevens, it would be the prize of the century. Miller was giddy, breathless, and bursting with excitement by the time he found the chief. It was like he had suddenly been told there really was a Santa Claus.

29

Peace.

It was a word Earl had never given much thought to before. All that had ever animated him was fear and anger. Except when he'd been with Brendan maybe. Maybe then for small and fleeting moments, when he was safe and warm in Brendan's love and acceptance, he came as close to peace as he was ever capable of being. But those moments were as quickly torn apart by jealousy and fear. Fear of being left. Alone. Left to carry on being Earl. And that was a hell he had found himself unable to face.

He was sitting in a forest shelter he had built when he was a child and used to visit to be by himself. It was made out of branches and fern with the odd bough and had been built up and over to make a kind of wild wood cave. It sat on the mossy forest floor in the middle of a clearing. He used to come out here after school and after his dad had given him a beating, when the world was no longer comprehensible to him and nothing that he could do or say made his pain understood.

He'd come here now because when he thought of all the places that meant home to him, this was the only one that still truly qualified. The Logan Ranch was a home that had deformed around him into something he did not recognize. Slowly and without Earl even noticing it was happening, he had been evicted. Exiled from paradise. Brendan had been his other home, and now that had gone. Forever.

He could hear the rapid, sharp klee of a sparrowhawk and the rush of leaves and branches as they swayed back and forth. The earth was still damp, but the rain had cleared and night had settled. Earl listened to the forest. It was like a thing alive, and he wondered at who he had been all his life. His wallet was open on the ground amongst the cans of tuna and packets of ramen noodles he'd brought with him. Next to the wallet lay a photo of Brendan, his face distorted by Earl's tears.

Earl heard a faint mechanical sound, a sound not of the forest. As it grew and became more distinct, Earl could make out the whooping blades and knew it must be here for him. As soon as he saw the news coverage, he had guessed that they would come for him. They had probably placed him at Brendan's house. Witnesses maybe, traces of blood from where Brendan had cleaned Earl's wounds. The uncontrollable sobs and howls that possessed Earl's body heard by passersby. No one would listen to his side of the story. Earl Logan, infamously violent. Shunned and feared by nearly everyone. As soon as he was found, it would be all over for him.

Well, so be it. After he'd fled in a panic into the forest, into hiding, he'd begun to reflect with a clarity that he'd never had before. He'd come to a decision. Let them come and find him. It was no more nor less than he deserved. In one way or another, he'd had this coming for a long time. He'd abused people, hurt people, torn their lives apart. Now he was ready to atone.

Just half an hour more was all he wanted. Just a little more time to enjoy this strange new thing called peace. A sensation he had begun to feel growing within him right after he'd run into the priest. The priest. What had he done? What miracle had he performed?

He found that his hands were pressed together. So he began to pray. For no reason he could give, he prayed to the Archangel Michael. He didn't have any idea who the Archangel Michael might be, but he sounded like someone grand enough to have the power to save his soul.

30

Stevens looked to his right and could now see a line of lights from police flashlights arcing through the darkness. Next on from him that way was Officer Gray. He'd had his routine call in with the Shelby County police coming down from the north but got nothing from Walker or Miller. He tried again to raise them but heard nothing but crackles. Even if the search had moved outside the handheld radio's area of operational coverage, he should have been getting some kind of communication from the Chinooks. Goddamn, these guys were costing four hundred dollars a flight and not coordinating or producing any leads. Things were getting hairy. Stevens was trying to steer a huge, unwieldy ship without anyone telling him where the hell the icebergs were.

Then Stevens heard the whip of rotary rings and looked up see the beam of a searchlight far off. Quickly he grabbed his radio and tuned into the air-to-ground frequency.

"This is the incident commander, Deputy Stevens, over." There was a long continuous hiss, then a whine and finally a voice.

"Deputy Stevens, this is the new shift coming on."

"Thank God. I got nothing from the last crew."

"Yeah, sorry about that, the radio system was malfunctioning. We've had technical assistance, and now good to go. We're heading up to the north ridge to check out the heat signature the previous crew got."

"What heat signature?" There was a silence before the next reply. This wasn't going to be good. Silence was never good.

"The other guys said they called it in with one of your boys. Looks like there's someone hiding in a wood shack up toward Tar Ridge. It's in the middle of a clearing, otherwise we wouldn't have picked it up. A guy called Miller took the details. Said he'd pass them on."

Sons of bitches, thought Stevens, *they kept me in the dark. They're trying to get to Earl before me.* Why would they do that? To get the glory? To deliberately undermine him? Undermine all Stevens's work?

"Which direction is it?"

"Keep going northeast and look for our searchlight."

Stevens took Gray and a few other officers from the line and broke off toward Tar Ridge. He had one objective now: beat Walker and Miller to Earl.

31

It was like a ghost town in the middle of Halton Springs. Nine thirty at night, everyone locked up in their homes and not a police cruiser to be seen. Shops shut up, bars empty, and the streets deserted. Deserted except for Devlin and Fox, who were parked over the road from Halton Medical Center.

Although it was a fine thing indeed for big organizations like Freedom and Logan Enterprises to have given to the town, in truth the actual building was a very modest affair: a one-story, flat-roofed brick building painted gray. There were two turquoise awnings over the front window to give a bit of color, and a ramped entrance to the small sliding glass doors. But it was cheaply built and functional.

Devlin wore black gloves and a black jacket, shirt, and pants. He'd gotten a crowbar out of his trunk and held it discreetly down by his side. Fox wondered if Devlin was allergic to anything but black. Sure, black suited him and was practical for the task ahead of them, but she felt sure he was missing out on a whole wardrobe of other colors. She was in sneakers, a hooded rain jacket, jeans, and a sweater with her hair tied back. She was also nervous as hell, but she wasn't the type to ever show it. If she ever felt nervous, she just put on an even more confident front.

"Okay, Batman, how do we get in?"

"Round the back," replied Devlin.

At the rear of the medical center were two much smaller windows and a couple of white electrical boxes mounted on the wall. The building backed onto a deserted parking lot, which in turn backed onto a park.

"That's the best way in." Devlin pointed with his crowbar to the window nearest them. "No one's overlooking us, and the parking lot's empty."

Fox sized up the small window. "No wonder you couldn't get in. I'm not sure I can."

Devlin ran his eyes up and down Fox's body. "Yes you can. And you'll need to keep your hood up when you're inside. There'll be CCTV."

"What are you gonna do?" Devlin took out an old Yankees baseball cap from his jacket pocket and pulled the brim down.

"Stylish," said Fox.

"When you get in, you'll be in the restroom. As you come out of the restroom, there'll be a hallway to your right leading back to the lobby and a rear hallway straight ahead of you. Take the rear hallway. Halfway along is an emergency exit you can open from the inside by pushing down on the bar. Got it?"

"Got it."

"Good. One other thing. Soon as I break the window, the alarm will go off."

"What?"

"There was always gonna be an alarm, Fox. The place has prescription drugs."

"But what if someone comes?"

"No one investigates an alarm these days. Trust me. People

just don't want to get involved. And on a night when a murderer is on the loose? If anything the alarm will keep civilians away 'cause the police are all tied up out of town."

Fox wasn't sure whether to believe Devlin's line about no one investigating alarms anymore. She suspected it was more to give her false reassurance. But he said it with such authority, she let it go without argument.

Devlin took another look around for safety and walked over by the chosen window. It was about five feet off the ground with metal struts dividing it into four panes of frosted glass. He took out a roll of duct tape from his jacket and covered the lowest right-hand pane.

"Jeez, you really came prepared. A regular Boy Scout. You learn this when you were an agent?"

"No. When I was a teenager up in Vermont. You had to make your own fun back then."

"You get caught?"

"Yeah."

"So you stopped?"

"So I got better."

"It's a wonder you ever made a priest."

"People who say they've never sinned got no business preaching to sinners."

Devlin took one more look around and began to punch at the pane with the crowbar. Soon as the glass behind the tape gave, the alarm sounded. But Devlin didn't change pace. He kept his nerve and went methodically about the work of breaking in. Once the window had shattered, he was able to take the pane out in more or less one piece which had been held together by the tape. He cleared the bits of glass around the edge of the smashed window and stood back. Fox looked at the size of the gap.

"I'm not Keira Knightley, you know."

"You can do it. You hold your breath, and I'll hold your legs."

"Damn."

Fox took a pair of gloves out of her jacket pocket and put them on. She extended her hands and arms through the gap, tucking her head in and wriggling so her shoulders and chest would pass. Her waist was a little easier, but her hips took some maneuvering. Devlin had ditched the crowbar and held her legs so she kept her balance. She could feel how easily and deftly he supported her while she worked her way through the opening. Finally she was in except for her legs and feet. Inside the alarm was deafening. Her hands felt their way down the inside wall. With Devlin still holding her, she was able to look up, and though it was dark, she could now see her surroundings. She was in a bathroom stall. *Great*, thought Fox, *I'm breaking in through the john*.

She walked her hands down onto the toilet seat and called back to Devlin over the siren.

"You can let go now."

Devlin fed the last part of her legs and feet through. Fox's feet slipped along the wall down to the ground, and she stood up. Relief. She was in. Now to get Devlin in. She turned on her cell phone flashlight and made her way out of the restroom. She found herself at the meeting point of two hallways. Above her were yellow lights flashing in tandem with the alarm.

Fox walked straight ahead, taking the rear hallway, and, like Devlin had said, she found a red emergency exit door halfway along and pushed the release bar down. The door swung outward, and Fox was met by the cool night air and a view over the parking lot. She put her head out and was about to call to Devlin when he appeared right in front of her.

"Jeez!" exclaimed Fox. "You scared the hell out of me."

"We're the burglars, remember. We're not the ones who

should be surprised." Devlin pushed inside and shut the door behind him. "Okay. You go," Devlin shouted over the alarm.

"What?" Fox yelled back.

"That's all I need you for. Go!"

"But I just...!"

"I promised you you wouldn't get caught, but only if you do what I say. Now get out of here."

"I wanna stay."

"What?"

"I wanna help!"

"Great. I had to plead with you to do this, and now you won't go?"

"I'm a part of this now, whether you like it or not."

"I don't like it..." Devlin hadn't factored Fox's unpredictability in, but he knew time was of the essence. Now was not the time to fall out. "Okay. Follow me!"

They raced back to the point where the two hallways met, sweeping their flashlights ahead of them as they went. Then they turned left and headed to the lobby. Devlin ran by the receptionist desk with Fox close behind and rounded the corner into another hallway. This one led from the lobby back along the other side of the building, and Lazard's office was one of the rooms off of it. All the office doors had plates screwed on with the names of medics and doctors. About two-thirds of the way down, Devlin found the door with Dr. Lazard's name on it.

Devlin tried the handle. It was locked. He stepped back and shouldered it a few times until the lock busted and the metal latch splintered the wooden doorframe. He pushed the door and it swung open. Before them was Lazard's office. It consisted of a desk up against the wall, a couple of metal-framed chairs, a stainless steel cabinet with medical wipes and sterilizing hand pumps, weighing scales, and an examination table.

Devlin entered the office and set about wrenching and cracking the four desk drawers open with the crowbar.

"You check that side, I'll check this side." Devlin lifted out the contents of the top left-hand drawer. He placed them on the floor and sifted through writing pads, prescription pads, free clinic information leaflets, phone chargers, and cigarette lighters. But there was nothing of use. Nothing personal.

"Hey," yelled Fox. "I got his desk planner. Should we take it?"

"Yeah. Anything else?"

"Nah. Just medical information leaflets and cartons of Dunhill cigarettes. Jesus, who smokes Dunhill anymore?"

Devlin pulled out the contents of the second drawer, and in it was the orange plastic folder. The one Lazard had been so keen to keep out of Devlin's sight. Devlin picked it up and tucked it in his jacket.

"What's that?" asked Fox.

"Something Lazard didn't want me to see, so it's coming with us. Let's get out of here."

Within two minutes they'd exited the building through the emergency exit door and were back in the car. Devlin hit the gas and they rode off, the alarm fading away as they put distance between them and the clinic. Job done and not a cop to be seen.

"Congratulations, Fox. As of right now you're a professional burglar."

"Yeah. Now I see the attraction. You know, Lazard may well guess it's you who broke in."

"Good. About time I lit a fire underneath some asses round here. Now maybe they'll quit being so shy and start coming to me."

32

Stevens was frantic and speeding as fast as he dared through the dark, dense woodland following the lead of his flashlight. The other officers were trying to keep up with him.

Stevens had to get there first. But with the head start Walker and Miller had, it would need a miracle to beat them to it. He couldn't lose this one. He had to make sure it was handled right. It meant everything to Stevens. If they got there first, he feared the worst.

WALKER AND MILLER had been following their compasses and hoping that they hadn't veered too far off track. Then they saw the new shift from Wright Patterson fly over in the direction of what had to be the ridge. More certain now of where they were going, the two men quickened their pace.

EARL CAME TO ABRUPTLY. He had drifted off to sleep and awoken cold and terrified. It had gotten so dark, so black, he had trouble seeing more than a few feet in front of his face. And then a terror came over him. Why had he woken? Had there been a sound of some sort? He crept to the mouth of the shack and looked out. He scanned back and forth but could make out no definite shapes in the shadows outside. He crawled out of the shelter and stood and looked up at the sky. It was beautiful. The clearest of skies. There were so many stars. He could see the opaque wisps of the Milky Way and make out the North Star. For the first time in his life, he was able to lose himself in the night, in something else. Able to take peace from the knowledge that the universe had existed for billions of years without him and would go on existing billions of year after he had vanished. In the last twenty-four hours, something extraordinary had happened. His heart had been freed. The air was sweet and clear, his body and mind light and magical.

Earl heard the sound of helicopter blades, and this time they were getting nearer very fast. Like it was traveling in a straight line to him. Like they knew exactly where their target was.

Then Earl heard a twig snap, and before he could turn, a hard, cold barrel jabbed into the back of his head. He stood still, not daring to make a sudden move. There was no voice from the owner of the gun, just heavy, determined breaths. Probably a nervy cop, thought Earl. Spooked and psyched that they'd got to him first. A cop now waiting anxiously for backup to help with Earl Logan, the legendary thug of Halton Springs. Earl was happy to accept his fate whatever that might be, his just punishment for a life of sins.

He closed his eyes and put his hands high in the air and said, "You come to take me in? I won't put up a fight."

He waited for an answer and thought about the sparrowhawk up above and imagined himself up there too, insensible and free. He thought of the bald eagles he used to see when he'd come to Long Pine. Imagined his soul in their stomachs, running through their veins, powering their wings and thoughts. Up high, high above Halton Springs, free and untethered from its soil, free and untethered from his life.

"Hey!" barked Earl impatiently. "Are you gonna arrest me or what?"

But no one replied.

THEN DARKNESS FELL LIKE A HAMMER.

33

By the time Devlin and Fox got to Devlin's motel room, it was midnight. Despite the late hour, adrenaline from the break-in kept their minds and bodies going. Fox had thrown off her shoes and laid out on the bed on her front reading through Lazard's planner. Devlin sat beside her as she turned the pages, looking over her shoulder.

Lazard's spidery handwriting filled the days of the planner, a mass of dark webs of ink that obsessively recorded his movements and appointments. Times were meticulously noted so no minute was lost, as if, at some future point, he intended to charge someone for his time based on this document. Most of the days were blocked out with some kind of appointment. Tuesdays to Thursdays had "HMC" written down and the exact times of arrival and departure. Devlin and Fox assumed this must be the Halton Medical Center. Then there were flights to LA, London, and Mumbai marked down every few weeks with corresponding flight numbers and times and Lazard's appointments in those locations. But many of the days spent in Halton Springs simply had the words "Logan Ranch" written alongside "HMC" or on their own with a beginning and end time.

"According to this," said Devlin, "he gets to the ranch at 18:30 nearly every night and leaves at 2:00 in the morning. That's a long day on top of his duties at the center. What the hell is he doing there?"

They both cast their eyes over the dates for the next few days, and all of them had either "HMC" written down and/or "Logan Ranch." Then the established pattern came to an abrupt end on Friday, which had the letter *J* written by it but, unusually, without a time. Beyond that, for the next week there were no entries in the planner until the following Friday which again had one word noted down, "Mumbai," without a flight number or time.

"What do you make of that, Devlin?"

"I want to know what's happening up on the ranch that's taking up so much of his time, and I want to know what it is that causes such an established pattern over several months to suddenly stop."

Devlin went over to the chair by the window and picked up the plastic folder he'd taken from Lazard's drawer. He sat, opened it, and started to read through the documents inside.

"What is it?" asked Fox.

"It's someone's medical notes. Pretty damned detailed medical notes. I mean, there's blood pressure, pulse, BMI, height, and weight, the normal measurements you'd take. Then there's urine analyses and ECG results—again pretty normal. But then there's pages of other tests." Devlin flicked through. "A DMSA scan for the kidneys, ERCP results... That's for the pancreas, I think."

"You sound like you know about that stuff?"

"Yeah. I was pararescue when I first went into the Air Force. We were trained in trauma care, kind of a military ER. We were dropped into places to recover and treat injured people. It's a long time ago now, and not exactly second nature, but this is still familiar territory."

Devlin flicked back to the front page. "That's odd..."

"What?"

"I can't find a name on here. There's nothing that says who these tests belong to. Looks like the front page is missing." Devlin checked back in the document folder, but it was empty. He put the documents back in the folder and dropped them into his lap. He sat back in his chair and breathed slowly and deeply. His head dropped and his mind started to tick away under its own tired but steady momentum. His thoughts sifted through ideas and fragments of fact in an effortful search to make connections.

Fox was lying down, still idly flicking through Lazard's planner and only partly paying attention to Devlin. Her fatigue had started to cause her attention to wander, so she sat up, drew her knees up under her chin, and wrapped her arms around her legs. She spotted Devlin's cell phone lying by her on the bed. She picked it up and flashed up the home screen. The background picture was a very attractive brunette in her twenties.

"Who's she?" asked Fox.

"What?" The question derailed Devlin from the track he'd been going down. He got up, put the folder down, and sat on the bed to see what had grabbed Fox's attention.

"Oh, that...yeah, she was my wife."

"Oh. She's pretty..." Fox suddenly looked puzzled, her tired eyes opening a little wider, and she said, "Wait, your wife?"

"Yeah. She died a few years back...before I became a priest."

"Oh...oh, I'm sorry."

"That's okay. I'm the one who keeps the picture on my cell." There was a moment's silence, and Fox almost did the sensible thing and didn't ask the next question. But being Fox, she went ahead anyway.

"Do you think it's good for you to have her photo on your cell still? I mean, after all this time it's a bit...morbid...don't you think?"

For the first time in a long time, Devlin actually looked hurt. "That depends, doesn't it? Have you ever been bereaved? Had the closest person to you taken away?"

"No...I...I'm sorry...I didn't—"

"No you didn't."

Fox felt terrible. And also that somehow this was the one part of Devlin's life that he understandably couldn't see with the same clarity that he saw everything else. After a moment Devlin's scowl began to melt away and was replaced by a guilty embarrassment.

He said sheepishly, "I acted like an ass, didn't I?"

"You have every right to act like an ass."

"You don't deny I acted like an ass though?"

"No. You were ass-like. But I was insensitive. I speak before I think. It's my thing. I'm sorry. Forgive me."

Devlin gave a small smile and said, "Forgiven. Of course you're forgiven." Another moment passed as Devlin reflected and cooled a little more.

"You're right. It is a bit morbid and maybe not totally healthy."

Fox looked at Devlin. He was a big handsome man with a powerful physical presence. Not unworldly at all. Not what you'd have down as a priest. There was a brute force about him, in his dimensions, his stare, his manner.

"So tell me about you and God, Devlin." Then she added with a twinkle in her eye, "Tell me how you put aside worldly things."

Devlin raised an eyebrow and said, "I don't think I put them aside. I canned them up."

"How long you been a priest?"

"Seven years."

"That's a lot of canning up."

"I have cigars."

"You must get through a hell of a lot."

"I do." A lull followed while the two looked at each other, momentarily relishing the fun of the conversation.

"You don't long for women? I'm guessing it's women." Another twinkle in Fox's eye.

"It's women," replied Devlin. Fox was breathing slightly faster now. Each step into the conversation was a little closer to Devlin and felt a little more dangerous.

"You must take lots of cold showers?" said Fox.

"I've managed seven years. It's a day-by-day thing."

"How much longer do you think you can manage?" They were staring across the bed with some intensity now. The tension found expression in Devlin's hands as they dug a little into the comforter.

"I mean to say, Devlin," Fox continued, delighting in fanning the flames, "have you got it under control?"

"I keep on top of it."

"Maybe you don't get that many opportunities."

"You saying I'm not easy on the eye?"

"On the contrary."

"Thing is, it's been so long, I figure it's best that I don't...lose control. Seven years...all that...canning up...could be dangerous." They were close now, both leaning in over the bed.

Fox placed her hand over Devlin's. It was tiny by comparison. "You saying I'm in danger?"

They were close enough they could hear each other breathing. Close enough to imagine they could feel the warmth of each other's lips.

"I'm saying stand clear, or climb on board."

"Oh, God, no wonder the Gypsies left town the night you

arrived." She was close to closing her eyes, her face falling toward his. Devlin's thumb was stroking the inside of her index finger. Then it stopped. Abruptly. Devlin backed away and became alert and wide-eyed.

"The night the Gypsies left town...!" he whispered as his mind began to race.

"What?"

"That's got to be it! I've been a fool. I've been the biggest fool." He got up, quickly changed into a fresh shirt, and put his clerical collar and jacket on.

"Devlin? Where are you going?"

"I've got to go. Listen, you can stay here for the night if you want or head back if you want to." Devlin reached the door before realizing he'd forgotten something. He went back and grabbed Lazard's folder from the chair he'd been sitting in.

"I'll call you in the morning," he said as he again headed for the door.

"Devlin?" Fox called after him, but the door closed and Devlin was gone.

"Jesus! If you were looking for a way out, all you had to say was, 'I'm gay'!"

As Devlin raced through the night, a fleet of police cars were heading the other way. Back to the station.

34

Most of the officers drafted in had packed up and left Long Pine. Walker and Miller, who had been first people to arrive at the scene of Earl's death, were still waiting for the all clear to go. The first wave of police who had arrived after them stayed to give their account to their senior officers. After their statements were taken, they had to take a twenty-minute hike in the dark to the state park office, where helicopters were on hand to fly them back to the highway at the south end of the forest.

Stevens kept Walker and Miller hanging on until last. They stood in silence as he finished speaking to the CSI and walked back over to the address the two men.

"Tell me exactly what happened," demanded Stevens.

Walker was silent, so Miller spoke for them. "We heard a shot and raced up here and found him like he is. Like this." Miller gestured toward the body surrounded by yellow tape. Earl's corpse lay outstretched, sprawled out on his front on the wet earth, the side of his face missing and brain, tendon, and blood oozing onto the forest floor. A couple of feet away, a snub-nosed revolver had come to rest, as if released at the moment of death. Stevens didn't look satisfied by the explanation.

"Honestly, Greg," Miller protested. "That's all that happened." Stevens looked at both of them, his gaze flicking from one to the other.

"What the hell's the matter, Greg?" yelped Walker, "you got him. You led a hunt to find a double killer and you got him—maybe not alive, but you got him. So take the stick out of your ass and let us go."

But Stevens couldn't let them go. Not yet. "I know you communicated with the helicopter crew and took off toward Tar Ridge without letting me, the incident commander, know what was happening."

"Greg, they couldn't get in touch with you on the radio," said Miller. "I waited for you to reply. I had to respond. It was a critical situation."

"Did you attempt to contact me?"

"We'd moved out of range."

"I've spoken to half a dozen officers who were stationed across the chain, and not one of them heard any attempt from you to pass on this information."

"I guess I was impetuous."

"Leave the kid alone," Walker butted in. "He's a young cop wanting to get to the action."

"If you were in my shoes, Caleb, Miller here would be heading right for a suspension. So don't you start messing me around."

"You may be the incident commander, but I am the senior officer up here doing legwork on a hell of a lot of goodwill, so you just watch your mouth. Just what the hell are you insinuating?"

"I'm saying maybe it wouldn't have ended this way if someone else had got to him."

"How dare you? Are you out of your mind? It's obvious to a retard what happened here. Earl was surrounded; he's wanted for two homicides. He decided to kill himself rather than face the law."

Stevens didn't have a comeback. He knew it was the obvious answer. But he didn't trust Walker and Miller. Not one inch.

"I think this whole investigation's gone to your head," said Walker. "But you better watch what you say, Stevens. You go throwing serious accusations around and it'll be a long, lonely walk out the door. Trust me on that because I'll be the one slamming it behind you. And if I were you, I wouldn't be attempting to spread any blame around. Good and bad, this one's all on you. After all, you have a press conference tomorrow."

"Press conference?"

"Of course! You wanted to be the big man, the incident commander. That comes with certain responsibilities, and one of them is that you handle the press conference. It's usually held after lunch at the Clifton Graham Center, but you should check that with the Halton Springs information officer. Now, if you'll excuse us, we've got a long trudge out of this hellhole up to the state park office."

Walker and Miller slouched off together into the dark woodland. Within minutes they were lost to sight. What Stevens wouldn't give to hear their conversation on the journey out of the forest. Then his thoughts turned to Walker's parting words. *Great*, thought Stevens, *all this and then a press conference. What the hell does a person say at a press conference?*

35

Devlin took the road north out of Halton and turned onto the 70. By the time he'd got to Columbus, it was five in the morning and he was dog tired but had reaped the benefits of clear highways. The odd headlight flashed by in the dark as traffic, even at this early hour, began to show signs of building.

He stopped to fill up halfway between Columbus and Cleveland. Business was still slow, and the guy behind the counter looked like he was coming to the end of a long shift. He struck up some conversation as Devlin paid up.

"You got an early mass or something, Father?"

"No. I'm just on my way to Cleveland. I've driven up from Halton Springs."

Devlin wandered over to the magazine and newspaper rack and picked up a copy of the *Cleveland News-Herald*. On the front page in the bottom bar was an article on the Romani travelers arriving in Cleveland. He read through the article, which said the travelers had moved from their initial spot in Hudson and had pitched by a river in Cuyahoga Park.

Devlin dropped the paper on the counter and paid for it.

"How far's Cuyahoga Park from here?" asked Devlin.

The cashier looked at Devlin through bloodshot, heavy-lidded eyes and thought for a second. "It's a couple of hours' drive from here. You wanna stay on the I-70 and then take the I-271."

Devlin paid up and got back on the highway, heading now toward Cuyahoga.

He drove until he hit the state park. He carried on for another three or four miles through the park but saw no sign of a river or a camp. He began to doubt the information in the article. He passed an elementary school and at last saw a sign for a bridge over the Cuyahoga River. He took a right off the highway just before the bridge. The turn took him down a smaller road, and he stopped at the point where it withered away into a footpath that ran parallel to the river bank.

Devlin got out of the car and had a look around. It wasn't light yet; the sky was beginning to illuminate with the promise of sunrise, but real daylight was still an hour away. There was nothing much in the immediate vicinity: an old iron asphalt roller, a stack of damp timber, and a rusty old container. But farther down, about a quarter of a mile off through a line of trees, he caught sight of what he'd driven through the night to find: a group of trailers. The camp was still quiet, and no one had stirred yet. Devlin got back into the Ford and felt in his jacket pocket for his rosary. He took it out and ran through his decades for penance. After that, he said his morning liturgy, then switched on the radio for company. There was a news bulletin reporting Earl's death and describing it as a suspected suicide. Devlin frowned as he considered the idea that Earl had committed suicide. It just didn't feel right. For some reason he couldn't articulate, despite everything that had happened, he felt Earl had still been open to salvation. He wouldn't have taken his own life. Then the news bulletin handed over to a phone-in, and within minutes he was sound asleep and, to his slight astonishment, dreaming about Fox.

36

Dr. Lazard was making his way to the community medical center to begin a day of work. As he drove, he took long and purposeful drags on a Dunhill cigarette perched in his gloved hand. He was having to get used to driving himself around these days, since he'd lost his chauffeur.

Though it was May, he wore a suit, a long tweed overcoat, a silk scarf, and black gloves. He even had his heated steering wheel on, the one feature his luxury Jaguar XFR possessed that really pleased him. Though what he discovered when he pulled up by the medical center didn't please him or warm him up any. There was a police cruiser parked outside the clinic.

Lazard popped his head around the door cautiously. The receptionist was talking to a young black female police officer, who was listening without a flicker of empathy and appeared to be tired and irritated. The receptionist turned to Lazard, looking distraught.

"Dr. Lazard!"

"What's happened, Helen?"

"We've had a break-in, Doctor. Maybe someone after drugs."

"A break-in?"

"Officer Gray, this is Dr. Lazard," said Helen. "He comes down to work here a couple of days a week."

"Hello, Dr. Lazard."

"Officer Gray."

"I'm afraid Mrs. Fletcher here is right; your office was broken into last night," said Gray. "Although nothing seems to have been taken. But I'd appreciate you taking a look and letting us know if you notice anything that might be missing."

"Of course," said Lazard. "How distressing this all is. Didn't the alarm go off?"

"Yes, it did. We just turned it off," said Gray.

"Well, really! What is the point of having an alarm if no one takes any notice?"

"Someone from Halton PD would have attended the alarm much earlier under usual circumstances, Doctor. But last night the police department, myself included, was fully occupied by the hunt for a double murderer. I'm at the end of a fourteen-hour shift, so I'm really in no mood for this."

Sensing that Officer Gray was on a short fuse, Lazard contained his profound annoyance. "I see," he replied curtly. "I'll need to take a look at my office, then."

After Officer Gray left, Lazard and the receptionist restored order to his office, tidying away the contents of Lazard's drawers that had been dumped onto the floor.

"Your desk is ruined, Dr. Lazard."

"Yes. No matter. I shall have another one ordered."

"It's mindless, that's what it is. Pure hooliganism. Why would they only break into your office? Your office is in the middle of the hall; why would they go past all the others and start with yours first?"

"Because they were probably out of their minds on drugs or withdrawal. Trust me, Helen, I've seen this sort of behavior before. It has no pattern that is comprehensible to the sober mind. Now, I'm sure the reception area is already filling with patients..."

"Yes, of course." Helen turned to leave.

"Oh, Helen?"

"Yes, Dr. Lazard?"

"If you could give me five minutes before I see the first patient? So I can take a moment for myself? And may I also have a cup of tea, please?"

"Yes, of course, Doctor."

"You're very kind."

Helen left and Lazard pushed the door closed behind her. Then he made a call on his cell.

"Hello, Stein. It's Claude."

"Lazard? What's up?"

"I have some troubling news."

"What?"

"My office at the medical center was broken into last night. Just mine. No others."

"You sure it wasn't kids looking for drugs?"

"Yes. Devlin was here yesterday, and now I have a break-in. It's not a coincidence. My desk diary and important patient notes are missing."

"What was in the diary?"

"General things. Nothing detailed."

"Why did he take the notes?"

"I don't know. But they were important notes."

"What kind of important notes?"

"The most important kind. But they were entirely anonymous. Thankfully I took the precaution of removing the patient's personal details. Even so, I will have to take precautionary measures and bring things forward. It is far from ideal. I don't need to tell you this is another complication that we could desperately do without."

"If we're talking about distractions, it was your chauffeur that turned out to be a snake in the grass. I'm the one who keeps getting the cleanup bills for your dirty laundry."

"I did not choose that man as my chauffeur. Stein, I would remind you that you are quite dependent upon me. I am integral to your business—"

"Yeah, yeah, Gloria Swanson. I'm going to call a crisis meeting. We have to get on top of this right away if we're to hit our delivery date. After all, D-Day is only forty-eight hours away."

"What about this man—Devlin?"

"Oh, don't you worry your pretty little head about him, Lazard. Fortunately for everybody else, I've been a busy boy on that front. I got a little guerilla warfare coming his way."

Stein rang off and Lazard stood still for a moment, very still, cradling his cell phone. Then he spat out two words in a thick Bosnian accent, "Stein! *Jebi se*!"

37

"Walker and Miller." The two names rolled around in Stevens's head continually.

Stevens's eyes stung, and his body ached with fatigue. Extreme exhaustion was fueling paranoia, allowing Stevens to entertain theories that a more rested and settled state of mind would have been equipped to discount.

He should have been at home getting some sleep. He shouldn't have come straight from Long Pine to the police station. He should have been doing anything other than sitting in his office obsessively running through the events of the night before. He had started checking through police reports. He just had to know what Walker and Miller were doing up to the point of Earl's death. He was consumed with finding some detail that would unlock a conspiracy between the two. So he'd started by going back over their movements for that day.

Stevens sat at his PC scrolling through the H: drive, the shared drive which held all the departmental records. He checked back through Miller's daily activity log for Wednesday's day shift. The log stated that Miller had initially been on the road check with Officer Lincoln. Then it had him checked in with Chief Walker at Long Pine in Walker's cruiser. So Walker must have personally pulled him off the road check, and that was unusual. The chief going all the way out to the road check to pick up a patrolman was pretty irregular, maybe even a sign of the conspiratorial behavior he was so desperate to find. Stevens's mind began to race. His heart quickened as he allowed himself to entertain the possibility that he had found something significant. Something that could nail the two men. But even in his ragged and sleep-deprived state, he knew it wasn't nearly enough.

Stevens wanted to cross-check the daily activity log, so he went back to the squad car check sheet to confirm it. But as he flicked through documents in the folder for May, he noticed quite by chance that one log sheet wasn't there. It was the shift log for the previous Friday night into Saturday morning, the 20:00 - 04:00 shift. That was strange. He looked through the previous couple of months, and all the other logs were present and correct. It was just that one shift. Maybe it was a mistake. Someone had deleted it by accident. So he decided to look through the other reports for that Friday-night shift. But as he scrolled through the H: drive clicking on the various different folders and subfolders, he realized that all the logs and reports for that shift had been deleted. That couldn't be an accident. They had to have been deleted deliberately. Now Stevens had entirely forgotten about Miller and Walker. He had become hooked on a new mystery. He was on a completely different track.

And then it hit him. A strike of lightning out of the blue that really shook him up. The missing logs were from last Friday's night shift. The shift that coincided with the time of death of the Long Pine victim. His heart thumped hard now, and his tired eyes suddenly burned with urgency. Who was on shift that night? He opened the folder with the lineup reports. The lineup report had to be there. They were filed and saved thirty minutes before the start of each shift. Even if it had been deleted, a copy would have been sent to the emergency communications center. But the report was there, and there were four names: Miller, Gray, Lincoln, and Taylor.

How could Stevens find out what these officers were doing on that night? As all the paperwork had been deleted, he decided the only way was to ask them. He sent separate emails to each of the four officers. The subject field read "Missing records for night shift. Friday 4th May." He explained that the records hadn't been saved on the drive and asked each of them to resubmit records for their daily activity and their cruisers on that shift. He could picture their reaction when they opened the email. Well, screw them. He'd haul each of them in individually if he had to.

His discovery prompted the obvious question: Why would someone delete those particular files—the files of the night of the Long Pine murder? The answer to that question filled him with doubt. For seconds that seemed like minutes, Stevens entertained the appalling thought that Earl Logan might not be the tidy solution to the havoc that had been visited upon Halton Springs this past week. It was too terrible to contemplate, so he forced it to the back of his mind, out of his conscious thoughts to a place where it could only fester.

There was a knock at the door. He looked up to see a thin woman in a checkered suit dress and round glasses standing in the doorway.

"Deputy Stevens?"

"Hi."

"I'm Catherine Goretzki, the information officer. We should really go through things for this afternoon's press conference."

"Oh. Of course."

She looked him over with a critical eye and asked, "Have you slept at all, Deputy?"

"No. No, I haven't. But I guess it's too late now?"

"Ah, yeah. I'm afraid It is. We have rather a lot to do. But this should be a breeze, Deputy. After all, you found and tracked down the man who brutally killed two people. Get through the press conference and people may be calling you a hero."

38

Devlin had felt terrible when he'd woken up. He'd had an hour's shut-eye at most and had a cricked neck and an aching head. Now, he was hungry as hell, and he must have smelled pretty bad too.

So he lit up a cigar. Well, that was a kind of breakfast. The dry leaf crackled, and a ball of smoke fled into his lungs, sweeter than air.

The Gypsy camp had slowly stirred into life. At first, one by one, a few individuals had emerged into the early-morning sun, and then, a little later, the greater part of the community had risen and started to go about their day. Young men and women were heading into town to work or look for work, and kids and toddlers were running around the trailers making their own fun. The people leaving the camp walked along the riverbank to steps that led up to the bridge and into town, so Devlin got a good chance to check out whoever left the site.

Nearly half an hour passed during which Devlin scoped out the camp from his car. He figured he could pretty much see all of it from where he was parked. There were in the region of thirty trailers. Most were parked in two rows side on to Devlin on opposite sides of a strip of land, but a few at the top and bottom of the camp were parked end on to where he was sitting. There were cars and panel vans dotted around too. Devlin reckoned he had seen around fifty different individuals. So if every trailer housed on average three people, and this was clearly a guess, there should be, even by this conservative estimate, at least forty more people he hadn't seen.

Devlin smoked some more as he watched the camp. There wasn't a lot going on. The morning spike in activity had died, and the camp had settled down. So he picked up and reread through the patient notes he'd found at Lazard's.

He got to the last two pages and noticed that there were two sets of identical tests that had been performed but with slightly different results. Devlin held the two pages up side by side and compared them carefully. Why would there be two sets of nearly identical results? What medical value would there be in that? Just based on Lazard's reaction when Devlin had seen the folder, he felt sure that the notes must hold some special importance. But so far, Devlin couldn't see what it was. He placed the notes back in the folder, dropped them back on the car seat, and resumed his surveillance.

About an hour and a half and two more cigars had passed by the time Devlin became curious about one particular trailer. It was now eleven, he'd been parked in his car for four and a half hours, and he'd seen people come and go out of every trailer—every trailer but one. This trailer was smaller and older than the others and out on the edge of the camp. It had the name "Wilderness" stenciled on it and faded light brown stripes around the middle. He had seen signs of movement, drapes twitching and a window opening, so someone was definitely in there.

Devlin got out of his car and walked toward the line of trees that divided him from the land the camp was on. He followed the trees away from the river and turned into the field adjacent to the camp and separated by a wire fence. He walked the perimeter of the fence up to the corner where the Wilderness trailer was positioned. He took a look around and then scaled the fence as quickly and as efficiently as his tired body allowed. He hit the ground on the other side harder than he would have liked, but it was grass, so not too loud. Then he moved up to the side of the trailer facing away from the camp and edged closer to an open window. He could have just knocked on the door, but he felt sure he was dealing with a nervous animal that could get easily spooked. He put his hand through the open window, pulled back the curtain, and peered in but could only make out a TV on a kitchen worktop playing *Dr. Phil.* A figure entered the kitchen humming and still in his robe, but Devlin couldn't risk a good look to make him out clearly. The guy in the dressing gown settled in a chair with his back to Devlin and started watching the TV.

Devlin felt confident enough now to crane around the edge of the window and take a closer look. In the dark of the trailer, he could see past the back of the guy's head and make out the TV screen. Dr. Phil was laying into some old guy about letting his thirteen-year-old daughter go off with a cult leader. In amongst the flailing arms and indignant posturing on the TV screen, Devlin could just about make out the reflected face of the occupier of the trailer. He strained farther in as the screen went to black for a commercial break, and Devlin finally saw the reflected features clearly enough to blurt out, "Ed?"

The guy in the chair whipped around and saw Devlin, just as Devlin felt a sickening thud on the back of his head that rang through his body like a bell and put his lights well and truly out.

When Devlin came to, he was slumped in the dinette area of the trailer and could dimly sense other figures standing around him. He immediately grabbed the back of his head where strokes of debilitating pain were emanating from. Then he heard a deep, reassuring voice say, "Here, take these," and a pack of Tylenol Extra Strength was slid across the table toward him. Someone placed a glass of water in front of him, and Devlin fumbled open two pills from the pack and downed them in one. They could have been arsenic, but with the pounding head he had, it would only have been an improvement.

"You're out of practice, Gabe," the voice said, and Devlin realized it was familiar. He rubbed his eyes and looked over at the person sitting on the opposite side of the dinette. The hair was grayer and the face heavier, but he recognized it, and it took a couple of seconds for Devlin to say the name.

"George? George Brennan?"

"Uh-huh."

"What in the name of God...?" Then Devlin looked to his right and saw a guy in a suit, a Fed maybe, standing by the door, most likely the one who had snuck up behind him and given him the mother of all headaches. And past George at the other end of the trailer stood a forlorn figure, stooped and defeated. It was Ed.

"Hi, Gabe," he said, looking a little ashamed.

"Ed... Finally," exclaimed Devlin. "Now will someone tell me just what the hell is going on?"

39

At fourteen hundred hours promptly, Stevens entered one of the meeting rooms at the Clifton Graham Center. He was accompanied by Chief Walker, the Greene County and Shelby sheriffs, and the town information officer. He stood behind a microphone and a wooden lectern perched on a desktop and waited a moment for the scraping chairs and the voices of the audience to die.

Stevens started to speak. He began with the police identifying Earl as a person of interest and whom they wished to interview about both Halton Springs homicides. He described what they thought they knew of Earl's relationship with Brendan McKenzie, his subsequent disappearance, and Congressman Logan's assistance in tracking Earl down to Long Pine. Then, in some detail that had been painstakingly rehearsed that morning, Stevens described the hunt. He described the heat pattern that had alerted the police to Earl's presence and the scene that greeted officers when they finally tracked Earl down.

Stevens believed he had done a good and thorough job and couldn't see how he'd let anything slip between the cracks. The media had been only too ready to buy the simple theory that Earl had committed both murders and, once surrounded and cut off, taken his own life.

Even so, as he stood at the head of the room facing the legions of reporters that had crowded in, he felt a little nervy. He casually wiped a couple of beads of sweat away from his temples and turned around to see Catherine Goretzki looking calmly back at him. Beside her was Walker, who avoided any eye contact. Stevens also noticed that Officer Gray had crept in while he was speaking and was standing alongside Walker, which struck him as odd. Gray had been out all night on the manhunt, and despite the fact she must have been dead on her feet from lack of sleep had still come to the press conference. Maybe, reasoned Stevens, she really wanted to show her support, even though it wasn't entirely in Gray's character to be outwardly supportive to anyone. Then he began to wonder if she had got his email about the missing shift report, but his thoughts were cut short by Goretzki's voice asking for questions. In response, hands shot up across the crowded room.

The first question was tricky. A lady from WDTN wanted to know if the police were convinced Earl had worked alone. Stevens leaned into the microphone.

"We have no evidence that would link any other parties to the two homicides. All the evidence we have gathered points solely to Earl's involvement."

Another journalist raised his hand, and Catherine pointed to him and nodded.

"Has Clay Logan given any comment on his brother's involvement?"

Catherine whispered into Stevens's ear, and he listened attentively and then replied, "I believe Mr. Logan will be making his own statement later this afternoon about last night's events."

"Is there any information on who the Long Pine victim was?" shouted a voice from the back row.

"No. At this moment I'm afraid that is something we haven't been able to confirm. A check of the national database has not yielded a match. However, the Bureau of Criminal Investigations is contacting international law enforcement agencies to cross-check their databases."

The room had fallen quiet, and Stevens felt calm for the first time. Maybe this was going to be a comfortable home run.

Then a voice, high and harsh and from the back of the room, came sailing over the heads of her colleagues.

"Deputy Stevens, what can you tell us about 'God's Detective'?"

Stevens was taken completely by surprise by the sudden change in tack. "I'm sorry? I don't understand the question, Miss...?"

Stevens sensed movement behind him, a sudden restlessness and unease amongst his colleagues. The journalist spoke again, abruptly, impatiently, as if Stevens were an idiot.

"Linda Chambers, editor-in-chief of the *Dayton Sun*. Did you use the services of a Father Devlin on this case, known to your colleagues as 'God's Detective'?"

Catherine Goretzki stepped forward and spoke into the microphone. "I'm not sure this is really what we're here to answer questions about."

Two arms shot up amongst the sea of reporters holding a newspaper aloft which carried the headline, "Halton PD Hire 'God's Detective' with Troubled Past." Linda Chambers, who was holding the newspaper, now bellowed back, "This is today's *Dayton Sun* headline, Deputy. My paper asks some concerning questions about your judgment, and the people of Halton Springs deserve answers. Did Father Devlin assist you with this investigation?"

Stevens heard Walker behind him cough and mutter, "I could have told you so."

Goretzki looked at Stevens with a puzzled expression. He whispered to her, "It's okay. Let me answer." Then he addressed the crowd.

"Father Devlin assisted me in the ruling out of the initial line of inquiry due to his familiarity with—"

But Stevens didn't get a chance to finish. Chambers burst in on Stevens's reply. "Did you know he had a history of alcoholism, Deputy?"

Stevens should have carried on answering Chambers's first question, but he was flustered and reacted to her new line of attack. "I knew he had a history, but it was a history—"

Again, before he'd fully explained, Chambers came back with another challenge. "A history? Didn't you know he spent a night in a Boston PD drunk tank last week?"

"No...no I did not."

"Were you aware he told his congregation that he didn't believe in God?"

"I...I really couldn't speak to that."

"Is it true that Father Devlin had a vicious fight in the street with Earl Logan the night before he took his own life?"

"I... It's possible. Yes, I believe that he was attacked—"

Again Chambers didn't wait for a full answer and came back at him. "Were you aware that Father Devlin had a violent past?"

"No, I was not. I mean, I don't think he has—"

"You don't 'think'?" Chambers had now adopted a tone that combined indignation with exasperation. "So you are not aware that Father Devlin has a conviction for violent assault?"

"I...I wasn't aware, no..."

Chambers was now full of righteous indignation as she went for the final blow. "Deputy Stevens, did you vet Father Devlin before he was brought on board the investigation into the Long Pine murders?"

"I...er..."

"Yes or no, Deputy Stevens?"

"No...not formally. I interviewed him myself and was satisfied he would be an asset to the investigation."

"Did you do a background check?"

"No. No, I did not."

"Would you say that your failure to make such a check—I believe I'm correct in saying a mandatory check—in the most important and tragic case in Halton Springs' history is a matter for resignation?"

There was a deadly hush. It would only be broken by Stevens's answer to Chambers's question. Stevens's reply was halting and hoarse. "I think it was perhaps a mistake. I should have checked."

"That is not in doubt," screeched Chambers. "The question you must answer now is, will you resign, Deputy?"

Stevens had been ambushed and had no means of defense. He was like a punch-drunk boxer staggering around the ring in search of a final blow to end his misery. He had run out of words, and exhaustion had now possessed him. Chief Walker came to his side and spoke into the microphone.

"Folks, I think we should wrap this up now if there are no more questions on last night's shooting. After all, that is what we came here to answer questions about."

"What about 'God's Detective,' Chief Walker?" challenged Chambers.

"What about him, Miss Chambers? This is a press conference about the Earl Logan killings. When we have a press conference about Father Devlin, you can ask about Father Devlin. Thank you all for coming."

As Walker and a shell-shocked Stevens exited the room,

Walker patted Stevens on the back and said with undisguised pleasure, "Maybe, Greg, the priest wasn't such a good influence after all."

Over in downtown Columbus, Trayder Stein had watched the press conference in his office. By the time it had ended and the news station returned to the anchor, he was beaming like the Cheshire cat that had just got all the cream. He reclined in his high-backed, leather executive chair and had himself a celebratory shot of bourbon.

"That's what I'm talkin' about! God's own alcoholic detective!"

His cell buzzed and Stein took the call with pleasure. "Hi... Yeah, you saw it too? Magnificent, wasn't it? I told you my two boys would come through with the goods... You're welcome... It ain't over yet as far as Devlin is concerned. My boys are all over that guy like a fat kid on a cake, and who knows what more they'll find my friend... Who knows?"

40

George Brennan wore a light brown suit with a dark brown tie. His hair had grayed at the sides, and he looked jowlier and heavier-set than the last time Devlin had laid eyes on him. But he was still as dapper and graceful as Devlin remembered. Devlin had known Brennan from Special Investigations. He had been Devlin's supervisor on his first case out in Kabul. One of the few black airmen of his generation to be awarded the top honor, the John Levitow Award, at Airman Leadership School, he was a stellar agent. For a kid out of Roseland, Chicago, Brennan had come a long way.

"I heard you'd become a priest, Gabe. Doesn't the church give you a clean change of clothes these days?" Brennan joked.

"I look like this 'cause I've been up all night looking for Ed," said Devlin, massaging the back of his head.

"Well, you just found him. You gonna tell us how the hell you knew he was here?"

"It was just a pretty compelling hunch which I should've worked out before now. If you want to be invisible, take a ride with the people no one else wants to see. And the Gypsies left town round the same time Ed did."

Ed spoke up. "They saved my life, Gabe." He was looking very sorry for himself. "They took me in and gave me an old trailer to myself. They gave me kindness where I had no right to find it."

"I can see that, Ed. As long as you're safe, that's all I care about. That's all I've cared about since I spoke to you last Saturday."

Ed didn't answer. Nor did George. And the guy in the suit who had given Devlin a sore head didn't look the conversational kind either. Devlin realized they were going to try and stonewall him, keep Devlin out of their operation. But he wasn't going to let that happen. Not after all he'd been through. Over his dead body.

"So what's going on? Why were two private detectives tracking you down, Ed? Tracking me down too? Why did you lie to me and tell me this was all about gambling?"

More silence.

"Anyone gonna tell me what you're all doing huddled up in a trailer in Cuyahoga Park?"

Again, nobody replied. The three men stared blankly back at Devlin.

"You're kidding me?" said Devlin. "I came five hundred miles to make sure Ed was okay and no one's gonna tell me why he's here?"

"I'm sorry, Gabe," said Ed dolefully. "I couldn't tell you what was going on when you called. I was under orders."

"We can't tell you anything either, Gabe," added George.

"I come all the way from Boston by way of DC, have your boy here knock me out stone-cold, and I don't get to know why?"

"It's classified government business," said George stiffly.

Devlin sat back gingerly in his seat, careful of his still-raw head, and gave the men a disdainful look. Then he said, "Okay.

You know what? You don't need to say anything. I know what's going on here anyway. I know that and plenty more."

"You can keep bluffing and working it, Gabe. Won't make any difference."

"I wouldn't be so sure, George. See, I've been in Halton Springs for less than a week, and I've gotten to know a fair bit." Devlin leaned forward and stuck a finger at Ed. "Ed here was working at the Logan Ranch and chauffeuring for Lazard. I know that much."

Brennan was a man not given to facial expression. He took professional pride in how hard he was to read, so he kept his poker face. Ed, however, couldn't hide his surprise that Devlin knew this.

"I know that on Saturday," Devlin continued, "without warning, Ed upped and left his job and disappeared into thin air. A week later, I find him hiding in a trailer being looked after by two government agents. One of whom"—at this point Devlin turned to George—"if his past form is anything to go by, probably holds a very senior rank by now. So my guess is, you, George, ran Ed as an agent, but for some reason his cover got blown. So that's why he's here. And the fact he's all the way up in Cuyahoga being babysat in a trailer by a suit with a gun tells me his life is in danger. And if you're running that kind of operation, you must have moved from the Air Force to somewhere like Homeland Security by now because this sure as hell isn't any Air Force business. So if Homeland's running Ed as an agent on the Logan Ranch and having him driving for Lazard, then you suspect Logan Enterprises and Lazard of some kind of major criminal activity."

There was a pause. Brennan was starting to lose his poker face. He was starting to look uncomfortable.

"He knows, George!" Ed exploded. "You should tell him."

"Shut up, Ed. Shut the hell up," yelled Brennan, his usual

composure escaping him for a moment. Then he regained his calm and said to Devlin, “We weren't running Ed as an agent. We had him there as eyes and ears on the Logan Ranch. Nothing formal. An informant, not an agent.”

“Not far off though. And I take it, then, you are Homeland now?”

“You found Ed, he's okay, it was nice catching up, but you should go,” said Brennan.

“I'm not going anywhere.”

“You'll go if we tell you to go,” said the guy in the suit.

“Nobody was talking to you, junior,” said Devlin.

“I hope you're enjoying that headache I gave you,” sniped the suit.

“Not now, son, the grown-ups are talking,” said Devlin. The suit muttered a curse under his breath, but Devlin paid no attention and continued to address George. “If you tell me what you're up to, then I'll let you know what I got. And I think you'll find you get the better end of that deal.”

“You always were a smart S.O.B., Gabe, but somehow I doubt you got anything we haven't,” Brennan replied.

“Maybe. Maybe not. Let's just say for starters, just to give you an appetite for what might be to come, I got a link running from a guy called Trayder Stein through the Freedom Medical Company through an offshore back to Logan Enterprises.”

“Crap,” Ed blurted out.

“I was always the better detective, George. You know that,” said Devlin.

“It's a load of bull, Gabe. You're reaching,” said Brennan.

“Okay. Then I'll say goodbye and take what I know. And seeing as you think what I'm trading is worthless, then it'll be no loss to you.” Devlin stood. “Happens of course that I have the kind of information you've been working months to get even a sniff of. That probably cost your operation hundreds of thousands, maybe more, in taxpayer dollars too. But you're obviously very confident I got nothing, so not knowing what I got evidently won't keep you awake at night, George. Goodbye."

Devlin looked toward the suit. The suit looked back at George.

"Well, boss. Should I let him go?" said the suit.

"Push comes to shove, son," said Devlin. "I don't think it'll be down to you what I do."

"I put you out cold pretty easy, old man."

"Yeah, but this time you're coming at me front on, not on twinkle toes. See how far you get before I bust your head open. Son."

"Leave it, Errol," snapped Brennan. "Both of you. Errol, you go outside and keep a lookout."

Errol looked sore as hell but left and slammed the door behind him. Devlin sat back down and looked at George expectantly. George loosened his necktie and said, "Okay. You tell me what you got."

"That wasn't the deal, George."

"I didn't say anything about a deal. You were always a friend and a good man, Gabe, but you either tell me what you know, or I'll have you arrested for obstructing a Homeland investigation. You tell me what you got, and then I'll be the judge of whether you've done enough to enter our little secret circle."

Devlin considered the situation for a moment. He'd found Ed, but he had some big questions he badly wanted answered now. Things that didn't make sense that he wanted to forge sense out of. For that, much as it pained him, he needed a seat at Brennan's table. He needed to make himself useful to Brennan.

"Fine," said Devlin. "I know that Freedom Medical has been plowing huge funds into Logan Enterprises via an offshore company, funds that have turned the ranch around. I know that the Secret Service was investigating the trail of money but that they got nowhere. I know that there was an investigative article on Trayder Stein dropped from the *Dayton Sun* due to pressure from Stein's lawyers. I know that Freedom Medical and Logan Enterprises have set up the Halton Medical Center in such a way that its accounts can't be scrutinized. In short, George, I know that you, me, and the Secret Service suspect something shady is going on, but nobody has been able to nail it down."

It wasn't everything he'd got, but it was as much as he wanted to say out loud. He watched for Brennan's reaction. Brennan casually brushed down his tie, placed his hands on the dinette table, and said in an unimpressed tone, "That it?"

"That's it."

"Okay. Most of that I knew. Only some of it I didn't. The newspaper thing, I didn't know that, but it ain't much."

If Brennan was going to play hard to get, then Devlin wasn't going to beg for a piece of the action. So he took another tack. A gamble. "You're not fooling anyone, George. You may act like the big guy who's running a high-stakes table and has all the cards, but I can see that's not the way it is. Ed was your only way into the Logans, wasn't he...?" A beat of silence. Brennan neither confirmed or denied it.

"I knew it," said Devlin. "You're cooked, George. You've played your one hand, and now you have to leave the table. Your investigation's stalled."

"You think insulting me is gonna get you what you want?"

"No. I think helping you get back on track is going to do that."

"How the hell can you help me, Gabe?"

Devlin was now thinking on his feet, hearing things coming out of his own mouth that even he found alarming. "Because you can run me as an agent, a real agent, and I can find out just exactly what's going on. You know my track record as a special agent. Hell, you practically begged me not to leave the OSI."

"Yeah, I did beg you, but you went and left anyhow, and now you're a priest. Why the hell would you want to go back into this line of work? After all these years?"

"It's a good question. One I'm still figuring out myself." Devlin took a moment to get his thoughts in order and then continued. "I've been in Halton Springs a week, and all I've done is try to find Ed. That's all. Yet nearly everyone I talk to has lied to me. The more I asked around, the more I saw something wasn't right with that town and the more I wanted to find out what that is and cut it out."

"That's all very admirable to hear," said Brennan.

"You, George, more than most, know how good I was. How accomplished a special agent I was."

"The only word I really heard in that sentence was 'was.' You're an older man now."

"And I'm a hell of a lot wiser. And I can do things that you or the Secret Service people can't. I'm not accountable because I'm not linked to you or Homeland, and if I mess up, you don't even have to care. No hiding me in a trailer paying for some greenhorn to come guard me. No phone calls to superiors explaining the mess. No missed promotions. In the short time I've been here, I've already got as much intelligence as your outfit got in, what? Months?"

George didn't answer this time. He was finding it difficult to pull reasons together to push back. Devlin saw an ambitious man with a big headache that threatened to upturn his career progression. He saw a gap and continued charging through it.

"The other reason I have is personal. I came here to find Ed. But I think I'm meant to be here. I was meant to crash into all these people's lives that I've crashed into. I'm meant to follow this to the end. It's a mission."

"Don't start getting all spiritual on my ass. You know I'm a non-believer. That sort of preacher spiel doesn't cut it with me."

"Okay. Bottom line. Truth is, George, I don't see where your investigation goes from here. You're all played out. Not only am I your best bet, right now I'm your only bet."

Brennan didn't say anything immediately. He took a deep breath and ran through his options. Then he calmly asked Ed to get him a glass of water. Ed filled up a glass from the faucet and set it down in front of Brennan. Brennan drained it one go and dabbed his mouth dry with the back of his hand. He spread both his hands on the countertop and studied them for a moment. Then he made his decision.

"Okay," said Brennan. "I'll tell you what our operation is. Obviously, this is between us. I wouldn't be telling you, no matter what you claim to know, if we didn't go way back and if I didn't know you as well as I do. Then we can discuss what it is you can do for me."

"You know I wouldn't betray you to anyone, George."

"Yeah, I guess I do." Brennan scratched his chin thoughtfully, looking for the right place to start, then leaned forward and spoke. He was measured and exact, just like Devlin remembered he'd always been.

"As you say, the Secret Service has been investigating Freedom Medical for the last three years for financial irregularities. Massive funds were being routed offshore and not being declared to Freedom's shareholders. It was thought to be part of a tax avoidance strategy. Thing is, when they managed to follow the money trail, it finally led to Logan Enterprises, specifically to the cattle fertilization plant. The Secret Service suspected the lab was a way of moving capital off Freedom's books to either avoid paying tax or just using the plant as a last stop before the money disappeared into unknown private bank accounts. But they didn't have the remit or budget to go after Logan Enterprises. Some more paranoid people say the secretary of state shut it down for conspiracy-type reasons. That Clay was protected up the chain. Whatever. So they turned to us for help. Personally, I didn't believe for one minute that fifty million had disappeared into Clay Logan's little cattle lab, no matter how much he crowed publicly about it, about how groundbreaking it was. I thought the Secret Service was onto something, and we saw Ed as a light-touch, off-books way of getting eyes on the lab. He'd just quit the Air Force and lived local. Like you, I knew him from back in the day working investigations. Congressman Logan makes great play of his support for the Air Force and his connections with the Wright Patterson base, so he welcomed Ed with open arms. It was a great fit. Then Ed was asked to drive Lazard around. He was fully embedded, and we couldn't have been happier."

"So what went wrong?"

"I don't know for sure. If I had to jump one way, I'd say it was the Secret Service. They were the only agency outside of my own unit to know we were running Ed. I think they must have referred it to the secretary of state's department, and that maybe got leaked to Clay Logan. He and the secretary of state are close friends. And that leak nearly got Ed killed by a guy named Packer, who works for the Logans."

"I know the name, but I've never met him," said Devlin.

"He's a monster," Ed butted in. "Scary mother. About seven foot tall and the size of a house." Devlin suddenly had a strong feeling that he had met Packer after all.

"Got one eye completely clouded over," Ed continued. "People say he's got the evil eye. While I was driving for them, he looked over my shoulder every step of the way. Gave me a separate GPS to navigate when I was delivering and told me not to use my cell. Packer said it was 'cause of the cattle lab. We used to pick up medical and chemical supplies. Clay was paranoid too. He didn't want anyone getting hold of the methods they used on their cattle." Ed had moved forward now. He really wanted to tell Devlin his side of the story and George wasn't stopping him. "I had a feeling something wasn't right. I thought I was getting paranoid—everywhere I went these two guys were following me, a bald fat guy and a tall thin guy, and not doing much to hide the fact they were following me."

"Believe me, I'm right with you. They sound like the clowns who tailed me down to DC," said Devlin.

"Well, it got me really wired. I started losing my head, and that's when I went and got a ticket out to you."

"The guys tailing you had that ticket when I ran into them. That's when I called you," said Devlin.

"Yeah, I'm sorry about not telling you the truth and spinning you the gambling story. But you know why now—I was working for Homeland, and I was scared. Getting the ticket seemed like a great idea at the time. I know we hadn't seen each other in years, but we were best buddies in Osan. You looked out for me, and everybody who knows Gabe knows there's nothing he wouldn't do for a friend in trouble. And the fact you were a priest just gave me this idea that you could give me sanctuary. I figured I'd just up and go if I needed to. Made me feel better I had that exit plan. But things got really serious really quickly. And then I just thought there was no way I could tell you what I was mixed up in. I was sworn to secrecy, and it had already started to get so ugly."

Ed had walked over by the dinette and leaned against the door. He was animated, jittery as he recalled what had happened.

"First thing I knew about it was that son of a bitch Packer coming up to my house. Lucky for me, once the weather warms up a bit I like to take a bottle of rye and sit by the trees out front of my place. So there's me winding down one night 'bout a week ago when I see a car pull up a hundred meters or so down the highway. This figure gets out and starts walking toward my house. He doesn't have to get close for me to realize it's Packer; the guy's so big it's obvious. I'm covered from sight by the trees, and he isn't even looking for me there. For some reason, instinct or whatever, I just stayed where I was, I didn't move or make a sound. I just had a bad feeling about it.

"Then Packer walks up the drive to my house and starts snooping around. He takes a look around the back of the house and up to the garage. So now I know something ain't right. At one point he's only about ten feet away from me, and I'm tucked behind a tree trunk. I tell you, I nearly crapped my pants. Then, once he's seen the coast is clear, he rings the bell. Some lights are on—course, my truck's parked up, and it looks like I might be home. As he's waiting to see if I answer, he pulls out a great big monster knife and hides it down by his side. I couldn't believe it! He's there to kill me! Out of the blue. Without any warning. If I hadn't come out for a drink, I'd be sliced open and dumped up at the damn gut pile.

"Anyhow, course the door doesn't open, and so he gives it a couple of minutes and goes round to the garage and I hear him bust the door open. Once he's inside, I just ditch the bottle and run like a maniac. I ran and I ran till I was sick in the road. Then I ran and walked till I reached the Gypsy camp. I wasn't intending to go there, but when I saw it up by the highway, I just threw myself on their mercy. And God bless these people, without question they took me in. They gave me a way out till I could get in touch with George."

"We figured it was the safest place for Ed to stay for a week or so," said Brennan. "Out here in the camp. Especially when the murders started happening. All the crazy stuff that's happened with Earl Logan just complicated things for us. We just wanted to get the hell out. Halton was becoming a mess. We have Errol here keep an eye on the trailer, and he buzzed me when you showed up. Of course, if I knew it was old Gabe, I would have gone easier on you. So that's it. Ed was compromised, and we got no way back into Logan Enterprises."

"What about the cattle lab? Did it check out?" asked Devlin.

"Well, it's there and it's operating," answered Brennan. "Far as we can see, it's all legit. But a fifty-million-dollar investment in a cattle lab? No way. I think it's a front, and that's why the money's taking a roundabout route. And if Logan's fully legit, why did they want Ed killed? Sure, they'd have been upset as hell when they found out he was working for Homeland, but if they had nothing to hide, why did Packer come after him?"

"I didn't see anything that didn't look legit going on down there," said Ed. "I just delivered regular equipment for them."

"What kind of equipment?" asked Devlin.

"Lots of stuff. You name it," said Ed.

"No, Ed. I want you to name it. Tell me what you drove up there."

"Well, stuff you'd expect... I went through it all with George's guys. Chemicals, pharmaceutical stuff. A lot of liquid nitrogen, lab supplies like beakers, blood collection tubes. Exactly the kind of things you'd expect for their cattle fertilization plant. There were box loads of anesthetics for heifers. Mostly this one called...pro something...prop..."

"Propofol?"

"Yeah, that's it. How did you know the name?"

"I worked in pararescue, remember? We used to drop into the middle of war zones weighed down with painkillers and—" Devlin stopped suddenly, and he sat up. "Ed, did you ever take delivery of ketamine?"

"Ketamine?" Ed thought for a moment and said, "Yeah, yeah we did. It was a veterinary anesthetic they brought in. In fact, that's the main one they used for cattle. Lots of that and other pharmaceuticals like prostomate, BioLife..."

"Why the interest in ketamine?" asked Brennan.

"Oh, nothing," said Devlin casually, leaning back in the chair. "Professional interest is all. Once a pararescue, always a pararescue."

George looked at his watch. "Well, much as I'd like to talk about the stuff you injected people with when you were a PJ, I got a meeting in Columbus this afternoon. So, let's cut to the chase. What is it you think you can do for me, Gabe? What's God told you 'bout all this he hasn't told anyone else?" said Brennan with a chuckle.

"I think there's a better way into all of this than you or the Secret Service found," replied Devlin. "And it's got nothing to do with bank accounts."

"What way's that?"

"Dr. Lazard. Everybody's followed the money, and that's usually the best way. But I don't think that's the case here. Marie Vallory and Clay Logan are both too powerful. Vallory is a CEO of a billion-dollar business. Logan is a congressman with high-up allies, and he's cozy out in his ranch, away from prying eyes."

"What about Stein?" asked Brennan.

"Stein is too shrewd. Too smart. I have a feeling that guy has been hustling and scamming since he could walk. I'm not saying I couldn't crack him, but it would take longer. No, Lazard's the best bet. Whatever his function is in all of this, he's the most exposed, the most isolated. He's my best in."

Brennan pulled his wallet out of his inside jacket pocket, opened it, and lifted out a card and flung it across the table at Devlin.

"Okay. You do what you think you need to do and check in with me every twenty-four hours or whenever there is a significant development. Whichever happens first. I can't do squat to help you if you get into trouble. We got no resources, people, or leverage on this. You're out on your own and fully deniable. Just tell me what you find."

"That's fine by me. Absolutely fine. You won't have to lift a finger. For now."

Devlin appeared relaxed and laid-back when he said his goodbyes and left the trailer. But when he got into his car, he sat rigid in his seat. For a while he didn't move. He stared over the steering wheel, his eyes locked into the middle distance for a long while.

Then he picked up Lazard's plastic folder and riffled through the test results. Finally, he laid them against the wheel and sighed in frustration. Devlin just couldn't get past the lack of any name or patient details. If he had those he could chase them up.

He looked back through papers again and it was then that Devlin saw the identical sequence of a letter prefix and numbers: "FDH 4488983" on the bottom of the pages in faint ink. The patient ID number, thought Devlin, for billing reasons if nothing else. It seemed pretty clear that the prefix must be for Freedom Dayton Hospital. Devlin looked up a number for the hospital on his cell and rang.

There was a short dialing tone, and a bright and helpful voice answered. "Hello, Patient Records, Laura speaking. How can I help you?"

"Good morning. My name's Dr. Lazard, I'm calling from Halton Medical Center." Devlin forwent any attempt at an impersonation.

"Hello, Doctor." The voice was still bright and helpful.

"I'm just going over test results of a patient of mine you sent me, and, well, we had a little mix-up a while ago; we had the wrong number assigned to this particular patient. It really messed up our end of things and made billing your end a nightmare."

"Oh dear. That shouldn't happen..."

"Tell me about it. I can't tell you how much work it caused for everybody. Took weeks to unravel. So, could I just confirm, for the sake of my own paranoia, that I have the right patient number on the results you've sent me? I've got 4488983 down on the test papers in front of me."

"Sorry, could you repeat that number?"

"Of course. The number is 4488983."

"Right, got that. Let me have a look..." There was a pause, and Devlin could hear background voices scattered around the office and the clack of long fingernails against a plastic keyboard. After a minute's wait, he heard the woman say, "So, Doctor, the name you should have is Miguel Alvarez. Is that right?" Devlin didn't reply for a moment. The name was familiar, and he hadn't expected it to be. He'd heard it somewhere before.

"Hello? Doctor?"

"That's perfect, thank you."

"He's in the Leeman Urological and Kidney Unit. They're usually excellent up there if that's any reassurance? Very efficient."

"Oh, that is reassuring."

Devlin hung up and leafed through the papers again, stopping this time to study the last two identical tests. He held them up side by side to scrutinize them. His eye scanned down to the patient ID number at the bottom of the two pages. And it was then that he noticed an anomaly. He realized that the numbers weren't the same. The patient ID on one of the identical tests had the FDU prefix, but the numbers were for somebody else. One set of results was for another person. Devlin checked back through the other pages, but all of them had Alvarez's ID. It was just that one page. He threw them back on the passenger seat, the papers spilling off the edge and into the footwell. Devlin started up the car, turned, and roared back up toward the highway. There was one person he had to talk to. One person he needed to talk to. And that person was Fox.

41

Stevens sat in the police car lot with his forehead resting on his steering wheel. Cutter had seen Stevens's performance and the *Dayton Sun* article written by Linda Chambers and had issued one of his beloved press lines: "Neither Halton Springs council or the chief of police were aware that Father Devlin had not been formally vetted, therefore Deputy Stevens is suspended with immediate effect. There will be a review of Deputy Stevens' decision to consult Father Devlin on what was an investigation of the highest sensitivity and seriousness without first carrying out the mandatory background checks."

He felt utterly defeated. And worse even than his suspension, his misgivings about Earl Logan's guilt, triggered by the discovery of the missing shift reports, had begun to emerge again. Again he pushed it from his mind.

Then his cell went. Stevens took a breath and answered.

"Mr. Stevens? It's Dr. Kumar from Miami Valley Hospital."

Of course, thought Stevens, the tests were back from a couple of days ago. They really couldn't have chosen a worse time.

"Dr. Kumar, hi."

"Hi, Mr. Stevens, how are you?"

Damn, thought Stevens, *don't do the pretend have a nice day stuff, just tell me the way it is*. Even so, Stevens couldn't help but reply out of courtesy. "Okay. I'm okay. How are you, Doctor?"

"Oh, fine. Y'know, busy as usual." *Come on*, thought Stevens. *Get it done. Get it done*. At the same time, he was also wanting not to get it done, to not move to the next stage, to stay where he was a bit longer.

"So, listen, Mr. Stevens, we got your results back and—"

"Yes, Doctor?"

"Well, it's unexpected. Things have changed a lot faster than we thought."

Stevens's heart plummeted. "Yeah, okay," Stevens butted in impatiently. "How long are we looking at?"

"No, hold on, you don't understand. That's not what I rang to tell you. I'm ringing to tell you that the cancer hasn't progressed. In fact, it's the opposite. The tests came back and, well, it's extraordinary, but the cancer has reduced. You are in what I would cautiously term partial remission."

Stevens had stopped breathing but just managed to whisper, "What?"

"It's good news, Mr. Stevens. You have more time."

"I don't understand. I was told there was no hope..."

"These things—well, sometimes...extremely rarely actually —they can be unpredictable, even with the best science we have. I do have to tell you that sustained long-term remission from metastatic pancreatic cancer, while not impossible, is extremely unlikely. I also have to tell you that we would like to have you come in again, because we want to make sure as the results went completely against our prognosis. But I'm sure you understand in the circumstances. So are you able to book in with the nurse? Mr. Stevens? Mr. Stevens? Are you there...?"

Stevens had let his cell phone drop from his ear and was staring over the steering wheel into the parking lot. All of a sudden the world looked a hell of a lot brighter.

42

Devlin crammed down the plate of steak and fries room service had brought up like his life depended on it. Fox sat with folded arms, looking unimpressed.

"Easy. You're going to give yourself indigestion."

Fox had met Devlin back at his motel. Devlin noticed she was frosty and short with him but decided to let it go. Whatever beef she had would come out one way or another.

"I'm ravenous," said Devlin.

"I can see."

Devlin swallowed down the last mouthful, dropped his head back against the bed headboard, and let out a sigh. He'd got to the hotel room, showered, changed, and eaten and only now was feeling like he was human again. All he needed was a cigar. He opened a window, lit himself up, and then lit Fox a cigarette.

"So, you found Ed?" said Fox.

'Yeah. I guess. I guess I did what I came here to do."

"But? 'Cause I can hear there's a 'but' coming."

Devlin had promised he wouldn't tell anyone what Brennan had told him. But he had to tell Fox; he had to get her on board.

"I found out a hell of a lot more than I was bargaining on," said Devlin. "Turns out Ed went into hiding because he'd been caught spying on the Logan Ranch for a guy in Homeland, a guy we both knew from years back in the Air Force."

"Wow..."

"Yeah. This guy, George Brennan, had Ed working on the ranch because he's investigating the funds that Freedom plowed into Logan Enterprises—the funds the Secret Service and your friend were looking into. Seems the whole world at some point has got interested in what Logan and Freedom are up to, but no one's managed to crack it."

Devlin sat in a chair opposite Fox. He waited a moment before he spoke again and fixed her a tired but deeply serious look. "But I have this idea."

Fox sat forward. "What do you think is going on?"

"Okay, it's...it's unusual. I started having this crazy idea, which just hasn't gone away, and the more I consider it, the more it makes sense of everything that's happened in this town."

Devlin paused, but Fox ushered him on. "Go on, what is it? Tell me!"

"It started when I was in the trailer with George and Ed. Ed mentioned they used ketamine up at the Logan Ranch as a veterinary anesthetic. Well, the bloods from the Long Pine murder victim contained ketamine. The coroner guessed it was taken recreationally. But it could have been used for another reason. When I was a PJ, we used it as an emergency anesthetic."

Fox almost flinched at the suggestion, such was her initial disbelief. "It's more likely he'd have taken it to get high."

"Yeah, when I first heard about it, that sounded like the most likely reason. Now I'm not so sure. The other thing I found out is who Lazard's test results, the ones we took from his office, belong to. Even though there was no name on the test papers, the patient ID was there, and it checks out as belonging to a guy called Miguel Alvarez. The name rang a bell, but I couldn't think who it was. Then I realized, it was a kid I met when I was at the Logan Ranch. A hand that worked there. And I looked at the tests again and there were two antigen tests run on him, which is just plain odd."

"What's an antigen test?"

"It's a blood test, and it's done for a number of reasons. When I was in pararescue, I mostly knew about it for testing for infectious diseases, but it's also done to match tissue types for donor testing."

"Donor testing?"

"The other thing that bothered me is that I looked at these particular test results, and I just couldn't work out why he'd had them run twice. And then it hit me: the patient IDs on each test were different. They weren't two tests for Alvarez; they were two tests for two different people. Only one of them is Alvarez's results. The results of both tests match incredibly closely, close enough on first inspection to take them for the same person. But they're not from the same person. They're from two different people who are highly compatible for organ donation."

"You think he's been lined up to donate an organ?"

"Yeah. I do. But not just him. I think the first victim was doped up on ketamine because he was being prepped for surgery."

Fox was stunned. "But, if that's so, that couldn't be legal, could it?"

"No way. I think Lazard and Clay Logan have got into black market organ trading. That's why Lazard is up at the Logan Ranch nearly every night."

"My God...but that's a hell of a reach, Devlin. So then, why did the Long Pine victim end up getting killed?"

"Because something went wrong. The deal went sour."

"That means Earl was involved in organ harvesting too?"

"No. No, I don't think he was at all. In fact, I don't think Earl had anything to do with any of this. Maybe he was even completely unaware it was happening. I certainly don't think Earl was the killer."

"But they found his DNA."

"He's been framed, Fox. It wasn't Earl," Devlin said adamantly. "The coroner said that whoever cut up the first victim was right-handed. And that kept niggling away at me. And then I realized why. Earl was left-handed."

"How do you know?"

"Earl fought southpaw. When I fought Earl, he led with his right and followed with his stronger left hand. I'd bet the shirt on my back he was left-handed."

"Come on, Devlin, the news report said they found Earl's DNA at the scene? Him being left-handed? It's slight to say the least."

"Maybe, maybe not. But if Earl went to Brendan's after the fight with me, he would have likely left blood there. Maybe he got cleaned up there. He was bleeding heavily. That's a good enough reason why his DNA was there. But the other thing, the thing that bothers me about the two murders is that they were fundamentally different." Devlin took a mouthful of smoke and reflected for a couple of seconds. Then he said, "When I was back in seminary, we were taught philosophy, and Aristotle said—"

"Aristotle?"

"Hold on. Hear me out. Aristotle was always looking for the 'quid rei,' the essential nature of things. Well, the essential natures of the two murders are completely different. The first murder was an improvised act born out of desperation. Done in the lashing rain at the edge of a forest. The second murder was deliberate and cold, done to replicate the first in every way but motive. Done to implicate Earl."

"If all of that's so, if everything you say is true, it still doesn't account for one big thing—the one thing that needs accounting for. It doesn't explain what's happening with the fifty million dollars. That wouldn't be swallowed up in an operation like you're suggesting."

"Yeah, I admit, right now I don't exactly see where all the fifty million is going. But look at all the other things that don't add up. Why's Dr. Claude Lazard, a heart and lung specialist, treating people at a free walk-in clinic?"

"Maybe he's just a charitable guy! Maybe he just wants to give something back. Someone in your line of business shouldn't find that so hard to believe"

"No. Not Lazard. Don't buy it. You're telling me there's no one else can do that? No one less qualified? I think the Halton Medical Center has been set up by Freedom and Logan to screen for suitable organ donors, to screen vulnerable people, illegal immigrant workers. People without insurance. People who need money. To match their tissue types to paying customers. The chances of Miguel Alvarez's tests randomly matching another person's so closely are astronomical. Those two test results have been selected with extreme care."

The silence was heavy. Fox's expression was distinctly stony, unmoved.

"Come on, Fox, it makes perfect sense," said Devlin. "If you wanted to find young, healthy men who were invisible, had no records anywhere but were maybe desperate for money, the kind of instant cash an organ donation would make, the illegal workers on the Logan Ranch would fit the bill."

"What about the Long Pine victim? Everybody knew about him."

"Yeah. And that's why I think it was a mistake. For some reason, it went badly wrong. Maybe he bailed at the last moment. That's why he was found out near Route 36. He almost got free, but someone stopped him. He was a mistake they had to fix there and then. And that's why they cut him up; they knew that would be enough to prevent identification. Because he was an illegal, because of the total lack of records they knew a DNA search would be unlikely to reveal a match. And Brendan McKenzie was a setup, to make Earl the fall guy for the first murder."

Fox still looked very skeptical.

"It makes sense, Fox," said Devlin. "More sense than Earl suddenly turning double killer. That's why the medical center is so secretive, and it's why Lazard is the key to this. He and Alvarez are our way in. I've said to George, the guy running the Homeland operation, that I'd help him. I'd find out what Clay Logan is up to. Where the fifty million dollars has gone. And I will. I'd like your help, but I understand if that's something you don't feel convinced enough to give."

Devlin was done talking. He'd await Fox's response however long it took and whatever it was. She took a drag, blew a cone of smoke, and then asked, "You didn't catch Greg's press conference, did you?"

"What? No. Why?"

Another drag and Fox looked at Devlin with a directness, scrutinizing him. "I watched it on WTDN. My paper did a take-down job on you. Asked Greg why you were involved in the investigation. They said you were an alcoholic, you didn't believe in God, that you have a conviction for violent assault."

Devlin fell silent for a moment, let the smoke drift out of his mouth, and picked out a flake of tobacco from his teeth. "It's 'cause I've been asking around about Ed," he said. "Because I took Lazard's notes. Someone's looked into my past and leaked it to a journalist at your paper. They're coming after me. Well, good. If there squealing, then I'm poking in the right places."

Fox didn't look remotely satisfied with Devlin's answer.

"Is it true?" she asked.

"Is what true?"

"Were you really an alcoholic, Devlin?"

"I was. I am."

"But you're clean now?"

"Apart from one slip, yes, I am. Clean for seven years."

"Do you have a conviction for violent assault?"

"That happened twenty years ago. I was a young man in a bar fight, and I was provoked."

"Did you say you didn't believe in God?"

"Maybe. Probably. Sort of."

"Sort of? You sort of believe in God, or you sort of don't believe in God?"

"Yes, I believe in God. I believe in God, but I think God is the mystery. We are all at the edge of existence, at the very edge of the light staring into darkness, feeling our way toward the unknown fraction by fraction. And, to me, that unknown is God. Anyway, I've never said I didn't believe in God. I have said God could be something more...strange and interesting." Devlin crossed his arms and fixed his gaze on Fox. "I know what this is about, Fox. This is about who I am and how much you trust me."

"Well, I am a journalist. And it occurs to me that I don't know anything about you."

"I don't know anything about you," Devlin shot back.

Fox shrugged. "What's to know? I'm a workaholic, I'm uncomfortable with commitment, I left my husband crying in a ball on the carpet when I walked out on him. I hate gossip. I hate people who are two-faced, I once ran over a dog and didn't go back, I hate Christmas. I love Susan Sontag, and I slept with one of my tutors when I was at UPenn." Devlin nodded his head as he listened. "You working out my penance, Devlin?" asked Fox.

"No, because that wasn't a confession. You were playing your hand because you want to see mine. You figure there's something...something unresolved."

"Yeah. That's right, I do. I really do. I guess I wonder why you just upped and left your church all of a sudden. I guess if this were your profile I was doing, the question I would ask as a journalist is, just what is it you are hiding, Father Devlin? What are your secrets?"

Devlin saw this moment for what it was: his confession. Not to be forgiven, but because he had asked so much of Fox and would ask more. And Fox was a very smart, very shrewd individual. She wanted to know who the hell exactly she had fallen in with. Devlin was suddenly possessed of an intense belief that he had to tell Fox everything. And either that was something Fox would find a way around, or it wasn't.

"You want to know what I'm hiding?" asked Devlin.

"Yes."

"Okay. I'll tell you. And I'll begin by telling you that I have only told one other person. And that was done within the seal of confession."

43

Father Hector Hermes walked the path from the sidewalk up to the rectory entrance rolling a large suitcase behind him. The rectory, like the church itself, was a grand gothic affair and, also like the church, in winter hellishly drafty. Now, even in late spring, it was incredibly stuffy, despite fans having been placed everywhere. Hector shut the door behind him. After three days leading a youth convention in Wilmington, he was mightily relieved to be home, even though home could do with better AC. He stowed his case in the hallway, hung up his coat, and started toward the stairs. But he stopped short of the staircase, feeling certain he'd heard a noise in the living room. Was it the cleaner? She kept odd working hours, but at this time?

Hector called out, "Mrs. Quinlan?" But there was no reply. He reassured himself that he was being paranoid about burglaries like he always was when he had been away for a few days. Even so, he decided to check the living room just to be sure. He opened the door, walked in, and froze. A fat, bald man in a suit was sitting in the chair by the fireplace.

"Who are you?" yelled Hector. "Get out of my home—I'm

going to call the police!" But as he backed away, he came up against a body standing behind him. He turned and saw that it was a tall, thin, sweaty man also in a suit.

"Sit down, Father," said Bradley softly. "We've been waiting an awful long time for you to come home. There's no need to be alarmed. No harm will come to you if you tell us the information that we need."

Hector sat pensively in the middle of the sofa facing the two men. Otterman sat in the chair by the fireplace, and Bradley stood by the door, which he had closed.

Bradley spoke first. "Father, we need to talk to you about a man named Gabriel Devlin."

"What about him?" Hector answered nervously.

"We know that he came to you last Saturday. We know he confessed to you. We just want to know what it was he confessed."

Hector glanced nervously from left to right, rubbed his clasped hands gently, and said quietly, "I'm afraid I can't reveal anything that he said to me on his last visit."

"Father," said Otterman. "It's really in your interests that you tell us."

Hector's breathing quickened, and his mouth twitched.

"We don't believe in a heaven or hell," said Bradley. "So our actions here, whatever those may be, are of no consequence to us."

"If I were you, I'd make things easy on yourself," said Otterman.

"I can't," replied Hector.

"I'm sorry? I don't think I heard you right. 'You can't'?" said Otterman.

"What Father Devlin said to me was said during the sacrament of confession. I can't reveal what he said in confession."

"Yes you can," Otterman said. "You just tell us. It's that simple."

"No, you don't understand, I am forbidden..." Hector insisted and then repeated a passage learnt by heart: "Whoever shall dare to reveal a sin disclosed to him in the tribunal of penance we decree that he shall be not only deposed from the priestly office but that he shall also be sent into the confinement of a monastery to do perpetual penance."

Otterman gave Bradley a weary look. Bradley shrugged. Otterman turned to the priest and said, "Yeah, forget all the *Game of Thrones* crap, Father—we're not interested. Tell us what we want to know, or we'll break your fingers one by one. And that's for starters."

44

Devlin put his smoking cigar in an ashtray by the bed and paused while he considered where the best point to start was, absentmindedly running his tongue around his teeth looking for stray bits of steak.

Fox waited patiently for Devlin to speak. She watched his strong brow crease in thought, his bright blue eyes search for the words, his thick tanned arms tighten across his broad chest in concentration. She wondered what it was going to be. Knowing Devlin, if he had this much trouble telling her it must be big. And that worried her, because it had the potential to change how she felt about him.

"About nine years ago," Devlin began, "my wife was killed by a heroin addict in a 7-Eleven parking lot in Maryland. She was shot. The man who shot her was imprisoned for eighteen years, some leniency being given for his situation and the circumstances of the crime. He was an addict with no previous arrests for violence. My wife had struggled with the assailant when he forced his way into her car, and the prosecution could not prove that the gun had gone off with deliberate intent to kill or maim. I was at the trial every day. I gave my services tirelessly and continually without rest to prove that the suspect had intentionally shot my wife. But it wasn't possible. Given all the evidence in the car and what could be gleaned from CCTV, I was not able to definitively establish what had happened in that car that night.

"So you see," continued Devlin, "for all my glittering commendations and successes as a detective, I could not find the truth about the one person, no, the two people I loved and cared for above all others."

"Two people?"

"My wife was six months pregnant when she died."

Fox placed a hand on her heart as if to ease its shock. "Oh my God, Devlin. I'm so sorry."

"But time passed and in desperately seeking to find a new way to live, a way to make sense of my loss, I decided to train to be a priest, and most importantly, I actually forgave that man. And I thought that was an end to it.

"About three months ago I happened to be up in Baltimore for a conference, and I'd gone downtown to do some shopping. I'd come out of a store and was crossing to my car when I spotted a guy who looked familiar to me. He'd walked around the corner onto the sidewalk opposite me. He kind of stood out anyway because he had long hair and a beard that was tangled, greasy, and unwashed, and his clothes were filthy, old military surplus. But it was him. I immediately knew it was him. The man who had killed my wife. And it was like I had been hit in the guts by a direct strike of lightning. And if God was testing me, then I was only too glad to fail. Here was the man who took the life I should have had from me, and he was walking the streets freely.

"I followed him a couple of blocks until he got onto the subway. When he got on the train, I jumped on the next car down and traveled out to his stop. He got out, and I followed him back to his apartment. So now I knew where he lived.

"I looked him up and discovered that he'd served half his sentence due to good behavior. It shouldn't have been a big surprise; I was told that was a possibility when he was sentenced. And over the next few weeks, I watched him come and go. Watched him so I got to know his routine. When he stayed in. When he had visitors. When he was alone.

"One night, a midweek night, when I was as sure as I could be that he would be recovering from partying over the weekend and be alone. Not long after his dealer had dropped by. I took the gun I kept in the safe in my study and drove over to his place and parked a few blocks away. Then I walked to his front door and tried the bell. There was no answer. I figured there wouldn't be. I figured he was high and wouldn't answer to anybody calling if he wasn't expecting visitors. So I picked the lock and entered his apartment. The entrance hall was dark, and I could hear the TV playing. There was one light coming out of the bathroom and one coming out of the TV room. So I went to where the TV was playing and stood in the doorway. And there he was, sitting with his eyes half-open in a battered threadbare armchair. He was so bombed out of his head he didn't even notice me until I called his name."

"What was his name?" asked Fox.

"Felix. Felix Lemus." Devlin said it like he knew it better than his own name. "When he saw me, he clasped the sides of the armchair and screamed. I put my finger against my lips and gestured for him to be quiet. It did the trick. I grabbed a chair from the kitchen diner and sat down opposite him. And for a while, I just looked. I looked at this guy. This weak, frightened, dirty, stoned little guy with his ridiculous beard and heavy, dark eyes who had taken my life away from me. He was exactly the kind of person I should give all of my protection and love to. Meek and lost.

"He asked me not to hurt him. Begged. I said that I wouldn't hurt him if he told me the truth—the truth about what happened that night, nine years ago in my wife's car in the 7-Eleven parking lot. But if he lied to me about that night, I would kill him. He asked me how I'd know if he was lying. I said that was my job. His job was just to tell me the truth. So, he told me on that night nine years ago that he was just another junkie that had to score but without any cash. When he saw my wife get into the car, when he saw she was pregnant, he thought she'd be a soft target. He said his whole body was on fire, he was shaking and felt like he was fighting to even get breath. He had to score. Just had to. Like he didn't have a choice. So he ran over to my wife's car and reached in through the open window and wrenched the door open. He pointed a gun at her and told her to move over. She did as he said, and as he slid in, she reached for his hand, the one holding the gun, and it went off in the struggle. That was exactly how it happened, he said."

"Did you believe him?"

"No. It was the same story word for word that he'd told in court nine years before. I didn't believe it then, and I didn't believe it after all that time. He pleaded with me that that was exactly how it happened. I said that all I was asking for was the truth. The truth had become more important to me than the consequences. So I asked him one last time to tell me the truth. He hesitated, weighing up his options. Seeing if he could trust my word to him. Then finally, after all the lying and the pain and the BS, he told me what really happened that night. He told me she wouldn't give him the money. She point-blank refused. So he shot her. Just shot her. Simple as that. And this time, for the first time, I believed him.

"But I didn't see my promise through. I found his stash and

said I'd let him live but not the easy way. I told him to eat all the heroin he had, or I'd shoot him. Kill him like he killed my wife and baby. If he ate it like I said, I'd call an ambulance. I threw it into his lap, raised my gun level with his head, and took the catch off. I told him to start eating, or I'd blow his head off. So he did. He only got to eat about half of it though; there was white powder everywhere, round his face, all over his clothes, on the armchair. It got that he was so high he wasn't even hearing me anymore. He'd eaten so much he was totally out of it.

"In the end, I didn't make the call. I placed him on the floor on his back so he'd more likely choke on his vomit, and I left."

Devlin paused and took a long, deep smoke and let it curl out. "A few days later, I saw a report that he'd died. And that's when I resigned at St. Jude's."

"Who's the priest you confessed to?" asked Fox.

"My old friend and mentor, Hector Hermes."

"So you've been forgiven?"

"No, Hector couldn't give me absolution. I needed to repent first and then to find God's forgiveness. But God can't forgive a sinner who hasn't repented. And that's before even considering the legal consequences I should face. Every night I see him in my dreams. Felix Lemus. Every night he appears to me in some form or another and asks me if I have repented what I did. And every night I say no."

"Every night?"

"Yep."

"That's pretty messed-up."

"Yep. I don't sleep so well anymore. Generally speaking."

There was a deep silence as both reflected upon the truth.

Then Fox said, "Well. I'm not God or a judge, but I forgive you. Without reservation or struggle. I forgive you. What was your wife's name?"

"Jane."

"You loved her?"

"I did. Love true as it was deep."

Fox wasn't appalled or shocked by Devlin's confession. But she did feel ashamed. Ashamed because she suddenly wasn't sure she had ever been in love. Or that she was even capable of it. Yet.

Moments ticked by, and then Devlin began to talk again.

"There's something else too...something I haven't told another soul about, not even Hector."

"What?"

"It's gonna sound crazy..."

"Crazier than organ trading?"

"Yeah. Without a doubt. Ever since I killed Lemus, I've felt the strangest thing...like an energy. I don't know if it's a curse or guilt or what it is. I could just be losing my mind. When I had the fight with Earl and it was all done, and he was out cold on the ground, I laid hands on him..."

"Laid hands on him?"

"Performed an exorcism."

"An exorcism? 'I compel you in the name of Christ,' that sort of thing?"

"Yeah. Exactly that sort of thing. I've never done it before. Once, a few years back, someone asked me about an exorcism. I told them to go find another priest. It's not me. But on that night, as Earl lay in front of me, I just knew it should be done, and the words flew out of my mouth. And, well, something happened—something passed between us. You can laugh, write me off as some sort of lunatic, but I know that something very weird happened. A huge energy traveled from me to Earl and he...he was released. By whatever held him. Maybe not demons but..."

"But his anger maybe, the anger that he was trapped in."

"Yeah. Although, it was more than just a psychological event. A secular explanation isn't it... Something's changed, Fox. That's all I know. Since I killed that man Lemus, something's changed in me. Changing in me."

"What? What's changing?"

Devlin took a minute to reply. "Since the murder, I feel like I've been inhabited by two entities that are battling for control of my soul."

Fox didn't reply. By instinct she was secular. She didn't buy religion any more than she bought astrology. But she was prepared to believe that in some way, a more orthodox way, Devlin did have an exceptional energy about him. Devlin, though, could see by Fox's reaction that he'd said enough.

"It's okay, Fox. You don't have to tell me what you think about what I said. It's more important I said it to someone."

"I guess if I were religious, then I'd say this is all God working out his wrath on you. After all, you could just turn yourself in. And you haven't. You haven't submitted yourself to man's law, so God's submitting you to his law."

Devlin considered Fox's reply. "Yeah. I'll take that."

More moments passed.

"So, what about Logan and Lazard?" asked Devlin. "Do you believe what I said about them, Fox?"

"I don't know. Maybe...maybe I do."

"Will you come with me to Freedom Hospital to check out Alvarez?"

"Yes. Yes. I will."

45

Hector lay balled up on the carpet in front of the fire. His hand was a strange thing to him now, useless and agonizing. His very soul was sick. In tiny whispers, as if words had the power to undo what had been done, he repeated over and over, "Forgive me, Father."

Otterman stood in the doorway and turned back toward Hector. "What a waste of three fingers. This could all have been done without a single tear being spilled. So long, Father."

46

A dog barked somewhere in the distance, and occasionally the wind picked up from the west, spraying a ripple of dust across the clearing. The buildings in the shadow of the Logan Ranch house were quiet, eerily silent. Night had brought peace to the ranch. No hands, no machinery sputtering and growling, no shouts of instructions, curses, laughter.

Then, in the space of ten minutes, three cars pulled up: a chauffeured Bentley Continental, a Cadillac XTS, and a Jaguar XFR.

Clay sat behind his desk waiting for his guests to arrive. The geniality so suited to his face had vanished. His mouth had set into a thin-lipped, sharp line, and his eyes had lost their twinkle and hardened into two dark stones. This was Clay Logan in repose. This was not Congressman Logan as his voters knew him. This was the man without the act. This was the real deal. He reached into his jacket pocket, brought out a pill case, and popped a tablet of propranolol.

Clay had been born with a withered conscience, a stump where something living and warm should have been. In exact opposition to his dead brother, there was a void in his center which gifted him, or cursed him, whichever way you wished to see it, with an almost total lack of feeling. Even so, from time to time an unnerving flash of guilt or empathy would burn in him like a solitary flare in the boundless night sky. And it terrified him, this alien feeling. When that happened he took his pillbox out and popped a pill. Lazard had prescribed the medication to ward off these moments, to re-numb Clay. Propranolol was used by soldiers to deal with post-traumatic stress. Lazard often warned that the increased dosages Clay was taking would lead inevitably to a higher tolerance and, in the end, immunity to its effects. No matter—when that happened, Clay would find something else.

Clay, of course, preferred to see his void as a gift. He could mimic what the people around him wanted from him without it costing him anything. He could fabricate charm, manufacture sympathy. His charisma, high intelligence, and physical presence had allowed him to effortlessly manipulate and control practically anybody he came into contact with. He was just so very brilliant at being exactly like a human being.

His three visitors entered, and each took a seat before Clay. Marie Vallory immediately recognized the version of Clay Logan in front of them. It was a version she'd seen more and more as she'd got to know him intimately. It was Clay stripped of his gleaming exterior put on for the voters and the media; it was the very core of the man, brisk, cold, efficient. And it excited her. There was a strength in his coldness, a power in his amorality. The feeling that anything could be done under his leadership.

The atmosphere was tense, the body language formal and restrained.

Marie Vallory was the first to speak. "Whatever happens, this delivery must go ahead. If it doesn't, then it will mean the certain ruin of Logan Enterprises and fatally damage Freedom."

"Agreed," monotoned Clay. "We've come too far, risked too much to draw back now."

"I for one think we can roll this baby across the line," added Stein.

Lazard didn't say anything. Jaundiced and stick thin, he sat motionless in his chair, caressing his leather gloves with nicotine-stained fingers.

Clay eyed Lazard. "Doctor?"

"I wonder," began Lazard, "whether we ought to push our deadline back, just by a matter of a week, until any further difficulties have been ironed out. The break-in at the center last night has—"

"Impossible," Vallory said flatly. "I have extremely important clients with incredibly busy schedules booked in. As you very well know, Claude, these are the kind of people you have to book years in advance."

"There's no way we're putting this off, Lazard," said Clay. "Too many sacrifices have been made to smooth the way."

"I am worried about the rushed and sometimes loose management of this project," replied Lazard. "Reeves and Campbell are being asked to accomplish tasks beyond their competency. They take shortcuts—"

"Lazard," interrupted Clay, "if we're going to talk about competency, it was your foul-up that forced us to take extreme measures."

"It was not my—"

Clay didn't allow Lazard to finish. "My men are trustworthy. We cannot bring anyone else in on this at this late stage for all sorts of obvious reasons. I'll remind you, Lazard, that of all of us, it's only you who has been paid so far. I might also remind you that your fee was breathtakingly large. A fortune. We paid you to make sure your experience and world-renowned skill delivered on time so that the rest of us get our money. The date will not move. Do you understand me?"

"But this man, Devlin...!" This rare outburst of emotion took Lazard's colleagues by surprise, but it cut no mustard with Clay.

"Do you understand me?" Clay barked.

"Yes. Yes. Of course. I see."

"Stein tells me the priest took very important notes from you," said Clay.

"Yes. However, they are exceedingly technical and do not say who they relate to. He won't be able to make much sense of them. Even so, I do not want to take any chances. As the delivery date cannot move, I will take precautionary measures."

Clay nodded and turned to Stein. "Where are we with Devlin?"

"I'm waiting from a call from my boys," said Stein. "They're following up on a very promising lead. Much better stuff even than the crap that rained down on him at the press conference. I have very high hopes."

"You sure we can't just find a way of killing him and disposing of his body?" asked Clay.

"It may come to that," said Stein. "But I think we should make our first moves intelligent ones rather than forceful ones. Right now the eyes of the country are on Halton Springs. It would be unwise, after what we've all been through, to bring any more heat down on us. We're approaching the most critical hour. I say we move strategically first."

"I agree," said Vallory.

Clay wasn't convinced. "I don't think Devlin is going to go away. Let's see what your men dig up, Stein, but I think we should be prepared to do what we have to do. I have a feeling the forces of darkness will soon be closing in on the good priest." Clay turned back to Lazard. "When's your brother Jakob and his team flying in from Beijing, Lazard?"

"Tomorrow. I'll bring them to the lab tomorrow evening to get them acquainted with the setup."

"Reeves and Campbell have kept a watch over the lab for you and your brother. Done the preparations you asked them to."

"Very good," replied Lazard. "I intend to go there now and begin my own preparations."

"What about the doctor's chauffeur?" asked Vallory. "Where are with that?"

"Packer's onto that," said Clay. "I'm expecting a call to confirm imminently. Now, we're all busy people—the next week will be harder than any previous week of our lives. So let's all get to work."

The three guests left, and Clay sat in silence watching his cell. His next call would be from Packer and would be of some importance to him.

47

Ed was sitting on the sofa still watching the TV on the kitchen worktop. He had a glass of bourbon in his hand and a quarter-drunk bottle on the table. He was watching some British chef telling Jimmy Kimmel how to make an omelet. Ed was laughing at the bleeps they'd put on 'cause the British guy had kept swearing. A voice from the trailer door broke Ed's boozed-up entertainment.

"Hello, Ed."

Ed recognized the voice instantly and swiveled around in terror, splashing bourbon onto his hand and sleeve. He saw Packer standing, hunched in the small trailer doorway looking like a giant. He opened his mouth to scream, but it was too late. Packer had already picked up the bourbon bottle from the table and was sweeping it down in an arc against the side of Ed's head, liquor spilling everywhere. The bottle exploded against Ed's head and sent his body sideways across the sofa, knocking him out cold.

And then there was blackness.

After the job was finished, Packer washed himself up as best he could in the kitchen sink. He walked past Ed's body that was slumped against the bottom of the refrigerator and stepped out into the camp. There was a group of men sitting on the steps of a trailer about fifty meters away, so he took care not to be seen as he walked back to his car. But he had to pass by one particular trailer close to where he was parked. He stomped up the steps of the trailer, reached into his pocket, and pulled out a brown package. He placed the package on the top step, stood, and knocked on the door five times but didn't wait for an answer.

As he drove off, the door of the trailer opened and a hand shot out to gather up the package and disappeared just as promptly. Then the door snapped shut. Packer watched it happen in his rearview mirror and gave a low rumbling grunt of a laugh. Then he put in a call to Clay.

48

Devlin and Fox parked up in the visitor lot at Freedom Dayton Hospital and walked over to the main entrance, a long glass strip overhung and shaded from the clear morning sun by a swooping concrete brim.

Inside they consulted the hospital map. The urology and kidney department was in building F, which stood right behind the building they were in. A long corridor took Devlin and Fox from the entrance past various departments and out the other side onto a large green lawn bisected by a tree-lined path. The path led up to a strip of road that ran in front of a tall, blue-green glass-and-steel tower. This was building F.

"Okay. Let's go pay a visit," said Devlin.

Miguel Alvarez had rarely felt so rested. He was sitting up in his hospital bed in a private room finishing a delicious breakfast of waffles with syrup, enjoying his last morning of top-quality health care. The tall windows hung with blinds that ran the length of the side wall and threw sharp strips of sunlight across his crisp white sheets and onto the spotlessly clean white floor.

In the few days he'd spent at Freedom, he'd been treated like a prince. There had been a nearly constant supply of food and drink and round-the-clock care.

And then there had been the news about Earl. The world seemed a paradise now that Earl had left it.

There was a knock at the door and Dr. Lazard entered.

"Miguel. Hello."

Alvarez put down his knife and fork and greeted him. "Hi, Dr. Lazard."

"How are you?" asked Lazard.

"Good. much better, thanks."

"Good. Are you feeling ready for the move?"

"Yes. I'm ready."

"We've set up everything very nicely for you at the ranch. You'll be able to continue resting there."

"You've been so kind to me, Dr. Lazard. I can't thank you enough for everything you've done for me."

Lazard didn't reply. In fact, he didn't even seem to hear what Alvarez had said. There was another knock and two nurses entered pushing a gurney, which they positioned by Alvarez's hospital bed. One of them slid the table with its remains of breakfast away from the bed, and then both assisted Alvarez as he slowly levered and rotated his body in preparation to stand. While Alvarez got comfortable again on the gurney, Lazard stood by a window peering through the blinds onto the quadrant of grass below. As he scanned the neat parkland in front of the building, he spotted two small figures below and his face suddenly flinched, as if he were in momentary pain. Then he turned to the nurses and clapped his hands abruptly.

"I don't mean to hurry you, but we only have the ambulance for a short time. We must be quick."

. . .

An insipid muzak version of "All My Lovin'" by the Beatles greeted Fox and Devlin as they entered the reception lobby of building F. Along the back wall was a curved metal reception desk, and to the side of the desk was a white spiral staircase that went up to a mezzanine level. Past the stairs were the elevators. A heavily made-up lady in her thirties wearing a white lab coat was standing at the reception desk working a PC.

Fox was first to improvise a plan. "Okay. You charm the woman on the desk. Divert her attention. You're probably bit on the old side for her, so it'll be a challenge."

"What are you going to do?" asked Devlin.

"I'll try and find out which bed Alvarez is in."

They split up. Fox broke toward the elevators while Devlin approached the receptionist behind the counter, putting on his most engaging and priestly manner.

"Hello there," said Devlin.

The receptionist looked up, saw the tall gentleman in a black suit and white collar, and her severe features softened a little. "Hello, Father."

"I'm supposed to be meeting the hospital chaplain here. But it's possible I'm early."

"Father Diaz?"

"That's right. Father Diaz. Have you seen him around?"

"I haven't. I can call him up for you if you'd like?"

"Oh no. I'll hang on a little longer..." Devlin looked down at her name badge. "Mrs. O'Driscoll. Are your parents from the old country?"

"My father was from Wicklow."

"Wicklow, is it? Have you seen the Wicklow mountains?"

"I haven't, Father."

"Well, come to think of it, neither have I. But I hear they're a wonder."

Mrs. O'Driscoll laughed as Fox slipped into the elevator with a group of doctors.

Fox read down the departments listed next to the elevator buttons. Floors four and five were the urology and kidney inpatients center. She got out on floor four with the group of doctors, keeping close to them as they passed the department nurses' desk in the entrance hall and turned into the corridor where the patient rooms were. Once she was at the head of the corridor, she slowed and let the group walk on. Then she began checking the patient names, which were written on the whiteboards outside of each room. She swept through the whole of the floor but could find no sign of Alvarez and came to a back stairway, which she took up to floor five. She did the same thing here, checking the rooms one by one and got to the end; again, no Alvarez.

She looked back and saw she'd passed a nurse who had now stopped outside one of the rooms, an empty one, and was busy writing a new name on the whiteboard. Fox charged up to her.

"Hi," said Fox. "Was a man called Miguel Alvarez in this room?"

The nurse was taken aback by Fox's impatient manner but answered, "Yes. He was."

"When was he moved?"

"You just missed him. He was taken a moment ago."

"Where to?"

"Excuse me, but are you a friend?"

Fox didn't blink and said with complete conviction, "I'm his wife."

"His wife?" The nurse was momentarily wrong-footed by the idea that a teenage Mexican was married to an American woman in her thirties. But she wasn't confident enough say it out loud.

"That's right," challenged Fox. "Oh wow? You got a problem with that? That is not professional!"

"Uh, no...no, of course not..."

"Good. Where did he go?" barked Fox.

"I...I'm...I'm not sure. I think I heard that Dr. Lazard took him to another clinic closer to Halton Springs." Fox didn't wait for any more information and took off back along the corridor to the stairs and sped down them, jumping half flights and swinging around the stairwells at high speed. She raced out into the lobby and saw Devlin at the desk still sweet-talking the receptionist.

"Devlin!"

Devlin looked up and saw Fox looking panicked. "I'm afraid I have to go. Tell Father Diaz I'll be in contact."

"Oh, okay. I will, Father."

Fox took off at speed out of the entrance, and Devlin caught up with her outside.

"What the hell's going on, Fox?"

"Lazard just took Alvarez."

Fox and Devlin looked up and down the road and saw an ambulance that had just loaded up having its back door pushed shut.

"There's Lazard," said Devlin.

Fox saw a pale, thin-looking man in a long tweed coat get into the back of the ambulance and shut the door.

"I'll run and get the car," said Devlin. "Keep an eye on the ambulance, and try and follow it as far as you can." And he sprinted off without waiting for Fox's reply.

The ambulance pulled off and rode down to the main route out of the hospital with Fox trying inconspicuously to follow. Then it took a right and before it was able to pick up speed came to a stop at a crosswalk. Devlin pulled up by Fox in his Ford and flung open the passenger door. Fox jumped in.

"We're okay, Devlin. We caught a break with the red light up ahead."

The ambulance took the 75 out of Dayton, then turned onto the 36 for a few miles heading toward Halton Springs' Main Street. It kept on going through the heart of Halton and out east. Devlin and now Fox too had no doubt where it was headed: out to the Logan Ranch.

Devlin slowed to a stop when he saw the ambulance signal left for the entrance into the ranch. They watched it turn off the highway and drive under the stone arch.

Fox turned to Devlin. "What are you going to do?"

"I'm going to follow it."

"Into the Logan Ranch?"

"Damn right."

Devlin turned through the stone arch and carried on up the track. The ambulance came into view again; it had passed the trailers, the barns, and the bunkhouse and was heading around past the ranch house.

"The cattle lab," whispered Devlin. "They're taking him to the cattle lab." Devlin began to speed up, then thumped his foot down hard on the brake and the Ford lurched to a standstill. Ahead of the car stood a man just about as broad and as tall as it was possible to be.

"Packer," said Devlin.

"You know this guy?"

"We have a history. He likes to dance with me."

"Is he a good mover?"

"Neither of us can agree on who leads."

"What's with his eye?"

"I don't know," said Devlin and then muttered to himself, "Woe to the idol shepherd that leaveth his flock...his right eye shall be utterly darkened."

"What?"

Devlin didn't respond. He was calculating that this was not the moment to go up against Packer, so he wound down his window and shouted, "We were just turning around. We headed the wrong way down the highway."

Packer said nothing. He just stood there, more like a monument than a man, his white eye unmoving, his right hand hovering over the sheathed hunting knife hanging from his belt. Devlin turned the car around and set back off down the 36. A run-in with Packer now would do them no good. Packer watched them go and unhooked his radio from his belt.

Devlin headed back in the direction of Halton. Fox stared out of the window in a state of confusion.

"Why take him back to the Logan Ranch?" she wondered aloud.

"Because that's where they're preparing him. Because that's what that lab is really all about."

"The lab?"

"The cattle fertility plant. It's a huge aluminum structure he had built. All that crap Clay spun me about the fertilization program, the R & D that increased their yield? Just a plausible front for a far more lucrative trade. Marie Vallory knows there is a massive demand for suitable, fresh organs from young healthy donors, a demand that Freedom can't legitimately supply. She understands that people will pay fortunes to get to the top of any organ list."

"My God. What the hell do we do now?"

"We have to get some evidence. We have to go back to the ranch."

Before Fox could question Devlin's plan, her cell rang. It was Stevens. Fox put him on speaker. They could hear heavy rasping breaths.

"Greg? You okay?" asked Fox.

"No. No, I'm not, Katy. Someone's just tried to kill me."

Devlin checked his mirror and suddenly broke and swerved, changing direction and heading back the opposite way.

"What the hell are you doing?" yelled Fox.

"Tell Greg we'll meet him at Ed's. It's a place off—"

"No, wait," interrupted Fox. "I got a better idea. A place I know. Somewhere we'll be safe."

49

Devlin and Fox stood side by side looking through a small cabin window out onto a clearing and thick woodland beyond. Fox had taken Devlin to her aunt's place in Hocking Hills that the family used for vacations. In light traffic and stopping once to fill up on gas and buy some provisions, they had got to Hocking County in just over two hours. Eventually, they had turned off Route 33 and, with Fox giving directions, wound down so many minor roads that Devlin lost all sense of where he was. Finally, they turned onto a dirt road that took them even farther from any passing traffic and came to a halt outside the cabin.

Inside the cabin, the place had been minimally furnished, enough for people staying a couple of weeks. There was a basic kitchen on one side, and set in the middle of the cabin were wooden stairs that went up to the attic room that had been split into two small bedrooms. On the other side of the stairs were an old sofa and armchairs set around a stone hearth fireplace. The bathroom was out back.

Now they were waiting for Stevens to arrive. As they stood motionless, the backs of their hands brushed together. Fox gently dragged her fingers along Devlin's and entwined her hand around his. Her small, neat hand became swaddled in his large, powerful, and gentle hold. Tiny as the gesture was, at that moment it consumed every atom of each other's feelings and thoughts.

Eventually, Devlin checked his watch and spoke. "I'd better call George. I'd said I'd check in, and it's been a while."

"Okay. I'll keep an eye out for Greg."

Devlin went outside to get enough of a signal to call Brennan. He sat on the porch and, as his cell rang, he thought about what he should say. He decided to hold back on any detail until he absolutely knew he had enough evidence. If Brennan didn't believe Devlin's theory, he might think Devlin had lost his mind. If Brennan did believe him, he might feel he was required to refer up, to brief a senior figure, and Devlin wasn't going to risk letting anybody muscle in until he had all but brought Clay Logan in himself. After all, as much as he trusted him, Brennan was a government agent and not absolutely out of the reach of Logan's Capitol Hill friends.

Brennan answered, but his tone was distant and serious.

"Gabe."

"George. I'm calling in like we agreed—"

But Brennan wasn't listening and went straight ahead and spoke. "Listen, there's been a development on my end." Brennan's voice was heavy now and ominous. "I've got some bad news. Very bad news. Ed's been murdered. And Errol too. The place up here is...well, it's a goddamn mess. Like a goddamn slaughterhouse. Whoever killed them, they were animals...a person or people who like doing what they do."

Brennan's words caught Devlin completely unawares. He felt numb and was unable to respond. It couldn't have been worse. The person Devlin had set out to help had befallen the worst possible fate.

After a moment he forced his mind back into gear and managed a reply. "How did they know Ed was there?"

"I don't know. Me, Errol, and you knew where he was."

"Well, you can damn well take it as a fact it wasn't me. I dropped everything to make sure he was okay."

"I know, Gabe. Of course. I never thought it was you. If I had to take a guess, I'd say it was someone on the camp who snitched. As to who actually did it, well, it doesn't take a genius to work out this Packer guy is the main suspect. The one who does Clay Logan's dirty work. The foreman on the ranch who came looking for Ed in the first place. But if it's about fault, then I feel like it's mine. I got Ed involved; I feel responsible for Ed and Errol. They should never have met an end like they did here. Nobody should."

"George, none of us had any idea what this was about. How dangerous it would get."

Brennan cleared his throat and said, "What do you know, Gabe? Have you got anything more since we spoke?"

"I have. I'm getting somewhere with this. Like I said, Lazard has given me a way in. But it's still not enough. Not enough to call it. But I will. I know I will. You're going to have to trust me; I just need one more day."

"Okay, Gabe." Ed and Errol's death had changed George's attitude toward Devlin. He was less combative now. More reflective. Maybe he felt like his only ally now in this nightmare was Devlin. "You got it. Truth is, I'm stuck. Everything that's happened just seems to point to Clay being protected somehow, either by people above me in Homeland or in the Secret Service. So it's all on you, Gabe. I want to mess these guys up, whoever is responsible for Ed and Errol's deaths. It's all I want to do. If you can do that, you got whatever I can do to support you."

"Just another day. That's all I need right now to do what needs to be done. I'll be in touch."

Devlin hung up and felt a bitter chill run through him. Ed, Devlin's friend, a man he had lived and worked with, a man he had resolved to find and protect, had been murdered. But tears would not call Ed back. There were other ways to channel grief. This Devlin knew all too well.

Devlin returned to the cabin. Fox turned to see him enter and noticed the sudden change in his mood, the darkness that had changed his features. She walked up to him and placed a hand up onto his chest.

"Devlin? What's wrong?"

"It's Ed. He's been murdered. Up at the trailer where I found him in Cuyahoga."

"What? Do you know who did it?"

"Yeah, I know who did it. The same people who killed the kid up in Long Pine, who killed Brendan, who killed Earl." Devlin looked at Fox. He saw her green eyes, wide and full of compassion. Something in his heart sparked, and he placed a hand on her face. "You shouldn't be involved in this. I was wrong to pull you in. This is a brutal business, and you're a journalist..."

"Devlin."

"No. You should go now. No one knows you're involved. You must walk away before your life is threatened. I can't have your life on my conscience. It's too much. It's happened to me before, and I can't allow it to... When Greg arrives I'll..."

Fox put a finger up to Devlin's lips and gently shushed him. She spoke evenly and softly but with absolute certainty.

"Shut up. Shut up and listen to me. I'm not Jane and I'm not Ed. What I do is my choice and never anybody else's. I am my own damn boss. I am not stupid. I know how dangerous this has got, and I'm not walking away, under any circumstances. When I get my teeth into something, I don't let go. It's the way I'm made, and you don't get to veto me out of this."

Fox stopped speaking, and Devlin didn't say anything. Instead, they held each other's gaze until the recognition of new feeling became unbearable and impossible to avoid acting upon.

"What happens now, Devlin? You're a priest after all..." whispered Fox.

The question hung in the air, and just as Devlin was about to break the intense silence with an answer, the sound of an engine growing louder beat him to it. A car had swung in from the dirt track. Fox and Devlin turned to see it lurch and bounce into the clearing. It was Stevens.

"Saved by the bell," said Fox. Devlin didn't reply.

They walked out onto the porch and beckoned Stevens in. He was pale and trembling. Whether from fear, from the strain of the past few days, from his illness, or more likely, a combination of all three, it was not possible to tell. They gathered nearly knee to knee around the small round kitchen table. There was a lot to catch up on. The last time Stevens and Devlin had been face-to-face was Tuesday, three days ago.

"What happened, Greg?" asked Fox. "Who tried to kill you?"

"I don't know. But I have a theory. You might think it's a little crazy..."

"Go on," said Fox.

"I think it might have been a cop. A Halton Springs cop...and I think I know why they went after me."

An agitated Stevens told Devlin and Fox how he had discovered the missing shift records for the night of the Long Pine homicide.

"It was the emails I sent," insisted Stevens. "I think that's what triggered it. Four emails to Miller, Gray, Lincoln, and Taylor asking them to refile the missing reports from last Friday's night shift. When I pressed Send on that email, I sent my own death warrant. Someone had broken into my house and was lying in wait for me. If it wasn't for a nosy neighbor telling me that they'd just seen someone in a hooded top sneaking in around the back of my house, I probably I wouldn't be alive. Thanks to her I went in around the back too and had the advantage of surprise. Had a firefight in my own damn house, and they ran off. I was just too worn-out to give chase. Thank God Rachel and the kids were at her folks in Hamilton. If they had been at home... Well, it just doesn't bear thinking about."

"Who do you think it was, which cop?" asked Fox.

"No idea. Whoever they were, they were hooded up and I didn't get a proper look at them. But it cannot be a coincidence that I asked for the missing shift reports and then I get ambushed." Stevens shook his head. "I think it's one of my own officers. One of the officers on that shift, the shift on the night of the first murder."

"But we don't know for sure," said Fox.

"Not for certain. But it sure makes sense to me." Stevens paused a moment for thought. "But there's something else that's shook me up even more, something on my conscience. It's the craziest thing..."

"What?" asked Devlin.

"It's since I found the shift reports had gone. I couldn't lose this terrible feeling... I've just had this his suspicion, this suspicion that Earl wasn't the killer. Despite the DNA, the evidence placing him at the scene, the revolver in his bunk, the manhunt I lead into the heart of Long Pine...despite all that that landslide of evidence, I can't push away the feeling I got the wrong man. How crazy does that sound?"

Stevens looked up at Devlin and Fox and was startled to see that they didn't think he was crazy at all, or if he was, they were too.

"We don't think he's the killer either," said Devlin. "We've had quite a busy few days too."

"What's going on, Gabe? Tell me now, what the hell is going on?"

Devlin searched for a place to start. Then he took a breath and said bluntly, "Ed James is dead."

"Ed? How do you know?"

"I tracked him down in Cuyahoga. He'd hidden out with the travelers that were camped in Halton. He was alive and well yesterday. I saw him with my own eyes. Just now I got a call he's been murdered. And by all accounts, it's not pretty."

"I'm sorry, Gabe. Truly sorry. Why would anyone kill Ed?"

"Because he was working on the ranch as an informant for Homeland."

"What was Ed doing working for Homeland?"

"Both Homeland and the Secret Service have been looking into money transferred covertly from Freedom Medical to Logan Enterprises. Fifty million dollars that seems to have been put into the cattle fertility lab. Ed was placed on the farm by Homeland to try and get intelligence on where the money really went. Clay Logan found out, and Packer came looking for Ed, to kill him for spying on the ranch. That's why Ed left town, disappeared."

"The Logan Ranch is into some pretty heavy stuff," said Fox.

"Like what?"

"There's something going on between Logan and Freedom," said Devlin. "I think they're using the illegal workers, offering money for...certain transactions."

"Transactions? What transactions?"

"They're selling organs to Freedom Medical taken from illegal workers on the ranch."

"Today," said Fox, "we saw a Mexican ranch hand transported by ambulance from Freedom Dayton Hospital to the Logan Ranch, we think to the building that houses the cattle lab."

"Remember Lazard?" said Devlin. "The surgeon who's working at Halton Medical Center? I got hold of tests he'd run on one of the Mexican kids working on the ranch, a kid called Alvarez, the one transported to the ranch today. Lazard had run tests for a donor match with another unidentified person. A recipient. I think Alvarez is an intended donor victim and the Long Pine victim was too. You remember the coroner found ketamine in the Long Pine victim's bloodstream? Well, I don't think he took it to get high. I think he was administered it in preparation for surgery. Ed told me Clay Logan buys in ketamine to use as a veterinary anesthetic. But I don't think it's just being used on the cattle."

"You think these men are selling their organs?" asked Stevens.

"Yes I do," replied Devlin.

"But why was the Long Pine victim killed, then? And cut up?"

"I think the deal went bad. I don't know why. But if he was an illegal worker, then whoever killed him knew he wouldn't show up on any national DNA database. Cutting him up would be enough to prevent him being ID'd. Earl was framed. We were all played. We were played by Clay and the people he has running the transplant business. As to who actually cut that body up, well, the coroner said the victim's bone marks indicated a knife. I'm certain the guy who attacked me at Ed's place was Packer. And he was carrying a big old knife. When Packer turned up here looking for Ed, he was carrying a hunting knife. That's who my money's on."

"Damn," said Stevens shaking his head. "Last Sunday we sat in my house and we were chasing two different things in two different directions. Now we've come full circle, and we're face-to-face again. But what I can't work out is why Earl killed himself? Surely that means he was guilty?"

"I don't think he can have killed himself. Someone must have got to him," said Devlin.

"It has to have been a cop," said Fox. "A cop working for Clay. One of the cops on the shift with the missing records. The one who tried to kill Greg. How could anyone but a cop have got through the police chain?"

"The first people on the scene were Walker and Miller," said Stevens.

"Do you think they could have killed him?" asked Fox.

"It's possible. And Miller was on last Friday night's shift."

"For now I think we have to assume all four cops on the night shift are operating rogue—Miller, Lincoln, Taylor, and Gray," said Devlin.

"Absolutely," agreed Stevens.

There was a weighty silence. No one spoke. Each sifted through the conversation they'd had to find some new revelation or connection.

In the end, Stevens said, "You really think Clay's involved in harvesting human organs?"

"I think it's the only explanation that makes sense of all the things that don't make sense. Lazard at the free clinic, Alvarez's test results, the money snuck into Clay's ailing ranch. Anyhow, I aim to put it beyond all doubt."

"How?" asked Stevens.

"I'm going back up to the Logan Ranch, tomorrow, in the light. I'm going to get a good look at that lab."

Stevens was completely blindsided. "If all of what you say is true, that sounds like a damn near suicidal plan."

Fox had been quiet for stretches of the conversation. She'd been letting Devlin lead. But now she felt compelled to spell it out to Stevens.

"Greg, at some point someone has to get access to the lab if they want to finally pin this whole thing down. It's where the money's going, it's where Lazard keeps going, and it's where Alvarez went. It's the curtain behind which the perpetrators are hiding. Like Devlin, I don't see any other way. If you don't buy what we're peddling here, that's absolutely fine. But we sure could use some help."

Stevens closed his eyes and for a moment looked like he was praying. But he didn't need long. Truth was he'd let this crazy idea take root that Devlin was responsible for his remission. Maybe not directly. Maybe not in the sense of some biblical miracle. But Stevens felt that Devlin's electric presence had been some sort of catalyst for his partial recovery against all the odds. He'd follow Devlin out to the edge of doom.

"Of course you got my help. There's a..." Stevens hovered for a split second over the next word, "a cancer at the very heart of Halton Springs. And it needs cutting out. Question is, how do we get into the lab?"

"Between the three of us, we'll work out a way of getting in," said Fox.

As the light failed outside and day shaded into early evening, the three uplit faces sat in a small pool of yellow light conspiring solemnly, working out how they would give themselves the best chance of getting into the heart of the Logan Ranch.

50

Lazard sucked the very last burst of warm smoke from his cigarette and let it soak into the walls of his lungs. Then he flicked it to the sidewalk and entered the Dayton Crowne Plaza Hotel. He surveyed the lobby. It was empty but for the receptionist and three gentlemen dressed in suits who were sitting huddled in a corner with large suitcases beside them. They had placed themselves behind one of the square purple pillars that were spaced out around the lobby in a grid formation. Two of the men were Asian and in their early twenties; the third was older by some four decades. He wore an expensive English tweed suit, an emerald tie, a gold tie clip, and matching gold cufflinks. He was completely bald at the top, but the gray-and-copper-colored hair around the sides of his head had been fastidiously pomaded back from his temples.

Lazard crossed the lobby and stood in front of the three men, his hands clasped together holding his driving gloves.

"So good to see you, Jakob," said Lazard.

"Likewise, Claude," said the older man. "I brought my hand-picked team with me. Allow me to introduce Chan Liu and Li

Wei. Trainee surgeons under my tutelage in Peking. Chan, Liu, this is my younger brother, Claude."

"Pleased to meet you," said Lazard. The two men nodded once, and Lazard bowed in return. Liu was broad and short, his chubby face still bearing traces of teenage acne. Wei was slim and wiry with his hair chopped short into a kind of punky mess. Both were wearing dark suits and ties like they were up for a job interview. They were reserved, probably nervous, thought Lazard. They knew what they had signed up to, what the paycheck would be and what the work would entail.

"Follow me. I'm parked outside," said Lazard. The three men followed Lazard and rolled their cases out into the street to the parked Jaguar. Lazard clicked his key fob, the car chirped, and the doors and trunk snicked open.

Jakob looked puzzled. "You don't have a chauffeur?"

"No. He...resigned. It's a long story." Lazard opened the trunk. "Please, put your luggage in."

"Dear God. You drive yourself?" asked Jakob despairingly.

"I'm afraid so."

Jakob rolled his eyes, and he and his two students placed their luggage in the trunk. They got into the Jaguar with Jakob in the front seat and the two young men in the back. Lazard started the engine and pulled out, driving in the direction of the I-75. They headed away from the Dayton skyline in a line of traffic, the streetlights sliding over the tops of other the cars that were streaming out of the city alongside them. Lazard hit the ramp onto the freeway, which was relatively clear of traffic, and accelerated. The speed brought a peace to the four occupants of the Jaguar.

"You're not too tired?" asked Lazard.

"No. One night to recover from jet lag was sufficient for us," said Jakob. "Is everything prepared?"

"Yes. Everything is in place," replied Lazard.

"What about the one who was damaged?"

"He is back to almost perfect health."

"Almost?"

"His right kidney will not be fully recovered for the transfer. We will not be able to fulfill that order."

"How much is that costing us?"

"Three hundred thousand dollars."

"That's a costly mistake."

"It's a fraction of the total price. It was a mistake made by the cowboys Logan uses on the ranch."

"First we lose an entire donor, now a kidney too. Why the hell are you using cowboys?"

"It was Stein's idea. To reduce costs and involve only those people we could of necessity trust."

"It's playing with fire."

"I agree. But I have overseen all the preparatory work. It's all in place and done to my satisfaction. And now you are here, we have all the expertise we need in place. A new chapter begins."

"It will be a hard week's work. The hardest we've ever undertaken."

"Hopefully one of many weeks to come, Jakob. And it will multiply your pension provision by a factor of ten. Besides, you have done this before. How many Falun Gong did you operate on?"

Jakob didn't answer immediately. They were driving over a river. He could see two bridges lit up either side of the one they were on. Ahead there was a billboard by the road advertising Rolex watches as if the journey toward his promised outrageous financial reward was being signposted.

As Jakob gazed out of car window, he totted a figure up in his head. Eventually, he replied, "Oh, thousands. Definitely thousands. Difficult to say for sure. We didn't keep records, for obvious reasons."

"And your two assistants?" Lazard angled his rearview mirror and peered at the two sleepy faces watching the freeway fly by.

"We've done plenty," said Liu, rubbing his red eyes and looking back at Lazard's face in the mirror. "We both extracted organs from executed prisoners in Beijing Municipal Prison. We know what we're doing and what we're doing here." Lazard noticed that Liu spoke English fluently with a slight hint of an American accent. Jakob had chosen very wisely indeed. There could be no communication difficulties if they were to meet their deadlines. Lazard moved the rearview mirror back into place and looked across approvingly at Jakob.

"I told you I'd bring you a crack team," said Jakob.

"I could always rely on you, brother."

"What are the donors like?"

"They are in the peak of physical condition. They have been handpicked for the closest possible match to their recipients."

"Wonderful." Jakob gave a broad smile, exposing his narrow nicotine-stained teeth. "It's the Bloomingdale's of organ transplantation."

"With price tags to match," replied Claude. "When we get there, you'll be able to examine the assets and read through their extensive medical notes. We have scheduled delivery to begin on Sunday morning when the first patients arrive at Freedom Hospital in Dayton. I will go through the schedule with you, but roughly speaking we are required to deliver for arrival at Freedom Hospital by ten hundred hours every morning, to ensure the assets are at their freshest and at optimum functionality. As you know, this will mean working through the night and resting by day for the next six days. Once we have finished the preliminary examination of the assets and acquainted ourselves thoroughly with the medical notes of each asset, I will show you to your bedrooms in the ranch house."

Lazard had arrived at the turnoff for the ranch. He left the highway and drove under the stone arch and into the dusty clearing. Then he motored on past the ranch house that stood illuminated in the dark and onto a grass clearing behind. He slowed his speed on the rougher terrain, anxious to protect his car, and came to a halt before the square, plain edifice of the cattle plant. The plant was deliberately tucked behind the ranch house, close enough to be accessible to large vehicles yet far away enough from the main ranch buildings not to be seen from the highway or by passing visitors. It was a huge, rectangular, light blue aluminum building striped with mirrored windows and with a sloping roof. Two trucks labeled Freedom Medical were parked up by the entrance, and Reeves and Campbell were heaving boxes back and forth from the trucks in through the brightly lit, wide front entrance. Reeves was a few years younger than Campbell with greasy black hair slicked back and shorn short at the sides. Tattoos covered his arms and torso and crept up around his neck. He wore headphones and the white cords ran into his jean pocket. As he worked he bobbed his head every now and then to the beat of the song blaring at full volume into in his ears.

"I see the cowboys are now doing the jobs they are most suited to," said Jakob.

"Yes," replied Lazard. He looked across at his brother and then over his shoulder at the two men slumped in the back seat, peeping back through half-shut eyes. "Here we are, then, gentlemen. Bloomingdale's. Like no other store in the world."

51

After a basic meal of canned soup and bread that they'd picked up on the journey from Halton, Devlin had gone outside to clear his head and smoke. By the time he had finished his cigar and entered the cabin, the lights were out. Stevens had insisted on taking the sofa and was stretched out fast asleep, already snoring. Devlin made his way quietly to the bathroom at the back and took a shower. Then he cleaned his teeth with what he assumed was Fox's toothbrush that she kept at the cabin, getting the woody tang of cigar leaf out of his mouth.

Devlin dried up, wrapped a towel around him and gathered up his clothes and shoes. He climbed the stairs to the attic bedrooms. As he passed Fox's bedroom, he saw the door was open and could see in. On the bed, under the window, he could make out Fox's slender body lying still, sound asleep under the blankets.

He willed himself away from Fox's doorway and walked into his own bedroom. It was cramped with a sloping roof. There was a single iron bed, a small nightstand, a closet, and a skylight that shed moonlight onto the floorboards.

Devlin folded his clothes and placed them alongside his shoes in the empty closet, he took off the damp towel and hung it over the closet door then pulled on his boxers, and knelt by his bed. He said a night prayer from the Liturgy of the Hours followed by a prayer for Ed. Then he got into bed and closed his eyes to the night and within minutes was in deep sleep and dreaming.

In his dream, he saw himself stand and walk over to Fox's room. He got into her bed and slide under the cool sheets, up next to her warm, soft, perfumed skin. His large, solid form enclosed around her. Still facing away from Devlin, Fox stirred and drowsily asked, "What's changed?"

"Everything," he replied

And without hesitation or a single thought, she turned and melted into him. He felt her hot, sleepy breath as she cradled his face and kissed him deeply, clasping her lips on to his. Her kisses grew more passionate and frenzied.

Then Fox was gone and Devlin found himself standing outside, in the middle of the clearing in front of the cabin. The temperature had dropped, and the cold night air bit hard. A little way off, within the woodland that surrounded the cabin, he could see a flickering yellow and orange light. He walked into the trees and toward the light. As he got closer, he could hear the licks and roar of flames and felt an intense heat that caused him to lift his hand and shade his face. Though the heat was blasting, Devlin wanted to see the fire, see its light, and came to a stop within a few feet of a tall, wide persimmon tree that blazed, consumed by violent sprays of fire rushing up to the stars. Out of the fire walked a small man in a woolen hat, a ragged military surplus shirt, filthy jeans, and sneakers without laces. Devlin recognized him as Felix Lemus.

Lemus stood within arm's reach of Devlin and said, "Are you ready to repent, Father Devlin?"

Devlin did not reply.

"I will ask you for the last time, are you ready to repent, Father Devlin?"

Again Devlin did not reply.

"Then I am here to tell you your true name, the name that has been given to you from this moment forward. It is Azazel."

Lemus reached out and grasped Devlin's hand, lifting it palm upward so that he held it flat between them. He spat into his other hand and laid it on top of Devlin's. Instantly Devlin felt a searing heat, and wisps of smoke escaped from the tiny spaces between their grip. Devlin yanked his hand away and looked at it. A faint pattern had been burned into the dip of his palm: the shape of a tree with a serpent wrapped around the bough.

Devlin wanted to speak to Lemus, to say that he had no regrets or wish to atone, but the intensity of the heat had become too much to bear and his closeness to the fire made his hand throb with pain. He was beaten backward by the growing, scorching heat, away from Lemus and deeper into the woods until he no could no longer see Lemus or the fire and no longer knew his way back.

The farther back he retreated, the thicker and darker the forest became until he did not know his way back and suddenly was afraid he would never escape the forest or the night.

Devlin awoke. He was in his bed in the attic room, alone. There was no noise except for an alarm clock on the nightstand that insensibly ticked off the moments. Perspiration covered his body, and his hands were shaking. He examined his right hand. There were no letters, no circle studded with triangles. But it hurt. Hurt as if it had been burned.

It was still the middle of the night, and morning was a few hours off yet. Devlin threw off his blanket, placed an arm across his face, and waited for the sun to return.

Friday morning.

The last day he would spend in Halton Springs. Whichever way things went.

He understood that now.

52

Campbell had been up early and out at the drop with Packer. He had then traveled back to wait for another delivery of medical supplies that were coming in that morning. At about eight o'clock, a Freedom Medical truck pulled into the ranch and drove up to the cattle lab.

He waved the truck in and helped unload thirty large unmarked boxes. The guy driving the truck offered to help Campbell move the load into the lab, but as always, Campbell was adamant there was no need. He instructed the driver to turn around and leave, and then he started shifting the boxes by himself. It was heavy work, and it took a couple of hours to carefully unpack the contents. When Campbell was finished, he checked his watch. Lazard, his brother, and the two Chinese guys would be due back soon. After they'd worked into the early hours of the morning, the three new arrivals had slouched off to their beds in the ranch house. As one of the select few on the ranch who formed Packer's inner circle, Campbell knew how critical today was. Once Lazard's brother and his team arrived, the hard work would really begin and Campbell would be needed around the clock. If he was smart he could catch some z's.

He switched with Reeves, who began a watch over the lab, and then he headed past the ranch house and the other hands on shift working the barns. He entered the bunkhouse and slumped on his bed looking forward to hitting the hay. But as he began dragging his boots off his aching feet, he heard the sound of a roaring engine in the distance. It built from a distant hum, getting louder and louder to a full-throated deafening rev as a Honda all-terrain vehicle skidded into the clearing and slid to a stop. The driver, Packer, got out and started screaming at the hands to round everybody up. He ran over to the bunkhouse and began banging on the side with his massive fists and hollering.

"Everyone out! Everyone out! There's a fire up at the bull pasture!" Packer carried on shouting and banging till all the men, including Campbell, had shown themselves and come out of the trailers and barns and gathered in the clearing. They were unsure and bewildered by the sudden turmoil. Packer shouted for them to be quiet and listen.

"We got a fire up in the bull pasture. It's a line of trees that are burning, and it'll spread unless we stop it. There's no way a fire truck could get up there. I need about a dozen men. I'll take everyone apart from the men working the shop. Load up the pickups with as many water jugs as they'll hold, and we can use the creek to put it out. But we gotta get it done now! Let's go!"

They loaded up as fast as they could, then started up the pickups and the Hondas, riding the herd of vehicles out from the nerve center of buildings up to the far edge of the ranch.

Five minutes of relative stillness and quiet passed. Then two figures appeared, climbing over the fence from the highway. Cautiously scanning the area for any ranch workers that had might have been left behind, Devlin and Fox made their way across the rough ground some way off from the main track, skirting around the back of the cluster of barns and trailers.

As they came to the last couple of outbuildings, they could hear noises. The sounds of hammering, drilling, and voices were coming from a large rectangular metal building. Devlin and Fox stopped at the corner of the building and paused. Ahead of them, they could see a rear door that had been left open.

"We'll have to go past the door," said Devlin. "You go first. Make it quick, fast, and light and hope they don't spot us."

Fox looked at Devlin and then back at the open door. She moved as quietly as she could up to the hinge side and stopped still for a moment, then peered through the doorway and saw two figures at work. One was taking a front tire off a pickup, and the other was drilling into the rocker panel of the same pickup on the opposite side. They both seemed absorbed in their tasks, so Fox took a breath and skipped past the opening to the other side.

Devlin followed in exactly the same fashion and caught up with Fox on the other side of the door. They looked at each other and listened. The hammering from the workshop went on and so did the drilling followed by some more fragments of low-level talk.

"I think we're okay," said Fox.

Devlin nodded. "Let's keep going."

They had moved past the far end of the workshop and were creeping by the last of the ranch buildings when they heard a voice call out from behind them.

"Hey."

Devlin and Fox turned to see a dark-haired, gray-bearded ranch hand in his forties smoking a rolled-up cigarette. His skin was brown, lined and weathered from constant sun.

"Can I help you?" asked the hand. He spoke with a Hispanic accent.

"Yeah," said Fox, improvising. "We're hiking and kinda got ourselves lost. Would you happen to know the quickest way to get over to Long Pine?"

The ranch hand studied Fox and Devlin for a moment. Then he said, "You can't get to Long Pine across here. This is private property. You'll need to get back on the highway and walk a mile or so toward Halton. You can get on a path to the woods from there."

"Oh gee, really?" said Fox. "That's a shame. We'd really like to take a look round the ranch here too. Looks like a beauty."

"'Fraid not. No public folk wandering about on the ranch. The boss is strict on that."

Devlin and Fox exchanged a glance, but they were out of ideas for a response. Fox sensed Devlin beside her begin to physically tense, intention and purpose seeming to fill his body. She guessed he was preparing for the next nonverbal phase. And Fox also noticed that the hand had turned his attention on Devlin. He was staring directly at him and frowning, his face growing more serious.

"I know you," said the ranch hand, pointing at Devlin.

Devlin remained still, expressionless, and replied in a monotone, "I don't think so."

The ranch hand took a couple of steps forward to look at Devlin more closely. Devlin's fists tightened a little, and Fox's heartbeat quickened as she prepared for all-out conflict.

"Yeah. Yeah I do," said the hand. "You were down here a few days ago. Talking to one of the new workers here. To Alvarez. You're the priest, aren't you?"

Devlin didn't respond.

"Yeah. You are. You're the guy who beat the hell out of Earl Logan."

"Think you've got the wrong man, my friend."

"No. No, I don't think I have. I got a good memory for faces.

And what you did to Earl was all over town and on the news. Nice job you did there."

"Excuse me?" said Devlin.

The bearded guy's face transformed in a split second. Suspicion and hostility vanished and was replaced by a grin revealing a row of yellow-brown teeth. "You should have said you were the guy who cleaned that son of a bitch's clock." He walked up to Devlin and took a smoke of his cigarette, then flicked it away and held out his hand. Devlin did likewise and they shook. "Well done, Father. You don't know how much I wanted to work that bastard over myself. He had it coming for the longest time."

Devlin and Fox didn't reply for a moment. They'd braced themselves for most eventualities but not this one.

"So...are we okay to carry on?" asked Fox. "I mean, go across the ranch to the forest?"

The hand shrugged. "You do what you like, miss." He glanced around and then back at Fox and Devlin. "Looks like I'm the only one who's seen you. And I never saw you. Far as I'm concerned, the man who gave Earl what he deserved can go where he likes." Then he chuckled and wandered back off, disappearing between the workshop and the last trailer.

"Looks like you got yourself a fan, Devlin. Let's go before we run into someone who actually liked Earl."

Devlin and Fox edged to the end of the last trailer, checked no one was about, and darted around the side of Clay's ranch house, keeping low and moving stealthily.

Behind the ranch house, Devlin and Fox got their first view of the cattle lab. It lay a few hundred feet away and was set in the middle of about four acres of grassland. Directly in front of them, much nearer than the lab, was a small red metal hut with ventilation slits. Devlin guessed it must house the generator that Clay had told him about back when he'd first visited the ranch.

They made sure the coast was clear and snuck in closer to

the lab, about fifty meters away. Devlin now had a clear view of the front and the left side of the silver and blue rectangle glimmering in the sunshine. There were black pods positioned on the corners where the roof met the walls.

Devlin pointed to the pods. "Sensors," he said. "Infrared."

"Is that bad?"

"Sensors aren't magic. They have limitations. They can only cover a certain area. There's a sensor on each corner covering one side of each face of the building. So there is a blind spot we can exploit if we move in a diagonal line to the nearest corner. It helps if we move slowly and keep low; we'll give off heat similar to the background heat. And the sensors have to be set up to ignore any small animals, otherwise they'd be going off every five minutes in the middle of a ranch."

The two began edging slowly across the grass and got to the side of the building. Once under the sensors, they slid along the front of the lab to the entrance.

Devlin examined the door. "It's a heavy-duty lock. Give me the gun."

"They'll hear in the house."

"Maybe, maybe not. We're about a hundred yards away in open ground. It's a ranch; gunshots have to be more common here than other places. Anyway, it's a chance we have to take. I can't see another way in."

Fox handed Devlin a Glock that Stevens had given them back at the cabin. Devlin took the catch off, aimed at the lock from a few feet away, and pulled the trigger. The shot ruptured the metal, burning the lock out. Devlin gave the gun back to Fox, lifted his leg, and repeatedly kicked at the door until it flung wide open. Then he peered around into the plant. No movement. No sound.

Devlin and Fox moved warily inside.

The front part of the building was very underwhelming and

very ordinary, like a big clean cattle shed. There were runs for the cattle and stalls to hold the bulls and heifers. Along the left side was a lab bench with beakers and other equipment laid out and shelves stacked with glass containers holding different chemicals. Along the right-hand side were banks of canisters in tall metal cages on wheels with the words "liquid nitrogen" stenciled on their sides.

"Well, so far, so normal. And no sign of fifty million dollars," said Fox.

Devlin walked to the back wall, which was hidden away behind a row of stalls. Set into the wall he found a wide double door without windows, inconspicuous-looking and the same drab brown color as the surrounding painted cinder blocks.

"What's behind there?" asked Fox.

"Whatever it is it makes up most of this building and it's worth protecting." Devlin pointed over to the right of the door. "There's a finger scanner."

Installed into the wall was a black box with a blue LCD screen above a numerical keypad. Beside the screen and keypad was a square gap, inside which was a small finger pad that glowed red.

"Oh crap," said Fox. "We're never gonna get through that."

"It's another challenge, that's for sure."

"A challenge? It needs a fingerprint. How the hell can we get through if it needs a fingerprint? I've seen these things in films—you need to go and chop some guy's finger off and then use that to get in."

"Wait, hold on. It isn't that bad. They had one of these at Scott Airforce Base in Illinois to control who had access. They're just like all the other security devices. Doesn't matter how much money they throw at these things, some new guy turns up and needs to get in and they haven't done the paperwork and put his fingerprint on the database. So people found a workaround. We discovered that all you had to do..." Devlin bent down and cupped his hands and gently and slowly blew warm air onto the scanner. As he did, a fingerprint impression flashed up onto the LCD screen above the keypad with the words, "Reeves. Access Granted" alongside in green. The locks clicked open.

"How the hell...?"

"Warm moisture in your breath attaches to the oil and residue left by the last person's finger," said Devlin. "They've set the fingerprint recognition parameters tight because they think it makes it harder to get in. It doesn't—it just makes the machine way oversensitive." Devlin pushed open the double doors and looked in.

Now they were way beyond normal.

53

"There's the fifty million dollars," said Fox.

Both Fox and Devlin thought they might find Alvarez in the cattle lab. Maybe. Neither had been exactly sure in fact what kind of operation lay in the secretive aluminum building. But in their wildest nightmares, they had never expected to find the scene that confronted them now. On the other side of the door, spread out before them in a cavernous, strip-lit space that resembled an aircraft hangar, were twelve beds arranged in an arc, each one occupied by a young man who had been wired up to a bank of monitors. The beds were dwarfed by the inside space and the banks of medical equipment and supplies. The roof sloped about thirty feet above them supported by metal struts. The place was alive with the sound of digital machinery that hummed and chirruped. Spare, unoccupied gurneys were dotted around the edges of the hangar. It looked like an extremely high-tech intensive care unit crossed with an operating theater, but far grimmer, for the suspicion was that this place existed not to stabilize the men and then nurse them back to health but to keep them in stasis.

"I'm going in," said Fox, bringing the Glock up from her side and readying herself.

"No. I'll go first," Devlin hissed back.

"I got the gun—you stay here."

Before Devlin could get out a reply, Fox had stepped through the door, the curiosity of a journalist overriding any instincts of self-preservation. She stood inside the hangar and gazed in wonder at her surroundings, at this warped Aladdin's cave. And then, out of the shadows of the chamber, came an unfamiliar voice, and Fox froze.

"Drop the gun, blondie."

To Fox's left, standing by what looked like a medical station decked with a bank of monitors, was one of the ranchers, a tall guy with greased-back dark hair and plenty of tattoos, wearing a flannel shirt, slim jeans, and a pair of muddy woodsman boots. He was holding a gun and aiming it at Fox. For a split second she considered trying to swivel and get a shot off, but realistically she knew it would be a shot in a hundred.

"I'm so sorry," stuttered Fox, looking around and realizing that Devlin must not have followed her in. "I took a wrong turn and…"

"Shut-up and drop the gun," said the tattooed guy. Fox let the Glock fall to the ground, knowing she had Devlin waiting out of sight behind her.

"I don't care why you're here," said the tattooed guy. "It's your bad luck either way." He had closed in on Fox and had his gun trained on her. "Now, back up through the door you came in."

Fox did as she was told and began to retrace her steps, walking through the doors and back into the cattle lab. The tattooed guy followed her, closed the double doors behind him, and reached a hand out to hit a red Lock button. But before his hand made contact with the button, he was hit from the side by a metal crate loaded with gas cylinders that knocked him off balance and sent his gun rolling across the floor. The force of the collision left him shaken and confused. As he lurched forward to get to his feet, scrambling in the direction of his lost gun, another collision, this time made of flesh and bone, grounded him for good.

Devlin stood over the ranch hand, who was out cold on the ground, his long limbs crooked and limp.

"That's a mean right cross you got on you," said Fox, admiring Devlin's handiwork.

"I used to box. A long time ago," replied Devlin, retrieving the gun from the floor, a Smith and Wesson M&P .45, and checking the magazine. "Next time let me go first, okay?"

Fox shrugged. "It turned out okay, didn't it?" she replied, nodding at the ranch hand laid out on his back.

Devlin shot Fox a stony look, then turned to the guy on the floor. "Let's get him hog-tied so we don't have to worry about him again."

Devlin and Fox hauled the ranch hand back into the main lab and got hold of rolls of bandages from the shelves of supplies that ran along the walls of the hanger, using them to gag him and tie his hands and feet.

Then they began to explore their extraordinary surroundings properly. They moved among the beds occasionally, looking over to each other to check and share their reaction. Devlin moved his hand over some of the men's faces, but there was no response. He lifted their eyelids and checked their pupils.

"They've all been put under general anesthetic. Like an induced coma." Devlin looked over at Fox as they both felt the same rising horror.

"They're not selling their organs, are they?" said Fox. "They don't even know it's happening to them. My God, Devlin. This is madness. We have to do something. Could we free them somehow?"

"Where would we start? What might happen if we disconnected the tubes? We have no idea what cocktail of drugs they're on. It could send them into shock. We'd be putting their lives in even more risk. God knows what they've been given to keep them like this... Although it doesn't look like any of them have been operated on...yet."

There was an eerie quiet punctuated by the beeps of machinery and the rhythmic percussive chorus of twelve different heartbeats. Devlin looked at the bed he was standing by and realized he recognized the young man lying in it.

"Over here," said Devlin. Fox joined him and looked down at the bed's occupant. "This is Alvarez."

Fox reached down and unhooked a plastic folder that hung from Alvarez's bed rail. There was a reference number, FDH 4488983, printed on the front of the folder. She flicked through the contents, and Devlin peered over her shoulder. The folder contained the same notes that Devlin had found in Lazard's office. Measurements for blood pressure, cholesterol, blood type, and many more in-depth tests. She searched through the rest of the paperwork, and Devlin turned to the next bed and started checking through the notes on another of the men.

"I'll bet they're mostly O blood type too," he said.

Fox flicked back through Alvarez's profile. "Yeah, Alvarez is. Why?"

"Because if you're O blood type, you're a universal donor."

Devlin had stopped at a page and was studying it. "It looks like they've made antigen matches for all of them. The more antigens that match, the better the chances of organs not being rejected. It's a bespoke transplant service. The money they could charge rich clients for perfectly matching organs and tissues delivered absolutely to spec, it would be astronomical. It's the very highest end of the organ black market."

"Look, Devlin, there's a list for Alvarez's organs." Fox showed him a page marked "Alvarez - Inventory." It was a list of every different kind of organ and tissue: eye tissue, lungs, skin, heart, thymus, liver, kidneys, pancreas, bowel, intestines, bone marrow.

"They're stripping them like car thieves," said Fox. "These men have no idea what's happening to them."

"This was why the first murder happened," said Devlin. "One of the victims must have escaped. Poor devil almost made it to the highway before he was caught and cut up. That has to be what happened. That's why he still had ketamine in his system."

Fox was still reading through Alvarez's documents. "Devlin, there's a date here for delivery of Alvarez's organs. It's tomorrow at ten hundred hours. Jesus, the whole thing's being shipped to deadlines."

Devlin and Fox stood motionless and wordless, grappling with the enormity of evil being done in this place. They were surrounded by a grotesque experiment the orchestrators of which had lost all human empathy.

"These poor souls are in purgatory," Devlin whispered.

54

On the far side of the ranch, Packer and the men had beaten the fire. The tree trunks were still smoldering, and the side of the field the trees bordered along was scorched and charred. But the bulls had been rounded up and moved to safety, and the men had started to fill the pickups ready to go. But Packer wasn't satisfied. Why had a fire broken out on the trunks and branches of the trees? It didn't make any sense at all. It wasn't nearly hot enough for a wildfire. He inspected the charred tree trunks more closely. Among the fire damage, he could make out traces of what to him looked suspiciously like pour patterns. He put his fingers up against a trunk and rubbed up and down. Then he put his fingers to his nose.

"Gasoline."

Packer looked over the field to the edge of the forest that started on the other side of the fence. He got curious and walked up to the fence. Then he climbed over and entered the woodland.

A little way into the forest, Stevens had ditched the empty gasoline cans, crouched behind a bush, and watched the men beat back the fire. He'd planned to call Devlin and Fox when they'd put out the flames and were on their way back. He'd held out as long as possible to give them as much time as he could. But now, as Packer moved closer toward him, he was beginning to regret hanging about. He started to back off slowly, trying not to give his position away while keeping an eye on Packer's movements.

Packer wandered about fifty feet farther into the forest. Then he stopped and listened with all his attention to the sounds around him. He heard nothing unusual, only the hoot and song of birds and the breeze troubling the treetops. Standing still as a deer, he looked back and forth across the forestscape. Birds flitted from tree to tree, and the occasional small animal, a raccoon or squirrel, darted across the forest floor. Nothing out of the ordinary. But Packer waited it out. He waited and watched intently until finally he saw the movement he was searching for, a shadow of human height in the foliage. Packer took off toward it instantly.

Stevens saw Packer thundering in a direct line toward him. His heart did a somersault, and he turned and raced through the woodland as fast as he dared. The branches and leaves stung and stabbed at his skin and caught his eyes, making them sting and tear up. As fast as Stevens could run, Packer's giant strides were still making ground on him. Stevens risked a look over his shoulder. Jesus, he thought, Packer was closing in so fast. It wasn't that Packer was quick; he just didn't care about the low-lying branches. A man of his extraordinary size and bulk, he had virtually no physical fear. He just plowed the hell on through.

Stevens could sense this was a race he could not win. It was a good mile back to his car, and at the rate he was being gained on, it would be game over long before he got there. But what could he do? He had to keep on running, though he knew it was useless. Choking back fear, he ran and stumbled on, thinking of all the time he had a moment ago. All the time with his beautiful children, the pearls of his life, with his wife that he was so stupidly lucky to have. All gone in this nightmare in which, at any moment, he would feel a pair of giant hands on his shoulders. His imagination raced with the images of the many different violent ways Packer could rip his body apart.

And then the earth itself seemed to give way and the day vanished.

55

"We should go, Devlin." Fox was by now extremely agitated.

"We don't need to go yet. Greg hasn't called."

"I don't know, it feels like we're pushing our luck. We've found out what we needed to know."

"I want to know who these organs are going to be delivered to." Devlin walked to the station at the head of the beds and began searching through the drawers beneath the worktop.

"They're not gonna write that kind of information down."

"Maybe not deliberately, but maybe it's buried here somewhere."

"Devlin," said Fox anxiously. "I got a bad feeling. We should go."

"Just give me a minute longer."

56

Packer stood scratching his head. It wasn't possible. It just wasn't possible. There was someone there. A person. He'd seen them, he swore. And now they were gone, like they'd been lifted out of the forest. A shout came from behind him. It was Campbell.

"Packer! What the hell are you doing? We're going back."

Packer turned and walked back to the pasture, shaking his head and glancing back every so often, as if he might catch whoever it was by surprise. As if he were playing Red Light/Green light.

The truth was that the earth itself had given way. Stevens was lying in a shallow, sloping lift shaft that gave on to an old mining tunnel. Surface mining that'd been covered over he'd bet. He looked up. The disturbed earth where he fell through now mostly covered the way in. He could just about make out a narrow chink of daylight. But no Packer. Then he looked down along the gradient of the tunnel he'd fallen into. He wondered how far it went on for. This forest must be riddled with these old mines, he thought. Maybe deeper ones than this. And then it dawned on him. How someone could have got through the police search to Earl two nights before. Someone who didn't have to be a cop. Who might not be Miller or Walker even. Of course! For God's sake, why hadn't it occurred to anyone that there would be old mines running underneath them? Someone could have walked into the forest underneath the feet of hundreds of unsuspecting police officers.

Stevens got to his feet. The shaft itself wasn't so deep. There were rocks and branches in the wall of earth that he could use to get out. It wasn't time for the dirt to claim him yet.

57

"Come on, Devlin!" Devlin had lifted out a pile of papers from one of the desk drawers and was frantically rifling through them. Fox was beside herself with panic.

"Wait, Fox. Greg hasn't called yet."

Fox was getting angry. Finally, she gave up. "This is crazy. I'm going to go start up the car and bring it to the ranch entrance. Throw me the keys." Devlin fumbled in his jacket pocket and flung them over to Fox.

"Stevens hasn't called yet," he repeated without looking up.

Fox sprinted out of the lab entrance and was gone. Devlin continued to work through the papers he'd found, scanning each sheet from the pile and then throwing them to the floor. They seemed to be mainly receipts for supplies from Freedom Dayton Hospital and older medical tests dated from a couple of weeks back that had been kept. He'd got about three-quarters of the way through the paperwork when he hit oil. A list of names Devlin figured had to be the recipients of the organs, the main reason being that none of the names were Hispanic. The other reason was that the list included names with titles: a Lord

Selwyn, a General Belinsky, a Sheikh Mansour Sajwani. Rich people. Alongside the names were dates and the numbers of suites in Freedom Dayton Hospital's premier wing. That was it, the final piece.

He was about to congratulate himself when Devlin heard the crunch of feet on concrete. He dropped the clutch of papers in his hand, which fluttered to the floor around his feet, and looked up. A massive figure loomed in the doorway, dipping his head to get into the lab. He glowered back at Devlin, a shaft of light illuminating his right eye.

A cold realization ran through Devlin that he was completely unarmed. Fox had taken the Glock, and he'd left the Smith and Wesson on one of the supply shelves on the other side of the hangar when they'd bandaged up the ranch hand. He cursed himself for getting so engrossed in the medical paperwork and not thinking more clearly.

Packer's attention had been caught by a muffled sound and movement down to his right, Packer looked to the floor and saw Reeves tied up, squirming and moaning.

"You useless dumbass, Reeves," hissed Packer. Then he looked back up at Devlin.

"Okay, priest. This time is the last time."

Devlin stood across the lab, diagonally opposite from Packer. He had a clear chance across the row of beds to take another look at this strange, giant man. Not many people had this opportunity before getting to grips with him, so Devlin used it to his full advantage. He was the biggest he'd ever gone up against. He'd take some damage, but it wouldn't be impossible. Packer's reach was longer, and his strength was greater. But he was human. And if he was human, for all his strength, Devlin had one good option: fight dirty.

Packer moved over toward Devlin, weaving through the beds. Devlin moved from side to side, threatening to move one way, then another, using the beds as an obstacle. Packer closed in until he was a bed apart from Devlin. Devlin took hold of the bed and started to move it on its wheels. Packer froze. He knew that Devlin was wheeling around millions of dollars of merchandise. Whatever happened, no harm could come to that asset. Devlin started using the bed as a shield. When Packer went one way, so did Devlin and the bed. When Packer attempted to reach over, Devlin pulled the bed toward him, putting Packer in danger of toppling over on the bed and patient. The movement of the bed meant the wires between the patient and the monitors were being stretched to their maximum.

Devlin's tactics were enraging Packer, who'd had enough and pulled out his knife. He reached over and swung it in arcs, trying to cut Devlin. Devlin saw the steel blade coming toward him and rammed the bed into Packer, causing a monitor to let out a high-pitched alarm. Packer panicked and leaped away from the bed, stumbling backward and giving Devlin a couple of seconds' advantage. It was enough time maybe to make the exit but not enough to try and retrieve the Smith and Wesson in the half-light of the hangar. Devlin took off toward the door. He had to take the fight out of here. It couldn't happen in the lab; he'd taken enough chances already with the men lying there in comas, prone and vulnerable.

Devlin ran through the doorway, turned, and saw Packer lumbering after him. Then he caught sight of the scanner and a red Lock button. He closed the doors and pressed the red button, activating the locks. On the other side, Packer pushed at the shut doors and realized what Devlin had done. He looked down to his side and placed his finger on the exit scanner. The display flashed up "Access Denied" in red. He roared in frustration and wiped his hands on his chest and tried again. The display flashed up "Packer. Access Granted" in green. He pushed against the door. It didn't give. Something was stacked up against the door on the other side.

Packer punched the door and bellowed in anger.

He pushed again but no dice. He stepped back and took a run-up, shouldering into the doors, which gave only a little. On the other side, he could hear the jangle of metal rattling. Packer forced the doors ajar and could see that Devlin had pushed as many cages of liquid nitrogen as he could up against them, rows upon rows. Packer pushed his way through, clearing each cage one by one with his great muscular span. Eventually, he stamped out of the lab into the light. But it was too late. Devlin was gone. Packer could barely contain his rage.

The next time he'd catch the priest and rip off his face, arms, and legs with his bare hands.

58

Devlin had skirted the other way around the ranch house from the way he and Fox had got in. He could see that the ranch hands had parked and were back at the trailers. He moved around unseen, over on the opposite side of the clearing from the cluster of trailers and barns, and got to the fence along the highway unnoticed. He climbed the fence and ran along the roadside to the parked Ford Explorer, puzzled that Fox hadn't got the car started and ready to go. He opened the door expecting to find her at the wheel. But she wasn't there. As traffic whooshed past, he sat with the engine running and waited, looking anxiously in his side mirror at the road behind him and the entrance to the ranch. Fifteen minutes passed and nothing happened. No Fox.

Devlin slammed a fist against the window and growled, "Come on, Fox. Where the hell are you?"

Then his phone buzzed. He'd got a text from Fox's number. But it wasn't Fox.

The text said, "Meet me at the coffee shop on the corner of Oakland and Main in an hour. We met your girl and asked her to stick around. Clay."

An electric pulse of shock and terror lit up Devlin's heart.

"No. Not Fox… Please, God…" First Ed and now Fox. Before that, Jane. Devlin was close to despair.

Devlin dropped his face into his hands. He didn't surface for minutes. Then, slowly, he pulled his head out of his palms and gripped the steering wheel.

"No," he said out loud. "The devil cannot win. I will not allow it."

He clenched his jaw and thought through his options. There weren't many, but there was one way. One way he could get back a chance of getting into the lab and rescuing Fox and stopping Clay. It had been a long time, but he was certain it was achievable.

His cell buzzed again. This time it was Stevens calling.

"Greg? Where the hell were you?"

Stevens gabbled his reply quickly, tripping over his words. "I'm so sorry, Gabe. Packer saw me and came after me. Then I slipped down an old mine shaft. It was an incredible piece of luck—it got me away from Packer, but it took time to make sure the coast was clear and scramble back up. And I didn't have any damn signal to call and warn you that they were on the way back. But the thing is, it made me realize if Earl was murdered, then it doesn't have to be Walker or Miller who did it. Gabe, there are thousands of acres of forest on old mining land. Someone could have got through to Earl using an obsolete shaft."

As Devlin listened to Stevens's words, it dawned on him that his discovery threw the doors wide open again on who might have murdered Earl.

"Are you and Fox okay?" asked Stevens.

"No. No, we're not. Fox is still in the ranch. She got caught."

"What?"

"But we managed to get into the lab. Greg, it's much worse

than we thought. They've got twelve illegals doped up in there, ready to strip and ship against their will."

"Twelve? Dear God…"

"And Clay wants to meet me."

"What? No way, Gabe. He'll have you killed."

"No. I don't think he will. He wants to meet in a public place. I have to go. He's got Fox. And I want to go. I want to finally meet the real Clay Logan and look him in the eye. Greg, this town is a death trap now for both of us. There's nobody we can trust and a cop out to kill you. I want you to head out to Fox's cabin until I contact you."

"What about you?"

"I'll be fine. I think I've got a plan."

Stevens rang off. Devlin took out his rosary and thumbed and rolled it patiently. Then he dialed a number on his cell, and the person at the other end picked up.

"George, it's Gabe. I need to talk…I got a favor to ask."

"Tell me what it is you need, Gabe."

59

Devlin sat at an outside table at the place Clay had chosen, sipping a black coffee. He had his back to the wall and faced the busy sidewalk. It was late afternoon in Halton Springs and full of people. Schoolkids were making their way back home, and brilliant sunshine had brought the office crowd out in force. Devlin felt confident that his position there was secure.

A black Range Rover with darkened windows pulled up opposite. The driver's-seat window wound down to reveal Packer scowling out at Devlin. The rear door opened and Clay Logan got out of the back seat wearing sunglasses and a suit, and he sauntered over to join Devlin. He folded his elegant frame into the chair by Devlin and crossed his long legs. A waitress recognized him and greeted him by name. He responded warmly and asked for an espresso. Then he turned to Devlin, removed his sunglasses, and all humanity and charm emptied from his face, a transformation as sudden as it was unnerving. At close quarters, Devlin noticed a vacancy about Clay's eyes. It was as if he were utterly removed from the human race. It wasn't so much an abundance of evil, more a complete absence of good.

"So, priest. I have your girl," said Clay.

"Is she harmed in any way?"

"No. But she will be if you don't do exactly as I say. You have thirty minutes from the moment I leave this table to get out of Halton Springs and never come back. I'd prefer to kill you, but I don't have that option open to me right now. But I will kill the girl."

"I've been to your cattle plant. I know what you're doing. I know the truth—that you're engaged in mass murder for profit. Why won't I go to the FBI?"

"Because I'll kill the girl. And because I also happen to know something about you. I know about Felix Lemus."

A chill went through Devlin. "What about him? He murdered my wife."

"And you murdered him. We got the information out of your colleague, Father Hector Hermes."

Every fiber of Devlin's body screamed to get up and break Clay's head open. But he remained perfectly still. He would not betray himself, his inner thoughts.

"He's fine by the way," said Clay. "A few broken fingers is all. He held out well...for an old man. We also have CCTV of you entering Felix Lemus's apartment on the night of his death. It was the two private detectives that got us this information. The ones you covered in gasoline in DC. You really shouldn't have pissed them off so badly. They've done an outstanding job. Well, I don't need to tell you that, an ex-special investigations agent. I gather they're going to be making a call to Chief Walker, handing over all the information we've gathered on your secret little trip up to Baltimore. So, priest, I suggest that when you leave our beautiful town you keep going, and after that you keep on going. Because the law won't be far behind you. And if you're seen in Halton again, I'll let Packer loose on the girl."

"You'll kill her anyway."

"Maybe. We both know though that there are many ways to die. A whole menu of options. Let's just say, you get to choose how...peacefully that happens."

Devlin now knew why Clay had been so relaxed about coming here, to a public place, to meet Devlin. He held all the cards.

Clay looked up and down the busy street and said, "It's a beautiful town, isn't it? Look at all these well-to-do, comfortable-looking, healthy people. They all have jobs, homes, cars, health insurance, and pensions. I like to think of them as innocent, well-fed children." He looked back at Devlin and smiled a blank, cold smile. Then he asked, "Have you read *The Time Machine* by H. G. Wells?"

Devlin didn't answer, and Clay didn't wait for a reply.

"When the time traveler goes into the far future, he discovers two distinct races, the Eloi and the Morlocks. I like to think of the people of Halton Springs as the Eloi, so pretty in their innocence, while we, you and I, are the Morlocks who toil in the dark and know that the true cost of innocence is blood. We know that bad things happen to everyone, eventually. It's just a matter of time." Again, Devlin didn't answer. Again, Clay wasn't really waiting for one.

"I'm going to leave," said Clay. "You have a good day, and remember, thirty minutes is all you have. Take a step back into Halton and I will rain all hell down upon you and the girl." Then Clay finished his espresso and took a look at Devlin. "You really thought you'd ride into town, my town, like John Wayne and save the day?" There was a moment of silence as Clay triumphantly grinned his winning grin. Then, unexpectedly, Devlin laughed, a long, deep, relaxed, easy laugh.

"Oh, wait," said Devlin. "John Wayne? No, Clay, that's not how it is. You think I'm the good guy? No, no. That's not the roles we've been given here. See, I've got a theory about you and your brother. Earl was born into the world wrapped in sin; it covered him like a net. The harder he pushed, the tighter it became, like a curse. But I also believe that in the last days of his life, he might have found relief. Absolution. He knew he had sinned, but he also knew there was a power greater than him. A power he could offer that sin up to. But you, you poor wretch, you were born into the world without sin, without even the knowledge of sin. But here's the thing: I'm not an agent of God. God wants nothing to do with either of us. We're both damned. No. I'm the serpent. I'm the agent of your awakening conscience."

It was Clay's turn to laugh. "What are you? Some sort of witch doctor? Are you kidding me? Is that the best you got, preacher? You should be on TBN; you'd be a rich man. You fraud." Clay moved to leave, but Devlin grasped his wrist. Clay felt the iron grip, the promise of great strength, and knew he would not be able to wrangle free from it.

"You are at the beginning of your last journey," whispered Devlin. "It is the moment that you wake up to your guilt, to understanding what hell is, Clay Logan. 'Your evils have encompassed you beyond number; they are more than the hairs on your head.'" As the words left Devlin's mouth, Clay was overtaken by a sudden and startling rush of energy. Just as heat moves from hot to cold, as high pressure moves to low, so Clay's emptiness, his void, was an invitation to Devlin's excess of spirit. A life force surged from one man to the other, running along the million tributaries into Clay's heart and, where they met, filling him for the first time with the world outside. Among a crowd of voices in the street and with pin-sharp clarity, Clay heard a woman laugh and a child cry, and it touched him. He was now connected to humanity. The virus was free in him. Devlin dropped Clay's wrist and Clay instinctively moved away, out of his chair, staggering backward into a couple walking past. He nearly fell and they steadied him, recognizing Halton's own statesman. He hurriedly attempted to recover, pulled his jacket straight, thanked the couple, and turned back to Devlin, who had seen everything that had happened and was as alarmed as Clay at this inexplicable transaction.

"You have thirty minutes to get out of town," Logan snarled. He put on his sunglasses and tried to shake off Devlin's spell. But as he left the coffee shop, he felt a burning sense of keen discomfort deep within him. A sensation unpleasant and new. A sensation called shame.

Devlin sat still for a minute or two, shaken and breathing fast. Something had just happened, and Devlin had no idea what it was. It made him feel like a frightened, uncomprehending child. It made him afraid for his own sanity. Then he looked across the road and realized that Packer and Clay were waiting for him to leave, that at any minute a patrol car could come by, pull over, and take him in. He stood, threw twenty dollars onto the table, and headed for his car.

60

Watched by Clay and Packer, Devlin got into his Ford. He pulled out and within minutes of leaving Charley's, he was being tailed by another vehicle. There was a jeep a few cars back that stuck out like a sore thumb. Whoever it was, they sucked at tailing. But it served Devlin's purposes. He wanted to make it look exactly as if he were leaving Halton. So he continued on, driving out of Halton and south, his heart still thumping from his encounter with Clay.

Devlin carried on straight until eventually he ended up in Fairborn, cruising on for a while longer until he suddenly hit the gas and took the interchange back onto the state highway going south. As he got off the ramp, Devlin saw the highway going the other way was light on traffic. He took a sudden, sharp left over the grass meridian and sped onto the highway going north. His tires squealed in protest as he swerved and veered, cutting in front of two other cars that had to break to avoid him and slammed on their horns.

A minute later the driver of the tailing car joined the highway heading south and, seeing no sign of Devlin's Ford, picked up speed trying to catch him up. Devlin, now tail-free and heading in the opposite direction, drove on a few hundred meters and took another sharp turn over the meridian back onto the highway going south. Then he found the exit ramp a little way down and got back on the road to the Fairborn.

It was a fifteen-minute drive through Fairborn onto state route 444. Devlin remembered the route well and knew where to take the turnoff he needed. He took a right and passed the entrance sign for Wright Patterson airbase. A figure in a raincoat with his hands in his pockets stood waiting at the side of the road. Devlin pulled over.

"About time. Room for one more?" said Brennan.

"It's open, George," Devlin replied.

Brennan got into the passenger's seat. Devlin turned to him and asked, "You got me my favor?"

"Sure, Gabe, I got it. Hell of a favor. There's a Hercules leaving tonight for Youngstown Warren. You got your lift."

"You're a gent, George."

61

The high walls of the lab flickered with blue light and flashes of red as the equipment kept a record of the sedated men's conditions. Fox sat in a chair up against a row of oxygen canisters near to the entrance. She was gagged and bound. Reeves sat a few feet away holding the Glock and looking her up and down every so often, not even bothering to disguise his interest. It sickened Fox, but it would not demean her. She looked elsewhere, and when she did catch his eye, she gave him the impression of complete disinterest. Not fear, certainly not, nor anger, nor indignation, just utter indifference. After a while, it wore him down, and the interested, salacious looks became one of contempt. The hate he had for Fox became manifest.

Fox watched the four men who had evidently been tasked with stripping the twelve bodies. Lazard, the reptilian-looking guy whom she recognized from the hospital, the older, bald man with a stouter figure but similarly blank eyes, and the two young Asian men. They all had gowns on and were preparing for surgery. At the back of the lab along the wall was a long, silver wash basin which the four men stood in front of. Each hit their foot pump and the faucets came on. Although Fox could mostly only see their backs, she still could make out the various stages of the scrubbing in process. She could see them wet their scrub brushes and soap up their hands to the wrists, paying meticulous attention to the areas between their fingers. She watched them pick their fingernails under the sink before scrubbing them. Then they scrubbed each finger in turn after which they moved down to their palms, the back of their hands and along their forearms to their elbows. Lastly, they rinsed the lather off and held their dripping hands over the sink waiting for the excess water to fall away. The men carried out this preparation with the deepest seriousness. It was almost ritualistic. A piece of theater. The bald man, although generally more expressive than Lazard, had now adopted the same unmoved expression, as if there were nothing in the world that could possibly impress or delight him. Watching him, Fox had the dreadful feeling that this was work that he was extremely familiar with.

The two older surgeons led the two younger ones. They moved in among the living bodies but smelled of death, of stillness and uniformity. The bald man, Fox noticed, had the same sallow skin color as Lazard, and his fingers were also stained dark brown with nicotine. The two younger surgeons were equally impassive. But for all their reserve, the four were impressively coordinated and deft in laying their groundwork. They gave the impression of absolute competence and of a lightning-quick understanding and shorthand between them. They bustled around each body making sure they were all perfectly prepared for the ordeal ahead.

The victims' hospital gowns were peeled back, exposing their young bodies. Once this had been done, it became stunningly obvious why these men had been chosen. They were at the peak of physical condition, the best examples of their peers.

The two older men had begun using black pens on the men's

skin. Starting with the body on the far right, they drew a mass of dotted and solid outlines together with shading and letters and numbers so that by the end the skin was tattooed from face to toes with labels and instructions. All the while there was low-level talk and discussion between the four men over the continuous whir of fans and the chorus of digital pips.

The door buzzed and Packer entered with Clay. Fox grew anxious. She felt utterly afraid of them. Who of the two she was more afraid of she couldn't say. Packer was a brute, but Clay was cold. Empty. He looked over at her and smiled. Then he called over to Reeves. Reeves hadn't heard; he was busy sneering at Fox.

"Reeves," Clay called again. "Take the gag off." Reeves walked over and roughly untied it. The moment the gag came free, Fox yelled as loudly and for as long as her lungs would allow her. It went on for nearly a minute. She knew it was futile, but it was a howl of outrage and defiance more than anything else, a howl of protest from her very soul at the barbarism she was witnessing. The four surgeons turned to see what was happening, quietly furious at Fox's incredibly thoughtless disturbance. Finally, she stopped, exhausted. Packer, Clay, and Reeves looked at each other and began to laugh.

"Darling, there isn't anybody going to hear you scream in here," mocked Clay. "Why do you think we put the lab out here in the first place? Look over there." He gestured to the bodies on the beds. "Plenty of people have had more cause than you to scream in here. Oh, yeah. Screaming never got anyone here anywhere."

"Perhaps she was trying to wake these guys up," joked Reeves. Clay and Packer laughed.

"I hope not," replied Clay. "Best these boys don't wake up. It happened once before, and it didn't end prettily for anyone."

"What do you mean, it happened once before?" asked Fox.

Clay looked at Packer, and Packer looked back in an amused and conspiratorial fashion.

Clay walked over and set up a chair by Fox. "I think you know, Ms. Fox."

"Just call me Fox."

"I think you know, Ms. Fox." Clay almost stopped there and said no more. He studied Fox, ran his eyes over her pretty face and lean body, leisurely appraising her figure and finding it very satisfactory. In the company of this attractive woman, his ego began to surge to the fore, demanding to be fed. He desperately wanted to tell this fine-looking, intelligent woman who he had captive before him, what he had done, and if it didn't impress her, it would outrage and even torture her. And that would be just as enjoyable. Clay leaned back and smiled. His blue eyes crinkled, and he began to speak, delighting in his own voice.

"I'm talking about the first murder up at Long Pine. Somebody—and there's still some dispute as to who—got careless with the anesthetic and one of our boys escaped. It was almost curtains for us. Took us a while to track him down. He got out of the ranch and through half of Long Pine. He almost made it as far as the highway. But we stopped him just in time. Shot him in the head. Well, actually, we didn't. That was the work of a law enforcement officer." Clay, Packer and Reeves laughed again. "Fine work by Halton's finest. We couldn't drag the body eight miles uphill to the ranch in the rain. So we cut his head, hands, and feet off. I tell you, that was a sorry night. We lost tens of millions of dollars. We had to cut our losses. Literally." Clay laughed and slapped his thigh, even more tickled by Fox's appalled reaction to his joke. "We hoped they'd think someone was trying to hide the victim's identity. Truth was, we just wanted people thinking and guessing and making up the identity. 'Cause he was an illegal, he didn't have one. It was a solid gold bonus when the Gypsy story started doing the rounds."

"How did you get all these...men in here?" asked Fox, looking over the row of bodies.

"Oh, that wasn't so hard. We selected them."

"Selected them?"

"Yeah. We offer all our staff free checkups and medical treatment at the Halton Medical Center, including our undocumented migrant workers. We're very generous like that. Course, that allows us to run deeper, more useful tests on some of our employees. We just take a swab and blood sample, and we get all sorts of exciting information." Clay pointed to the men in the beds. "We built this group of specimens up over the course of a couple of months. Once we got an illegal worker that was a good match, that matched one of our orders, Packer would ask him to go out on a job with him. Then Packer would overpower him and chloroform him, and Dr. Lazard would arrive with his bag of treats. After we'd sedated the guy, we moved our new body in here. It became just like building up our own little collection."

Clay looked over at Reeves. "Reeves. Go and walk the perimeter with Campbell."

"Okay, boss." Reeves dragged himself out of his chair, stretched his arms, yawned, and buzzed the door open with his finger. Clay looked back at Fox. "We got a long night ahead, Ms. Fox. We got a long night ahead." Fox looked over at the four surgeons. Soon they'd start cutting into the bodies, right in front of her, butchering the young men while they slept.

62

Devlin and Brennan had driven into the base with Brennan guiding the way to a complex of buildings that backed onto a runway. They parked, and Brennan led Devlin to a large, brightly lit hangar. At the far end, the hangar door was wide open to the warm spring night. Devlin could see the illuminated runway outside and the lights of military planes standing ready beside it.

This particular hangar had been set aside for supplies and rigging, and it felt like being home again for Devlin. He'd done hundreds of drops as a pararescue, and for a few years this world had been Devlin's world. There was a line of wet chutes from a recent drop left hanging along a rope to dry out. The rope arced down from the roof and was secured onto the side of one of a line of yellow freight containers. Against the walls were rows of shelves and tables. The tables were piled up with chutes ready to be rigged and training bundles. The shelves held more chutes along with stacks of deployment bags and extraction chutes used for dropping cargo. Running along the center of the hangar was a varnished wooden bench, and midway along the bench lay a row of items that had been carefully prepared and set out.

Brennan and Devlin stood by the bench surveying the equipment.

"Everything like you wanted," said Brennan. "The rigger and the loadmaster have both checked it over. There's an MC-4 chute and Extreme Cold Weather clothing system with oxygen, just like you asked. And a Beretta M9, loaded with fifteen rounds and an extra fifty rounds. There's a night training flight I got you onto scheduled to go out at twenty-two hundred hours, A C160. You got a few hours till then. They can take you over Halton Springs, but you'll need to give them the exact GPS. They said they can give you a twenty-six-thousand-foot drop."

"Thanks, George. It's everything just like I asked."

"Yep, it is. But the crew have asked questions. I just said it's a joint exercise drill with Homeland and local law enforcement. Insurgent detection and capture."

"Did they buy it?"

"They bought that it was an explanation. They don't think it's the actual honest-to-God truth, Gabe. Who would?"

"As long as they think someone's gone to the effort of making something almost believable up. Better than no explanation at all."

George looked at the kit on the bench. It was high-spec military equipment, serious stuff.

"Gabe, it's a long time since you were pararescue. You okay to do this? A high-altitude night jump?"

"I'll be fine, George. I kept my hand in at the Boston Skydive Center. Besides, I'm jumping into the middle of Ohio, not behind enemy lines in Afghanistan. Now that was difficult."

George accepted the answer, but there were others he wanted too.

"So what's going on at the Logan Ranch?"

Devlin's answer was short and frustrating. "Something big. What's going on is as big as it could possibly be." But that was all Devlin said. He would not say any more, so Brennan stood locked in a back-and-forth conversation that was happening all in his mind. He was thinking a hell of a lot but nothing that he could say. Caution and political savvy were holding him back. Devlin let him off the hook he was squirming on.

"Let me answer the question you got going on in your head, George. No. I'm not going to tell you. Because if I do, you'll have to do something about it, and that will give you the biggest headache of your lengthy and patiently built career. It's so big that if you kept it to yourself and someone found out that you knew, you'd be humiliated and sacked. Career over. But if you try and take it somewhere, and it would have to be the Secretary of Homeland Security and up, whoever it is they'll wish you'd kept it to yourself. And they wouldn't thank you for it, but they'd remember you for it. You're a career man, George. You're ambitious and you're good at being ambitious. So, because you're my friend and my comrade, this is my advice to you: you never saw me, you never talked to me. Give me my rig and my ride, and read all about it in tomorrow's papers. Goodbye, George."

Devlin extended a hand. Brennan hesitated, then shook.

As Brennan got to the door, he swung around and added as an afterthought, "Oh, by the way, about that other matter you raised. The two PIs. I made a call. We have it in hand."

"Okay. Do I need to know anything else about that?"

"No," George said with the hint of a smile. "You just need to know we got it in hand."

63

Devlin got suited up. He checked his altimeter, chest-mounted GPS, and compass were all in working order. He then rigged up the oxygen mask and sat on the bench with the mask fitted over his helmet and cupped against his mouth. For about forty minutes, he breathed only pure oxygen to prevent hypoxia occurring during the fall.

Devlin had only just removed the mask from his face when he heard the clack of boots on concrete and looked up. A squarely built Master Sergeant in his forties with a gray buzz cut walked into the hangar.

"You Devlin?"

"Yep."

"You ready to go?"

"Yep."

"Well, hurry the hell up, princess, your carriage awaits."

Devlin stood and picked up his backpack. His bulk and height were emphasized by the layers of camouflage uniform, Gore-Tex, the Mr. Puffy suit underneath, and Gore-Tex boots.

"Let's go," he replied. Then they walked out shoulder to shoulder.

"You gonna tell me what this is all about?" snapped the Master Sergeant.

"I can only tell you what you've already been told."

"Well, it had better be important. We've had to reroute and clear with commercial flights."

"It's important."

As the Hercules taxied onto the runway, its huge engines rumbling, Devlin got the coordinates from his cell that he'd given to the crew and put them into his GPS unit. The occupants of the plane were the three flight crew up front in the cockpit, Devlin, who was sitting back in the fuselage, and the Master Sergeant, who sat opposite Devlin. Devlin wasn't in any mood for talk. He wanted only to find Fox, save the young men before they were butchered like the cattle they were kept with, and kill anyone who tried to get in his way. He silently repeated the motto that he'd sworn by as a pararescue: "That Others May Live."

The Hercules took off with a deafening roar. There was a red light illuminating the inside of the aircraft so that Devlin's eyes would be adjusted to see more clearly in the dark when he began the drop. He did one more check of his equipment to make sure everything was in order, and then he took his rosary from his pocket and began rolling each bead between his thumb and index fingers. The Master Sergeant noticed the beads and shouted over.

"If you need God, you must be in a heap of trouble!"

"When you step out into the darkness, you need all the light you can get," Devlin yelled back.

The beast thundered and bellowed in the vast night, and Devlin hoped desperately and fervently that Fox was still unharmed as he sat in its belly preparing for the fall.

64

Campbell had done another walk around the front of the ranch, patrolling from the barns and trailers across the face of the house and down to the highway and back again. Then he stopped by the calving shed, rolled a cigarette, and leaned up against the shed entrance for a smoke. There had been no sign of the priest. Pity. Campbell was itching to be the one that came face-to-face with him. He had heard about what the priest did to Earl, how he had whipped Earl's ass. Although he had never been an admirer of Earl, knowing some bum had come breezing into Halton and bested Earl in a fight still bruised his pride. He ached to get a chance to square things with this Devlin guy. Campbell, Reeves, and a few of the other men formed a core that was fiercely loyal to Packer and the Logans. Over the years, Packer had assembled an inner circle of a few hands who he could trust absolutely and who were not to be messed with. Men who were hardened and indifferent to the younger hands who came up to work. Men who, like Earl, felt they had earned some deference in their hometown and some special treatment from the local police.

Campbell had been told to shoot the priest on sight. He had

been told that if the priest were killed, the perpetrator would be protected. Legal consequences would be unimportant. Campbell knew Devlin had broken into the cattle plant and was suspected of homicide so had no personal qualms about killing him stone-cold. He took another drag and blew the smoke out of his nose, admiring the spare beauty of the Ohio nightscape. He hadn't traveled much, but for Campbell the Logan Ranch was the one place where he felt safe and content. It was his corner of the world.

The perfect peace was broken by a bang coming from back in the shed and the sound of a heifer snorting. Campbell threw his smoke down, heeled it into the dirt, and went to investigate. Halfway down he saw that a gate had come loose and a heifer had wandered out into the gangway. He calmed her down and guided her back into her jug. Then he secured the gate, took one last look to check the heifer had settled, and felt a dull crunch that propelled his head forward and back off the top bar of the metal gate. Blackout.

His unconscious body collapsed back into the arms of Stevens.

"Whoa, easy there. Sweet dreams, son."

Stevens threw Campbell over his back. He was long rather than stocky, so carrying him was awkward rather than straight out exhausting, which was lucky, because it was a good trudge up a slight incline to Stevens's next stop, the generator. It was housed in a red metal hut and secured with a padlock like Devlin had said. Stevens dropped Campbell, took out a pair of pliers that had been wedged into his belt, and cut away the padlock hanging from the door. Then he dragged Campbell inside. The generator itself was in a large, orange metal casing with various tubes and wires running from valves along the side. At one end was a black metal structure that encased a fan.

Stevens took his cuffs out and secured Campbell to one of the sturdy black metal bars that supported the fan.

And then he waited.

Devlin's orders to Stevens had been clear: stay by the generator, follow Devlin's instructions, and get out as fast and safely as he could. But already Stevens had a hankering to get a little bit more involved. He walked outside and stood looking at the outline of the lab sitting enigmatically in the middle of a large clearing, the last building before you were out into the pastures. And Stevens started to get curious.

65

Clay was dreaming and it was such a strange alien dream. He was sleeping with Marie. They lay on his bed in a glow of summer sun streaming through the windows. He had never felt anything for Marie, but in his dream he felt such tenderness, such vulnerability, that it made him cry. Real tears, tears that would not stop and which grew into a river and carried Marie off, leaving Clay alone. Abandoned. And he was scared. And his fear turned into a serpent that coiled around him, trapping him. The serpent's scales began to sear Clay's skin, to burn and fry his flesh, and Clay heard the serpent say, "For evils have encompassed me beyond number; my iniquities have overtaken me, and I cannot see; they are more than the hairs on my head; my heart fails me."

Clay screamed.

He did not stop.

He went on screaming and screaming until he was shaking. But the shaking was because someone was pulling him back and forth. It was Packer.

"Clay!" Packer growled. "Clay!" Clay was shaken awake and saw that everybody in the lab was looking at him wide-eyed, including Fox. He rapidly set about pulling himself together. Hiding the state of shock he was in.

"It's okay. I'm tired is all. Take no notice. Carry on."

He could feel Fox's eyes in particular staring at him, and he chose to ignore her. He took out his pill case and popped half a dozen tablets of propranolol. Now he felt Claude Lazard staring over at him. The doctor had seen how many tablets Clay had taken and was concerned.

"Carry on, I said," snapped Clay. Lazard looked away quickly and continued with the body he was working on.

In fact, the four men were now working away with incredible intensity. You could feel the ferocious yet completely controlled concentration that they worked with. If it wasn't so utterly abhorrent, Fox might actually have admired them. They had begun working on two men occupying the beds closest to Fox but were now solely focused on one of the men, Alvarez. Lazard was making an incision in the flesh which was also visible on a monitor. The other three were providing assistance, monitoring the anesthetic and handing Lazard surgical instruments to suck away excess blood from the site of surgery. Fox could only watch helplessly, knowing that with every minute that passed, Alvarez's life was becoming less and less redeemable. His body was being stolen while he slept.

"They're good, aren't they?" Clay had noticed Fox's fascination and leaned over. "Hell, they're better than good; they're world-class. Claude has got it down to a work of art. In fact, he's like an artist. It is breathtaking. Mind you, he comes with an astronomical fee. So does his brother, Jakob." Clay pointed to the older man.

"They're murderers. You're a murderer. Worse, this is systematic. You're like Nazis. You're as close to evil as I've ever seen."

"But we're also saving lives—the lives of people that have contributed huge amounts to the world. People who have earned billions and paid vast amounts of taxes, employed armies of people, developed and innovated new technologies. People who have the ears of presidents. People who will pay heart-stopping amounts of money for the freshest human parts made to order. And trust me, they ain't asking where we're getting the organs from. It's the deluxe end of medicine, baby. Look, if you examine someone's worth, and in this world we do it all the time, these men lying here are odds-on never going to contribute anything to the progress of the human race. Zero. Let's keep the entrepreneurs, the innovators alive. That's what I say. Besides, this is recycling. By the time we've finished here, these boys will be nothing but bits of skeleton."

Fox looked at Clay in horror. "You've lost every drop of humanity you have."

"I just make the decisions other people are too afraid to make."

"I never thought I'd hear myself say it, but I wish you had died and Earl had lived."

"Ha! That boy died like a dog," Clay scoffed. "You want to know how Earl died? Me and Packer followed him out to his favorite little spot in the woods and blew his brains out. Like taking the family dog into the backyard and putting him down. Y'know, we took one of the old mining shafts that runs out from the north pasture deep into Long Pine. I know! Astounding! We calmly strolled in under the noses of every police officer in Halton, Shelby, and Greene County. Best thing I ever did for that boy. He's found more peace now than he ever had in Halton Springs. All of us at the ranch knew he was a sexual deviant. Packer went looking for him the night he had the fight with the priest. Course, none of the cops on the night shift wanted to get involved. They knew from experience that Earl was bad news. They gave him a wide berth. So Packer found him up near Fairview stumbling about like a madman, dripping in blood, watched him throw himself on his boyfriend's mercy. And that's when we saw our opportunity. It meant blowing the Gypsy story out of the water, but by that time Earl was making himself such a pain in the ass it was worth it. To make Earl the fall guy for the Long Pine killing and get rid of him for good. Get that little bastard out of our hair so we could do business without him bringing heat down on us. And it all worked out pretty nicely. Don't you think, Miss Fox?"

"You know Devlin will come back here?"

"No, he won't. Even if he did, he isn't going to get very far. We got men out front and around the back. We got a chopper out covering the ranch for any sign of him. Anyone who sees him has been told he's a suspected murderer trespassing on private property and is to be shot on sight. He doesn't stand a snowball's chance in hell of getting in here. And if by some miracle he does, he knows that right after we kill him we'd kill you. So, forget Devlin. That ship has sailed."

It was about as bleak as it could get. Fox's wrists burned with the tightness of the duct tape that bound her. She rolled to get as comfortable as she could and felt a small hard object in her back pocket. At first, she couldn't place what it might be until she realized it must be Devlin's lighter, the one he'd given her back when they first met. With her hands bound behind her, she slipped two fingers into her pocket and tweezered out the lighter with her index and middle finger. She lay it on the chair and picked it up in her palm and flicked it. She felt the flame burn her hand and almost dropped it. *Okay*, she thought, *now it's about how and when I play this card.*

66

Devlin took a breath and sat up straight. His lungs were begging for the reassuring warmth of a Corona, but he had to put any luxury like that out of his mind. He had sensed activity up at the front so guessed they must be nearing the drop zone. The Master Sergeant had comms mounted in his helmet and looked like he was listening intently to flight information from the crew. He barked over at Devlin.

"Wind speed ten miles an hour, ground temperature sixty-three degrees with light rain."

He operated the release lever and immediately the hydraulics kicked in. There was a dull whine and the top rear cargo door opened, then the lower door, revealing the great, dark, formless void. Swirling, chaotic winds raged around the Hercules. The Master Sergeant walked over by the opening, and Devlin watched him intently as he held up two fingers signaling two minutes to the drop. Devlin walked to the end of the ramp with eyes locked on his instructor. Finally, the ready signal, a thumb up to the ceiling followed a moment later by the signal to jump, the Master Sergeant pointing to the door. And that was it. Here it was, always the same—the moment, against every sensible thought in Devlin's head, against every instinct he had telling him to stay inside the plane, that he made his body do the final step onto the precipice and fly backward out into thin air, the wind instantly hitting his chest.

Time to meet the angels.

Devlin was hit by a sudden massive surge of adrenaline, a feeling in the pit of his stomach like plummeting down a roller coaster, his body shuddering against the wind. At the same time there was a sudden quiet and peacefulness. He was surrounded by so many stars. They were overwhelming.. The Milky Way really lived up to its name up here.

Devlin reached terminal velocity, 125 mph, at around ten seconds. He was in free fall and knew that at this height, it would last a couple of minutes during which there would be nothing to tell him how fast and how far he was going. All he could feel was the air pressing against him and rushing into his helmet and the sound of his own breathing into the oxygen mask. The light switch was on by the altimeter on his wrist, illuminating the reading. There were only thirteen thousand miles on the dial, so it would whizz around nearly twice before he had to deploy. It read 4,000 feet, so Devlin knew he was at 17,000 feet. It was all he had to guide him up this far. Night was always the hardest time to jump mentally because you were in limbo, halfway between heaven and earth and nothing to tell you where you'd come from or where you were heading. But it was the best time if you wanted to be invisible.

Then Devlin hit the cloud deck. The internal pressure of cloud threw him momentarily, and he was soaked through as the pressure of the water particles leaked into his supposedly waterproof suit. He strained to see signs of the ground ahead. And then he was out, as quickly as he'd entered the clouds, back into the night air. Devlin checked his compass and looked at the landscape. Below him, he could see the lights along the highway coming east out of town. Up ahead he could see the lights from what he was pretty sure was the Logan house. Just like that first night he rode by, it was lit up like Christmas and stood out from all the other smaller, isolated buildings scattered around.

He checked the GPS on his chest using a chemlight he'd strapped to his arm, which confirmed he was tracking in in the right direction. Then he checked his altimeter: 6,000 feet. From here until 5,000 feet, he hardly took his eyes off it, and when the dial read 5,000, Devlin began the pull sequence. Even though he was jumping alone, he still checked over his shoulder to make sure everything was clear, an old habit from all the group drops he'd done as a PJ. He pulled on the D ring like he was slugging someone with a punch from the shoulder, and there was a massive jolt as he was jerked roughly back up into the sky and then began the descent in.

Devlin checked his compass again and took a left ninety-degree bearing into a heading of seventy degrees magnetic, which took him over the edge of Long Pine and closing in on the ranch. He could now see the cattle lab lights at ten o'clock behind the main house about four klicks away. He had eyes on the target. Devlin was able to maneuver into the wind so he stood a good chance of a safe, braked landing. And he'd need to because it was a tough target. Devlin was aiming for the roof of the lab.

When the roof finally came, it came rushing in toward him and was shiny with light reflecting off it from the ranch house. What the hell was the roof made of? thought Devlin. It couldn't be glass panes; Devlin wouldn't have missed a glass roof on the lab when he was in there. Then it clicked. Solar panels. Worse. Wet solar panels. Damn. The moment his feet hit the roof, his legs went from under him and he slid at speed down the ramped paneling. He was going to fly off the roof and plunge thirty feet to the ground.

He reached out and caught his arm around the top of a yellow steel ladder attached to the side wall, bringing him to a hard, painful and juddering stop. He was finally motionless. Thank God. He'd almost hit the roof and bounced right back off. His right arm and right side aching and bruised, he snaked back up into the center of the roof and began to collect in his chute. A chopper flew by about a mile away, one of Logan's no doubt. It turned and headed back out to where the forest met the ranch. It was skirting the boundaries, looking for Devlin. Well, thought Devlin, it had failed.

67

Light rain had turned into a downpour, drumming fast on the aluminum and glass skin of the lab. Inside the lab, in amongst the rattle of the downpour, Packer thought he heard something. On most nights he would have paid it no attention, but tonight was not most nights. Clay, also in a hypervigilant mode, noted his concern.

"What is it, Packer?"

"I thought I heard a sound outside. Probably nothing," Packer said and gestured to Reeves. "Reeves, go and do a walk-around again."

Devlin had only just removed his helmet and goggles and gathered and yanked his chute in when he heard the bang of a door somewhere below. He flattened his body down on the paneled roof. It was incredibly slippery; a wrong move could send Devlin sliding down and off the side of the building. He chanced a look up over the edge of the roof and glimpsed a figure walking out ten feet or so from the lab and scouting around it, making sure it was clear. Devlin lay perfectly still and prayed for whoever it was below to just go away. He clutched his chute close to him, listening intently for footsteps to detect which way they might be heading. But in the increasingly heavy rain, it wasn't so easy to hear that kind of noise from where Devlin was. He lifted his head up to peek over the edge of the roof again and heard the click of safety catch. Someone was behind him.

"Very slowly now. Just turn around and get up with your hands where I can see them." Devlin looked back over his shoulder. Reeves was at the top of the metal ladder with a gun trained on Devlin. He had one leg on a rung and one planted on a solar panel.

"You can throw that gun you got on you over to me too," said Reeves.

Devlin turned and sat up and complied reluctantly.

"You gave me one hell of sore jaw, you son of a bitch. Never mind. We'll soon be even. From now on they'll call me Reeves the Priest Killer."

Reeves lifted the gun, aiming at Devlin's head, and stepped off the ladder, planting both feet onto the wet, glassy surface of the roof. Devlin frantically searched for options. As Reeves's trigger finger tightened, Devlin twisted sharply and slung his chute around toward Reeves. The nylon material spread and billowed on the air between them, stifling Reeves's attempt to get a shot off. In the seconds it took Reeves to thrust the chute down and away from him, Devlin had pushed himself off, skidding low along the rain-covered, near-frictionless solar-paneled slope. He collided into Reeves's legs, knocking him off balance and sending him stumbling and slipping backward off the edge of the roof, his arms windmilling frenziedly as he plummeted to the ground. Devlin's body hit the top of the ladder and took a bump, sending him rolling over the top rung, which he managed to grasp with his left hand. He hung from the ladder with his legs dancing around for a foothold and looking down at Reeves, who was lying prone and still on the sodden ground, his legs and neck bent unnaturally.

Once Devlin had got a foothold, he scrambled down the ladder to search Reeves's lifeless body and took his knife from the leather sheath on his belt. Then he paused and studied Reeves's face, feeling a stab of guilt. He genuflected over the dead man and quickly ascended the ladder back up to the roof. He crouched by a solar panel on the back right-hand corner of the lab, calculating it to be the farthest point away from the beds and the lab entrance and hoping it was the least visible way in, especially in such a large space. Using Reeves's knife, he stripped back the rubber seal around the panel. The rain streamed down his face, and Devlin had to keep wiping the water from his eyes while he worked away in the dark. Finally, he managed to loosen strips along three sides of the panel, which let him lift it a couple of inches and get a very narrow view in.

Beneath the panel, through the metal roof supports of the lab, he could glimpse Fox sitting by Clay and about half of the beds, but he couldn't see Packer or Lazard. Devlin took out his cell and opened the video app, then pressed the record button and slipped it through the gap he'd opened up. He pointed it hopefully in the direction of the line of beds and moved it from side to side. Then he pulled his cell back up and looked at the grainy, low-res footage. He could make out a hulking figure that had to be Packer, who was over by the monitoring station. There were four other figures—Lazard maybe and three other guys who were already operating on one of the bodies. He pocketed his cell so he could examine the solar panel's attachments. They were screwed into a roof truss on either side. He twisted the knife into the screw heads and wound them loose. Now the panel could be lifted up like a flap. It left a gap of about five and a half by three and a half feet, possible to get through even for Devlin.

It was a good thirty feet to the lab floor, so Devlin needed to work out a way of getting down. He retrieved his canopy from the edge of the roof. It was a standard stealth rig, three hundred and seventy square feet of material with a nearly thirty-foot span. Devlin knotted the chute hard around his waist and reached in and tied the other end around the roof truss. Then he took a deep breath. He pulled out his cell and opened the text app. He typed one word—"now"—sent it to Stevens, and waited around thirty seconds for the response.

In the lab, Lazard had his scalpel poised, ready to sever Alvarez's ureter tubes when they were suddenly cast into darkness. The only illumination came from the pinpoint light of the LEDs on the medical equipment and the monitor screens. Lazard squealed in an even thicker accent than usual.

"Turn the lights on! Turn the goddamn lights on!"

Clay was on his feet. "Don't panic, Lazard. The generator's shut down. We can run the lights from the main grid like the equipment."

Packer had already run to the side wall and lifted up a metal panel. He turned on his flashlight and searched furiously for the fuse switch on the right circuit.

In the dark Devlin had flipped open the solar panel completely, climbed in through the square gap, and sat on a metal rafter. Then he lowered himself so his legs were wrapped around the chute and descended hand over hand, the night rain falling in around him. He was about six feet from the ground when he lost his grip on the wet material and jerked around uncontrollably in the dark. Desperately he tried to free himself from the knot he'd tied so hard. The knot then gave with an unexpected suddenness and he dropped the remaining two meters on to the floor. The noise was loud and obvious. Everyone in the lab, including the four surgeons, stopped still.

"Packer!" cried Clay. "There's someone in here!" The lights started up, and Packer swung around to see the hanging chute material and took great strides through the beds over to the far corner. Devlin saw him coming and scrambled away, pulling out his Beretta.

There was a sudden animal scream. "*Don't shoot*!" Packer and Devlin froze and looked over at Clay, who had Fox at gunpoint.

Fox yelled out, "Just kill him, Devlin!"

Clay racked a round into the chamber and placed his barrel against Fox's temple. "Just give me a reason, priest... Throw down the gun."

Devlin couldn't see any way out that spared Fox's life. So he dropped his Beretta. *Great*, he thought, *I threw away my whole entrance. I got nothing left*.

At that moment, the lab door clicked open and Stevens appeared, holding a gun.

"Let Fox go, Clay," he ordered. For a moment Clay was stunned and just looked at Stevens, his eyes wide with surprise. Then the momentary lull was shattered by a sudden boom—the sound of a gunshot. At first no one knew where it had come from, or who had fired. But after a moment of confusion, all looked over toward Stevens, who in turn was looking at his stomach. A red circle was growing on his shirt, indicating massive blood loss. Stevens slumped to his knees, revealing Officer Gray behind him holding a smoking gun that shook a little from being gripped too hard.

There was a silence. Then Clay laughed. He laughed almost uncontrollably until it petered out into a crooked smile. "Look who it is. It's Officer Gray. Our secret weapon and our trump card."

Stevens looked up at Gray and gasped. "Gray...? Why...?"

Gray didn't answer and instead, Clay interrupted with a blunt order. "Just kill them. Just take them outside and kill them. And when you've killed the priest, Packer, come back for the woman."

Packer took the Beretta and Reeves's knife off Devlin and marched him out of the lab past Stevens's semiconscious body, through the cattle lab, and out into the night. Gray grabbed Stevens's upper arms and followed, dragging his limp body along the floor.

Clay threw Fox back into her chair and screamed, "Come on, Lazard! Keep going! We got hundreds of millions riding on tonight's work!"

The four men were under crippling stress and took a moment to clear their minds and try and summon back the immense focus they needed.

Clay stood, watching them, his concern growing. And then he had what he could only describe as an attack. Without warning, from deep within him, a volcano of scalding grief erupted. He saw again with paralyzing clarity the moment Packer put the rifle up to Earl's head and blotted out his life. He saw the blond waves of hair on his brother's head the moment before Packer pulled the trigger. It was the same head of hair he'd often seen walking ahead of him to school. The same head of hair his mother used to tousle and play with as they both sat on the sofa watching TV. Tears and shame threatened to overwhelm him. Clay was stricken, as if his soul was in mortal terror. He stumbled back into his chair, pulled his pillbox out of his jacket pocket, and swallowed down a fistful of propranolol. Then he waited for the merciful release of the pills.

The brothers were far too busy now to notice Clay's difficulties, but Fox wasn't. She was using every moment she could take to heat the oxygen cylinder behind her with Devlin's lighter.

She'd seen enough. She'd blow both her and Clay into eternity if she had to.

68

Gray shut the lab doors and lifted Stevens so he was propped up by an empty steel cage. They were huddled in the front part of the lab, the cattle lab part. As she stood back and drew her still-warm gun, he began to come to. She held the gun in both hands and focused. She should do it now. It would never be easier. She had to do it before he came around. *Pull the trigger now*, she thought. *Do it like you did it up at Long Pine.*

"Come on, Gray," she ordered herself. "Pull the trigger, you coward." But nothing happened. This was different from Long Pine. It was the second time, and the terrible nightmares since the first murder gave her pause. The same pause that had gotten in the way of her killing Stevens the first time around at his house.

And this was Stevens she was shooting at point-blank range. She knew Stevens. He was a good man. She knew his wife and his kids. It was so much harder this time around. She did everything she could to will herself to the act, but it was already too late. Stevens was staring up at Gray.

For a moment he just stared. Not out of fear—out of pity.

"You were the one that deleted the shift reports, weren't you? That tried to kill me in my home? Why, Gray? Why?"

"Shut up, Stevens. You should never have grown a pair of balls. You were just an ordinary cop who got ideas above himself. It's your fault it's come to this. And don't look so goddamned surprised."

"I never had you down as a cop that could be bought. That's all. If it were Miller or Walker? Hell, it wouldn't have surprised me so much. But you? I thought you had ethics."

"Shut up, Stevens." Gray raised the gun in preparation. But Stevens didn't seem to react.

"They must have paid you a hell of a lot, Gray. That's all I can think."

"It isn't about money. It was never about money."

"What was it about, then?"

Gray shifted back and forth on her feet with the gun aimed at Stevens. She was trying to find her resolve to do the damned thing.

"What was it, Gray?" Stevens asked again.

Gray thought for a moment. Then she spoke.

"I'm only saying this because I don't want you dying thinking things about me that aren't right." She licked her lips nervously and sighed. "My mother is dying. Okay? She needs a lung transplant, and this is the only way we can possibly afford that. We would never stand a chance with somebody my mother's age and with her insurance. Clay Logan has given us a lifeline."

Stevens nodded and answered. "Okay. I see that. I understand."

"She is the only one who ever stood by me. The only person who thought I amounted to something. You don't understand. You don't know what it's like to be this close to losing a loved one. And everyone is telling you there's not a goddamned thing to be done about it. Clay Logan is the only one who offered me a chance. The only one who listened. Who gave me something that wasn't more despair, that gave a damn."

Stevens nodded and then groaned a little in discomfort. The wave of pain and nausea passed, and then he spoke, quietly but clearly.

"Okay. But you're wrong about me not understanding Gray."

"No, I'm not."

"You are. You see, I'm dying, Gray." Stevens laughed and then winced, looking down at his gut. "I mean to say, I was dying even before this happened. I have cancer. It's inoperable."

"You're lying."

"I wish I was. Isn't it obvious, Gray? Haven't you and the other officers commented on how much weight I lost? It's one of the reasons I grew some balls, to use your phrase. I knew I was dying, and suddenly I got some perspective. I knew how short time was. So, do you see? I do know what that's like. I don't know your mother, but if this is what it took to save my life, I would never ask my loved ones to do...this. To help Logan do what he's doing to those innocent men. And I'm pretty sure your mother would feel the same way."

Gray's eyes welled with tears, and her breathing quickened.

Stevens continued in the same calm voice. "If saving my life meant a member of my family willfully taking another's, then I would not want any part of that. Before that would happen, I would say goodbye to my wife and my two children. I would. I wouldn't want that extra time with the people I love at any cost. And neither would your mother."

Gray's arms dropped to her sides, and her shoulders rose and fell in quiet sobs.

"Dear God! What have I done?"

"Walk away, Gray. Right now you can walk away."

Gray collapsed to her knees weeping. Stevens reached over despite the pain and put his hand up to her face.

Gray whispered, "I killed the guy in Long Pine. I did something that can never be undone."

"You have a choice now though. You can leave here and choose not to be a part of it anymore. It isn't too late to do the right thing. Instead of spending your time here, chasing around for Clay, you should be at home treasuring the time you still have. Trust me, Gray, I know."

Gray held her gun in her hands, the handle wet with her tears, and made her decision.

69

"Turn around."

Devlin turned and felt a hard blunt object hammer into the side of his skull. He wheeled back violently against the side of the lab, his face numb and blazing with raw pain, his senses at sea. Packer had walked him out and down by the side of the lab, away from the view of the ranch house and the trailers. The rain had stopped, and the ground was still soft underfoot. He felt Packer take his left hand and slam it at shoulder height against the cold aluminum. Then Packer tucked his gun in his belt and took out Reeves's knife. Devlin felt a sharp point in the middle of his palm and then paralyzing agony radiate out from his hand as Packer drove the blade through skin, tendon, and bone and into the sheet metal behind.

Packer was only an inch from Devlin's face. He laughed, mucus rattling in his throat. The stench of his stale breath and sweet cologne hung in the clear night air. "I've been waiting a long time for this. Ever since you pushed me through that damned window. If the police hadn't come, I would have sliced you up there and then. And that would have been kind. Because now, not only am I going to cut you up, but I'm going to crucify you too, priest. I killed that runt friend of yours, Ed James. He cried like a baby when he died. I'm afraid he wasn't a very brave soldier."

Packer put his hand against the knife pummel, ready to drive it all the way through Devlin's hand to the hilt. Devlin could feel Packer's long thick fingers on his chest. He knew he had only seconds to find a delay, a space in which to attempt to free himself. With his free right arm, Devlin summoned up every piece of energy available to him and grabbed at Packer's little finger, wrenching it out and backward from its socket. Packer roared, as much out of surprise as pain, and instinctively brought his hands together. With Packer's guard down, Devlin rammed the edge of his good palm into Packer's nose. Packer rolled back with blood spurting over his front. Devlin seized the chance to lash out with a front kick into Packer's stomach, sending him farther back onto the wet grass.

For what Devlin had to do next, there were only seconds left. Packer was already rising from the ground with the fury of a bull looking to gore. Devlin reached across with his right hand, gripped the knife pinning him down, and ripped it out, screaming as the blade came free. Packer was nearly upon him, so he sliced wildly back and forth, slashing into Packer's forearms that he'd brought up instinctively as a guard. Packer was hurt, not something he was used to. Devlin held the knife out, and they circled each other, Packer's arm reaching for his belted gun.

"You're not going to shoot me, are you? You coward!" Devlin sneered. Packer already had the gun in his hand and paused. "You gutless coward! You got forty pounds, nearly half a foot and one arm up on me, and you're gonna shoot me?" Devlin slung the knife away and snarled, "Do it like a man!"

Packer stood to his full height and spread out his shoulders.

He threw his own gun behind him, spinning up and far out into the longer grass. Then Devlin's Beretta followed. Packer breathed in deeply and exhaled slowly through his swollen, bloodied nose. "I'm gonna rip your body apart while you watch it happen."

Devlin took stock. He was an arm down, but he didn't have a gun pointed at him. Packer was big and he was strong with a long reach, but he was slow. There was only one strategy that Devlin could think of: get him as riled as he could and fight as dirty as he could.

Packer was already coming at Devlin with his big fists hanging in the air. A boulder of flesh came out of the right, heading for Devlin's head. Devlin sprung low with his knees bent and head down, letting the punch ride over his back and shoulders. As Packer followed through and came a fraction off balance, Devlin threw his fist into Packer's groin, taking his breath away and leaving him bent over double and momentarily stranded. Devlin surfaced up by his ribs and bit down savagely on his right ear. Packer howled like a beast that had been speared and caught Devlin with a wild swing of an elbow, snapping Devlin's head backward. As Devlin reeled back, he took half of Packer's earlobe with him, trapped between his bloody, gritted teeth. Devlin spat out the lobe, and Packer felt for his ear, which was dripping blood, and roared with anger.

Packer came at Devlin again, and Devlin danced back, causing Packer to keep coming, lurching forward. Devlin feinted left and then ducked right, exposing Packer's left side, allowing him to grab Packer's trailing hand and pull hard on his damaged little finger. Packer reared back and spun, yelling from the sharp pain. Then he came stampeding back and rammed Devlin, picking him up and squeezing him, crushing him, attempting to snap his ribs open. Devlin's left arm was busted, but he reached round Packer's huge head with his right arm and grasped what was left of his bloodied ear, digging in behind the cartilage.

Devlin couldn't hold out much longer. Another thirty seconds and either his ribs would explode or he'd pass out. Or both. He had the root of Packer's ear by his fingertips and wrenched at the cardboard-like cartilage until it clicked and tore. Packer's grasp faltered, but then he battled through the damage and pain and went for one last crunch. Devlin desperately pummeled at Packer's great cranium until his thumb found the wet, soft mass that was Packer's right eye. As Packer came close to breaking Devlin in two, his eye was being pressed against the bone of his ocular cavity, the membrane reaching bursting point. With moments to go before Devlin's body would give way and sustain devastating internal injuries, Packer's eye burst like a water balloon, and Devlin's thumb, free of resistance, was propelled through the thin bone into the soft yielding mass of the frontal lobe. The release was instant. Devlin dropped to the ground and rolled backward across the grass and mud. Packer's purpose and intention were gone. He was still standing, but that was all, a great black mass now in the place of his milky eye. Devlin got to his feet and took a vicious swing at his neck, sending him crashing down on the grass.

Packer had fallen and lay motionless. Devlin collapsed onto his knees beside his foe's great bulk and wiped the soft organic material from his hand onto his jacket. He looked skyward toward a heaven and a God who led him to ever darker places. A God that pushed Devlin on into realms of evil that, in the end, were only inhabitable by humans.

"If you do evil, be afraid..." he whispered, "for I do not bear the sword in vain. For I am God's servant, an avenger for wrath to the one doing evil."

Devlin stood up and located his Beretta amongst the mud and grass. Then he went to find Stevens and Fox.

70

When Devlin walked into the cattle lab, there was only the light from the ranch house and the moon crisscrossing the cages and stocks. He was about to try and bust his way into the main lab when he heard a moan. Down amongst the shadowed floor, a streak of silver light ran across Stevens's drained features. He was slumped and on the cusp of consciousness.

Devlin crouched down to examine him. He was paper white and drenched in sweat.

"I'm fine," whispered Stevens. "Gray couldn't kill me. Didn't have it in her. She's gone. Go, Gabe. Go put an end to it." Then he pulled something out of his shirt pocket. "You'll need this. It's how I got in before." He was holding out Campbell's finger. "You said there was a scanner to get in, and I had the pliers to do it anyway. Campbell's got nine other fingers to make do with." Stevens gave a weak laugh. Devlin took the finger in his right hand, turned to the lab door, pressed the tip into the scanner, and the door clicked open. He dropped the finger, and with one hand he genuflected, then unholstered his Beretta, taking the safety off.

Devlin stepped into the lab, and Clay's face said it all. He'd been expecting Packer. It never for a moment crossed his mind that Devlin would come back alive. The surgeons stopped working and eyed the two men nervously.

"Drop the gun, Clay. It's over," ordered Devlin.

Clay was wild with terror. Devlin now exercised a power over him, shared an intimate and awful connection with him. But Clay wasn't about to give up. Not even now. Especially not now. Instead, he raised his gun and pulled Fox off her chair, dragging her with him behind the row of beds. Claude, Jakob, Liu, and Wei scurried to the side of the lab and cowered along the lab wall, as far away from the line of fire as possible. Devlin tried to get a shot off, but with the bedridden men lying in the path of his bullets, there was no way he could safely fire. Clay had the advantage and let off a volley that peppered the wall behind Devlin, forcing him to the ground.

Clay drove his gun barrel into the side of Fox's face. "You come near me and I'll blow her head off! Put the gun down now, Devlin! Put the gun down, or I blast her pretty face off!"

Devlin had sidestepped around until he was standing by Fox's upturned chair.

"There's a SWAT team on the way, Clay. It's over." As Devlin spoke he noticed Fox gesturing with her eyes at the floor. What the hell was she trying to tell him?

"A SWAT team?" Clay yelled. "You just called up a SWAT team? A priest on the run from the police for murder. You got a SWAT team to come down here? What a load of crap."

Fox was moving her eyes furiously now, but Devlin had no idea what she was trying to communicate.

"I'm going to count to three, and if you haven't put the gun down, I'll pull the trigger," shouted Clay.

"You're all alone now, Clay. Packer's dead, so's Reeves." Fox was still gesturing manically with her eyes.

"One..." said Clay.

"Gray's gone too. Give up, Clay."

"Two..." Devlin desperately wished he knew what Fox was doing. Then he glanced down by his feet in the direction that Fox was frantically indicating and saw a lighter on the floor.

"It's over, Clay."

"Three..." Clay moved his head back and straightened his gun against Fox's head.

"Okay! Okay!" Devlin had no choice. He dropped his Beretta to the ground.

"Thank you. Now kick the gun away—hard." Devlin complied and the Beretta skidded and spun under the beds. Clay moved from behind the beds, dragging Fox with him so that he now stood on the other side of the lab with a clear path to Devlin. He pointed his gun at Devlin and snarled, "Goodbye, priest."

Just as Clay was about to fire, without warning, he was blinded by a vision of a dark, thunderous night, rain pouring down like the deluge, he and Reeves drenched and standing around while Packer cut a young man's body into pieces. The scene felt more real to him now than it had at the time. It was a horrific apparition and robbed Clay of his self-control.

He screamed out, "No! Not now! You bastard priest! What have you done to me?"

Fox had worked her gag free and turned her head. She dug her teeth into Clay's outstretched bicep. Clay screamed again and his gun went off, putting a bullet up in the roof. Now free of Clay's hold, Fox yelled so loudly it might have shredded her vocal chords, "The oxygen cylinder!"

Devlin turned to see an oxygen cylinder behind him with scorch marks along the side. Now he got it.

Fox hit the floor. With one large span of his working hand,

Devlin was able to pick up the hot oxygen tank and take aim. He pointed it toward Clay and slammed it hard into the ground. The immense heated pressure ruptured the brittle nozzle, and oxygen ripped out torpedoing, the cylinder across the lab taking the top left quarter of Clay's cranium with it before ripping a hole in the lab's aluminum sheet. So quick and clean had been the impact that Clay stood for a fraction of a second, not comprehending his own catastrophic mutilation before he slumped to the ground, like a puppet whose strings had been severed.

Devlin retrieved his gun, went over to Fox, and tore the duct tape off her wrists. Then Fox kept a gun trained on the four men huddled against the wall while Devlin checked over Alvarez. They'd extracted and packed one kidney and made an incision along his chest but had yet to open up his thorax.

"Is he going to be okay?" asked Fox.

Devlin checked over the monitor's signals. "I think so. They've done a good job of keeping him stable." He turned to the four surgeons. "You got him this way, you need to fix him."

Fox leveled her gun at the men. "Now," she insisted.

Jakob and Claude looked at each other. Then Claude said slowly, "I really don't think so..."

Without hesitation, Fox let off a round that whizzed past Lazard's head. Lazard's thin, feeble body spasmed and shuddered pathetically with terror. For a man who had no qualms about cutting other people open, he was an absolute coward when it came to his own physical safety.

"Okay! Okay!" he screamed in a high-pitched whine. "Please stop shooting!"

The four men followed the direction of Fox's barrel over to Alvarez and set about undoing their harm.

"What about you? Are you okay?" asked Fox, looking at the sorry state of Devlin's left hand.

"Right now I'm one of the healthiest people in this whole damn building. I'm fine."

"What do we do now?"

"We call George." Devlin surveyed the vast, flickering aluminum chamber. "If there's anyone I know can clear this mess up, it's George Brennan."

After Devlin put the call to in to Brennan, he remembered Stevens. "Dear God! Greg's lying outside with a gun wound in his gut. He needs immediate medical attention."

"Well, in that case, we're in luck," said Fox, looking at the men tending to Alvarez. "You—" Fox pointed her gun at Liu, figuring him by build to be the best candidate. "—help him get the policeman in here."

Liu nodded eagerly.

Devlin rolled one of the spare gurneys that had been stored in the lab out to the front building, and Liu followed. Between Liu's two good hands and Devlin's one, they managed with great care to get Stevens up onto the bed. Then they rolled him alongside Alvarez's bed, and under Fox's orders, Liu scrambled to work immediately, hooking Stevens up to a drip and respiratory and cardiac monitors.

As they worked under Fox's watch, Devlin walked over to Clay's butchered body, his cranium and most of its contents sprayed out across the floor. Just below Clay's outstretched hand, Devlin's eye was caught by a silver tube with a yellow label. The silver had dulled and tarnished. The top of the tube had come free, and small white pills had spilled out. Devlin picked up a pill, but it was blank. No name, no company. Then he picked up the tube and examined it. It had a design engraved on the tube, a design Devlin recognized, of a tree and a serpent wrapped around the trunk. Devlin placed the pills back in the container and slipped it into his pocket.

Then he walked through the cattle lab out into the morning

sun. Early light had arrived. Devlin looked out beyond the ranch for signs of George and his team's arrival. He took out his last cigar and was about to have the smoke he had been yearning for since he'd left Wright Patterson when the peace was ruined by the sound of blades. Coming in from the horizon was the Logan helicopter. As it got nearer, Devlin could make out a figure in the cockpit aiming a gun on him, waiting for a shot. Just a little closer, thought Devlin. He dropped his cigar, readied his Beretta, stood square on, and bided his time. Just a little closer yet. For a moment Devlin wavered between the tail and the cockpit. Which to go for? Then he made his decision and stuck to it. As the chopper loomed over the lab roof, shots kicked up the turf by Devlin's feet. But Devlin didn't flinch and let off all his fifteen rounds into the cockpit. The pilot was hit and the helicopter started to spiral out of control, spinning faster and faster and whipping into the beautiful, flawless Kansas brickwork of the Logan Ranch. The fuel tank blew, and flames spewed from the embedded wreck, traveling with unnatural speed until the entire building was burning like the fire itself had a score to settle.

In the distance, a line of black vehicles filled the highway and began to turn up the dirt track into the ranch.

Devlin bent down to pick up his smoke. Finally, he had his cigar.

71

Fox and Devlin stood a way back in the dusty clearing among the vehicles from Homeland, the Bureau of Crime Investigation, and the emergency services. They had given detailed accounts of night's events and the last few days to George Brennan and his senior agents. Paramedics had given them both the once-over and treated Devlin's wounds. They gave him something for the pain, then bound his hand and put it in a sling.

Devlin and Fox stood watching the firefighters trying desperately to contain the inferno that had engulfed the ranch house. But it looked fairly certain that everything worth saving had gone. Beyond the fire, the entrance to the lab had been screened off, and teams dressed in white coveralls were coming and going, like worker bees flying in and out of a hive. Inside they were operating feverishly on Alvarez and examining and stabilizing the other eleven men. The bodies of Packer, Reeves, and Clay had been bagged, and Campbell had been treated for his amputated finger and given a police escort to the hospital.

Stevens was stretchered out to a waiting ambulance. He was critical but stable. Devlin and Fox stood by as he was wheeled up and into the patient compartment. Without raising his head, Stevens whispered to his attending medic, who looked back at Devlin and beckoned him over. Devlin stepped up into the back of the ambulance, and the medic cleared some space for him to get in by Stevens. Devlin stooped to hear Stevens's breathless and weak voice. He spoke in short, halting sentences.

"I need to say thank you," said Stevens.

"What the hell for?" asked Devlin.

"I didn't tell you... The doctor at Miami Valley...he told me my cancer...is in remission..."

"Greg, that's astonishing. I thought it was untreatable?"

"It was. I know how it happened... It was you, Gabe...you did it. You changed something...fundamental in me. Something I hadn't had the strength to do all my life... You arrived and the strength was there..."

Devlin was resolute and unwavering in his reply. "No. It was never me. I don't have that power. I would never want that power in a million years."

"That's because..." Stevens was really struggling now, and the medic looked ready to intervene. But he made one last effort to explain. "That's because you're an unwilling servant of God, Gabe...and the unwilling ones...well, they're the only ones worth trusting... The willing ones are all madmen."

Then Stevens was packed up and the doors to the ambulance slammed shut. The siren screamed and dust flew up in its wake as it sped off under the stone archway. And Stevens was gone. Devlin stood in the settling sand looking troubled.

Fox appeared by Devlin's shoulder. "I got a ride back to Halton with a couple of the BCI guys."

"Okay. I need to hang around and clear up some stuff with George. The stuff that happened in Baltimore."

"Lemus?"

"Yeah. Lemus."

Fox nodded. She had a puzzled look like something was bothering her.

"What the hell happened in there with Logan? When Clay was screaming? He said that you'd done something to him? He looked like he was having some kind of attack."

Devlin hesitated. "I'm not sure."

Fox studied Devlin's face. She wasn't convinced. "You think it's the same thing you talked to me about at the motel, don't you?"

Devlin looked at Fox, paused, and replied truthfully. "Yeah, I think it's the same thing. Me and Clay met while you were being held at the ranch. And while we were talking, something happened, same as what happened between me and Earl. Something moved between us. Something that sent Clay over the edge."

"I don't want to get all reasonable on your ass, but it might all not be so scary, y'know. There could just be a conventional explanation."

"You're right. There could be. I could say stuff like what happened to Clay was a long time coming. That Clay Logan was a man on a precipice. A man in full-tilt denial. I made him hear the right words at the right time. That's all. Sometimes maybe that's all that's needed to cause a man's conscience to begin to unravel. He did the rest for himself. It was nothing to do with me. I guess you never know when you'll have your conversion on the road to Damascus. I could say that...but that wasn't what really happened."

There was another pause. Fox chewed her lip and, unusually for her, looked a little anxious.

"You're not gonna stay in Halton, are you?"

"No. No. I'm not."

"Where are you going to go?"

"I have no idea. But I have to go. I have to find out what's going on, why all this stuff is happening to me and being asked of me, and that's not going to happen in Halton Springs. Like you said, I haven't submitted to man's law, so I'll have to submit to God's law. I'm sorry, Fox. I'm sorry I can't stay here and give you more. Give you everything I should do. Want to. I'm sorry for you, and I'm sorry for me."

"Don't be sorry for me. Never be sorry for me. It's your fault anyhow for giving a girl ideas."

A car horn sounded, and one of George's guys yelled over at Fox.

Then there was a silence, and they both watched it happen —the moment that could have been. Him leaning in and taking Fox's face in his hands and she, eyes closed and up on tiptoes, her mouth seeking out his. Then the locking of soft lips. He would hold her waist close to him while they fully embraced. And at that moment, Devlin saw how it might be. Saw himself throwing it all away, letting his vows and his beliefs go hang for a moment in a woman's arms and a way back to a normal life. He imagined the nights and the mornings to come. Never waking alone again. Imagined how life would taste living it the way everybody else did, drop by normal drop, his life marked out by the seasons and love given and loved returned. The life that had been stolen from him. But as he witnessed this alternative life flash before him, he also knew with absolute certainty that it was not his path.

A horn sounded again and the moment that never was evaporated. Devlin let it go. Fox walked off to her waiting car, her hair tangled and her face covered in scratches and dirt but still looking beautiful in the pure May morning sun. And Katy Fox was gone.

. . .

Brennan was talking to a couple of guys from the med team, so Devlin waited patiently until he was able to break off. Then Brennan flashed him a smile.

"Good news, Gabe. Alvarez is okay. He can be moved to a real hospital, and guess what? It ain't gonna be Dayton Freedom. The other eleven are gonna need a long time to recover physically and emotionally from the sheer volume of sedatives and anesthetics they've been pumped full of. They won't know which way is up, poor bastards. And a team of our guys just arrested Marie Vallory at her office. We got enough on her now to put her away for life. Well done, Gabe. Well done. You want the glory? We could make sure what you did here gets to the all the right ears."

"No. Thanks but no thanks, George."

"No. I figured not. You always found that stuff kind of painful."

And indeed Devlin did look uncharacteristically awkward, vulnerable even. Something was clearly troubling him. As he spoke he almost stuttered.

"George, did you sort out the other...problem?"

Brennan sensed his unease and didn't play on it. He gave Devlin the release he needed. "Yeah. Yeah, Gabe. It's sorted. There was no CCTV. Never was any. It was a bluff. There's no evidence linking you to that...incident." Brennan paused. He could tell Devlin how Otterman and Bradley were at that moment being held at a black site in Poland. How by the time Brennan's team had finished with them and finally given them back their liberty, they would never want to even think about Felix Lemus or Father Gabriel Devlin for the rest of their lives. But instead, he said, "And those two clowns that call themselves PIs. We intercepted them at Dulles Airport. Long story short, you never have to worry about them again. You have my word."

"I want them to see the inside of a court for what they did to Hector."

"I'll make that happen."

"Thanks, George." Devlin extended a hand, and Brennan shook it warmly.

"Believe me, it's small fish compared to the job you've done here."

"It was good to see you again, George."

"Likewise, Gabe. Likewise. Listen, one of my boys will give you a lift back to town… I mean, Jeez, it's the very least I can do." Brennan pointed to a black Subaru sitting in the clearing. "I'll go tell him he's got a passenger. A regular VIP."

Brennan chuckled and walked over to the waiting car. He tapped on the driver's window, and it whirred down.

The agent at the wheel greeted Brennan. "Sir."

"Hey. I got someone that needs a ride to back into Halton."

"No problem, sir. Who is it?"

"The guy over there." Brennan turned to point out Devlin. But Devlin wasn't there.

"Which guy, sir?"

"Where the hell's he gone? Dammit. Hold on." Brennan marched back to the spot where he'd been talking to Devlin a moment earlier and scanned the ranch. Then he asked anyone in the vicinity if they'd seen a big guy with dark hair and an arm in a sling. But no one had. It seemed like the priest had vanished off the face of the earth.

EPILOGUE

The truck pulled out of a stop a few miles east of the town of Anna, Ohio. Refueled and refreshed, the driver was ready for a nine-hour haul eastward. Just as he turned onto the highway and began to pick up speed, he spotted a shambling figure a little farther up walking along the shoulder. As he passed, he noticed the man had his arm in a sling and his clothes were stained and ripped. The truck driver had never stopped to pick up anyone in his entire time on the road. He was never in need of any other company than the radio and was no passing Samaritan. But this time, for some inexplicable reason, he felt a pang of guilt, and in a split second he decided to pull over. The eighteen-wheeler groaned to a stop, and the rig hissed and complained and settled. Then he pushed the cab door open. After a few moments, the man in the ripped clothes appeared by the side of the road and looked up at the truck driver. The driver saw that he was a tall, broad man with a kind of battered nobility.

"Hey, fella. You need a ride?"

"Yeah. Yeah. As matter of fact, I do. Where you headed?"

"East Hampton."

"How about that. Me too."

"Okay. Get up here, my friend."

The passenger climbed up into the cab and slammed the door shut, and the truck began its slow acceleration again. Devlin got his aching body and limbs comfortable in the wide cabin seat and glanced down at the silver tube he had in his good hand. He lifted it up and inspected the letters inscribed into the bottom of Clay Logan's pillbox. "Montauk Jewelers. East Hampton."

How about that, thought Devlin. *Looks like I'm being shown a path.*

As the truck ran through its gears and hit cruising speed, Devlin stared out at the flat Ohio landscape.

And then the word came back to him, the word that had told him what he was. His punishment and destination.

"Azazel." The fallen. The banished. Wilderness.

AFTERWORD

You've finished the first Gabe Devlin thriller and you can go straight on to the second thriller 'The Salvation Man", just click the link below...

http://mybook.to/TheSalvationMan

Please click below and subscribe to my newsletter if you'd like to hear about latest news and releases...

http://eepurl.com/gdVyyX

Thanks so much for reading 'The Redemption Man".

Best,

James.